THE PARK STREET SECRETS

A NOVEL

Every life has a story and every story has a life

Yvonne Van Lankveld

YVONNE VAN LANKVELD

The Park Street Secrets
Copyright © 2022 by Yvonne Van Lankveld

All rights reserved. No part of this publication may be reproduced, distributed, or transmitted in any form or by any means, including photocopying, recording, or other electronic or mechanical methods, without the prior written permission of the author, except in the case of brief quotations embodied in critical reviews and certain other non-commercial uses permitted by copyright law.

tellwell

Tellwell Talent
www.tellwell.ca

ISBN
978-0-2288-6926-9 (Hardcover)
978-0-2288-6925-2 (Paperback)
978-0-2288-6927-6 (eBook)

Indie Reader Rating: 4.8/5. The Park Street Secrets is a well-written, well-thought-out, slice of life story fraught with engaging characters and situations
~ *Florence Osmund for Indie Reader*

Yvonne brilliantly writes about The Park Street building as a character in the story. It is old, worn down, refurbished, safe, loving, gentle, and charming. I could imagine it, and wanted to live there with the characters. I absolutely loved this book and didn't want it to end. I fell in love with some of the characters (especially Winnie) and was fully engrossed in their lives
~ *Whistler Independent Book Awards Review*

I loved it. I found myself reading much later than I ever do, and kept reading only a paragraph at a time, as I didn't want it to end. I loved the characters, the organization, writing style and the social issues that were addressed so well. It's just a great novel
~ *Randi Evans, Program Coordinator, Canadian Authors Association (Niagara Branch)*

DEDICATION

The Park Street Secrets is dedicated to the people I have had the honour of caring for. They have defined adversity, gratitude and respect in such unique and distinct ways. While none are represented here, they planted the seeds in my imagination, most of them long after they were gone.

*"I think happiness is largely a matter of temperament,
a disposition or attitude, a generic inheritance."*

James Hillyer in Nightfall
by Richard B. Wright

Other Works:

The Road to Alright

All of the characters in this novel are a creation of fiction. *The Park Street Secrets* is set in the historical Dominion Public Building at the corner of Park and Zimmerman Street in Niagara Falls, Ontario, which has been vacant since 1978. The front cover image is the entrance door from Zimmerman Street, which the character Sonny would have used. Steps away, the cat colony under the old railway bridge still flourishes at the time of this writing.

The Residents of Park Street

Name	Age	Unit Number	Comments
Winifred (Winnie) Firestone	80	1A	Husband: Alexander (deceased) Children: Allen (San Francisco) Annette (Boston)
Marcello Portobello	70	1B	Single: (fiancée was Valentina) Cats: Mona Lisa and Michelangelo
Lily Jamieson Rose Miles	45 50	1C	Divorced Single: Lily's sister
Bryce Turner Talia St James	30 29	2A	Romantic Partners
Mitch and Sally Penfold	55 45	2B	Married
Adrian Common	35	2C	Single
Gracie Sheehan	53	The Loft	Widow

> **Obituary Notice**
>
> **Firestone, Alexander Richard (Alex)** - With heavy hearts, we announce the recent passing of our beloved husband and father. In his 83rd year, Alex succumbed to a lengthy and courageous battle with Parkinson's disease. Devoted husband of sixty years to Winifred (Winnie), loving father of Allen (Kimberley) and their children Alexander and Whitney of San Francisco, California; Annette Simpson (Richard) of Boston, Massachusetts, and her children Brooklyn, Dallas and Savannah. Alex was generous in his time and devotion to many service organizations and charities in Niagara Falls, Ontario. At Alex's request, a private family service followed his cremation. In lieu of flowers, donations to any local charity would be appreciated.

SEPTEMBER 1ST
Weather forecast: sunny skies

Suite 1A: Winnie Firestone
1:30 p.m.

*"Nothing can take away the love
that a heart holds deep ..."*

The moving truck holding Winnie's possessions preceded her arrival at Park Street. She had come and gone through this building for a few of her eight decades, never thinking that as of today, it would become her permanent address. She still felt the sting of "the intervention" that her children Allen and Annette arranged when they last visited in July. They coerced her, adamant that her frailty was a barrier to her remaining in the home she and Alex cultivated their marriage—and them—in. The business of leaving home and moving here happened too fast. Before she could process it, her house was sold and the movers packed everything, including her underthings still hiding in dresser drawers, into the big truck that was parked in front of her.

She sat beside Mason in his shiny, black Cadillac at her new but very old front steps. Mason doubled as her lawyer and power of attorney. If you'd care to know a secret, some days she trusted Mason more than her children. He was also the son of her oldest friends, Mason Sr. and Alice, who were fortunate enough to have left their home feet first and within six months of each other. Mason lost his own wife five years ago but rarely discussed it with Winnie.

Mason arrived after breakfast; together they took a final stroll around her well-appointed house and yard. He supplied fresh tissues for every corner she wept in. He brought Winnie to his downtown office to process the real estate transaction. His secretary Aida, a demure woman who was much too thin, brought her tea on a tray that Winnie knew was Mason's mother's. Earl Grey steeped in a teapot beside its matching cup and saucer. Aida supplied more tissues and today's newspaper to distract Winnie until Mason wrapped up his business for the morning.

Just before noon, Mason drove from his parking spot behind his office to the street entrance. He got out and opened the passenger door as Aida escorted Winnie out, holding her purse while Winnie folded her withered frame into his car. Alex used to hold her door, one of many endearing gestures that she took for granted and now dearly missed. Mason closed her door quietly, then whisked her away, funding soup and a sandwich at her favourite local diner.

Winnie fell asleep during the ride to her new condominium on Park Street, almost four hours after being coaxed out of her vacant house. Appreciating her exhaustion, Mason parked his car and answered emails on his phone for another half hour. Winnie woke up with a startled snort, took inventory of her surroundings, and then her chauffeur. He smiled affectionately at her as she checked the time on her tiny, gold wristwatch.

"I fell asleep, didn't I?"

Her voice always reminded him of Jessica Tandy in the movie *Driving Miss Daisy*.

"Just for a second."

"Now be truthful, Mason. How long was I sleeping?"

"Not long at all."

He always spoke in a calming tone. Mason opened a yellow manila envelope and shook out her newest and most important possessions. Ceremoniously, he awarded her a green and a blue key attached to a lanyard. In Winnie's opinion, this was just an old federal building turned into apartments, not condominiums. And apartments were for people lacking the financial means to afford a home. She sighed as her arthritic fingers curiously fondled a small, unfamiliar white disc also attached to her lanyard.

"It gives you a little extra protection, Winnie. And look at this. If you need help, just push this red button and someone will call you on your phone to see if you're okay."

"Hmmm ... what will they think of next?"

She eyed the safety device and shook her head. She didn't need any protection, but if it made Mason happy, she would keep it just for him. He picked out the green key, shiny and new like the blue one, but bigger.

"This green key is for your condo door, and the blue key opens your mailbox. Remember blue is the same colour as the mail carrier's uniform. Now let's have a look at your new digs."

Another thorn needled at her thoughts. Her children decided she would move to Park Street, not Winnie. Did she already tell Mason that?

"Mason, I'm not so sure that living on this side of town is a good idea. What would your mother have said about this place? Unlikely that she'd visit me here."

"Winnie, she'd visit you if you moved to the moon. Remember that my dad worked here as a judge, so he's watching over you."

He gazed over the building.

"Wow, look at this place. They've done a great job renovating it. Did you read the articles I brought you about the downtown re-development?"

"Yes, but it doesn't feel like home."

"It will very soon, and you'll be as happy as a lark before you know it. Look, the movers are already unloading your things. Let's go inside. They need you to tell them where to put everything, especially Alex's piano."

Even though her husband was no longer alive to play it, Winnie wouldn't part with it or any sentimental treasure. She hoped to feel his same presence sitting at the bench, playing a concerto for an audience of one.

Winnie grasped Mason's strong arm, both for courage and support. She panned the limestone structure, gazing to the third floor while his other hand gently touched her back for security.

"When was this place built?"

"In 1885. Other than the outer and supporting walls, almost everything is new."

"I can't believe I'm moving into a building that held jail cells …"

She shook her head, planting one orthopedic shoe solidly on the first step. The warmth of Mason's arm was the only comfort she felt. As he guided her up the outer stairs, Winnie felt very alone, again resenting her children for forcing this move upon her. It was this place or a retirement home, which, in her opinion, was equivalent to a geriatric prison for people who were abandoned by their family. The opposite of their flashy brochures, to Winnie they were dismal places where adult children transferred their caregiving role and messy chores to someone else. Where the noise from weekly casino jaunts would never replace the happy chatter of a family gathering.

> **Retirement Announcement**
>
> Friends and co-workers are invited to celebrate the retirement of **Marcello (Marco) Portobello** on September 30. At the young age of seventy, Marco completed ten years of service as a translator for the Niagara Falls Tour Guide Service. He was well-respected by countless visitors who had the pleasure of meeting him. Come share your memories and best wishes with Marco at the Family Restaurant on September 30th (5:00 – 8:00 p.m.).

SEPTEMBER 1ST

Suite 1B: Marcello Portobello
2:00 p.m.

"Women are a force to be reckoned with."

Marcello navigated in his light green Fiat into its newly designated spot behind Park Street, his cherished Mona Lisa and Michelangelo in their carriers beside him. Their meows were merciless, and his cooing did nothing to settle them. Excited about his move, he was the first tenant to register at Park Street. He fell in love with the building long ago because it reminded him of the architecture that surrounded him growing up in Venice. He admired the impressive, predominantly grey building that was capped by a slate mansard roof and centre gables on each facade. Massive, rounded archways protected the corner dual stairs facing Park Street in the heart of Niagara Falls, Ontario.

What also stirred Marcello's senses was that Marilyn Monroe repeatedly climbed these steps when she filmed the movie *Niagara* in 1952. To Marcello, she was the most beautiful woman in the world, full of lust, and second only to his beloved Valentina. Both had abandoned him decades ago, Marilyn by her own demise and Valentina by deserting him. And just like Marilyn, Valentina's dalliances with political dignitaries humiliated him. Reconciling with Marcello and promising to leave her sins in Italy, she agreed to follow him to Canada, providing he first prepare their new home. Crates of wedding gifts from his family were shipped across the Atlantic to Niagara Falls, where many remained unopened for years.

Tainted as Valentina was, Marcello waited patiently for her to regain her dignity and her senses. Her first arrival was delayed because of her mother's bronchitis, which progressed to a month's hospitalization for pneumonia, then rolled into seasons of prolonged rest under Valentina's care. Marcello sent touristy gifts and pleading letters to join him in the honeymoon capital. Eventually he lost hope of someday carrying her across their front door threshold. Since then, forty-five years had passed.

Today, however, he turned a page and this move was a new beginning. A cool breeze circulated through the open windows of his Fiat where his tabby cats waited for him to secure the condo for their move inside. He walked purposefully from the parking lot, located between the main building and a small, one-storey secondary structure. The ornate wrought iron gates were unlocked, and they sparkled with fresh black paint. According to the property manager, security cameras and a remote locking system were slated for installation. As Marcello rounded the corner to the front of the building, an elderly woman about ten years his senior was being escorted from a black Cadillac up the front stairs by a tall, distinguished man in a good suit. Marcello guessed he was a proud son giving his mother a tour of his new place. He followed the couple in after displaying his matching keys and commented that they would be neighbours. Unlocking his door and admiring his new surroundings, he hoped both he and his cats would retire peacefully there.

> **In Memoriam**
>
> **Miles, Annaliese (née Smith)** - In memory of our mother, who passed away suddenly five years ago today. Pre-deceased by her husband, Harold, and infant son, Harry.
>
> To hear your voice and see you smile,
> to sit with you and chat a while,
> every day in some small way,
> memories of you always stay.
>
> Always in our hearts, lovingly remembered by daughters Rose Miles and Lily Jamieson.

September 1st

Suite 1C: Rose Miles and Lily Jamieson
3:00 p.m.

"Sisterhood is like electricity. It's an invisible but powerful connection."

The truck Rosie Miles reserved was too small, and Lily's insistence to upgrade to a larger vehicle fell on deaf ears. Most of the packing and over-stuffing the cube van was done by Lily because Rosie was working. As usual, Lily felt it was an unfair division of labour, but she was somewhat appeased by Rosie paying to clean their parents' old house before the new owners moved in. Lily spent every waking hour of the last month purging their mother's and her own belongings. Both sisters had left home, and by different circumstances, eventually returned. They bickered about why they kept their mother's things so long. Rosie cited sentimental reasons; Lily was convinced Rosie couldn't be bothered to dispose of them.

Lily filled dozens of garbage bags with outdated shoes, clothes and other junk. She felt no remorse in dumping them at the thrift shop front doors at night, violating the requests for donations only during business hours. She knew the old kitchen utensils, linen and worthless trinkets would be rejected or trashed. Pressed for time, she saved a few heavy boxes, sealed decades ago and labelled "ROSE and LILY" in her mother's perfect handwriting, for after the move.

More tragic than their mother's sudden passing was the reading of her will. The sisters were forced to live together for five years together despite their animosity towards each other. Even after death, she held a tight rein on her daughters, hoping they would repair their relationship. The consequence of non-compliance meant the house would be sold and the proceeds donated to the local animal shelter. So, the sisters remained in the family home for exactly four years, siphoned what they legally could from their mother's estate for home maintenance and spent their own money on themselves.

Lily was particularly miserable because Rosie, in management at an upscale hotel, was unable to take a day off during the peak of the tourist season. Lily, self-appointed as the housekeeper and groundskeeper, was supported by her ex-husband, Everett. She never worked while married and felt Everett should continue to support her in the lifestyle she was accustomed to before their divorce. Her university scholarship and degree completion went by the wayside when she became pregnant the summer before her final school year. A lavish wedding was hastily arranged, and by the time she miscarried in her fifth month, her only attraction to Everett was his family's wealth. Their marriage stretched into ten miserable, childless years that was equivalent to the duration of Everett's alimony commitment. To Lily, it was collateral damage for him ruining not only their marriage but others. Due to expire next year, Lily planned to bridge the alimony loss with her mother's inheritance until she could snag a new husband.

Lily sat waiting in the cube van, guarding their possessions and calming her nerves with a jumbo bag of low-sodium potato chips. The sisters both knew the Park Street building when it was sagging with neglect. Originally constructed as a post office, then used as a customs house, it was finally refurbished to house the city's police department until it was evacuated in 1978. The condo website boasted it as "An impressive Romanesque revival." Lily's memory of this building from her high school history class drew her back here. She wanted an address with a commanding presence, at least until a handsome man with money and a thick head of hair unlatched her from Rosie.

Rosie drove her lemon yellow VW Beetle into the parking spot marked 1C at the back of the building one hour after Lily's arrival. She opened her door carefully to avoid scratching the Fiat beside her. Soft meowing drew her to the crated cats in the front seat, but the vibrant foliage in the back seat distracted her. She inhaled deeply, disappointed that instead of cannabis, she smelled an assortment of potted herbs. Her new neighbour would have pleased her more by harvesting plants instead of cooking with them. Rosie walked purposefully to the truck bearing the rental company logo she booked that was parked across the street from the condo entrance. Circling around to the driver's side, she startled Lily by slapping her open hand hard against the van's driver's side door where Lily sat licking grease off her fingers.

"Are you eating again?"

"Shut up."

"Did you pick up the keys?"

Lily dangled them in front of Rosie like bait.

"Then what are you waiting for? Let's get on with it," Rosie said, adjusting her over-stuffed purse over her shoulder and marching ahead of Lily up the double-sided front steps.

Lily paused, lingering outside the main entrance. The tree-lined street was carpeted in leaves the colour of pumpkins, and the pristine air from the Niagara River just two blocks away circulated between them. Three weeks ago, Lily and Rosie signed a one-year lease, their bridge to independence.

They bullied each other as they lugged the lighter boxes onto moving carts and into the condo, then went their separate ways. Help for the heavy things was arriving tomorrow.

> **Engagement Announcement**
>
> Jack and Alice Turner, and Jessica and Mark Stemple are pleased to announce the engagement of their son **Bryce Turner** to **Talia St. James,** daughter of Stewart and Kim Stevens, and Gregory and Annie St. James. A summer wedding is planned.

SEPTEMBER 2ND
Weather forecast: rain all day

Suite 2A: Bryce Turner and Talia St. James

"The more things change, the more they stay the same."

Unknown

Bryce and Talia couldn't unpack fast enough. The rain hastened their steps as they ran back and forth between their vehicles and the condo, wet clothes plastered to their skin. Park Street was their first official co-habitation effort, encouraged by Bryce's family but scorned by her divorced Catholic parents. Talia was determined that living together would solidify their relationship. Acutely aware of both their parents' fractured marriages, she was convinced any blemish in her and Bryce's union would heal before it became a permanent scar.

This building was her only choice. A familiar name in its historical description picked at her memory until she recognized its significance. In her first year of university,

Talia served as a page at the legislative buildings in Ottawa. Thomas Fuller, the architect for the original parliament buildings in Canada's capital city, designed this treasure and therefore connected her past to her future in this building. Mindful that the rent was steep, she felt confident that their career goals would quickly advance beyond the call centre that meshed them together. She wasn't worried. And Bryce was brilliant.

Arms full of clothes still on hangers, Talia entered the front lobby, noting the open and overstuffed mail slot for Suite 1A. She remembered handing a blue mailbox key to Bryce for safekeeping because, unlike her, he was meticulous and organized. Heaving her final load up the stairs, she knocked against their door gently with her soaked sneaker. Bryce opened the door cautiously, naked and aroused. He took the clothes from her and dumped them on the sofa. He peeled Talia's clothes off and carried her to the spacious steamy shower, stifling her squeals with his hungry lips.

September 2ⁿᵈ

Suite 1C: Lily and Rosie

*"Someone you have overlooked in the past
will cause great changes in your life."*

Chinese Proverb

Lily took full advantage of Rosie's co-workers as they emptied the truck and re-arranged the furniture until she was content. They drove Rosie to work on time and returned the rented vehicle while Lily organized the kitchen, pleasantly surprised that most items found new homes quickly. The high ceilings offered generous cupboard space for unused wedding gifts. Her new bedroom was triple the size of the one she just vacated. Her massive four-poster wedding suite, previously split between rooms at her mother's house, was re-assembled and accessorized with items her lawyer cautioned her about taking. Only a night table and dresser fit in her childhood room, contrasting sharply with her white single canopy bed. Rearranged now as it was in her matrimonial bedroom, a brief flashback of a passionate night circled her back to the present.

Tomorrow morning Rosie would sleep in, and Lily would shop for new linens and accessories for her bedroom. She walked over to her window and scanned the parking lot. Rosie's car was parked between Lily's white Honda and the green Fiat, the only cars in the lot. She counted out ten parking spaces, including two marked for visitors.

Lily sat down on her bed, the bare mattress exhaling the mustiness of her mother's basement. In contrast, the cedar lining of the armoire drawers she then opened was still appealing. She unpacked a forgotten mattress protector from its aging packaging, a very practical wedding present from her side of the family. Only Everett's side made use of the bridal registry. Her side didn't acknowledge such frivolities. She threw the protector onto the mattress, walking freely around the bed in the spacious room. She pulled the first corner at the head of the bed and tucked it easily between the box spring and the mattress. She grabbed the second corner on the opposite side of the bed and pulled hard enough to take the creases out of the fabric. The stretchy fabric, designed to cover the depth of the mattress, separated from its elastic banding. It didn't matter because the cover's intent was to protect her mattress, not be displayed. She circled to the other side of the bed and tugged at the fabric near the headboard. It disintegrated in her hands. Shreds of the fabric floated lightly, like leaves, to the floor. Groaning as she forced the fabric over the final corner, it also tore away. She sat down on the mattress cover, skimming her fingertips lightly across the pilling of the fabric surface. She'd first opened this gift nineteen years ago. What else should she have expected?

Lily glanced wearily at two sealed boxes in the corner of her bedroom. She knelt down beside them, peeling away the tape that was separating from the cardboard. Opening these meant unlocking memories. And yes, there they were. Her acceptance letter to university. A full scholarship, providing she passed and finished. A dried bouquet from some long-forgotten date. A rare picture her mother took of just Lily and her father, a towel wrapped around her ten-year-old shoulders as the pair sat dangling their feet in the water off a dock. It was the only summer cottage their family ever rented. She looked helplessly in the box, tears dripping onto her sweatshirt. Other photos slid from her lap and scattered across the floor. Lily left them as they landed and walked to the kitchen. There was nothing she could eat to soothe her. Nothing in the fridge would help. She swung the cupboard doors open, scanning containers of food that required time to prepare. She craved sweetness, remembering the bakery she passed down the street. It was a ten-minute walk, including two minutes to ready herself enough to blend in with the regulars on the street.

The fall air was like a salve on Lily's skin. Her feet moved her in heavy, purposeful steps. She paused at the bakery window to find rows of cooling cinnamon buns nesting in waxed paper on trays in one window and a round, two-tiered wedding cake with silver ribbon circling each tier in the other window display. The real gems were only visible once she pushed the glass door open. Euphoric with the sweet aroma of warm baking, vanilla and butter, Lily approached the glass counter. Staring at the rows of cupcakes with icing swirls that peaked like soft ice cream, she swallowed saliva and placed her order. The two-for-one sale eliminated the need to narrow her choices; Lily bought them all.

> **Garage Sale**
>
> Huge garage sale Saturday morning! Seven families are cleaning out their closets, basements and garages! Lots of treasures, some antiques and lawn equipment in excellent condition. Look for the signs on Morrison Street. Everything must be sold!

SEPTEMBER 3ʳᴰ
Weather forecast: cool with sunny skies

Suite 2B: Sally and Mitch Penfold

"Cultivating a relationship is like peeling an onion:
It's a lot of work and it can make you cry."

Unknown

Sally Penfold longed for wonderful things, including her new husband, Mitch, but she also wanted happiness. Their marriage began with a clean slate, and the garage sale was an effective way to leave their old lives behind. They chose only significant items from their last addresses, agreeing to ditch any negative physical or psychological reminders of their past relationships.

Mitch, a police officer and now detective, had followed in the footsteps of his father and grandfather. It was a stressful life for both of them, and Sally learned from partners of other police officers to have faith that Mitch would leave and return home after each shift, exhausted but alive. His workdays were long and unpredictable. She never interfered or asked him to change. He was born and bred for this career, and his life revolved around the institution of law enforcement.

Mitch's father spent much of his career working on Park Street when this building housed the old police station, so it didn't surprise Sally when Mitch suggested they move to the same floor that his father ended his police career. Mitch believed his father's legacy would bring them good luck here. *Lord knows*, Sally mused, *Mitch could use a little more luck.* In his divorce settlement, his ex-wife, Georgia, kept their house. Their lengthy legal battle tarnished his relationship with their adult sons, who adored their ever-present and nurturing mother, making him the villain.

Sally's ex-boyfriend Robin was in jail for corporate theft thanks to the endless hours Mitch invested in the case, and in Sally. She never expected to fall for a man who knew every intimate detail of her life. Gently and methodically, Mitch peeled away the layers of her existence: phone records, texts, credit card statements and holidays taken over her ten years with Robin. There was enough evidence to convict the bastard for the same length of time they were together. Mitch suggested a reputable lawyer from other cases he had testified at because he knew how they operated behind the scenes. Her chosen lawyer was both fearless and energetic, billing her at a discounted rate and allowing Sally to retain her job and her dignity. She sold her house to eliminate its baggage and upkeep. She and Mitch were starting fresh. Sally called him her knight in shining armour. Mitch called Sally Barbie Doll.

Sally waited on the stone front steps of the building on Park Street for Mitch, soaking up the warm sun. He pulled up in an unmarked cruiser within minutes, just as she and Lily exchanged greetings. Lily was the younger of two sisters who had already moved in and was about her age. When Sally introduced Mitch to Lily, she made a nice first impression. Mitch was courteous but, as always, cautious with unknown people. Sally knew it was the nature of his business.

Sally's heart fluttered as they climbed the stairs. She couldn't wait to officially share the same address with Mitch. Good times were just around the corner.

Human Resources Announcement

R & R Customs Brokerage is pleased to announce the promotion of **Adrian Common** to the position of Account Manager, International Logistics. Adrian comes to the organization with extensive experience in our European and Asian locations and will be relocating to our Niagara Falls office. Congratulations on your achievement, Adrian.

September 3ʳᴰ
Weather forecast: cool and sunny

Suite 2C: Adrian Common

"He's like a bull in a china shop."

Jacob Faithful by *Frederick Marryat (1834)*

Adrian whipped his matte black BMW into the parking spot marked 1C, narrowly missing the little Fiat and ignoring the designated 2C spot in his lease; it was the closest walk to the front door. Adrian often took self-imposed privileges on a first come, first served basis. Quickly surveying the building, he thought whoever was responsible for choosing this dump should have paid more attention to his condo preferences. It was substandard, but at least it was close to the customs office and the border. Kelly, his new administrative assistant, told him he could monitor the bridge traffic between Canada and the

United States from his bedroom window. He wondered how she knew that. Kelly also mentioned that aside from the building's historic and architectural significance, it also served as the original Canada Customs location.

Adrian re-adjusted his laptop and overnight bag, feeling his pockets for the blue and green keys that Kelly pressed into his hands just minutes earlier. His company always set up his accommodation. In his own mind, Adrian was an aspiring logistics expert, and he expected others to match his pace. He travelled often and re-located annually. Adrian's contract demanded an upscale home office, a new mattress on a king-sized bed and quick access to the border. So far, the proximity to the border was the only good part.

The green key unlocked tall, double-leafed wooden doors. They reminded Adrian of castle doors in animated movies where princesses were protected from dragons and other demons. A frail old lady in matching slacks and tunic stood in the front vestibule, her bony fingers picking at junk mail on the marble floor. She looked up and started to approach him as he walked across the lobby. He ignored her and skipped up the stairs two at a time.

"Is that you, Alexander?" she asked, eyeing him curiously.

Being the sole person within sight, he assumed her question was directed at him.

"No ma'am."

"Well then, what's your name, son?"

He hesitated; no harm would come from sharing this personal detail.

"Adrian."

"What is your surname, Adrian?"

"Common. Adrian Common," he said, checking his watch and phone but failing to register his impatience with Winnie.

"You look so much like my grandson."

"That's nice, ma'am."

"Do you live here, too?'

"Yup. Just moving in. And if you'll excuse me, I'm late for a virtual meeting," he lied.

The only senior he had any use for was his own grandmother, who still sent him twenty dollars via his mother every birthday and Christmas because she couldn't keep track of him. He should call and thank her, but the thought vanished as he reached the top of the stairs.

Winnie was still trying to process what a virtual meeting was. She thought Adrian was a little abrupt with her, but she shifted her attention back to the envelopes and flyers on floor. She had no idea how her mail arrived so fast, forgetting that Annette arranged her address change. Her thoughts ruminated on her old home. Despite her protests, Annette and Allen argued that the upgrades and upkeep costs far exceeded any benefit to Winnie remaining there. The gardener's and housekeeper's salaries increased annually. Suggestions turned into battles. Neither Annette nor Allen had time for what Annette described as trivial nonsense. For months, Winnie shifted what precious free minutes they had for meaningful dialogue to arguments about her outdated house.

Annette and her second husband, Richard, lived in Boston. Allen and his wife, Kim, lived in San Francisco, a five-hour flight to Niagara Falls, New York, excluding traffic to cross the Canadian border. Mason was their primary contact and trusted lifeline to Winnie's legal, financial and personal affairs. He was well worth the chip out of their inheritance to cover his billable hours.

Annette and Allen alternated calling Winnie on the first and third Sunday of every month. It was the most efficient way to manage their commitment to their mother. Of course, birthdays and other special occasion expenses were funded equally via a "Mother Firestone" account they both contributed to. Their administrative assistants sent her cards, flowers or gifts on the appropriate dates. They agreed that they "managed" Winnie as efficiently as their schedules permitted. With some flexibility in his insurance business, Allen scheduled quarterly weekend visits. Since Annette's booming corporate real estate career demanded her availability on short notice, she returned to her Niagara Falls roots bi-annually for two days, at best. It would be much easier if Winnie flew to Boston, but that only happened every other Christmas when Allen's family joined Annette's.

Winnie retrieved a grocery bag from the lobby garbage can and gathered the remaining flyers from the floor, bracing her hand on her knee to straighten her degenerating spine. Blowing dirt off her hands, she scanned her new neighbours' names listed on the other mailboxes. Seven polished steel squares were recessed into the freshly painted wall. Five mailboxes were labelled. Winnie pulled a pen from its cover, which was attached to the lanyard hanging from her neck, and recited each tenant's details aloud as she wrote on the back of an envelope:

Suite 1A – myself
Suite 1B – Portobello (like the mushroom)
Suite 1C – Jamieson/Miles

Suite 2A – Turner/St. James
Suite 2B – no name – maybe empty??
Suite 2C – A. Common (looks like Alexander)

Suite 3 – no name – maybe empty too??

Winnie re-checked the information on the mailboxes; she also felt better after tidying up the foyer. And maybe just a little more settled. She unlocked the heavy, leaded glass door that separated the foyer from the hallway leading to her main floor unit. Maybe tomorrow she'd climb the stairs to the second floor to see if Suite 2B was occupied. She walked to the end of her hallway, double-checking the numbers and suites on the first floor against her own written inventory.

> **Posted Ad: Furnished Condo to Sublet**
>
> Beautiful, newly furnished condo Loft to sublet. Available immediately for short or long-term stays. Recently renovated historic building boasting spectacular views is a short walk to downtown Niagara Falls and most amenities. Must see to appreciate. Secure parking spot included.
>
> For more information please contact Grace at (555) 555-5555

SEPTEMBER 3ᴿᴰ

Suite 3 (The Loft): Gracie Sheehan

> *"A woman is like a tea bag:*
> *You can't tell how strong she is until*
> *you put her in hot water."*
>
> *Eleanor Roosevelt*

Gracie Sheehan had signed the lease agreement for the furnished Park Street Loft on September 1st but was having trouble processing her decision to be alone again. Blair, her husband of twenty-eight years, died a few years ago of metastatic lung cancer, leaving her a widow with their daughter Tess to support through university. To make matters worse, she lost her job as a benefits administrator at a large steel company when her site location closed. That all happened within a span of eight weeks.

Blair had smoked anything he could get his hands on, but mostly cigarettes. Gracie's persistent and vocal nagging forced him to quit long enough to purchase a life insurance policy, which was her nest egg, or secretly her vindication after his early death. He messed up by telling his oncologist and dental hygienist that he periodically enjoyed a cigarette. After he died, the life insurance company audited his medical records and denied the claim, which listed him as a non-smoker. Her $100,000 nest never materialized. She hated him then, and although she thought she had forgiven him, she hated him again today. Her life, mundane as it was, would be very different if Blair had the insight to realize how negatively his choices affected his surviving family.

Gracie worked tirelessly to rebuild her life, and met a wonderful man named Fred by sheer chance. She often wondered if she made a mistake by leaving all things familiar in Toronto and moving to a little hamlet called New Pelham to be with him. Maybe yes, and some days, maybe no. Today it was maybe both because she wasn't feeling particularly confident about anything she had done in the last year. She called the property manager to cancel the Park Street condo lease, citing renter's remorse. After pleading with him, the manager verbally agreed to cancel the lease but withheld the first two, as well as the last month's rent. He suggested she sublet and would advise her if he found an interested party. To Gracie, three months of lost rent was a lot of money, but it was better than losing out completely. She felt like she was regressing instead of moving forward.

September 4th
Weather forecast: sunny skies

Suite 2A: Bryce and Talia

"The best things in life are free."

Message in Chinese Fortune Cookie

Bryce slid the tiny, frayed slip of paper out from the secret spot in his wallet and read it again, as he had done countless times over the last two years. He took a picture of it. The most precious thing in Bryce's life was Talia. From the first day he sat behind her at the call centre employee orientation, he felt hopeful and happy. By week's end, he'd mustered up enough courage to invite her to dinner. She declined, but by the second week, Talia opted for a rain check. They ate Chinese food, and the tiny paper in his hand came from the fortune cookie he opened that night. It began a life he was determined to keep whole. Chinese food on the first Friday of every month became their ritual from that day forward. Sometimes for lunch, sometimes for dinner, and sometimes leftovers delivered to the one that had to work. He never wanted this to end.

Talia was perfect. Her straight hair was the colour of chestnuts that shone like a wet stone. There was never more than a few brushstrokes of make-up on her flawless skin. Her clothes were not flashy but attractive enough for him to always want her. Her voluptuous breasts, inherited from her mother, were an odd fit on her slender frame. Slim hips and square shoulders awarded her a confident gait. He would watch others, both male and female, turn their heads and watch her as she went about her business, oblivious to the silent commotion she created. She was like a magnet that drew him and others to her. She never did or said anything wrong, and Bryce knew after the first date that he wanted to spend his life with her.

Bryce's parents divorced when he was young, soon after his anxious mother discovered his father's infidelity. Bryce saw his father and misery as one and the same. At any event which his father deemed appropriate to bring a companion, there was always a new face. Bryce ignored their names because they weren't around long enough for the need to remember. His father's alcohol-fuelled comments and demeaning stares remained consistent with each changeover of partners. His marriage to Alice lasted long enough to include her name when Talia's parents posted the wedding announcement. Bryce's mother, in contrast, was a saint. She raised Bryce and his sister Kate by juggling multiple jobs to supplement their father's intermittent support payments. She was Bryce's rock, spending what little energy she had left after work to inspire and educate her children. Bryce's mother was firm yet fair, and he avoided doing anything that would make her unhappy.

Bryce's mother always complimented him on his attention to detail and cleanliness. He liked things organized and consistent. He set the table and loaded and unloaded the dishwasher, neatly assembling plates and cutlery on the machine racks. The more havoc his father created in his mother's life, the harder Bryce worked to ease her burden. When things were calm at home, he was calm. These systemic timing patterns worked for everyone, and he hoped that Talia would accept him for that. For now, he had some flexibility. Keeping her happy was his main priority despite his inability to escape the revolving patterns in his mind.

Suite 1B: Marcello Portobello

Marcello's fourth day on Park Street was less pleasant than the first three. The wide-silled palladium windows made great napping spaces for his cats on sunny days. One window doubled as an emergency exit to a wrought iron fire escape. Mona Lisa and Michelangelo could venture outside if the window was opened wide enough. This irritated Marcello because the building safety plan prohibited protective gates from being installed to keep his cats from roaming and getting lost.

New stainless steel kitchen appliances, far superior to the ones he left behind, gleamed in the sunlight. Marcello's herb garden was acclimatizing nicely on the kitchen window ledge. Intending to expand his culinary skills, Marcello retrieved the box of treasured recipes inherited from his family, hoping to impress the rare lover he took on in a moment of weakness. Selecting a few meandering stems of lemon basil, he found a recipe his mother used with this fragrant herb. He sat down on his gold brocade, plastic-covered sofa, a piece that matched his eclectic combination of Venetian antiques and ornate replicas. He pulled a small green envelope from the front of the recipe box which held the invitation to his own retirement party.

Dark and bitter days followed Marcello when his tour guide/translator career ended abruptly, a job that came about quite by accident ten years ago. He used to frequent the botanical gardens in Niagara Falls on Sundays after mass, not only for the visual stimulus but also to hear his first language spoken by Italian tourists. He took every opportunity to preserve his own dialect, beaming with pride when he recognized it in the crowd. Always impeccably dressed in public and very well spoken, one could easily mistake him for a wealthy businessman living off the tourist industry rather than describing it.

His career took hold when a mature tour guide with a pleasant voice butchered his Italian language. It pained Marcello and others until another Italian tourist asked Marcello to interpret instead. The guide readily acknowledged her weakness and agreed. In fact, the bus full of tourists applauded when she offered Marcello a free ride in the seat beside her for the rest of the guided tour.

By chance, she was also a supervisor, so between stops she pummelled Marcello with intrusive questions until the last stop, when she offered him a temporary assignment. He started the next day wearing a name tag labelled Marco; his supervisor explained that many tourists found Marco easier to pronounce than Marcello. This deeply offended him because he had proudly inherited his father's name. However, from then until his last day, Marcello remained Marco to his supervisor but Marcello to everyone else. The social interaction inspired him to work from Easter to Thanksgiving. He was also granted a seasonal city bus pass in return for promoting local attractions, and he enjoyed a complimentary buffet lunch with the tour at its host hotel. This afforded him an annual trip to Italy in the off season to replenish his custom-made suits, shirts and leather footwear that displayed his devotion to fine Italian couture. Rarely did he allow Valentina's name to sour the conversation with family and friends when he returned to Venice.

Marcello maintained an active lifestyle until a nagging backache cramped his easy stride. To compensate, he reduced his work schedule, walked cautiously and avoided the scrutiny of his supervisor. Eventually she explained that business was slow and she had to lay him off. A co-worker, greedy for more shifts, complained that he couldn't keep up. Marcello preferred the truth than to be cast aside like a broken animal, devalued by its owner.

Marcello's retirement party was his supervisor's idea, and despite repeated protests of not wanting one, a date was set. He dreaded the thought of going beyond the consolation of a free meal. He threw the invitation on the coffee table and hissed; his cats, who lifted their heads, looked lazily at him and resumed their naps.

September 8th
Weather forecast: rainy day and foggy night

Suite 1C: Rose and Lily
Just after Midnight

"Life's tragedy is that we get old too soon and wise too late."

Benjamin Franklin

Rosie locked her bedroom door, adjusted her bedside lamp to its softest setting and forced the huge window wide open. Stripping off her hotel uniform, she eased her nude body into a white lace camisole and roomy pajama pants. She perched her petite, flannel-clad bottom on a folded towel, stretching her tired legs along the perfect length and width of the deep inside windowsill. Pulling the flannel down to cover her toes, Rosie carefully lit a joint, flicked the match outside and watched it fade into the foggy night.

Small drops of rain bounced off the outside window ledge like crystals in the haze of the street lights. The solitude of her room blended with the relaxant between her fingers and calmed her quickly. Occasional splashing of car tires against the wet pavement below her gently reminded her that few others shared this quiet. If she cranked her neck far enough, she could see the flashing lights of the casinos on both sides of the border. She often walked to work, even though most of her workday involved standing. It refreshed both her mind and body. She took a long pull of the thin roll and held it in her lungs for as long as she could. God bless Ramone, who gifted her first with a small package of edibles after a supervisor's meeting. They split her first joint on her fiftieth birthday ten months ago. She tilted her face up into the drizzle of the night sky, feeling the cool wetness on her eyelids.

"Forgive me, Mom, but perfect I'm not," she whispered as she exhaled slowly.

Rosie saw Lily less since the move, frustrated with her fumbling through life and making bad choices. Yet Rosie loved her. At this stage of their lives, both were single and childless. Rosie remained content while Lily was always searching for something—or someone—beyond her reach. Like their mother, Rosie was petite and lean. Lily was her father's clone, inheriting his tall and stocky frame. Lily never accepted her extra pounds, compounded by her mother's criticism of her weight. Lily's insecurities were shrouded in misery. She threw words at Rosie like weapons, then feeling remorseful, overstocked the pantry with junk food they both enjoyed. Rosie hoped that one day Lily would forgive herself, move beyond her past and learn to value the good between and within them.

Other than distant or disinterested relatives, they were each other's only family. They never healed their wounds because neither knew how. Rosie thought about the spa certificate she was gifted today from her director for her exemplary paid and volunteer work. Maybe she'd leave it on the kitchen counter one day for Lily with some kind words.

Chilled and damp as she finished the joint, Rosie eased herself off the windowsill, her back stiff from a long day. Preparing for bed, she left the window open enough to let the misty night air circulate. She crawled under the new white duvet cover Lily washed before making Rosie's bed, and was asleep within minutes.

SEPTEMBER 9TH
Weather forecast: more rain

Suite 1C: Rose and Lily
Afternoon

"Children begin by loving their parents.
As they grow older, they judge them.
Sometimes, they forgive them."

Author Unknown

Lily reverted to the routine she and Rosie kept before their move to Park Street. Rosie was promoted three years ago at the hotel. Managing people is what she did best, with the exception of Lily, who was certain Rosie worked the afternoon shift just to avoid her. Lily woke early and retired to her bedroom before Rosie got home, and she was often gone before Rosie got up mid-morning. They rarely shared a meal, which Lily assumed suited them both. It was baffling that these siblings were created by the same parents.

In childhood, Rosie was the peacekeeper while Lily sought out reasons to create havoc. Rosie earned the "favourite daughter" status early, even though their parents gave them love, attention and material things equally. Rosie earned praise for good grades and helping the needy while Lily did the opposite. Rosie attended the local university and earned privileged access to the second family car. When Lily was home from school, she monopolized the car and left Rosie to clean up after her. Conflict was as routine as night followed day.

Just one more year until I can unlatch myself from Rosie, Lily thought today. She opened the first box of her mother's things, which still smelled of fried egg sandwiches and cigarettes. She transferred most of it into another box for charity and filled the rest with clothes she outgrew. She blamed Rosie for everything that ate away at her. Instead of preparing meals, she picked up the daily feature at the nearby diner, bakery or coffee shop. Lily set a goal to start a new diet once all the sealed boxes were purged. Her previous diets had all failed, and she vowed that her next diet would be different—and better, depending on what her inclusion or exclusion criteria was that day. Which diet she would choose needed more research than she had the time and willpower to invest today.

Suite 2B: Sally and Mitch Penfold
Early Evening

Even though it was still raining, Sally took her time going home from her job at the bank. Their condo was near the bus and train stations. Ambitious travellers often left these terminals and walked along the fast-moving Niagara River, drawn to the thundering sound of Niagara Falls before seeing them.

Sally continued down the main street toward the river, then followed an alternative route under an abandoned train bridge half a block from her building. A faint meow came from somewhere above her. In the dark gaps between the stone wall and the rusty undercarriage of the old bridge was a deep ledge spanning the length of the underpass. From a safe distance, two sets of green eyes interrogated hers. As her focus acclimatized to the dark, a third set of amber eyes widened when she inched closer. A fourth creature growled softly by the time she was able to focus on a half dozen cardboard and Styrofoam boxes filled with hay. Someone purposely recessed the containers deep enough into the space to protect this little colony from predators. Plastic margarine and sour cream containers were partially full of water or dry cat food. The scent of food, hay and mustiness reminded her of her grandfather's barn on his cattle farm. As she walked by, she wondered if other feral creatures invaded this cat haven and what sort of pecking order determined entitlement to room and board here. She caught a quick glance of a lanky male figure dressed in baggy jeans and high-top sneakers, his head shrouded under a black hoodie as he walked away.

Sally's building looked wet and dreary as she approached it, and she hoped the landscaper would dress it up soon. She entered the vestibule, reflecting that the only tenant she'd met after a week was Lily. She opened her condo door and took a deep, relaxing breath.

Sally had set up the condo quickly, arranging her and Mitch's odd mix of furniture as best as she could. The bathroom, kitchen and bedroom linen came from her inventory. Mitch's went straight into the rag bag. The newlyweds planned to spend Mitch's next precious day off shopping for condo accessories. With the gas money she saved by walking to work, she secretly opened a "Hawaii

Honeymoon" account, a destination they both talked about. It was something exciting to save for. She texted Mitch a quick love note, knowing it might be hours before he responded. His work hours were endless, but he usually texted back if he'd be really late.

She changed into worn jeans and a red sweater, Mitch's favourite colour. She worked hard to stay fit and well. Making love was less fulfilling to Mitch now than a few years ago, but it was still important to her.

Mitch met Sally during the criminal investigation of her ex-boyfriend, Robin. Their first official date progressed rapidly from a restaurant to her bedroom. Mitch knew her room well, because he had once sat on the bed beside Sally in his suit writing his detective notes. Sometimes he asked intimate questions, such as her sexual partners before Robin or if she had any addictions. He said it was all part of the process, but when he started writing less and edging closer, she sensed it was a different kind of investigation. He kissed her only once, softly and tenderly like she had hoped, before the case wrapped up. When Sally saw Mitch in uniform for official events, he took her breath away.

Despite her patience, she sometimes resented Mitch for staying out late to have pizza and beer with his colleagues after a tough day instead of coming home. He called it debriefing and said it was critical to his well-being; it made him a better husband, he said. She hoped his work routine would become more predictable soon but remained grateful for his contributions to make her world safer.

Suite 3 (The Loft): Gracie Sheehan

A week ago, Gracie regretted her hasty decision to lease the Loft, but changed her mind again, for good reasons. As of today, no one was interested in subletting her condo. A pair of senior travellers considered it briefly, then backed out because her third-floor unit had no elevator access.

Gracie was fortunate enough to transfer her part-time library job to a Niagara Falls branch. She wouldn't lose her rent money and could walk to work. It was a nice place to call home and heal. Perhaps she would learn to love herself again, even though it would take more effort this time around. She needed to re-learn the importance of looking after herself before looking after others. She stopped by the condo to check her mail, which was re-directed from Fred's house in New Pelham, where she had lived for about a year.

After Blair's death and Gracie's job loss at the automotive plant, her manager suggested she rent part of a neighbour's estate in the exclusive Toronto area he had lived in. Gracie became fast and close friends with Livy Bless, a dynamic divorcée who lived in the mansion. Livy loved life and travelled extensively as part of her job. A series of unexpected events led Gracie to take on new roles she was unprepared for including lover, dog sitter and respite caregiver of Livy's distant uncle, a crotchety recluse with secrets of his own.

At that time, a much less confident Gracie was forced to question her own values, judgment and life goals. She shifted between her Toronto roots and helping Livy's uncle in New Pelham, where she met Fred, a teacher who lived next door. Although neither were looking, their losses drew them together.

With a clearer mind, Grace understood that, although Fred was legally separated from his wife, what remained of her relationship with him was much too complex to allow them to plan a future together. It took months for them to formally acknowledge this. Fred had lived in the tiny hamlet of New Pelham forever. Grace was transplanted there, and loved country living, but couldn't compete with the responsibilities that Fred continued to maintain, be it the result of guilt or pressure from his daughter.

Fred was Fred, and she realized soon enough that she could never "fix" him or his life. After many sleepless nights and heart-wrenching "discussions," they parted, both with wounded hearts. Gracie left with what little she brought, except Wilson, a golden retriever who took to country living like a duck to water. When she moved to her daughter Tess's apartment in Toronto, there were no pets allowed, and it was mutually decided by all that New Pelham was the best place for Wilson. Tess's apartment furnishings were from the home they lived in before Blair died, and until Gracie was in a position to decide where her next residence would be, only her personal possessions would move with her.

Gracie fingered the platinum and diamond eternity ring that Fred purchased from Livy's family's estate. When they parted, he insisted she keep it, respecting her closeness to Livy. Determined to turn that page, she slowly twisted it over the knuckle of her left ring finger and repositioned it on her right hand. The first time she'd seen the heirloom was on Livy's hand. That seemed like such a long time ago, even though it was just a few years.

September 12th
Weather forecast: unseasonably warm

Suite 1B: Marcello Portobello

"Everybody wants to go to heaven, but nobody wants to die."

Anonymous

Marcello's dinner for one consisted of pasta al dente with marinara sauce that simmered all afternoon on the stove, followed by a tossed salad with a fresh herb vinaigrette. The sun faded peacefully, as did Marcello in his favourite chair, listening to an Italian symphony with a second glass of red wine in his hand and Mona Lisa on his lap. A warm breeze circulated through the open windows as he heard a fading siren responding to someone's emergency. Michelangelo, soaking up the remaining warmth on the window ledge, popped his head up suddenly, then sat up. Mona Lisa shifted her position in Marcello's lap. Marcello checked his feline family with heavy eyelids, murmuring comforting Italian words. A faint wail came from somewhere, possibly down the street. He leaned back lazily in his chair. It came again, with the same level of intensity. He finished the last sip of wine, gently moved Mona Lisa to the warm spot where his bottom had been and walked to the window. The wail returned, followed by a retching sound. No one was visible on the street below. He waited, and hearing it again, linked the noise to the condo next door. It must be the old woman. She might be sick or crying. Not one to meddle in another's business, he returned to his chair, but the next cry overshadowed any desire for sleep or privacy. He changed from slippers to his worn Italian leather loafers and gathered his thoughts before knocking softly on the door marked 1A. A floral paper sign with "Winnie Firestone" penned in an elaborate script was taped to the door. When the next episode of retching stopped, he knocked louder. Still no response and no sound. Abandoning his well-polished etiquette, he banged louder.

"Mrs. Firestone, are you there?"

No answer. He pounded the door with his fist.

"Mrs. Firestone, are you all right?"

The sound of something metallic hitting the floor followed by a desperate cry startled him.

"Mrs. Firestone! It's Marcello, your neighbour! Please open the door! I am afraid for your safety!"

He continued banging the door until he heard the slow shuffle of feet approach. With his palms splayed flat against the steel door, Marcello felt the vibration of a deadbolt unlocking, then heard the click of a second lock. The heavy door opened a crack, still secured by a thick link of chain. He gasped when Winnie's glassy, grey eyes met his. He saw sallow, ashen skin, and but for the fact that she was still standing, she looked dead. A pathetic, frail bird. The stench of vomit stopped his breathing.

"Mrs. Firestone, you are sick!"

"Oh, oh, oh, you can't come in … I've made such a mess," she cried.

"My God, someone has to help you," he said as a wave of nausea swept through him.

"Who can come and help you?"

"No one."

"No one? *Merda*, Mrs. Firestone, then I will help you," he offered with mild regret.

"I've made such a mess. No, no, no. You can't come in."

"But someone has to help you … we will worry about the mess later. Let me in and I will help you."

She looked both skeptically and pathetically at him, leaning heavily against the door frame.

"Who are you again?"

"Marcello, Mrs. Firestone. Marcello from next door."

"How do I know that?"

"I met you at the mailbox."

"You did?"

"Yes. Twice. And if you open the door, perhaps I can help you."

She eyed him suspiciously, then shut the door. As Marcello contemplated his next move, he heard the sliding metal of the chain lock. The door opened slowly and the sight of her in full view humbled him. The front of her flannel nightdress, slippers and matching housecoat were drenched in vomit. It was in her hair, under her chin and on her hands. Not sure if the sight was worse than the odour, he feared he would lose his own dinner—and worse: fine, imported wine. He took a cotton handkerchief from his pocket to shield his nose.

"Come and sit down, you can barely stand up," he said, his eyes watering.

He coaxed her to a kitchen chair. Her head heavy, she cradled it in her hands, which rested against the table as she whimpered.

"Don't cry, Mrs. Firestone. Please don't cry," Marcello whispered.

He was helpless when women cried, and he blamed Valentina for that. The floor, not two feet from where she sat, was splattered with undigested food around a stainless-steel cooking pot. He surveyed the mess, following the spatter marks sprayed across the lower cupboards and appliances. *What a mess*, he thought silently in his native tongue. *How could such a tiny woman empty so much from her stomach?*

"Can I call anyone to help you?"

"I have no one," she sniffled again, producing a used tissue from somewhere in her nightclothes.

"You have no family?"

"I might as well not have."

He looked puzzled. "Have you a friend I can call?"

"They're all dead."

She can't be serious, he thought. But then again, estimating her age, he thought maybe she was.

"Where is your family? Can I call them?"

"You can call them, but they won't come."

"Why not?" Marcello was mildly irritated. Although his distant relatives all lived in Italy, family was important to someone who was old and in need.

"My daughter, Annette, lives in Boston, and my son, Allen, lives in San Francisco," she sniffled, then retched again.

Nothing came up, and again Marcello felt the nausea roll in his belly.

"Hmmm. You must have someone nearby I can call."

"Only Mason."

"Who is Mason?"

"He's my lawyer."

Marcello scratched his forehead. No lawyer was coming over to clean up vomit. He inhaled through his mouth and surveyed the mess. It was confined to the kitchen, but the immediate problem was the poor soul in front of him.

Yielding to sympathy, he said, "I will help you," but he had no intention of assisting her beyond the door to her bathroom. The only female he had ever bathed was his cat, and this was no time to start. Leaving Winnie seated with her head and arms still on the kitchen table, Marcello peeked into her bathroom. She had an easily accessible bath and a shower unit, and if he could help her to the door, perhaps she could manage beyond there. Shuddering at the possibilities, he knew better than to make other suggestions, so he returned to the kitchen.

Winnie's head was still on the table. A shower was not going to happen, and he was frightened by the sudden thought that she may think he was a predator. Marcello's thoughts flashed back to just ten minutes ago when he was snoozing in the comfort of his own tidy home. He looked at Winnie. Like a frail bird, she was unsafe alone in her nest.

"Winnie?"

She looked up at him, head still on the table and only one eye open.

"Let me help you to your room. Maybe if you sleep, you will feel better. Then you can bathe yourself after you rest."

A suspicious frown returned to Winnie's face. A speck of the vomit had fallen from her hair and was dangling precariously from her eyebrow. She looked down at her soiled clothes and whimpered faintly. Marcello felt as despondent as she did, and Winnie sensed he was quite sincere in his offer of help.

"Have you more bedclothes?" he asked. "Do you feel strong enough to change into clean ones? You, you, you will have to change yourself. I can put your clothes in the washing machine," he stuttered, again regretting his offer and not sure how he was going to manage either. Her expression was pitiful.

"I can't ask you to do that."

"You are ill, Mrs. Firestone. We all need help when we are sick."

Why am I here? he asked himself silently in Italian. He took a deep breath, then approached her slowly and gently guided her to her feet. Her upper arms felt smaller than his wrists, and they were the only part of her clothed body he could safely grasp. He estimated her weight to be under a hundred pounds.

The pair shuffled in unison to the bedroom, the bulk of Winnie's torso leaning into Marcello. He guided her steps gingerly across the lush Persian carpet and turned her around cautiously to face him, encouraging her to feel the back of her knees against the bed before she sat down. She looked bleakly up at him, lids half-closed.

"Now what do we do?" she asked, her mouth forming a crooked smile.

Holding her shoulders gently, he returned the smile. Her sunken eyes were inches from his when she spoke.

"Only one man has ever put me to bed, and I never thought there would be two," she squeaked.

He grinned widely.

"Mrs. Firestone, if the neighbours knew, they would talk."

"I think, considering these circumstances, you can call me Winnie."

"If you could, Winnie, then please tell me where your clean nightclothes are so I can get them for you."

She pointed to a dresser about eight feet away.

"And which drawer?"

"The second."

He eased his hold from her shoulders and walked quickly to the dresser. The second drawer held socks and neat piles of cotton underwear in various pastel colours, but no nightgowns. Marcello's face flushed as he spoke.

"No bedclothes in the second drawer. Perhaps the third?"

"Perhaps."

Marcello turned from the sweaters folded neatly in the third drawer to see Winnie rolling from the bed onto the carpet.

"Merda!" He yelled in Italian and rushed to his patient. "Winnie!"

She opened her eyes, met his and closed them again.

"Winnie, look at me!"

No response.

"I'm calling 911."

Instantly, her eyes fluttered open, wide as saucers.

"No! No! No! You are not!"

"Yes. I must."

"No!"

"Why not?"

"No! No! I insist!" she yelled.

"But maybe you broke something," he pleaded, his own heart pounding fiercely.

"Please! Please, just let me sleep."

"No, Winnie. Not here. I can't let you sleep on the floor."

"I just want to sleep."

"Then I will at least help you into your bed."

She closed her eyes again and opened her mouth. It was an effort for her to speak, but her words were clear.

"If you must, but I beg you not to call the ambulance. Please don't call them. I do not want to go to the hospital. They'll send me to a nursing home and then I'll die. Please, I beg you again not to call them. I just need some sleep."

Her eyes sealed shut and did not re-open, but they released a single tear that followed the crease of a wrinkle and landed onto Marcello's arm. Marcello understood, briefly envisioning his own destiny of growing old alone. Winnie was eighty. He was seventy but felt her age today. It terrified him, and he sensed Winnie had experienced this feeling before.

Marcello carefully arranged his arms around Winnie and awkwardly brought her to a seated position. Questioning his own strength, he tightened his flaccid abdominal muscles and, with great effort, heaved Winnie onto her bed. Her eyes flashed wide open with surprise, then shut again. Anchoring himself against her bed, it took every ounce of strength he had to stand up, his back instantly retaliating from his rescue effort. He looked at Winnie as she lay across the bed, exhausted and misaligned like a discarded rag doll. Marcello gently rearranged her into a more anatomical order. Still, she lay too close to the edge of the bed and was susceptible to a second tumble off of it. Knowing neither his back pain nor his strength would permit him to re-position her safely again, he limped to the other side of the bed and tugged at the bedspread until she was centred on the bed.

She looked like a corpse until she mouthed the words "Thank you." He took the half of her bedspread which was on the carpet and rearranged it over her. He gently eased two of the three pillows out from under her head and lay them on either side of her like an overcautious mother with a newborn. He sighed heavily, slightly less concerned for her safety. He found a face cloth in the bathroom, wet it and lathered it with her lavender soap. He gently washed the drying vomit out of the bony hollows of her face and hands as she lay still, and perhaps felt better than Winnie when he left her snoring softly. He wondered what prompted him to do something so personal for a woman he barely knew, until the distant memory of caring for his own ailing mother explained everything.

Marcello surveyed the disaster in the kitchen. It would be impossible for Winnie to feel well enough to clean this mess. A housekeeper, if Winnie was more privileged than him and had one, would not appreciate scraping up dried emesis. Marcello again thought of his own mother. If she was alive, he would never allow her to face this when she rose from her sickbed. And that vision is what prompted him, a rapidly aging man with a self-inflicted episode of chronic back pain, to tackle this project. He looked under the sink a found the needed supplies, save for a large silicone spatula he used to scoop up what mess he could first. He wiped, washed and re-washed the cupboards and floors and everywhere else Winnie had lost her meal.

Over the time it took to clean the kitchen, Marcello's back pain tripled in intensity. It was far worse than he could remember. At the one-hour mark, he could barely stand or even straighten up. His conscience tugged at him not to leave Winnie in case she got up and fell, so he limped over to the living room and eased himself onto her sofa. He fingered the fine but worn burgundy leather and imagined that many good conversations had transpired sitting on this furniture.

Rummaging through his pockets, Marcello found his antique pill box. Electric shocks from aggravated nerves and old discs pulsated from his back right down to his toes. A pain level of nine out of ten justified taking two prescription pain tablets instead of his usual one. And the half litre of wine he consumed earlier was starting to wear off. Needing all his strength to elevate his feet onto the sofa, Marcello knew he would be unable to bend over to remove his shoes, let alone put them back on again. Well-medicated and lubricated, he, too, fell asleep in minutes.

A half-hour later, Winnie stirred, aware of the dampness and stench of her clothing. The phone beside her was ringing. She sat up quickly, her heavy head pounding. She looked at the pillows on either side of her, totally confused about what she was doing in bed in this arrangement. Was it morning? She answered her phone on the third ring, her parched throat reducing her voice to a raspy whisper. Mason's voice immediately soothed her.

"Winnie? Is that you?"

"Who is this?'

"It's Mason."

"Yes, Mason. What time is it?"

"It's seven thirty. Were you asleep?"

She looked at her bedding.

"I guess I was. I have a terrible headache."

"Are you sick?"

She frowned at her soiled clothes.

"I guess I was."

"I'm just leaving the office. Do you need anything?"

"I don't know. I don't know if I need anything."

"Would you like me to pop over for a few minutes?"

"That would be nice. I haven't talked to a soul today."

"Why don't I come in about fifteen minutes?"

She pulled back the covers and looked at herself.

"Make it thirty."

"All right then, I'll see you in half an hour."

Winnie sighed wearily and wiggled her way to the side of the bed, feeling slightly better but not sure from which ailment. More apparent than her pounding head was the vile stickiness in her throat. She eased her feet onto the floor, her head spinning. Waiting until her balance permitted her to stand up without falling, she looked at the partially open top drawer of her dresser where a clean nightgown lay folded over the drawer. She didn't remember opening the drawer or choosing a nightgown she didn't particularly care for. Leaning against her bed, she removed her dressing gown, turned it inside out and placed it back on the bed. Knowing better than to bend over, she grabbed the sides of her soiled nightgown and tugged at it until it was up over her hips. She sat safely back down on her bed. She struggled to get it over her head without smearing the pasty patches against her hair and skin. Off came her baggy underpants, and Winnie stood up, her naked reflection staring back at her in the mirror. Her skin, and wherever hair still grew, was all the same dull grey. Her hips and ribs protruded like a carcass of angular bones, covered with skin as thin as paper. Her breasts, once supple and firm, now hung like withered flaps of flesh.

Remembering Mason was coming, she shuffled her way into her walk-in closet. She put on the strategically placed nightgown and closed the drawer. She took the matching bathrobe off its hanger, again trying to make sense of why something she was not fond of was right there in front of her. She supported herself against her dresser and slipped it on. She would bathe after Mason left.

Winnie exited the bedroom towards her living room, planting each foot strategically apart from the other to stabilize her gait. With the back of her sofa just a few more steps away, she would rest against it before going into the kitchen for a drink of water. She spotted the worn pair of Italian loafers on her sofa arm, toes pointing up to create a V. *Mason would never come in without knocking, let alone put his feet on my couch*, she thought. Startled, still nauseated and thoroughly confused, she grabbed hold of the closest thing to her, which was a large china figurine on the side table. Armed and ready to throw it, she lost her balance, toppling a treasured Tiffany lamp over and onto Marcello.

"Holy mother of God!" Marcello yelled as he jumped awake, wincing aloud as another electric shock pierced his back.

Winnie's fall was interrupted by the armrest, and it prevented her from landing directly on top of him. Both parties yelled, a frenzy of deconditioned legs and arms untangling themselves in very slow motion. Winnie grabbed Marcello's hair and pulled as hard as she could. Without enough strength to do more than make him appear even more dishevelled, Marcello managed to get himself seated and on the opposite side of the sofa from Winnie. The china figurine lay on its side between them, miraculously intact.

"You! What are you doing here?" she squealed, her raspy throat burning with bile.

"Mrs. Firestone, I am terribly sorry. My back pains me deeply. I took my pain pills and, and, and I must have dozed off."

He replaced the figurine and up-righted lamp on the coffee table beside him.

"And terribly sorry you should be, Mister. I thought you were an intruder!"

"A change of clothes," Marcello said, pointing to her clean clothing, relieved she managed to change on her own. "Ah, that's good to see, Mrs., I mean, Winnie. Are you feeling better?"

"Somewhat. Yes, I did change my things." She eyed him distrustfully. "How did you know I changed my clothes?"

Marcello was suddenly aware he had been just steps away from a very precarious situation, and Winnie's expression acknowledged she interpreted his thoughts.

"You better get out of here, Mister, because I'm expecting company in five minutes."

That was all Marcello needed to hear. He used the arm of the sofa to assemble himself into a semi-standing position. The double dose of medication dulled his back pain but also made him unsteady on his feet. She watched him hobble to the door.

"What's wrong with you?" she squawked.

"Winnie. You were sick. Remember? You were ill and threw up on the floor."

"So I was," she responded, taking a whiff of her staleness.

"I washed your kitchen floor, your cupboards, et cetera, et cetera," he told her.

"You did?" she looked around.

"But as you now can see, I have a very bad back, which makes such a simple task very difficult for me."

She looked into the kitchen. Whatever mess she vaguely remembered was gone. She had indeed vomited.

"I ralphed."

"Why, yes. Yes, you did."

Marcello leaned heavily against the wall for support.

"And I helped you to your bed, but you slid off and landed on the floor. Do you remember that, Mrs. Winnie?"

Her recollection of that part was foggy, but Marcello was adamant about defending himself.

"If you have some scrapes or bruises, it may be from that fall. Do you not remember begging me not to call the ambulance?"

Winnie's eyes met his. That she vividly recalled.

"Yes. Yes, of course. Now I do. And I do thank you for that."

She was exhausted. And she stunk.

Marcello smoothed his wrinkled clothes, fingering his thinning hair back into place with minimal success. He looked at Winnie. She was still pale but no longer the shade of death. The nap did them both good, if only a little. Limping, another stab of pain shot down his leg as he opened Winnie's door. She also realized that with the intensity of Marcello's pain, neither was a threat to the other.

"Will you be all right by yourself, Winnie?"

He could barely stand. She was touched by his concern.

"I'll be fine, and thank you again for your help."

"Take care not to fall."

He took his pen and an old receipt from his breast pocket, wrote his full name and phone number down and handed it to her. She put it on the coffee table.

"If I can be of assistance, this is my number. Suite 1B. Just next door."

"I'm sure I can manage on my own. I've looked after myself since my husband passed away."

"Ah, such a terrible loss. I'm sorry for you. And I am sure you can manage, but just remember how ill you were, so please take a few days to rest."

"I'll be all right, young man," she said.

"I wish I was a young man," he said, flattered. "Do you need anything before I leave?"

She paused, moving a shaky hand to her forehead.

"Maybe a painkiller —and water. I have a headache."

"You may be dehydrated," he said, wincing as he hobbled to the bottle on the kitchen counter and brought it to Winnie with a glass of water.

She fumbled with the pill bottle, six tablets spilling into her hand. Marcello hesitated at the door, aware of the potential overdose in her hand. She waved him off.

"Don't worry, I'll be fine."

"Ciao," he said, but still watched her place all but two of the tablets back in the bottle and swallow them before he felt comfortable enough to close the door.

Winnie carefully studied the printed phone number and letters spelling Marcello's first and surname.

"Huh. Portobello. Like the mushroom," she said aloud to herself as she folded the paper and put it back on the coffee table.

Marcello unlocked the door to his own condo just as he heard the visitor's buzzer at Winnie's door. She was obviously welcoming someone who was familiar to her. What a night. Nothing peaceful and quiet as he had expected.

Same Time ...

Adrian walked into the front vestibule to see an older man in a custom-made suit, carrying a weathered leather briefcase, buzz one of the occupants. He checked his mailbox. It was empty, as expected.

"Winnie, it's Mason," the suit said.

Probably her son, Adrian thought. Mason nodded slightly to Adrian, who reciprocated. He heard the security buzzer click at the door to the first-floor hallway.

"Are you seeing the old—I mean older—lady?" Adrian asked.

"Why do you ask?"

The men eyed each other, aware they shared expensive taste.

"No reason. She reminds me of my grandmother."

"I'm her lawyer," Mason responded assertively, sending a clear message to Adrian that Winnie was carefully supervised.

"She gets a lot of junk mail. Really none of my business, but the mailman mentioned it."

"And he's paid well to bring it to her. Have a good evening."

Mason caught the door release and made a mental note to ask Winnie about it.

Winnie was waiting in her doorway for Mason as he walked down the hallway towards her. The thick, patterned carpet runner had a zigzag of fresh vacuum marks. The sour odour lingering around Winnie stopped him abruptly. He noticed her pallor.

"What happened, Winnie? Were you sick?"

"I have a headache," she said, pressing the back of her palm against her forehead.

He walked through the doorway. The condo smelled clean. As he bent over to peck Winnie on the cheek, he realized the stench was from her.

"I took a pain killer, so it should be working soon."

Mason put his briefcase down at the front door.

"I'm sorry to hear that," he sympathized.

It brought back memories of the days when his parents were ill. Mason surveyed the condo. The furniture transplanted from Winnie's old house, although slightly congested, fit quite nicely. He looked back at Winnie. Her white hair, cut in a bob and usually pulled neatly back with a velvet hairband or barrette, was a mess. She was also minus her slippers.

"When did you get sick?"

"Not too long ago. Mr. Port-mushroom came over and helped me."

"Who's that? And how did he help you?"

He recalled the young man in the lobby. Mason played many time-consuming roles related to her care but thinking of what he expected for his own parents always brought his patience back. A cleaning lady came every two weeks. Maybe he should bump that up to weekly, not for housekeeping but rather for checking in on Winnie. He typed a reminder into his phone to suggest to Annette and Allen that it may be time to hire a caregiver to ensure Winnie bathed regularly. Maybe he'd use a falls prevention strategy to lobby for that. With more paid support, he'd worry less about her, which he genuinely did. Winnie loved his mother, and his mother adored Winnie. It wasn't the obligation, even though he was fairly compensated for it, but rather knowing that his parents' friend was safe.

"He washed my floor."

Mason scratched his forehead as he returned to the present.

"He what? What happened to your floor?"

He followed Winnie's gnarly, pointed finger to the kitchen. The smell of floor cleaner confirmed her statement. The sink had bits of food debris and a wet dish towel hanging over it to dry. He left the kitchen and peeked through her bedroom doorway. Her soiled bed clothes lay on the new carpet. Another reason to get more support.

An Hour Later ...

Laying on his back on his sofa with his knees up to ease the pressure in his back, Marcello was very aware from past episodes that he would remain there until he needed more pain medication or his bladder forced him to move. He pictured himself to be as helpless as Winnie in a few years. Was this in fact his fate? A loveless existence of loneliness and misery? No one to care for him or worry about him? Mona Lisa shifted her plump body from the windowsill and settled herself back into Marcello's lap. As she kneaded his thighs, it depressed him that his life was reduced to managing his crumbling body and parenting his cats. A tear spilled from the corner of his eye, landing on Mona Lisa's outstretched paw. She lazily watched it bead on her fur, then licked it off.

SEPTEMBER 14TH
Weather forecast: seasonably warm

Suite 2C: Adrian Common

"So young, but with a heart and soul that's empty."

Anonymous

Adrian returned home from work, checked his empty mailbox and then his phone. He raced up the lobby stairs in case the old lady was hovering in the front entrance again. His conscience nagged him about his own grandmother, whom he'd thought about more since he'd moved to Park Street. She was also helpless, and he wondered how she spent her days. Did she subscribe to junk mail, too, hoping to win big money? Adrian's mother was a kind person who, between priding him for his successes, slid subtle hints about calling his nana. Adrian had a fleeting thought about getting her a nice pink housecoat and nightgown set like the old lady was wearing when she was shuffling through the junk mail in the lobby. Maybe Kelly at his office might suggest something.

Adrian unlocked the solid steel door to his apartment. The cleaning lady had done what few dishes were in the sink. The glass shower stall sparkled. Adrian examined himself proudly in the huge bathroom mirror. His clothes, crested in labels, came off carefully. Pants were returned to their special hangers, and his shirt went into the dry-cleaning bag. The white-and-black tiled floor cooled his feet as he adjusted the shower setting. Water splashed off the large white slabs of grey-veined marble as the pulsating jets bounced hot water off his spine. He rotated slowly, tensing and then relaxing as his flesh reddened. Eyes closed, Adrian inhaled the steam deeply. His phone ringtone indicated his office was calling. He had just left there, so he ignored the call in favour of savouring a few more minutes in the shower. He reached for the towel that the housekeeper replaced, clean and fragrant, and he dried himself off. The call on his voicemail originated from his office, but it was from a co-worker from Vancouver, where Adrian had spent the last year.

"Hey! Where are you?" the voice came over the line. "I'm standing here beside Kelly in your office. Kelly, what street is this? Never mind, anyhow, I'm here on business and wondering what your plans for tonight are. Here's my number because Kelly is protecting you by not giving me your new number. Text me and we'll go out."

Adrian had no plans. Frozen pizza, milk and cereal, the only edibles in his condo, were not an appealing dinner.

Primped, adorned in costly clothes and lightly scented, he locked his door, cursing the inefficiency of carrying extra keys. Adrian stopped to admire himself in the lobby mirror, framed in thick, gilded wood. *Perfect*, he thought as he heard light footsteps tap quickly down from the second floor. Adrian glanced at Talia, who was rushing to work, her long legs carrying her effortlessly down the stairs. He was mesmerized by her shiny chestnut hair that slid over her ivory silk shirt. She smiled politely, flashing perfect teeth. She was soap and water beautiful.

"Hey, just moved in?" he asked.

Talia saw the familiar keys in his hand.

"Yup, but of course, everybody just moved in," she said, giggling.

When Adrian's eyes followed her slim hips to her beautifully round breasts, he was not embarrassed when she noticed. He flashed a confident, then inquisitive smile, imagining how they would feel in his hands. She extended both her middle fingers up to her forehead, then combed her hands through her hair, positioning her elbows high enough in the air to allow him an unobstructed glare. She turned and walked purposefully out the door, leaving Adrian to watch her bottom sway under snug, cherry red jeans until she left his sight. He headed towards his car, then stopped and returned to the building lobby to check if this girl might also live on the second floor, literally steps away from Adrian. He studied the mailbox labels for the first time since moving in.

Suite 1A – Firestone
Suite 1B – Portobello
Suite 1C – Jamieson/Miles

Suite 2A – Turner/St. James
Suite 2B – Occupied
Suite 2C – A. Common

Suite 3 – For Lease

The Park Street Secrets

If the third floor was still unoccupied, she must be "Occupied" or "Turner/St. James." Struck by the vision of her hands in her hair and her lingering scent, Adrian re-arranged the swelling in his pants, hoping to meet her again and confirm that her breasts were not purchased. He walked to his car, revved the engine and psyched himself up for an evening of adventure.

September 14th and 15th
Weather forecast: hot and unseasonably humid

10:00 p.m.

"The value of a secret depends on whom you keep it from."

Anonymous

Mitch loosened his tie and shifted his position in his cruiser's overused seat. He glanced at the time again on his screen; he was starting the third hour of a twelve hour shift, the second in his four night rotation. It was a shitty shift after a shitty dinner where he and Sally argued over money. Again. Sally wanted to invest in decorating, which he saw no value in. The place was new and full of character. They parted with a compromise of agreeing to discuss it, again, which would make for another shitty conversation. He expected tonight would be a quiet shift and therefore a long night. He rolled his window down enough to feel the fall breeze against his face. He was working solo because his partner, Stewy, called in sick. Mitch knew his colleague was burned out, with two toddlers and a wife working opposite shifts from him as an emergency room nurse to minimize childcare costs. His partner needed a break to do something as simple as snuggle with his family and watch cartoons. He always covered for Stewy because Stewy covered for him.

The Park Street Secrets

The new dispatcher's voice broke the silence in his car. Mitch was still getting used to her low drawl. He recognized the address and confirmed he was responding to the call. No need to write it down.

He drove through town, past a church and a small strip mall, and onto the side street. Contrary to what the dispatcher said, he knew there was no "suspicious person" in the backyard. There never was. He parked the cruiser three doors down and locked it. He looked around, checked his phone and walked around the back of the house. It was a dark night, and those familiar with it would notice nothing unusual in this backyard. Unless it was dropped or planted. This time it was planted. They were pink. They were always pink, and the game was to figure out where she left them. It was easy today. They were hanging from the clothesline by the crotch. He walked to the back door, scouting out the adjoining yards. Not a light on beyond distant shadows from the street lights.

The back screen door was unlocked, as was the main door. He knocked lightly, then let himself in and locked the door. It was quiet. He unlaced and slipped off his boots. His sock had a hole in it, which bothered Sally, but not Mitch.

He walked slowly up the stairs, the middle step squeaking under the weight of his foot. The pizza box was on the kitchen counter. He guessed correctly as he lifted the lid. Half of the vegetarian slices were gone and the other half with pepperoni and hot peppers was his midnight meal. He moved quietly from the kitchen to the living room. Most of the furniture remained the same. She did all right, managing her small mortgage from her hotel chambermaid job and his support payments. The bulge in his pants grew as he scanned the bathroom. *Unchanged, just like the kitchen,* he thought as he entered the bedroom.

Georgia lay under the covers, playing by their agreed upon rules. No make-up, no perfume and no talking. He sat down quietly on the side of the bed and undressed slowly in the glow of the night light. He pulled the sheets away, revealing her round folds of skin. She'd grown heavier after they separated and more so after the divorce. The extra weight erased her facial lines. At fifty-five, Mitch was two years older than Georgia. He gave her almost everything she wanted and was still giving it to her when she needed it. She was warm, soft and responded to his desires like a well-maintained machine. Predictable and reliable. He kissed her softly on her neck, holding her breast in his hand. Georgia took his other hand and moved it gently between her thighs, responding quietly to his touch. It was peaceful, familiar, and neither knew who needed the other more, or less.

Mitch lay with Georgia nestled in his chest waiting for the timer on his phone to ring, the regular segue to his exit. He wanted to sleep. The second shift was always the worst. He held her, caressing her dark hair as she circled his nipple with her index finger. He didn't hold her accountable for anything now. What made him return to her, and her respond to him, remained a mystery. They argued constantly when they were married, but now there was nothing left to fight about. Did guilt bring him back? Was it the years his job took precedence over her and their sons? He'd screwed up and he knew it. He'd followed in his proud father's footsteps, despite his militant control over them all. What difference did it make now? It didn't. His body lay limp and relaxed when the timer rang. Shit. Tears sparkled in Georgia's eyes as he dressed. He heard her sniffle.

"Please don't," he whispered, and he left as quietly as he arrived.

Quickly re-lacing his boots, he locked the back door with one hand, pizza box in the other.

Mitch's shift dragged on, interrupted with spikes of remorse. When sleep called to him, he'd get out of his car and walk, chewing periodically on an antacid. By the time he got home in the morning, he was beyond exhausted. Sally was still sleeping when he crawled into bed beside her. She snuggled up to him, her petite body, firm and ten years younger than Georgia's. Sally caught the tail end of his burp rebounding off the sheets.

"Lemme guess: cold pizza," she mumbled.

"How'd you know?"

"I still love you."

"Me too. Now let me sleep."

September 20th
Weather forecast: rain

Suite 2A: Bryce and Talia
8:30 a.m. and continuing into the day

*"I must silence my in-house critic. Yes,
that voice in my head ..."*

Author Unknown

Bryce was rarely happy without Talia nearby. She was his inspiration to wake up each morning. When she worked, he had time to complete his share of the chores. Talia sometimes did the laundry and most of the cooking because she could create a feast from nothing and have it on the table in thirty minutes or less. Bryce needed time to clean the floors, the bathrooms and the kitchen. Talia admired his tidiness but thought he went overboard to be sure it was done *right*. He did his chores when she was at work because it gave him uninterrupted time. "Everything has a place, and everything in its place," his mother always said. Bryce habitually progressed from the cleanest to the final and dirtiest task, which was the bathroom. He glanced at the clock. It was 8:30 a.m., and Talia would be home by 4:00 p.m. He had lots of time.

Bryce started with the fridge. Everything came out, and he scrubbed each shelf and drawer, drying the top shelves and replacing them in their slots so, should there be a wet spot, it would fall on a dirty level instead of a clean level. Once that was done, he wiped each bottle, jar and container. He re-positioned the shelving units to accommodate the short containers, then the mid-sized containers, with the tallest shelf reserved for everything else. He eyed the contents of the fridge that were still sitting on the kitchen counter. He re-arranged them according to height as he replaced them in the fridge, which was a new integration into his ritual. *Yes, this will work.* All labels faced out. *Beautiful.* He closed the fridge. *Is it right?* He opened the fridge and re-checked the order. *Is it right? Yes.* He shut the fridge, checking to be sure it was shut tight. He felt much better.

He checked the clock. It was 10:00 a.m. Next time he would work faster.

Bryce cleaned the stove, which was easy because it didn't get as messy as the bathroom. He needed to budget his time carefully to finish before Talia returned. He walked into their bedroom and opened her closet door. As much as it pained him, she forbade him to re-arrange her clothes. They were all over the place. Jeans parked on door hooks, shirts still within sweaters hanging wherever. Socks tossed into drawers. In due course, she would give in. It would just take time to convince her.

Bryce opened his closet door, content that his inventory was in order. Shirts all faced right, first long-sleeved, then short-sleeved. Light colours progressed to dark. Sometimes he needed to check the striped shirts with one eye closed to confirm that the order was correct. Light background colours were easy; it was those complicated colour blends that made him prefer solid colours. Much less confusing.

He closed the door, hand still on the door knob, then reopened it to switch two shirts. Once, twice, then he closed the door and let it go. He looked at the bedside clock.

Time: 10:20 a.m. He was a little behind. He moved quickly to Talia's drawers. She let him keep these in order. He removed all of her underwear and spread it out on the bed. *Beautiful, beautiful things*, he thought. He smelled them, clean and soft, but ah, so tricky to fold. He arranged them, also alphabetically according to colour. "A" was for the one aqua pair. "B" was for the three black pairs, including one thong, which sat on top of the other black panties. "C" was for chartreuse, a colour he researched before categorizing one pair. Talia hadn't caught on; she just knew he liked to re-arrange her undies "to make them look pretty."

Time: 11:10 a.m. *Keep going, keep going.* He scrubbed the floors, first the living room then the kitchen, which led to the halls, saving the bathroom for last.

Time: 12:30 p.m. *Keep going, keep going, keep going.* He didn't have time to eat. Once he finished the bathroom, he would eat.

Time: 2:00 p.m. *Oh boy, keep going, keep going.* His timing was back on track, and he was now in the bathroom. It was all new and much easier to clean than his mom's bathroom. Bryce started with the huge glass shower. He sprayed all the walls at once, rather than individually, with a pungent antibacterial cleaner to avoid over-spray landing on a finished wall, requiring him to redo it. Six squirts on the smaller wall and nine squirts on the big one. And if the squeegee lines weren't straight, he'd have to start over. *Ready, ready, ready. It is time to start.* He took a deep breath in and started. Very carefully, after starting with horizontal lines from the top left-hand corner to the bottom, he completed the task in only two tries. *Perfect.* The fumes from the cleanser fuzzed up his thinking, but there wasn't enough time to stop. Talia would be home by 4:00 p.m. *Hurry, hurry, hurry.* He cleaned the sink. *Scrub, scrub, scrub. Toothbrush around the sink seal, one quarter turn, then rinse, second quarter, then rinse, third quarter, then rinse. Good, hurry, hurry.* Finally, the throne.

Time: 3:02 p.m. He was short two minutes. *Hurry, hurry, hurry.* He unscrewed the toilet seat bolts and put them in the toilet brush holder, spraying cleanser into the vessel until all the nuts and bolts were submerged in the solution. *They need to soak for twenty minutes; no more and no less.* He assembled six cleaning cloths in sequence of dirtiest to cleanest, cleaned the toilet tank cover with the first cloth, then used the same cloth to clean the tank. He used the second cloth to wash the base of the toilet and repeated the cleaning with the third cloth until he finished the second round of the toilet seat and the nuts and bolts with the fifth cloth. *Ready, ready, ready.* The sixth cloth did the final wipe, and Bryce was careful not to let the cloth touch anything other than the nuts and bolts when he re-attached the seat. He used the sixth cloth to wipe down the floor, always washing from left to right in a counter-clockwise motion until he was done.

Time: 3:58 p.m. He stood outside the bathroom, wiping the handle with the hand towel that was on the inside wall of the bathroom because it was used less and therefore cleaner.

Time: 4:00 p.m. *Perfect timing.* Bryce was exhausted and weak with hunger, sweat drenching his clothes. He just had to wait until everything dried.

Talia keyed in the building main entrance door code and entered the lobby. She gathered the discarded flyers from the floor and threw them in the recycling bin which she insisted the property manager put in the lobby. A business card that would have been easy to miss was tucked deep into the seam of their mailbox slot. She retrieved it and read the card and the handwritten note.

Adrian Common, BA, MBA
Account Manager, International Logistics
R & R Customs Brokerage

Hi, Suite 2C!
Met you Sept.14 in this lobby. Buy you drinks? A.

Talia threw the card in the recycling bin, wondering how he knew which unit she lived in. Adrian was arrogant but handsome—and educated. She'd completed university and dreamed of earning the same master's degree he had to advance her career. She started up the stairs, stopped and returned to retrieve the card, checking it against his mailbox. Suite 2C was on her floor and overlooked the river. Better views meant a higher rent. She inhaled his cologne from the card and wondered if he rubbed his skin against it so she could smell him. The scent was heady and seductive. According to the mailbox listing, he lived alone. Why was she even thinking about this? She tossed the card back into the recycling bin. It landed face up. She looked at the card again. Feeling guilty, she tore it into small pieces and threw all but one piece back into the bin, which she left face up on the floor, doubting he would notice it.

Talia climbed the stairs and smelled disinfectant as she reached for her front door. *Bryce is on another cleaning binge*, she thought. *Better to be fixated on clean than dirty.* She walked in to see him beaming and exhausted but welcoming her home with open arms. She kissed him lightly on his lips, not wanting his sweaty T-shirt to soil her silk shirt.

"Hmm ... I smell something different on you. What is it?" Bryce said, as he inhaled when he kissed her forehead and then her hands.

Caught off guard, she did not want to lie to Bryce. Little secrets like that eventually cost her parents their marriage.

"It's nothing. Cologne on some junk mail which I threw into the recycling bin downstairs," she answered. "You're going to have to shower if you want more than dinner."

September 30th
Weather forecast: intermittent drizzle

Suite 1A: Winnie
8:30 a.m.

"A candle burns brightest just before it is extinguished."

Author Unknown

When Marcello awoke, he was lying on his back. He lay still, opening one eye first, followed by the other. He looked at the ceiling. This was not his bedroom. In Italian, he silently mouthed to himself *Christ, what am I doing here? I am losing my mind.* He listened carefully, then looked to his right. *She's alive. Of course, she's alive,* he thought, calming the thunder in his heart. Marcello attempted to rationalize again how he had gotten himself into this situation. Remaining as still as a corpse, he relived the last twelve hours in chronological order, afraid to waken Winnie. She was sick again yesterday evening and looked deathly ill. This time she was convinced she would join her beloved Alex before the dawn came. He checked in on her yesterday after dinner, a daily habit that somehow started about a week ago. She was a feisty old soul, and although her memory was intermittently compromised, she was bright.

Winnie also shared Marcello's love and competency level of mah-jong. This game, which he learned from a

Chinese tour guide colleague, involved an equal mix of skill, strategy and chance. It was best played with four participants, but they played with only two. Winnie had played with Alex and Mason's parents, so when Marcello spotted the game on her bookshelf, she challenged him for the competition and his company.

Last night terrified both of them because Winnie had developed chest pains and then weak legs. He wanted to call an ambulance for the second time since they had become acquainted, but she stubbornly refused. Again. Winnie made it clear that she would rather be alone at home and dead than alone and expiring in an overcrowded emergency department. She refused to call Mason to sit with her and certainly would not re-expose him to the trauma of dying in his presence, as both his parents had years ago. So, Marcello was becoming a convenient neighbour to have for many reasons, and she was growing more comfortable with sharing an increasing load of her burdens with him. She had no reason to distrust him, even if he was Italian. For some unknown reason, Alex secretly disliked Italians, but they were the same as everyone else to Winnie.

As Marcello and Winnie alternated drawing and discarding the Chinese tiles at her kitchen table, she grew less chatty. Marcello watched her discreetly, with increasing concern. He pressed her gently for the reason she was quiet, and when they were down to the last few tiles, she confessed it was her sixtieth wedding anniversary and neither Annette nor Allen had called. With each excuse she made for her middle-aged children, Marcello's quiet reasoning calmed her. Then at some point, her skin became the same ashen colour she turned when she was vomiting a few weeks ago. Unsure why, he checked her feet. They were a mottled bluish-grey, and when he suggested she elevate them on the sofa, she shook her head.

"If I'm going to die tonight, it's going to be in my own bed," she said flatly.

She abandoned the game, unsteadily forced herself out of her chair and shuffled out of the room in silence. He reluctantly followed her to her bedroom, a knot forming in his gut from his memory of when she slid off the bed the last time he was there. He took a deep breath and was relieved when she pulled the elegant duvet back on her own and crawled underneath. Whatever stains were on the cover on that last disastrous day had been laundered out. He stood quietly at the foot of her bed, preparing his words about how to execute his plan.

"Winnie, I'm very worried about you. I'm calling 911."

"You'll do no such thing."

"I can't help you. I am not a doctor."

"Thank the Lord for that."

"It's for the best."

"No, it's not. It's for the worst. Now sit down," she ordered.

He obliged and took the chair beside the bed, listening again to her rationalizing her way out of the ambulance call.

"How would you like to be shivering and hungry on a cold gurney, wearing nothing but a flimsy patient gown, bare-bottomed and peeing in a pan while a frenzy of activity and neon lights brighter than Niagara Falls spin around you?"

Winnie came to life, waving her arms in the air to emphasize her point.

"Wouldn't you rather have a nice cup of hot tea in your own bed than warm tap water in a plastic cup, or worse: nothing at all? How would you like to be poked and prodded like a slab of rejected meat, waiting for the inevitable news?"

As she ranted on, her thinking clear and focused, he slouched deeper into the chair, defeated again.

"Yes sirree, and to be told that you are too old. Yes, too old and—" she counted each reason, raising another finger to correspond with each point: "A: that you can no longer live alone, which means, B: you can kiss your independence goodbye. Which means, C: that you'll be sharing a room with someone not only demented but despicable. And even worse, D: you will never eat another decent meal again, much less savour the taste of good cognac, which I'm sure—you being Italian—know the good kind. No. No. No! Thank you very much!"

Deflated and uncertain whether the reference to his nationality was a compliment or an insult, Marcello pictured himself in that situation and knew that, within her withering and fragile state, Winnie was right.

"Winnie—"

She interrupted him with another raised finger, eyeing him long enough to lose track of her next excuse.

"What?" she pouted.

"I agree with you."

She ignored his answer and kept talking.

"Now ... back to the Hennessy. Go and get it from the dining room credenza."

Marcello escaped from the bedroom, arguing again with himself about how he was so easily manipulated by this woman in her precarious state. He found the decanter that preserved the amber indulgence in Winnie's china cabinet exactly where she directed him to look. Sometimes her memory wavered, and other times it was better than his own. He chose two matching brandy snifters and delivered the items on a small, ornately engraved silver tray he found displayed among other treasures. He set the tray on her bedside table and poured equal thimblefuls in each snifter, handing her one.

"To almost sixty years of marriage," she said.

They clinked glasses. *Sixty years for her and none for me*, he thought as he sipped the golden liquid. Winnie gulped the drink, smacked her lips and extended her empty glass.

"I might as well die drunk and in your company because it's better than none," she said.

Marcello laughed despite himself and refilled their glasses. Winnie patted the side of her bed.

"Sit," she ordered, "but get the mah-jong."

He rolled his eyes, determined not to get himself into another mess, but then obliged by getting the game. What else would he be doing? Winnie's colour had improved, likely more from the cognac than their conversation.

There were only a few tiles of the game left to play. Marcello re-assembled them on the top of Winnie's TV tray and placed them on the bed. He stood still until she patted the space beside her on the bed again for him to sit down, emptying her glass more slowly.

"Sit here on Alex's side. I don't want to be alone when I die."

"You are not dying," he said, reluctantly slipping his shoes off.

It was easier than arguing. He sat stiffly on the edge of the bed, fidgeting as he would at his doctor's office before a physical.

"Now, Mr. Portobello. How are you going to play from way over there?" she asked, looking at him over the top of her bifocals, chin on her chest. Acquiescing, he leaned against the abundance of decorative pillows and put his feet up.

"Like I said, I'm dying. Yes, I am," she chirped.

Suddenly, as if on cue, she gasped. Her heart and mind had separate agendas, and Winnie knew it. The pain began with a strong and irregular beat, hammering loudly within her left rib cage, increasing in duration and frequency. *Is this the big one?* she thought. *Yes.* She was sure of it. She decided she would endure the attack patiently and wait for the good Lord to reunite her with her Alex. She reached for Marcello's hand and he felt her clammy, cold hand. He noticed the arteries in her neck—or maybe they were veins?—pulsating rapidly. He was certain he had not noticed this before. He moved his fingers to the inside of her wrist and found her pulse. It was irregular. He had no idea of how many beats were normal, so he didn't bother to count. But he took her hand and stroked it gently. She squeezed it lightly, then patted his back, a gesture which neither seemed to mind. *Maybe she is really dying*, he thought, and he morbidly wondered how the newspaper headline would be worded when he called to report he woke up next to a dead woman.

"Oh Lord, please help me," Marcello whispered in Italian.

Winnie eyed him, aware that he sensed her grief. She raised her eyebrows and paused.

"Does that mean I'm dying in Italian?" she whispered. "Because if it does, I already told you that I am."

"No, you are not dying. I can still feel your pulse."

It was a feeble excuse to mask his fear.

"Then so be it," she sighed.

"If you die now, what am I to tell the coroner? And Mason, and then your family, et cetera, et cetera?"

"You can tell them that at least one person cared enough about me to escort me safely to those pearly gates," she said, laughing feebly.

After a few minutes, Winnie's pulse became more regular, and they both exhaled heavily in relief.

"Mr. Portobello?"

"Yes, Mrs. Firestone?"

"Please, just ... please don't leave me. I don't want to die alone."

From the corner of his eye, he followed the glassy pools of saline slide down her cheeks. Marcello's heart sank, feeling pity for this fragile soul he didn't know a month ago. He did not want her to die, and especially in his presence.

And so the debate of whether Winnie was living or dying continued indefinitely, but with more careful rationing of the cognac. They drank and moved the mah-jong tiles until neither of them cared about who was winning or who was right. Winnie fell asleep first, and Marcello followed after he eventually lost track of the hours in the night.

Marcello awoke first, and suddenly it was morning. Of course, there was Winnie, purring softly and buried deep under the covers. She was very much alive. Her fragile ribs moved in rhythm with her calm and regular breaths, and here he was waking up in bed beside her. His dental plate was still secure in the roof of his mouth, but he had no idea where his glasses were. And he had forgotten about his cats! They must be very hungry. He quietly and slowly slid off the bed and stifled any urge to groan in pain as he bent over stiffly and retrieved his glasses from the carpet. He tiptoed out of Winnie's room in socked feet, carrying his shoes, before locking her door on his way out. He wondered about this new part of his life. Michelangelo and Mona Lisa met him at his door, meowing loudly to scold him for being late for breakfast.

Suite 1C: Rose and Lily
8:32 a.m.

Lily reviewed her ambitious list as she gulped the last of her bitter coffee, and then headed out the door. Black coffee was no way to start another diet day. Instead of her normal double cream, double sugar, maybe she would compromise with just a little of each. Consuming fewer calories was better than the poison lingering in her mouth.

Today, Lily's to-do list was simple:

1. Empty two more boxes
2. Buy laxative to kick start my weight loss
3. Groceries: lettuce, tuna, diet pop, diet candies, cookies and low-fat, sugar-free ice cream
4. Check out new dating website — ask Tracy!
5. Set up system for bills — and Rose pays half!
6. ? new running shoes

Rosie returned home from a double shift just as Lily tucked her list in her purse. Rosie wanted to bathe rather than shower before bed. Lily's bathroom had the tub while Rosie's bathroom had only a shower. Lily, resentful of being rushed through her morning routine, also knew that the quicker she went out, the less of Rosie she would have to see. Lily dressed in leggings and a floral swing top that covered her substantial bottom. She grabbed her rain slicker in case the weather prediction was right. She was down to three pairs of pants that fit. She snarled "Goodbye" to Rosie under her breath, knowing her voice was inaudible over the sound of the bathtub tap flowing. Lily was meeting her best friend Tracy for breakfast.

Today Lily was armed with willpower, and planning to eat a small breakfast was all about willpower. Then she could save her calories for lunch. It didn't matter how lousy Lily felt, Tracy always pulled her out of her misery and made her feel good. And today, she needed an extra dose of feeling good. In twenty pounds, which according to her new diet plan should take her two months to lose, she was going to re-claim her life and find herself a man.

Suite 2A: Bryce and Talia
8:33 a.m.

Talia kept her eyes closed as Bryce rhythmically pounded inside her, counting silently with him. His routine never changed, not that she minded because he consistently brought her to a sensational orgasm. It was really quite amazing how within a span of twenty-two to twenty-four minutes he could get his rocks off and satisfy her. Not twenty minutes. Not twenty-five, but somewhere between twenty-two and twenty-four minutes. She had watched the clock enough times to be certain. She drifted off, wondering if anyone had researched this or if he would reset his goal to fifteen minutes at some point. So far, none of Bryce's quirks affected their relationship. He was just a nerdy, good-looking guy who did everything within his peculiar world to keep her happy. Six minutes left and counting down; maybe it was a little too long today because her thoughts drifted to that Adrian guy down the hall a few times.

Suite 2B: Mitch and Sally
8:34 a.m.

Sally untangled the clean sheets as she pulled them out of the dryer, then reset the timer for an extra few minutes to fluff out the wrinkles before she made the bed. Two loads down with just the whites left. Mitch was working days, and this was not her favourite way to spend a day off. She didn't mind being alone, but she sometimes felt more single than married. Mitch didn't like to go out on his days off unless he had to, explaining that the more often he was seen in public, the higher his probability of being recognized. Sally didn't understand what the big deal was. He wasn't in an undercover job anymore, but according to Mitch, there were unresolved cases he was still connected to. He didn't like to take chances. On their rare dinners out, Mitch chose secluded booths, which was fine with Sally. She just wished he was a little more social with other people. Maybe she would make some new friends on her own. Maybe she should invite Lily over for coffee or a glass of wine the next time Mitch worked the afternoon shift. She decided she would.

Sally left the laundry area and found her stash of greeting cards in the spare room closet. She chose a blank card with puppies on it and wrote a cute note that invited Lily to go for a walk or meet for coffee. She sealed the envelope and wrote Lily's name on the front. She set it on the little table by their front door and would put it in Lily's mail slot later. She had gone back to her laundry when she thought about whether she should have included Lily's sister, but she forgot her name. Maybe next time.

Suite 2C: Adrian
8:35 a.m.

Adrian's sour stomach was the first organ to protest last night's foray. As he rolled over in bed to shut off his phone alarm, his head spun. After nights like the last one, he rarely saw morning. It was often well into the afternoon before he left his bed. Today he had a virtual meeting at 8:45 a.m. Niagara time, 9:45 a.m. their time. Who were they again? Where were they contacting him from? Oh, what a night!

Adrian only remembered the first two clubs he and his friend attended. He tried to hook up with a shapely brunette who brushed him off because his friend was rude. After that many beers, did she expect a prince? Everything after that was a blur. He swung his feet over the side of the bed and let them settle on the floor before the rest of his nude body wrestled itself out from the covers and into a sitting position. Adrian knew he was still drunk. And alone in his bed again. He would have to find somebody soon—somebody who wouldn't compromise his standards. That girl who lived on his floor would be a good start. He re-positioned his feet to a wider stance, hoping for more stability when he put weight on them. He needed coffee and something for his pounding head. He shuffled to the kitchen and inserted a Colombian extra bold pod in the coffee machine, head hanging low until his mug was full of steaming caffeine. He trudged back to his bedroom. He exhaled with a pursed mouth to cool the scalding liquid, then took a sip, swirling it in his mouth until he could swallow it instead of spitting it out. Adrian pulled yesterday's underwear and pants on, not bothering to zip them up. The socks could wait because anything requiring bending lower than his waist could produce negative results.

Suite 3 (The Loft): Gracie
8:36 a.m.

Gracie stood in the front lobby sorting through the mail that she was still picking up every few days. She'd been up to the Loft earlier before picking up her mail. She hadn't moved in, reneged on the lease agreement and now she was wavering again. The condo looked better every time she entered it, and Tess had been more than patient with her.

Gracie applied for a full time posting at the library. If she was successful, she would double her current hours and salary. She reminded herself of the easy walk to work from here, then left Sonny, the project manager, a message that she had reconsidered and would be moving in. For sure this time. Leaving the building, she looked back and admired its architecture, reassuring herself that everything would sort itself out.

Suite 1C: Rose and Lily
8:47 a.m.

Spent of energy and brains, Rosie dropped her clothes in a heap beside the tub as she undressed, lit four tall, scented candles and poured bath oil into the running water. She locked the bathroom door, dimmed the lights to simulate night, then eased her exhausted body into the steaming bathwater. She had finished her afternoon shift and then covered a night shift for Ramone. As night became day, it was—bar none—the worst eighteen hours of her career. She fired her best employee for theft in addition to managing an unruly busload of inebriated gamblers who were abusive to her already distraught and short-staffed crew. Security was ineffective. It was beyond chaos. Desperate to power down her racing mind, Rosie finished the large crystal goblet of red wine in minutes and lit a new joint Ramone had gifted her for taking his shift.

She sank deeper into the hot water, its surface iridescent from bath oil. Rosie eased her head back and flipped the jacuzzi switch on, pouring more wine into the intricately etched crystal glass, one of Lily's abandoned wedding presents. The huge oval bathtub was the best feature of the condo, and a little bit of heaven after a hellish night. The first drag of the joint soothed her within seconds. She rested her wine glass on her knee between sips.

She felt very relaxed, almost euphoric.

The tension in her mind and body melted away as the candle flames on the bathtub ledge smeared across her sight lines. Her breathing became calm with the alcohol and drug. Her grip on the wine glass loosened, merlot spilling and swirling into the bath water. The glass rolled off her knee and floated momentarily in front of her, then sank in the water between her legs. Her brain function failed to send the signal to her hand to pick it up. Her foot, which was resting on the bathtub ledge, slid heavily off, tipping two candles over. One candle landed in the water, glued with wax to its holder. The other candle landed in the heap of clothes on the floor beside her, the fire evenly consuming her clothing before it spread to the white faux fur bath mat.

The joint rolled out of Rosie's mouth and hissed as the water immersed it, bobbing on the surface and then sinking. She attempted to close her mouth, but was unsuccessful in keeping the bath water from seeping in. Her throat failed to elicit a choking reflex. Her breathing shallowed. Losing power to hold, inhale or exhale air, soapy water seeped into her lungs, then like a veil, covered her nose and her open eyes. Panic froze her facial features into a portrait of respiratory distress.

Then, as her body grew still and calm, she felt nothing.

Rosie passed peacefully from life into death. Her sinking weight crushed the submerged glass, shards of broken crystal puncturing her skin from the pressure of her thigh against the bathtub bottom. Flames traversed from the bath mat to Lily's fluffy bathrobe hanging on the door hook. The shade of Rosie's arms transitioned from pink to grey, her hands from grey to blue, and her lips and fingernails to a dull white. Her hair covered her submerged face like a nest, and she appeared asleep in the rose-coloured water.

8:58 a.m.

It took a just a few minutes before the smoke seeping under the bathroom door in Suite 1C activated the smoke detector, setting off the fire alarms.

Adrian heard the repetitive honking and ignored it, wanting to finish his virtual meeting and return to bed.

Talia and Bryce played in the steamy shower, blaming each other for not turning the fan on in the bathroom and setting something off.

Sally also heard the irritating noise, prompting her to open her door to find out what it was. She knew immediately by the smell in the hallway that something was terribly wrong.

Marcello and Winnie were back together and arguing that Winnie was not dying anytime soon. Winnie could only faintly hear the alarm and relied on Marcello to come to the conclusion that it was not a normal sound.

Lily was devouring a scone and savouring a latte with Tracy at a café six blocks away. She had just progressed into a robust second round of complaints about her sister.

8:59 a.m.

Sally called 911, then walked—not ran—quickly to the fire alarm location that Mitch oriented her to her on moving day. She pulled the lever even though the alarm was activated on another floor. Then she called Mitch, barely able to verbalize what was happening on Park Street. His phone went to voicemail, so she texted him.

The alarm wailed as Marcello threw Winnie's housecoat over her shoulders, set her slippers on the floor in front of her feet and, like a child, held her hand firmly and tugged at her until they were both standing outside his front door.

"Stay right here and don't move," he warned Winnie.

She looked at him, not knowing whether to lecture him on his manners or follow him inside. He called for his cats, who responded to the alarm by hiding under the bed. There was no time to chase them, so he shook the bag of cat treats. Only Michelangelo came close enough to allow Marcello to heave him up and throw him into his cat carrier. Marcello parked the cat beside Winnie, who by now was complaining about the noise and the smell of smoke.

"I'll be back. Watch the cat!" he yelled to Winnie for the sole purpose of keeping her distracted.

He re-entered his condo to search for Mona Lisa. He called and called to no avail, and then he looked in and under all the usual places she would hide. No success. Marcello opened the tall Palladian window adjacent to the fire escape stairwell, hoping she would recognize danger and exit the condo. He felt a backdraft, an urgent signal for him to leave quickly.

With Winnie's hand securely in one hand and the cat carrier in the other, he guided his troop down the hall, through the main floor fire door and entered the front lobby. His heart was pounding as a shaking Winnie held on tightly. The deafening alarm noise rebounded against the vestibule stone walls. Marcello was torn between the need to protect the two creatures that were safe with him or return to the condo yet again to look for Mona Lisa. She was only five years old, with many good years on her side. He could not lose another female in his life.

Bryce opened the steamy bathroom door to realize it was indeed the fire alarm.

"Tal, it's real! It's the fire alarm—let's go!"

Talia's nude body glistened, small streams of water from her soaking hair funnelling between her breasts. He threw his towel at her.

"Hurry and dry off—we need to leave fast!"

He ran to the bedroom and grabbed two sets of his T-shirts and boxer shorts. He dressed, and despite her resistance, helped Talia dry off and climb into the second set of his clothes. Because of Bryce's meticulousness in arranging clothes by colour, they were dressed the same: white T-shirts and red plaid boxers. No time for her to protest that they looked like camp counsellors—they needed to evacuate immediately. Barefoot, Talia grabbed her phone, purse, their shoes and ran with Bryce who was mumbling something about even numbers and stepping only on every other flower on the patterned hallway carpet.

Sally met Talia and Bryce, Marcello and Winnie and a very vocal Michelangelo in the front vestibule. She looked at the address boxes and did a quick roll call. Lily, her sister and A. Common in Unit 2C may have still been in the building. She took a chance, ran to Lily and Rose's suite and banged hard on the door marked 1C. She immediately retracted her seared hand after it came in contact with the hot metal. Smoke seeped under the door and followed the draft down the hall.

Sally became very afraid. Mitch would be livid if he knew she returned to the fire. She coughed from the smoke that was also burning her eyes. She covered her nose and mouth with her shirt and ran back to the front lobby. She pushed the fire door open and gasped for clean air. Relief spread across the faces of the small gathering in the lobby when they saw her. The little lady in the matching nightclothes was searching in her pockets for a mailbox key. Sally ordered everyone outside, and they assembled safely under the trees across the street like they all belonged to her.

9:00 a.m.

Lily heard the emergency vehicle sirens as she and Tracy were leaving the restaurant. At the same time, Mason watched the blaring fire truck and ambulance speed by his office window. He assumed they were responding to an emergency at the nearby clinic. He poured himself a third coffee, ignoring the nagging of his doctor to switch to decaf.

By now, Adrian connected the smell of smoke and the approaching sirens to the fire in his building. Zipping his pants up, belt still unbuckled, he grabbed yesterday's shirt, his laptop, phone and wallet. He shoved his bare feet into loafers as he opened his front door. He saw smoke filling the top half of the second-floor hallway. Miserable from the noise and his hangover, he ran down the stairs into the opaque cloud that was billowing into the lobby. He exited the building, coughing and sputtering, to see the frightened gathering of people under the tree. An older male paced like a madman, mumbling in another language. The old woman who reminded him of his grandmother had hair as dishevelled as the Italian pacer. She clung tightly to a petite blonde who was rubbing her back.

The Park Street Secrets

Adrian's eyes focused on the brunette from 2A. She and some shivering nerd next to her were dressed in identical clothes. *He's not worthy of her*, he thought. Her wet, tangled hair had dampened the top of her T-shirt. Adrian was as conscious of his own bare chest as he was of Talia's underneath her shirt, and he again realized that she was beyond beautiful. He put his own shirt on, watching her turn away from him and rub the nerd's shoulders in an effort to calm him down.

Sally spoke first, directing her words at no one but hoping all would listen.

"Does anyone know if the ladies in 1C are home? I think the smoke may be coming from their condo."

Marcello turned towards her and replied, "I don't know if anyone is there, but my cat is trapped inside, and I fear for her life!"

His plea, delivered in a strong and desperate accent, fell on deaf ears.

The first fire truck came into view, followed by two ambulances. Winnie looked around and then at herself.

"I'm not dressed! I need to get dressed. What is going on here?"

Sally detached herself from Winnie and approached the firefighters just as Winnie protested.

"Who called them? I'm fine! I'm not going anywhere!"

Marcello took her hand while soothing his screeching cat. He felt oddly like a father, which he had never been, trying to settle toddlers.

Sally maintained her charge.

"The fire is on the first floor. Two sisters live there, but we don't know if they're still inside."

"Which unit?" the firefighter asked.

Frazzled, Sally looked to Marcello. "Which unit are you?"

"1B."

"And Mrs. Firestone?"

"1A."

Sally turned to the fire crew and paramedics joining them.

"Then it's 1C," she said, her voice shaking as she realized the gravity of the situation. "The sisters—Lily and I don't know what the other one's name is."

Before today, Marcello's Mona Lisa hadn't met with danger but had enough instinct to sense that the condo was not a safe place to remain. She initially hid under Marcello's bed, but needing better air, she found the window that he wisely wedged open to the fire escape. She perched herself on the landing, contemplating her next move. It was a big, noisy and unknown world to her. The sirens kept her away from the front of the building where the condo residents and a growing crowd assembled across the street. Startled by a loud noise in the apartment next door, Mona Lisa fled down the fire escape, her paw pads not used to the uneven grating of the metal stairs. She cowered in an overgrown bush behind the building until the wailing of the sirens ceased. By that time, Michelangelo had also stopped hissing and howling, so she sat quiet and unnoticed by humans and other cats, hungry and pondering where to go.

Mid-Morning

The residents, now engulfed by inquisitive spectators, watched as the firefighters worked with organized efficiency to extinguish the fire. When Mason's assistant, Aida, alerted him to the fire's location, he was adequately fuelled with caffeine and adrenaline to run to the Park Street corner. He searched the clusters of people until he saw Marcello standing with his arm securely around a shivering Winnie.

Talia held on tightly to Bryce as they paced the street in unison, feeding into each other's fears. Other than their phones and laptops, their life's possessions were in that condo.

Confident his company's insurance would cover his wardrobe and toys, Adrian started his BMW, wove it through the emergency vehicles blocking the exit and across the front lawn of the adjacent property. His car was his baby, and he didn't want it damaged with debris or heat from the fire. He opened his car window, passed his business card and phone number to a police officer and drove the short distance to work.

Sally continued to act as the building's spokesperson while she waited patiently until Mitch arrived. Then she fell apart. He hugged her, reassured her that nothing but their safety mattered and that everything but people could be replaced. She knew he was right. He eased his arms out of hers and joined the cluster of police shielded by the half circle of cruisers to see what they would share with him. Sally rejoined her little group just as Mason arrived, out of breath and relieved to see Winnie. Marcello exchanged introductions with Mason, and with high praise from

Winnie, felt confident he was in Mason's good standing. Mason called Aida to update her, and she offered to run out and purchase something warm for Winnie to wear. After passing his credentials and accountability for Winnie on to police, he invited Marcello to join Winnie and himself at his office. Marcello declined the kind gesture, hoping that Mona Lisa would find him or vice versa.

Once the owners of the nearby coffee shop became aware of the fire, a delivery of food and refreshments arrived for the condo residents.

Lily, oblivious to the smoke and flames, was annoyed because of the road block; she had to take a wide detour to the shopping mall.

2:00 p.m.

Lily arrived home from shopping to see all the commotion around her building. A circle of lawn chairs supplied by neighbours had formed, guarded by the remaining emergency vehicles. Local media vehicles were parked nearby, their reporters mingling with spectators who volunteered second and third-hand theories about the cause of the fire, which by now was extinguished. Caution tape and orange barricades separated them from the authorities entering the building.

Lily recognized Sally, who burst into tears and hugged her tightly. Sally took her arm and guided her to Mitch, who introduced her to the fire marshal and investigating officer. It was then that Lily realized something was terribly wrong.

After confirming that the sisters occupied Suite 1C, the investigator asked Lily about Rosie's whereabouts. Lily described their morning and Rosie's decision to bathe instead of shower. She blanched when the fire marshal asked her to describe Rosie's appearance. He confirmed someone had drowned in Lily's bathtub. The death was under investigation by the coroner, who was in Suite 1C with the police. Marcello, Bryce and Talia edged towards Lily as she sank into a chair someone offered her.

By this time Adrian had left his car at the office after a client lunch and had walked back to Park Street. He watched Bryce clinging to Talia from enough of a distance that neither was unaware of him.

5:00 p.m.

The remaining Park Street occupants were summoned together by the fire marshal, who informed them of what they didn't want to hear. They could not return home until it was safe and the investigation was completed, which would take a minimum of a few days.

Sonny, the owner and property manager, arrived midway into the discussion. He was visibly disturbed that his newly renovated building was damaged and that the residents were inconvenienced, especially the renters in Suite 1C. The fire would delay completion of the landscaping and storage building. Not knowing the specifics of the fire, he re-introduced himself to Lily and offered his condolences. One deep breath later he also suggested she move into the unoccupied, furnished Loft on the third floor at the same lease rate as her unit once the residents were cleared to return. In the next breath, guilt washed over him. Hoping none of this was his fault, he also offered the evacuated tenants accommodation and meals at a small nearby hotel he had recently purchased. It needed renovating, but it was a small comfort for the inconvenience for the hardship they faced even after they returned to Park Street.

8:00 p.m.

Marcello had frequently limped away from his fellow residents to search as far a distance as his back would allow him. He carried Michelangelo in his carrier and called out for Mona Lisa. By evening, he was convinced she had perished from the smoke. Pain and hopelessness sent him back to his lawn chair after each unsuccessful search. He sat until it was dark and unsafe to remain there alone. By then, housed and homeless people had lingered and dispersed around the vacated building, some curious and others looking for trouble.

Today was Marcello's retirement party, which he had missed. He'd remember this date for a long time. Unemployed and limited in his skill and ability to perform physical work he was also unhoused, albeit temporarily. He hoped the same for Mona Lisa. At least he didn't have to worry about Winnie because she was safe in the good care of Mason.

Most unsettling, Marcello thought as he got up from the chair a neighbour was waiting to reclaim, *is that I am not only very tired, but very sad and very, very lonely.*

October 3rd

Notice Posted by Rosie's Employer

The corporation is devastated to announce the sudden passing of one of our exemplary employees, **Rosemary (Rosie) Miles.** Rosie died at her home on September 30. She was a dedicated member of our Niagara Falls team and led others by example. She delivered hotel meals and produce to the local shelters after each of her shifts ended. Rosie loved life and was loved by many. She was predeceased by her parents Alexander and Annaliese, and is mourned by her beloved sister Lily Jamieson. Details of her funeral service will be posted as soon as they are available. Rosie would be honoured to know you followed in her footsteps and continued to support the causes so dear to her heart. Anyone interested in continuing Rosie's legacy is encouraged to contact the Food Services Manager directly at ext. 242.

October 4th
Weather forecast: sunny but unseasonably cold

9:10 a.m.

"We know what we are, but not what we may be."

William Shakespeare

Obituary

Miles, Rosemary (Rosie) Jane – passed away suddenly at home, in her 51st year on September 30. Predeceased by her parents Alexander and Annaliese, and an infant brother, she leaves her beloved sister Lily Jamieson to mourn. Rosie worked in the Niagara Falls hospitality industry for many years. Funeral plans are incomplete at this time. Donations to the local Niagara Falls food bank would be greatly appreciated in memory of Rosie.

Lily approved the standard obituary draft notice which the funeral home director had prepared; she was all business today and was in and out of the funeral home in under thirty minutes.

Park Street Front Doors
9:30 a.m.

Gracie Sheehan left three unanswered messages for Sonny, and because of that, was in a foul mood. She drove to the condo to confront him, alarmed to see the yellow caution tape surrounding the building. A notice prohibiting entry unless authorized by the fire marshal was dated Sept. 30 and taped to the front door. Initially livid at not being notified, she calmed herself when she realized she'd avoided another tragedy. *What if I had been in the building?* she thought. This added to her confusion about being a tenant. She had signed the contract for the Loft and changed her mind twice. She walked slowly around the building. There were a few boarded-up windows on the first floor, with black residue above one of them. All of the other windows appeared intact, including in the Loft. She spotted a friendly looking tabby cat hovering over a fire escape ledge and meowing. It descended quickly, brushing against Gracie's legs until she stooped down to pet its matted fur. She was rewarded with a loud purr. It followed Gracie to her car. She placed her unfinished breakfast bagel on the sidewalk for the cat, who gobbled it up quickly and looked to her for more.

Gracie sat in her car stewing over the wasted morning. She'd driven the hour from Tess's apartment without seeing Sonny, and because he had her money, she had every right to know what happened. She left him a fourth message that was even less pleasant than the previous ones, spinning her platinum and diamond ring in frustration.

10:00 a.m.

Mason brought Winnie back to the security of his home right after the fire. His housekeeper, known to Winnie through Mason and his parents, worried with him about the challenges of caring for the ill and aged. Winnie seemed impatient to return to her new friend Marcello Portobello, "like the mushroom." Her children were updated, grateful to Mason for exceeding his obligations and accommodating her until she could safely return home.

Marcello was also out of sorts today. He drove around searching for Mona Lisa and found himself inquiring about Winnie at Mason's office. They had an odd exchange where Mason asked Marcello random questions until he felt reassured that Marcello was not a threat to Winnie. Marcello was still mortified about the precarious sleepover incident, and had she told Mason, this meeting would have a different flavour.

After the fire, Sally continued to take her role as the unofficial condo tenant representative seriously. She passed updates from Mitch on to the small group, with the exception of Gracie who was still unknown to them. Most of the tenants accepted Sonny's offer of free accommodation at his low-budget hotel during the investigation and clean up.

On the final night of their stay, Sally gathered them in the breakfast room and shared the sparse details of Rosie's funeral, which was scheduled for the following day. The only current picture of a smiling Rosie, taken from her hotel identification badge, was used for the obituary, layering another veil of sadness over Lily.

A few of Rosie's friends offered to help Lily with some of the funeral preparations, and she was more than happy to pass whatever she could on to them. With the exception of one woman she remembered from the condo move, they were all strangers. There was no funeral visitation or burial, only a mass at the very old Gothic Revival church her family had attended for years. Once Sally updated Marcello, he notified Mason, who had more pressing issues to deal with that day. But because it was Winnie, he agreed to bring her. Lily went to sleep that night dreading the funeral as well as meeting with the fire marshal, the coroner and the police whenever their investigations wrapped up.

October 5th
Weather forecast: just as cold as yesterday

11:00 a.m.

"Nothing ever happens by chance; everything is pushed from behind …"

Emily Murphy

The funeral mass was a brisk fifteen-minute walk from Park Street and also from Mason's office. Mason brought Winnie to work, and for the hour it took him to tend to his legal matters, Winnie sat in the waiting area interrogating Aida about looking like a waif.

"Most men prefer women with a little more meat on their bones," she said.

Mason and Winnie arrived at the funeral mass just as the bell tower chimed eleven times. The organist accompanied a well-rehearsed choir of eight, filling the air with heavenly voices. The church pews were almost full when Lily was escorted to her seat by an elderly usher who would have benefitted more if Lily escorted him. Taking her seat in the front row, which was reserved for her and a handful of distant relatives, she felt curiously detached, watching in wonder as others gathered to mourn her sibling. The vivid colours of the stained-glass windows and steep vaulted ceilings brought back the Sunday mornings of her childhood.

The assembly of funeral occupants was varied. Many young and middle-aged adults who Lily correctly assumed were Rosie's friends or co-workers from the hotel were there. The back pews were sprinkled with a half dozen saintly looking ladies who regularly attended funerals armed with missals, sturdy shoes and matching purses. These outdated fashionistas stood, then sat, then knelt in unison for prayer under the added holiness of the church. Their subjective opinions of the deceased and their mourners fuelled their chatter when they took advantage of the free lunch after mass, which was hosted in the basement by the parish's ladies auxiliary.

Rosie's urn sat on a tall, wheeled cart that was centred in the nave of the church. It was draped in white satin that fell to the floor and circled by a small wreath of white carnations Lily ordered from the florist her parents had used for decades. She was surprised that so many people attended Rosie's funeral, and she suddenly realized that her meagre choice of flowers was a reflection of her, rather than what Rosie deserved. Large bouquets of various white flowers from unknown senders and organizations dwarfed the urn on display.

Lily declined to speak at the eulogy, but she heard four others stand at the pulpit and describe a sister she didn't know. They spoke of the community events she organized, fundraisers she led at work, countless recognition awards she earned and her years of mentoring others. By the end of the service, Lily was reduced to tears, not from losing a sibling she squabbled with her whole life, but because this gathering of people loved her sister so dearly. It seemed like another sister she'd never met.

At the luncheon following the funeral, Rosie's friend Ramone approached Lily and introduced himself. She had no idea who this fidgety fellow was. Initially elaborating on their friendship, he moved beyond small talk to a question about the cause of her death.

"She drowned," Lily replied flatly, watching Ramone's colour go pale.

"That's terrible. I'm so sorry to hear that. Rosie covered my shift that night after working her own. She must have been exhausted, but how could she have drowned?" he whispered, visibly distraught, then distant.

"We should know more soon," Lily said, taking a step back from him.

"Soon?"

"There is a coroner's inquiry."

"Really?"

"And it's still classified as a suspicious death," Lily said.

Ramone's cheeks sagged.

"Oh my God. Our poor Rosie," Ramone said through a stifled cough.

Lily eyed him with suspicion. He gave her the creeps.

"Were you sleeping with her?" she asked, knowing it was an inappropriate question.

For the first time in forever, she felt the need to defend her sister. He gasped, then looked around to see if anyone nearby had heard.

"Oh God, no," he said, laughing nervously. "I have a wife and kids."

"That never stopped my ex-husband," Lily mumbled, taunting him.

Ramone took the cue that their conversation was over, repeated a standard condolence and disappeared.

Lily floated through the next hour, responding kindly to offers of sympathy and watching the small clusters gather like an outsider. Feeling distant and removed from everyone, she became aware that she was the outlier. She left as soon as she felt it was acceptable; she had no one to be accountable to but herself. Her shoes slapped against the stairs as she climbed them from the basement hall and returned to the sanctuary. She walked slowly up the centre aisle to the nave where her sister's urn remained. She kneeled at the same front right pew where she was an hour ago and numbly progressed through the motions of mass. She had not prayed meaningfully earlier, but this time she did. She prayed first for herself, then for her sister. She prayed that she regretted not making amends before Rosie died, and that she vowed to be more respectful of her.

The kind, elderly priest quietly observed Lily leave at the end of the mass, endure the luncheon and re-appear in the church. He remembered this family of faithful parishioners from decades ago; Harold, Annaliese, their daughters and the infant son who died at birth. Lily disappeared after she left for school and returned annually for Christmas mass. Once she married, she left again. It was a marriage he prayed would last, but rightly predicted would fail. Lots of pomp and circumstance but no solid roots to hold their union together. He wasn't surprised when Annaliese told him the marriage had ended.

Watching Lily from a distance, he busied himself silently around the church and the altar. He waited until she made the sign of the cross to end her prayers and slid back from a kneeling position to sit in the pew. He approached her cautiously and touched her shoulder.

"Are you all right, Lily?"

"Hi, Father. It's been a long week."

"It has. You can stay as long as you wish."

"Thank you, Father."

He bowed his head and slowly turned to walk back towards the altar.

"Father?" Lily said quietly.

The priest paused and turned his head, not sure if he had actually heard her speak. He came back to confirm he had heard her.

"Will you bless me?" she asked with glassy eyes.

The request came not from her brain but from somewhere deep in her conscience. She was barely aware of what she had asked.

"Of course, Lily. You are a child of God and He will always love you."

He put his thumb on her forehead and made a cross as he blessed her. Responding with her right hand, she crossed herself again and bowed her head in prayer.

"Thank you."

They shared a moment of silence together before she stood up and looked towards the urn.

"Can I take her home now?" she asked, realizing it was a redundant question.

"Of course you can. That is where she belongs."

Lily picked up the vessel which resembled a pearl Fabergé egg encased in a lacy silver scroll.

"Thank you for all your help with the funeral. I do feel better now."

"You are always welcome back. Anytime."

"I know," she replied in a voice just above a whisper.

Lily buttoned her fall coat with one hand and left the church. She buried the egg's small base in her purse and hoisted it over her shoulder. She clutched the egg in both hands, attempting to cover it. As if to protect it. She decided to leave her car in the church parking lot and walk the fifteen-minute distance to the condo, where she had not been since the fire.

The air refreshed Lily as she passed people going about their daily business. She walked by Mason's office, unaware that he and Winnie observed her passing them with her hands clasped in front of her. She walked past downtown businesses that included shuttered retail stores with dusty, outdated and partially dismantled window displays. She paused at an old building where the murder of a sex worker had taken place, long forgotten by those unaffected by it. Restaurants advertised their daily specials. Unlike most days, the Chelsea buns in the bakery window did not call to Lily. She cautiously crossed the street while other pedestrians socialized, texted or talked on their phones, as oblivious to her business as she was to theirs.

As Lily approached the condo, a middle-aged man was removing the caution tape. Three men watched her curiously as she approached the front entrance. She pointed to the front door and initiated the conversation with the fire marshal and Sonny, the project manager.

"Any news?" she asked Sonny.

"Yes. Good news. The forensic engineer said this old building's strong bones kept it structurally sound, and because the safety inspection and investigation are complete, the other tenants can return."

She looked to the other men, who validated Sonny's statement.

"Okay, but what about me? You know I can't go back there."

"Ah, Ms. Jamieson, yes you can, but not to your original unit. I have a key to the Loft if you'd like to see it."

Sonny had picked up all four of Gracie Sheehan's messages but had purposely not responded. Lily had no accommodation plan as of today and was unsure if she could even return to live in this building. Her last argument with Rosie was still swirling in her mind. It was either Sonny's suggestion or check into another hotel; Lily chose the path of least resistance.

"Okay, but don't pressure me into anything I'm not ready for," she said, embarrassing Sonny in front of the others.

Her right hand shielded Rosie's egg against her heart, and she took the key in her left hand. All three men were still distracted by why she was clutching the egg.

"It's my sister," she said, opening her hands to expose more of the egg. "Her funeral was this morning."

Almost in unison, they responded with different expressions of sympathy.

Sonny held the front door open for Lily and led the way to the Loft. The smell of smoke distressed her as they crossed the lobby and proceeded up the stairs. Lily avoided looking down the first-floor hallway where Rosie took her last breath. She held the egg tightly, cautiously climbing the last set of stairs. Winded when they reached the Loft, Sonny took the key back from Lily and opened the door. She was pleasantly surprised to see a very spacious, sparsely decorated unit with one bedroom much larger than hers. She inhaled clean air, free of fire smoke, which swayed her decision to move in. She had no other options.

"I'm sure this will be better for you," Sonny said in a persuasive tone.

"Probably."

"Same rent and fees as yours but, as you can see, a much nicer view. It's the least I can do," Sonny said, looking out a window.

"Yes, but one less bedroom," she muttered, peeking out another window.

"You have this office instead," he counter-offered as he opened the glass-paned French doors into a bright sunlit room that contained a desk, a dove grey leather love seat and matching recliner.

"The plan was to use this for short-term leases to local businesses," he lied. "That's why it's furnished, you know, with such high-end products, and considering your unfortunate circumstances, I'll let you have it for the remainder of your lease."

Lily asked for a few moments alone and Sonny left her in the Loft. She walked over to the white marble fireplace mantle, carefully pulled out the urn base in her purse and gingerly placed Rosie's egg in its cradle. She breathed loudly, walking between rooms and now aware of her fatigue. She sat on the bed, made up with a crisp grey duvet and white overstuffed pillows. Everything was new. *Kind of like starting again*, she pondered peacefully. *Almost like another chance*. She retraced her steps, touched Rosie's egg—now as cold as the marble it sat on—and left it there. She locked the Loft door and returned to the three men waiting for her at the front of the building.

Sonny was impatient to notify the other tenants that they could return today. A fire clean up and restoration crew had quickly restored the first-floor hallway where smoke seeped out from Rose and Lily's unit. A broken window had been replaced. Sonny also received clearance to start restoring Lily's condo, expecting her to work with her insurance company to sort out which of her contents were salvageable. It was too much for Lily to process today.

The third man Lily saw when she returned to Park Street was unknown to her. He introduced himself as Spencer and approached her slowly along with the fire marshal. He asked if they could meet with her later that day, however Sonny suggested she check out of her hotel first. Lily ignored him and asked if they were meeting all of the tenants. They said no, and when the detective said he was from the crime unit, it was like alarms went off in her head.

"The crime unit? What's wrong with meeting right now?"

"We would prefer somewhere quieter and more private," Spencer replied.

She pointed to Park Street and then to the unmarked police car.

"Is here or the car quiet enough?" she asked.

Spencer looked at the other two men, who nodded reluctantly.

Sonny joked, "Last time I was in the back of a police car was when I was sixteen."

"Care to share why?" the detective asked.

"Not really."

The detective opened the front passenger door for Lily, which impressed her because she didn't know she could not have opened it herself. Sonny and the fire marshal crawled into the back seat, both leaving their doors open with one foot on the pavement.

"Comfortable back there, gentlemen?" Spencer asked as Lily was taking in the police technology in front.

"How come there's no barrier between you and us?" Sonny asked.

"I can arrange that if you'd like," Spencer offered.

Lily wanted this meeting over as soon as it started.

"So, what did you learn?" she asked, already feeling claustrophobic in the car filled with men. She turned and faced the detective.

"A few things. First of all, did your sister smoke?"

"Nope, she never smoked. In fact, neither of us did," Lily responded, shaking her head for emphasis. "Why? Is that what caused the fire?" she asked.

Spencer turned to look at Lily. He reorganized his thoughts.

"Not exactly. But I'll address that in a minute. What the forensic and fire marshal's investigations found was that the fire started in the bathroom, probably from lit candles that fell off the bathtub ledge and landed on dry clothes or towels on the floor. Our working theory is that the fire was an accident."

Spencer allowed a long gap of time for Lily to process this, then continued.

"But what we also now know is that she did not die from smoke inhalation."

"What? Then how did she drown?"

"So, as you already know, an autopsy was completed because your sister's death was unexpected and suspicious. To spare you the grief, we identified her remains from her photo identification, which was verified by her employer."

Lily shuddered, flashing back to the same enlarged, framed picture that was used for her funeral. She attempted to speak, but Spencer slowly raised his index finger to finish his explanation.

"I apologize for interrupting you, Ms. Jamieson, but I will ask for your patience. And I will caution you first that this will be difficult for you to hear."

Lily took a few deliberately deep breaths.

"When we found your sister, she was submerged in the bathtub. Based on that theory, we initially assumed she asphyxiated first from the smoke and then drowned."

Lily felt faint. And dumbstruck. What a horrible way for Rosie to die. She resumed the deep breathing that a therapist taught her years ago when she was having panic attacks.

"I'm fine. Go on."

She searched the lines on his face as intently and carefully as he watched her. Spencer's intuition and expertise told him that Lily had no prior knowledge or involvement in her sister's death.

"The evidence also told us that your sister made no attempt to get out of the tub or to extinguish the fire. She didn't even try to leave the bathroom."

"I'm not understanding what you're saying. Like she was trying to commit suicide?" Lily's brain worked furiously to organize these facts.

"We've considered that, but it's not our main theory. We found a broken wine glass in the bathtub, which we assume tipped over or came loose from your sister's grasp and discoloured the bathwater. Based on the wine bottle contents, she may have consumed one glass and poured herself a second. That amount is usually insufficient to significantly impair the judgment of someone her size, even if she was a non-drinker."

"Rosie drank maybe a couple of glasses of wine once or twice a week. At least that's what I thought," Lily guessed, now doubting she could be certain of anything that her sister did, especially after hearing all those strangers talk about her at the funeral. "Go on," she said, refocusing on the present.

"What the autopsy concluded is that she died of respiratory arrest, which occurred before, not after enough bath water entered her lungs to drown her."

Lily rubbed her temples.

"Wait! What does that mean? Now I'm thoroughly confused," she said.

Spencer allowed a pause, then carried on.

"We also found part of a marijuana joint."

"You're kidding me? A joint? I don't believe it," Lily said, laughing nervously.

Then again, she was learning more about her sister by the minute.

"There was evidence in the water, and the lab reports confirmed it."

He watched her carefully again, solidifying his thoughts that the sisters lived together as a matter of convenience and that they were not close enough to know each other's habits.

"Rosie? She wouldn't touch a cigarette, let alone marijuana."

"You sound very certain of that."

"I am. My mother smoked, and we hated the smell of her breath and her clothes. I know that Rosie despised cigarettes."

"Interesting. The lab analysis showed that the joint was mostly CBD based, which is the type of cannabis that doesn't give much of a high or induce psychotic episodes. People usually use CBD for its calming effect or to relieve anxiety. Sometimes it helps them sleep. However, there was fentanyl and other toxic substances mixed in that joint."

Lily shuddered in disbelief.

"Fentanyl?" Sonny gasped.

He let out a long whistle from the back seat. His mother used fentanyl prescription patches for her painful back, and he picked them up for her with the rest of her medications at the pharmacy.

"Isn't that also the street stuff that kills drug addicts?" he asked, shaking his head nervously. "It's in the news all the time."

"You're mostly correct, but they are not all addicts," Spencer said. "Some are regular folks looking to buy cannabis discreetly. Sometimes, but not always, it may be cheaper to buy from an illegal supplier rather than a licensed distributor. We also know that many illegal dealers have difficulty keeping up with customer demand, so, unfortunately, they buy tainted stuff from disreputable suppliers. In the underground market, people have no idea what they are buying. Everything on the street should be considered to be more addictive and more deadly. And it's not like spoiled produce where you can return it to the store and get your money back."

Spencer let his words sink in as Lily's throat tightened so quickly that she couldn't catch her breath. A few moments lapsed before she whispered.

"I can't believe I'm hearing this. Was my sister an addict?"

Spencer looked towards her and waited for her to face him again.

"If you're asking me for a non-medical opinion, I'd say not based on the toxicology screen. There was some CBD along with fentanyl and other toxic substances found, but by her levels of CBD in the lab report, we can assume that she used cannabis products very occasionally. Considering more than a quarter of Canadians use it in some form or another, it wasn't a red flag to us. But what's critical here is that lab report confirmed that there was enough fentanyl and other toxins in your sister's bloodstream and lungs to paralyze her airways, so she could no longer breathe. Unfortunately, here we are."

Unable to unroll the back windows, the fire marshal opened his door wider to allow more of the breezy autumn air to circulate through the car. He'd heard this explanation many times and knew Spencer repeated it weekly. The stories were the same, but the setting and the loved ones left behind were different.

"I am stunned," Lily said repeatedly.

"It's also important to note that your sister didn't fit the typical profile of someone who overdosed on these addictive substances," Spencer said after a few minutes.

"We can't accurately predict who does or doesn't overdose, intentionally or accidentally. We assume that whoever supplied her the cannabis may or may not have known what it contained. Dealers come and go, and for every dealer we apprehend, two more are there to take over. The market is huge, and there is no such thing as a clean dealer."

"No more clean dealers ..." Sonny repeated to himself.

The others stared at him.

He put his hands up defensively.

"No. No. No! I don't do drugs. But I've got four teenagers. We shoulda had two, but my wife wanted a girl. So now we have four. Enough said."

Spencer wasn't concerned about Sonny because he had been investigated once and cleared. Sonny didn't know that, and there was no reason for Spencer to tell him, but today Sonny's statement didn't sit well with him.

Sonny was the first to exit the cruiser.

"I've heard enough. I'm going home to my kids. Ma'am, I'm very, very sorry your sister died. But I gotta go home and hug my kids. Then I'll yell at them and warn them about all of this stuff. And, and then I'll tell them what happened to your sister."

He paused.

"If that's okay with you."

"Go for it," Lily said, easing herself out of the car as Sonny hurried away.

Spencer got out as well, went around the car and shook her hand.

"I'm also very sorry about what happened to your sister. If it's any consolation, I can now also tell you there were at least a half dozen other reported suspicious deaths within a day of your sister's passing, so we are trying to determine if there is a connection. Of course, those in the underworld may already know, but for obvious reasons, nobody would tell us."

"Six more deaths? That's terrible. Who were the others?"

"A university student, a young mother, and a thirty-year-old female who was known to us."

Lily bowed her head.

"What a waste," she said. "And the others?"

"They were all adults. The thirty-year-old is of the most interest to us because she was a regular visitor to the local hotels. Mostly the upscale hotel and conference centres."

"A regular visitor—as in a prostitute?" Lily leaned heavily against the car as she rubbed her forehead.

"Yes. So, we are wondering if another frequent patron or perhaps a hotel employee was involved. You said you had no idea that your sister was using any of these substances, but do you have knowledge of a co-worker or friend who may have been close to her or whom she was in contact with?"

Lily shook her head slowly again.

Spencer surprised her once again when he said, "I was at your sister's funeral, as were a few other plain clothes officers."

"You were?"

"We were watching the attendees or hoping to overhear something that may have been helpful."

"Really?"

"Our intent was not to interfere with the event. We hoped you wouldn't have noticed."

"I certainly didn't. It was a blur. I hardly knew anyone. Honestly, I did not expect so many people to come."

"It was well-attended. Your sister must have been a very special person."

Spencer's comment saddened her deeply. All those years of conflict and bickering took precedence over any meaningful relationship between them. Sometimes weeks with no more than exchanging a few words or texts. What a waste.

"Lily?" Spencer said, turning towards her.

Her tears began when she looked up at him.

"Sorry. It's been a …"

She didn't finish her sentence.

"If I hear of anything, I'll let you know. Or if you become aware of anything that feels odd to you—even if it seems insignificant—here is my card. It could be someone casually asking about the cause of your sister's death or a question that sounds irrelevant … or something that doesn't make any sense to you. We'll keep in touch."

Lily thanked him and watched the cruiser leave. She didn't connect the conversation she had just hours ago with Ramone to Spencer's message.

In the Afternoon ...

Unlike dogs who become deeply ingrained in their family's emotional lives and thrive on the attention they get, cats are somewhat different. Although both were domesticated thousands of years ago, a cat's behaviours often remain unchanged from their feral ancestors. Mona Lisa was just like that. She was initiated by the street gang of cats who dominated the bridge's underpass less than a block from Marcello's condo. Lured by the scent of cat spray, food and hope of a better shelter than the neglected bushes and litter behind the Park Street condos, she was drawn to the feline community under the bridge. A protected and pampered city cat until now, Mona Lisa succumbed to the other cats' instincts to earn her the lowest peg of the pecking order in their colony. Her coat became matted as she roamed the streets, adapted to ancient hunting rituals and fit in nicely with her mangy street-smart gang. Her new, yet old home remained abandoned, and with the fire escape still locked every time she returned, she started her new life on the street.

6:30 p.m.

Sally was the first occupant to come home. She unloaded what little she had to tide her over for the past five days, leaving everything untouched and as it was before the fire. She positioned herself at the building's front entrance, welcomed her fellow residents back and invited them to dinner, which was donated by a local Thai eatery. Sally had set some folding tables and chairs in the lobby, complete with disposable dishes and cutlery but out of respect for Lily, she skipped the candles.

Sally greeted Marcello, who was the next to return after he searched the neighbourhood again for Mona Lisa. They were surprised to see the first-floor hallway restored and presentable. The fire damage was now limited to Unit 1C, which was across the hall from Marcello's condo. Unlocking his door, the faint smell of smoke was still apparent but was masked by the strong cleaners and fresh paint in the halls. The plastic coverings that had protected his furniture for years remained intact, and he was once again relieved not to have removed them. Other than a little film, nothing had really changed. This was good. Very good.

Mason decided to keep Winnie for one more night but, at the encouragement of his housekeeper, brought her to dinner and to catch up with the other tenants.

Marcello entered the lobby and welcomed his new friend back by kissing her hand. Winnie, flattered by the gesture, held his elbow as they toured the refurbished hallway with an amused Mason following behind. Mason declined dinner, opting for a few precious hours of solitude at the office.

Because Bryce and Talia worked opposite shifts, Talia represented the pair.

Sally set a place for Mitch, hoping he could steal away from work for just an hour.

Lily walked back to her car at the church after the meeting in the police cruiser, passing a tabby hanging around Park Street.

Just before 6:30 p.m., she had no place to go but Park Street. She felt a lump form in her throat when she saw Rosie's yellow car but was calmed by the greetings of her neighbours when she entered the lobby. By now they knew her even though they were strangers to her. Lily had carried a resentful attitude from years of arguing with her sister, her mother or someone about something, but there was none of that tonight. She was not accustomed to the uncomplicated kindness and compassion her neighbours showed her. As generous helpings of dinner and a bottle of wine was divided equally in plastic glasses, Sally toasted the homecoming and acknowledged the one missing at the table—the sister no one had met. Lily was speechless.

It was after 7:00 p.m. when Adrian pulled his car into his designated condo spot. Concentrating on not dropping his overnight bag full of laundry, a laptop bag and slices of take-out pizza, he unlocked the entrance door and was startled to see people dining in the condo lobby. Sally—rather than Adrian—apologized that he may not have received her emails, all of which he had trashed unopened. She invited him to join the group. As he was about to decline, he spotted Talia seated between Lily and Marcello, and no nerd in sight. A vacant chair and place setting sat across from her and beside Sally.

"Mitch is tied up at work, and there's lots of food left," Sally said, pointing to the empty chair.

Adrian couldn't remember or care about who Mitch was.

"That's great," Adrian said.

With the aroma of Thai spices reinforcing his hunger, Adrian winked at Talia, excused himself to change and ran effortlessly up to the second floor to drop his baggage off at his unit. Other than the faint smoky scent in the hallway, his condo was as he left it. He changed his shirt, applied more cologne and put his pizza in the fridge.

Adrian returned to the lobby just as Mitch walked through the front door, and Adrian made the connection to Sally. They acknowledged each other, both hesitating over who would occupy the vacant chair at the table. Mitch walked over to the pair of armchairs in the lobby near the windows facing the street and dragged one to a corner of the table as the others shuffled over to make room for him. He gestured for Adrian to take the armchair as Sally pulled out another place setting and handed it to a clearly disgruntled Adrian. Mitch took the spot across from Talia, who smiled sweetly and initiated the assembly line by passing him half-full containers of warm entrees and rice. Adrian sulked between Winnie and Marcello, who obstructed his view of Talia's glowing face as the food containers were circulated his way.

As Winnie cleaned her plate of food, she shifted her attention to Adrian.

"You need to eat a whole one," she pointed out as Adrian put half a spring roll on his plate. "You're much too thin." She watched his face, searching for something. "What is your name, son? You look just like my grandson."

"Like Alexander?" Adrian responded, remembering the name from their first conversation.

It caught her by surprise.

"My goodness! Do you know him?"

"No, but you mentioned him when we first met."

"We've met? Where?"

"In the lobby, last month."

"Last month? Some days I can't remember yesterday, let alone last month," Winnie said, chuckling.

Adrian smiled politely and slid the other half of the spring roll onto his plate. He pictured his own grandmother forcing second helpings on his plate for the same reason as Winnie just did. A pang of guilt stirred him for not calling her despite gentle reminders by his mother. His grandmother was proud of Adrian. He would call her tonight, he decided, and he would also call home.

Lily remained quiet other than to respond to Sally's kind words to keep her engaged. She wasn't prepared to share the crime unit findings, so she listened to the discussion about how well this building had withstood the fire. She flinched when Winnie said it was remarkable that no one else had died. Lily wondered what Mitch knew, his glances flitting occasionally between her and the other guests at the table. He was polite and smiled warmly at Sally but said nothing of value.

By 8:00 p.m., the lobby was empty, tidy and arranged back to its intended purpose. Everyone was re-acquainting themselves with Park Street. Except, of course, Mona Lisa. And Rosie.

OCTOBER 6TH
Weather forecast: rain, rain and more rain

Park Street Basement
8:30 a.m.

"The difference between who you are and what you want to be is what you do."

Anonymous

Sonny checked the furnace room in the basement of Park Street and was relieved that the historic artifacts uncovered and stashed there during the renovations were unaffected by the fire. He also kept dry food for the cats living under the bridge nearby, which was their reward for keeping the rodent population at bay. His small supply of his mother's prescribed fentanyl patches were stashed in a coffee can. She gave him a few patches after he wrenched his back, which worked wonders, and from then on, she donated her surplus patches to him. Not wanting his four sons to experiment with them, he hid them in the furnace room. When they were close to expiring, he sold some to a "regular guy" in the neighbourhood who guaranteed Sonny anonymity. Sonny used his proceeds to buy cat food and—rarely—he also exchanged a few patches for the services of a female acquaintance he periodically allowed to spend a few hours at his low-rate hotel.

Sonny phoned Gracie Sheehan and was relieved that she didn't pick up. He left her a short but pleasant message. He was new at this property management business and already had more than his fair share of trouble. A fire, a deceased tenant and this Sheehan woman who had signed the lease, backed out, then wanted the condo again. Nothing but a headache. The bigger headache was that she signed the lease agreement, but there was no exchange of signatures to void it. Thinking he was the good guy, he offered it to Lily not only to help the grieving woman out, but to be sure he was guaranteed an income if that Sheehan woman bailed. Some of his buddies who owned some legal and not-so-legal rental properties gave him an assortment of suggestions. He didn't know who or what to believe and was reluctant to seek legal advice. Retaining legal counsel would cost him more than the nothing he had budgeted for this unwanted and messy complication. If the fire restorations in Suite 1C could be finished in a month or so, he'd offer that unit to Gracie and fix that problem.

He tried to settle his nerves with another espresso. *Maybe I should have sold the building after I bought and renovated it*, he thought. Things had to improve from here, because instead of the freedom of autonomy, he was starting to feel the pressures of being self-employed.

OCTOBER 10TH
Weather Forecast: perfect for raking leaves

7:20 a.m.

"Secrets take on a life of their own …"

Anonymous

Mitch rolled over in bed and watched Sally as she slept, a storm of blonde curls covering most of her face and pillow. She was nothing like Georgia. Sally worked hard at self-preservation, kept a perfect house and dedicated her working hours to being a role model. She could make soup out of a stone. She prepared and served Mitch a hot, delicious meal when he stepped out of the shower after work. Georgia never served his meals. Whether a home-cooked dinner actually made it to the table or remained on the stove, everyone in his old life, including himself, fended for themselves. He watched Sally's tiny nose flare with every breath. Her lips remained in a pout even as she slept. He thought about their first encounter. A frightened woman in need of protection after being taken advantage of by her ex was a different version of the same problem he'd investigated countless times, but this one had a different outcome for Mitch.

Mitch and Georgia had separated long before then. Georgia devoted more time to their sons than herself. She got sick of waiting: for dinner, for family time and for everything because of his unpredictability. His work. His showing up late for the boys' school events or worse; not showing up at all. Recycled spats ignited heated discussions which burned into days of silence. Then weeks of nothing. The sex had always been good but not worth maintaining a marriage for. He and Georgia both knew that. They lived apart for about a year, and Mitch had no shortage of intermittent encounters with somebody's sister or friend until Sally entered the picture. That's when one segment of his life regained some sense of stability. In Sally's eyes, they were a good match. In Georgia's mind, he was the opposite.

Not far from where Georgia and Mitch lived shortly before their divorce, two homes were demolished and a halfway house was built to accommodate eight male residents transitioning from incarceration to their rehabilitated lives. Despite much opposition from the nearby community, the project went ahead with the city and police department's reassurance that no sexual predators would be housed in a residential neighbourhood. In contrast to those tucked safely in their beds when the moon came out, it was not unusual to see a single male emerge from what was labelled the "rehab house" and pace the sidewalks near Georgia's street in the dark hours of the night.

Mitch responded to the first call about three weeks after the rehab house was fully inhabited. Occasionally, a restless male was seen breaking curfew and going for a run or walk in the middle of the night. Mitch, alone on patrol that night, checked his old backyard and was surprised to see Georgia standing at the back door. Usually confident and unafraid, she was stricken with fear and unable to calm down. There was nothing of concern in the yard except a toppled garbage can and a raccoon feasting on its find.

Mitch hesitantly accepted her offer to complete his report at her kitchen table. She watched him quietly as he rambled through a standard series of scripted questions. He reassured her repeatedly that she was safe. She wore the same ivory flannel housecoat which smelled of the same detergent she used when they were married. When she leaned forward, he caught a whiff of her hair, clean and slightly damp from her bath. She always bathed at night, and based on her scent, still used the same soap. She was barefoot, and he saw her toenails were painted pink. Something new. She never painted them before. She watched him looking at her feet.

"The boys gave me a gift certificate. They said I needed to do something nice for myself," she said.

He looked around and remembered. Memories, lots of them, including endless arguments in this kitchen.

"They were right," Mitch replied, as he felt a small stirring, unexpected and unprovoked.

Georgia felt it, too, and as quickly as their eyes met, they both looked away. Mitch stood up and put his empty coffee cup, the same one he had used for years, among the dirty dishes in the sink. Georgia stayed in her chair, her back towards him. He inhaled the scent of her hair and paused. An unexplained, stupid thing to do. No reason for it. He thanked her for the coffee.

"I'm glad it was you who took the call," she said quietly.

He walked the five steps toward the back door slowly.

"Just make sure you keep your door locked. But not just because of the rehab house. Those guys are all on parole, and the last thing they want to do is break it and land up back behind bars."

"I know," she said.

The day he told her they were done, he was standing in the same spot as he stood in right now. Such a distant thought. She felt overpowered by a yearning to touch him, and he sensed the same. More stupid, foolish thinking. No explanation. *Stop it, Mitch*, he argued with himself.

"You're going to be fine," he said.

He looked at her, at the familiar nightgown he had taken off her—or sometimes just pulled up—before. Sometimes in this kitchen after the boys had gone to school or bed. That was years ago. What was he thinking?

Georgia knew exactly what he was thinking. She knew him too well. She had recognized that look in his eyes for years. Most of the time she didn't care. But today she did. It was not that she expected it. Not what either had expected.

"Mitch?"

"What?"

"Nothing."

"What?"

"I'm sorry."

"Sorry for what?"

"I don't know," she said.

Mitch took a deep breath and looked at her. She looked helpless. So unlike the determined, unabashed Georgia.

"I'm sorry too."

Their eyes met again.

"I'm sorry we fought so much."

"Me too."

Then, somehow, it happened. He was not sure who made the move, but as they had done many times at the back door, they kissed. It was the same type of kiss that was reassuring to both. From Georgia, it was a "please be safe" kind of kiss, and from Mitch, it was a "stop worrying, I'll be fine" kind of kiss. It just happened, and it sparked a fire that had been extinguished a long time ago. It was a stupid thing to do, and neither had expected more.

The second visit came a few months later on a night when Mitch was not scheduled to work, but had switched shifts with another officer as a favour. He was the back-up responder to a disturbance call a couple of houses down and across the street from Georgia's house. New young neighbours reported noises in their backyard and blamed it again on the "ex-cons from the rehab house." Just as before, Mitch found a family of raccoons fighting a losing battle with a sealed garbage pail. He saw the light on in Georgia's living room. She knew enough not to taunt danger by standing in front of a lit window. After settling the neighbours down, the first patrol car left and Mitch walked over to check Georgia's backyard. For what? More raccoons? She recognized his stature and his gait, watched him walk around to the back of her house, her heart pounding with anticipation. *Stop expecting that he'll come in*, she thought as she tried to clear her mind. She turned the backyard light on.

Mitch's search yielded nothing except a half dozen pairs of lacy underwear secured by clothespins on the clothesline he had tied between two trees when the boys were young. Mitch had never seen Georgia wear anything but three-in-a-pack, budget-store cotton briefs. She was there again, standing in the back doorway. Same frumpy housecoat and another of her favourite flannel nightgowns. The combination of that underwear on the line and the reassured look she was wearing was enough to arouse him. *You're a fool*, he thought. *Look what's waiting for you at home.* He approached the back door, and she opened it slowly.

"You should keep the back gate locked," he warned softly, trying to remain professional.

"So no one comes around and sees my underwear?" she said, chuckling quietly, anxiously.

"There was a call across the street."

"I know. I couldn't sleep. And I saw the cruisers."

Georgia shut the backyard light off.

"It was the same four-legged thieves that were in your yard a few months ago, except they've multiplied."

Even by the dim moonlight, she recognized the need in his eyes.

"Coffee?" she asked.

He looked at his watch.

"It's not break time."

Mitch had no explanation for what made him walk inside. He closed the back door carefully behind him and locked it. Georgia remained still and very close to him. Neither of them spoke. Again, he took in the scent of her clean skin. They stared quietly at each other.

"This is stupid," Mitch said, using the same word again.

Georgia didn't move.

"It is."

"And not a good idea."

"I agree."

"And dangerous."

"You're right. Your gun looks loaded," she said, pointing to his revolver and brushing gently against his pants. She'd used that expression for years.

"I'm leaving," he said.

But he didn't move.

"You can't leave like that."

She put one hand over his bulge, gently massaging it through his pants. Her other hand went to his back pocket. He leaned in, relinquishing any sense of control. She kissed him firmly, and he responded. Her hair felt the same—thick and luxurious. He pressed into her against the back door, content that he'd won the argument of buying a solid steel back door for safety reasons instead of the flimsy decorative one that Georgia wanted. He reached inside her housecoat and nightgown to her breasts. They were softer and more pliable, like the rest of her. She moaned softly. His hands gathered her nightgown up and found her naked bottom, then searched for the dimples at the base of her spine. Soft, familiar skin. Like coming home.

Georgia took his hand and put it to her naked breast. He slowly pulled the flannel gown up higher and put his mouth over her nipple. Georgia responded with a long, low moan. He pulled more of her breast into his mouth and sucked gently, taking in her responses before he moved on to the other. He licked around her nipple, then blew on it until it was erect, remembering how she always responded before. He leaned harder into her. There was no turning back. His hand moved down over the softness of her stomach and to the mound of flesh between her legs. Georgia took Mitch's hand and led him to the bedroom. The light from the hood over the range and a small night light that had always been in the bathroom guided their way. The bedroom light stayed off. The blackout curtains were unchanged since Mitch last slept in this bed.

Georgia heard the sound of Mitch's belt coming undone.

"Leave them on."

"What?"

"Your pants. Drop them but leave them on. And keep your boots on," she ordered in a throaty growl.

He laughed out loud.

"But my boots are dirty."

"I know. You might need to make a quick getaway."

He took a deep breath.

"That's not romantic."

"This is not about romance, Mitch. This is about sex."

Georgia was nude and on the bed before Mitch could think of how to respond. He took his boots off anyway. Mitch's hands repositioning themselves on Georgia's hips silenced them both. He caressed her body, running his hands over the extra folds and crevices that had grown around her middle. She was no longer self-conscious that her body had changed since he last touched her. She felt comfortable in her skin. This wasn't about pleasing him anymore. She had nothing to lose, and in the heat of the moment, Mitch forgot he had everything to lose. Every inch of skin he touched made her body come alive. His hands moved to the delicate space between her open legs. Gentle and kind, he massaged her and moved his mouth to her moist flesh as she slowly kneaded his engorged shaft. Georgia hadn't slept with anyone since Mitch left, so she was aroused by every move he made and climaxed easily. Mitch entered her carefully, pacing himself and rhythmically moving against the resistance of the bed. It was over for him with a long groan. His uniform shirt was damp, and she felt his sweat fall onto her face. He rolled over on his back and laid beside her, bent elbows pointing to the ceiling while his hands covered his face. They said nothing for what seemed like a long, long time. She fell asleep before he left, in silence, ensuring the back door was locked and the lights were turned off.

Mitch regretted what he had done even before he got back to his car. What bothered him most was that he knew it was going to happen again. It was clandestine, consensual and wrong. Georgia was astute enough not to discuss it. Sleeping with his ex-wife, or anyone for that matter, during his working hours was grounds for termination. The fallout would compromise Georgia and the boys if she lost her alimony payments. To never return to her was the right—and the only—thing to do.

Many scenarios Mitch was involved in during the course of his work exceeded his moral conscience. Even though his divorce created a significant emotional and financial burden, including a struggle to re-build a relationship with his sons, his life was still good. He had many co-workers, some of them close friends, who took chances and paid a hefty price for the trauma they were exposed to through their work. They investigated many well-calculated schemes that criminals got themselves into, which often carried on for years before someone made an ill-fated mistake. Sometimes the lines between their work and personal lives became blurred. Risky behaviour got good and not so good people into trouble.

Sally knew something was amiss for days after Mitch's encounter with Georgia because Mitch's demeanour and attentiveness to her changed. She attributed it to his job, which had happened before. He rarely spoke to her about what bothered him. Maybe it was a particularly distressing incident affecting one of their own, or something involving a child, which always put a damper on the whole department. As always, she allowed Mitch space, knowing that he usually settled down in time. She suggested he talk to the police chaplain or attend the counselling program that work offered him. He agreed to consider it, telling her that he appreciated her concern. It also sent a strong warning sign for Mitch to get over Georgia and move on.

But he didn't. Mitch bumped into Georgia again at a bank machine at the outlet mall a month later. A pure, unplanned coincidence. He was off shift. Sally was at work, and Georgia was heading home. She suggested he leave his car in the mall parking lot. She said she'd park her car inside her garage to avoid anyone seeing him and would drive him back. It was all too easy. He was horny before he even closed the car door. And it became routine after that. No strings attached. And as Georgia had said the first time, it was not about romance. It was the sex.

He felt terrible after each encounter, but he couldn't stop. And although he did not have an addictive personality like his father did, he understood first-hand what it was.

2:30 p.m.

Lily settled into one corner of the sofa and ran her hand mindlessly over its soft leather. She had moved into the third-floor Loft she rented. A week's worth of newly purchased clothing was still in her suitcase. Everything was a size larger, adding another layer to her despair. Her thoughts kept defaulting back to Spencer's words and how this information affected her. There were still boxes of her sister's belongings that she couldn't bear to open.

She had also seen her fire-damaged condo with Sonny. There was more destruction than she predicted. Because the bathroom with the bathtub was adjacent to Lily's bedroom, her belongings and furniture were unsalvageable.

Sonny offered to "fix the place up real nice" so she could move back but returning to where her sister died would only compound her grief. Entering it to gather what she could save reduced her to living on the couch in her pajamas for days.

Lily accomplished only a few things on the long list of settling Rosie's affairs. The condo insurance company was adjudicating her claim for damages. She was forewarned that an extensive review of the police and fire marshal's reports was required to rule out arson.

The hotel where Rosie worked contacted Lily to pick up Rosie's locker contents, which included casual shoes and toiletries. Lily asked lots of questions, including if she was dating anyone at work. Otto, Rosie's manager, said it was against company policy. She inquired about alcohol or drug use among staff. Otto sat up stiffly in his chair, waved his hand across his desk and said the hotel had a zero tolerance for drinking or substance use on the job. He asked if she was concerned about Rosie. Lily shook her head, and Otto reassured her that Rosie was the perfect employee.

Lily did not mention the autopsy findings. Spencer had investigated the hotel and if Otto knew something, he did not share it. Compromising the hotel's five-star rating was not good for business. Otto and Lily also reviewed Rosie's employment benefits. Because their mother was still listed as Rosie's beneficiary on her life insurance policy, Otto suggested she seek legal advice to sort out that unfortunate detail. One step forward, two steps back.

Lily was exhausted from the morning as she passed the bakery on her way home. Sweets were back on her radar as a coping mechanism to manage her stress. Lily purchased an apple strudel, today's featured special, for her dinner. And two butter tarts for dessert. She hurried out of the bakery, salivating as she inhaled the aroma of butter, apples and cinnamon. She walked home with a purpose—to eat. Eating to cope with grief, to manage a new set of complicated circumstances and, unlike others, a sister she was coming to understand more after death.

Lily fiddled with her door keys and precariously balanced the pastry boxes with her other bags. She climbed the three flights of marble stairs, stopping on each landing to catch her breath and noting how time had worn down each step. Safely locked in the Loft, she took a big bite of strudel without bothering to slice it. She exhaled slowly as she savoured the warm apple filling. After a second bite, she removed her coat and shoes and slumped onto the leather sofa. She began another argument with herself about the same thing—her weakness which started when her marriage fell apart. Elliott chided her often about her lack of willpower, and today he proved himself right again.

Lily's family's law firm, she learned today, was unsure Rosie had a will. If she did, it was not with that practice. She'd gone to Rosie's bank armed with enough documentation to convince the staff that she was Rosie's sister. The teller encouraged her to make an appointment, which Lily eventually did after making no progress. Lily needed to know what her financial status was outside of her income from Elliott, which would end in less than a year. She did find out that Rosie had a safety deposit box and multiple accounts in undisclosed amounts, so this would take time to sort through. One tiny step forward.

Well into the second half of the strudel, Lily felt no more comforted than before her first bite. Only that revolving circle of guilt. She was failing at her tenth or maybe even twentieth diet. Lily put her head back against the sofa and cried until sleep eventually took over.

4:00 p.m.

Gracie left her interview for a full-time position at the local library feeling hopeful that she got the job. She was done with traffic, commuting and living with her daughter. Gracie drove to Park Street straight from the interview. Winnie, who was pre-occupied sorting flyers in the lobby, let her in without asking questions and returned to her task. Gracie sank down into one of the armchairs and called Sonny again. As usual, his voicemail was full.

She chastised herself for being her age with no clear life path. She ruminated again about what went wrong in her relationship with Fred. Tess and Fred were amazing people but had competing personalities, as did Fred's daughter, Claire, and Tess. Any event involving the foursome ended in conflict, and both daughters encouraged the separation. Fred and Gracie still cared about each other, but beyond a cordial text, there was no chance of reconciliation.

Gracie was more than frustrated today because she signed a lease and invested her hard-earned dollars in what she anticipated to be an easy move, yet had not spent one night at Park Street. She had the main entry passcode and a mailbox key, but Sonny kept the Loft key. His excuse was that he could show the Loft on short notice to any prospective tenant because he lived nearby. The longer Sonny avoided her, the more questions arose. Was she still a tenant? Had it been rented out? Was she a victim of fraud? Had the locks been changed? She stood up and determined she would find some answers. She climbed the stairs to the Loft, leaving a pre-occupied Winnie in the lobby. Her heart pounded with anxiety as she thought she may get some answers on her own.

Catching her breath in the hallway, she looked around. Three doors on the third floor were labelled. One led to a widow's walk on the building roof, the second to what served as a maintenance/storage room, and the third door was marked Unit 3: The Loft. Gracie knocked quietly on the door. No answer. When she tried the door, it was unlocked. Her heart skipped a few beats. She slowly moved it open until a deadbolt chain blocked her. She and the startled voice inside yelled "Hello?" simultaneously.

A woman's sleepy and swollen eyes met Gracie's. She looked about Gracie's age but was heavier.

"How did you get up here?" Lily said coarsely, not expecting to be seen or interrupted.

She attempted to tame her hair, and rubbed her puffy eyes.

"I rented this place in September and paid for it, so I'm wondering the same thing. How did you get the keys?"

Sonny's story of holding her money as a "collateral investment" was sounding more and more illegal.

"The landlord or the property manager—or whoever he is—offered it to me."

Gracie's mouth dropped. She didn't want to say anything she would later regret.

"Something's very wrong here," she finally said.

Now, both women were confused.

"Who did you pay rent to?" Lily asked.

"Sonny."

"Well, Sonny is the one who gave me the key."

The door shut, the deadbolt was unlocked and Lily opened the door. The two women stood momentarily in silence, sized each other up, then determined neither posed a safety risk.

"Well, you might as well come in so we can sort this out," Lily said wearily.

Gracie took her shoes off and scanned what she could see, including an open suitcase, unpacked boxes and the disarray of someone not expecting company.

"When did you move in?" she asked Lily, and introduced herself.

"October 5th. I'm Gracie," she said.

"Well, Gracie, I'm Lily, and one of us has a problem. Do you want to sit down?"

Lily gave her guest a short version of the fire, the evacuation and losing Rosie. Gracie's grief from losing Blair paled in comparison to Lily's sudden loss, which was compounded when Lily said Rosie's beneficiary on her life insurance policy was their deceased mother.

"That's unbelievable," Gracie said, shaking her head.

"Not really. My lawyer said it happens all the time."

"That's not actually what I was thinking," Gracie clarified. "With my husband's life insurance, I was the beneficiary, but my husband breached the policy conditions. The insurance company investigated it and denied the claim."

"Really?"

"Yup. It was a $100,000 mistake. He was enrolled in the policy as a non-smoker but snuck the odd cigarette without my knowledge or weighing the consequences it would have on our daughter and me."

"That's just not fair," Lily said as she leaned back and stared at the ceiling.

Lily made coffee and served the butter tarts that she was too stuffed to eat as the women meshed the stories which them led to today. Gracie scanned the Loft again, but she didn't recall the silver encrusted egg on the fireplace mantle when she initially saw it. She desperately wanted to live here but uprooting a grieving woman was worse. Their solution was to call Sonny and ask him how he intended to resolve "his" problem.

The women traded phone numbers and agreed to keep in touch. Lily was more unsettled about the Loft now than she was five days ago, but she felt a warm connection with Gracie. Gracie felt the same as she walked down the marble stairs and ran her hands over the re-finished walnut banister. She stood on the last step and admired the lobby of this grand old building that Winnie had left uncluttered. She wanted to live on Park Street and decided to wage war with Sonny until she won.

5:00 p.m.

Mason brought fish and chips and some forms to review with Winnie over dinner. He walked into the vestibule while trying to keep his worn leather briefcase from making contact with the greasy package. An attractive woman stood pensively on the bottom step taking in her surroundings. He smiled warmly, wondering what her voice might sound like.

"Beautiful day for this time of year," he said.

Gracie returned his smile.

"It is."

Mason saw the mailbox key in Gracie's hand.

"New to this building?"

Gracie frowned, then sighed.

"Sort of, I'm supposed to live here."

"That's a peculiar answer."

"More convoluted than peculiar. I signed a lease on a condo that someone else is living in."

"That sounds complicated. Which floor?"

"Third. The Loft."

"And no alternative?"

Gracie watched Mason's awkward efforts to keep his paper bag of food away from his suit. She squinted to read the roster of resident names across the lobby.

"Not that I know of. As you said, it's complicated. Ah, is there a door I can open for you?"

"Thank you. Would you be kind enough to buzz Unit 1A?"

Gracie pressed Winnie's buzzer. The hall door unlocked and Grace opened it, and as she held the door for Mason to pass through, he caught a whiff of her light perfume. *Much nicer than fish and chips*, he thought. In contrast, the aroma of the food in Mason's hand smelled incredible to Gracie as she had only eaten a butter tart since breakfast.

"Lunch smells wonderful."

"Yes, indeed."

Mason paused enough to inhale a second breath of her scent before walking through.

"Fish and chips?"

Grace noticed Mason's suit was a cut well above common and thought he might be slightly older than her.

"Yes. From the diner just up the street. Today's special," Mason said, smiling warmly again and guessing that she may be slightly younger than him.

"Hmmm. Now I know what I'm having for dinner."

Mason wished he could join her.

"Best diner on this side of town. And if you need some advice on your lease, I'd be happy to help."

It was unusual for Mason to make this offer, especially to a woman he'd never met, but there was something wholesome about her.

"Really? That's very generous of you. Thank you—I will keep that in mind."

"If I can ask you for one more small favour?" he said, passing the greasy bag into her open hands. He noticed the absence of a wedding ring as he reached into his inside breast pocket and offered her his business card. She looked at his impressive credentials.

"Pleased to meet you, Mason, General Practice Attorney. I'm Gracie Sheehan, part-time librarian."

"And a pleasure to meet you, Gracie."

"I could certainly use your advice, but as a part-time librarian, I don't think I can afford you," she said honestly.

Mason had no intention of billing her.

"Would covering the cost of fish and chips be a reasonable fee?"

"As in, a lunch date?" Grace said with a blush.

This amused Mason.

"To be honest, I wouldn't want to compromise my intent. Maybe we could call it a lunch meeting."

Gracie was embarrassed, which further amused Mason.

"I'm sorry. I don't know why I said that. Of course, I can manage that. Thank you, Mason. That would be very kind of you."

Gracie passed the bag of food back to Mason and saw that grease had seeped onto her hands and then his. Grace put her index finger up.

"Just a minute," she said.

She retrieved a newspaper flyer from the recycling box, took the food container and placed it on the coffee table between the armchairs in the lobby. From her purse, she produced a small bottle of hand sanitizer, poured some onto a clean tissue and wiped her hands clean. Instinctively, Mason opened his hand, palm facing up. She paused, laughed, then wiped it too. Mason felt the slight tremble of Grace's hands as she touched his, bringing an unexpected bit of pleasure to his day.

"I'm sorry. I'm still such a mother," she said, laughing at her own behaviour.

He savoured her smile. A beautiful, genuine smile.

"There you go. Now you don't even need to wash your hands before dinner," she said.

Mason laughed aloud.

"It was a pleasure to meet you, Gracie."

"Likewise, Mason. If things don't resolve with my lease soon, I'll call your office to arrange the 'lunch meeting,'" Grace said, raising the appropriate fingers to illustrate quotation marks.

Mason walked purposefully down the hall to Winnie who was standing in her open doorway. Gracie watched his tailored suit move against his tall frame as he walked away from her. He turned back to give her a polite nod and was flattered that she was still watching him.

What a nice man, she thought.

What a beautiful woman, he thought.

What took him so long to get here? Winnie thought as she closed the door behind him.

5:30 p.m.

Adrian finally made the call he kept forgetting—or neglecting—to make. He couldn't recall the last time he spoke with his grandmother, but the guilt of the lapse bothered him. Moments where Adrian felt guilt came rarely. He dialled her number, trying to remember her birth date. He'd forgotten her age. The phone rang. There was no answer and no voicemail, and she didn't have a mobile phone. After ten impatient rings, he dialled his parents' home. It had also been a while. His mother texted him often; she was such a worrier. His father rarely did. His mother picked up on the third ring, and after the initial string of greetings, she asked him what was wrong.

"Nothing's wrong. I just called to see how things were at home."

"You never call. Something must be wrong."

"Everything's fine. Work is good. Busy, as usual. We had a fire in the building I just moved into."

"Oh my God, Adrian! I knew there was something wrong. That's terrible. Was anyone hurt? Are you all right? I knew I should have called. There was a full moon last night and I told your father we were going to get some bad news and oh, my poor child …"

Adrian paused, knowing from his past mistakes never to lie to his mother. Or worse, his father. Better not to tell them than to lie.

"It was contained to only one unit. Some careless smoker started it. It's no big deal, Mom. Everything is back to normal."

"I knew there was something wrong!"

"Mom, stop worrying. It wasn't even on my floor."

His mother had no idea where he lived and because he moved so frequently, she always checked before forwarding his grandmother's cards. Adrian switched subjects to avoid more questions or tell his mother that the fire was directly below his unit and that someone had perished.

"So, are you and Dad doing okay?"

"Oh, we're fine. Your dad is losing his hearing but refuses to get tested. So everything he turns on is at full volume. Some days, Adrian, he drives me crazy."

Based on those few comments, he already knew things were normal at home.

"And how's Nana? I tried to call her but there was no answer."

"You called Nana? Well, bless your heart. Nana had a fall last week, so the doctor said she should stay somewhere where there are no stairs for a little while."

Adrian remembered sliding down his grandmother's stairs on his bottom as a child with his sister right behind him. Adrian's parents still lived nearby her in the spacious four-bedroom home he grew up in.

"Is she staying with you and Dad?"

"Yes, for now. It was the easiest option."

"Hmmm, for how long?"

"Let's see …" she counted the days aloud, and he pictured her using her fingers to guide her. "Six more days, or maybe seven."

"And other than that, is she doing okay?"

"Well, the doctor is also worried about her memory. They did some tests and he thinks she may be in the early stages of dementia. But he can't be sure if it's from the fall or if this is really what's happening, so we're watching her closely for that too."

Adrian did not expect that news.

"What's she doing that made him think that?"

"Well, you know, sometimes she forgets to take her pills, and sometimes she forgets to eat or bathe. We didn't know how bad it was until we hired someone to come in and help her with her bath. When we started checking her mail, we noticed she was sending money to all these charities. When they call, she can't remember who they are. I witnessed it myself, and so did your sister. And when Chrissy notices something's wrong, it's worrisome."

Adrian thoughts digressed to Winnie's habit of sorting junk mail in the lobby. Usually insignificant, it bothered him.

"Should I come home? I know it's Thanksgiving and I'm supposed to be working, but maybe I could book a last-minute flight."

"We'd love that! Nana's in your room because it's nearest the bathroom. Chrissie's home for the long weekend, so you'll be in the guest bedroom."

Adrian hated that room. It was a mismatch of old furniture that his mother wouldn't part with. He decided he'd wait until his grandmother was back in her own place before he'd return home for a visit.

"I'm checking flights as we speak, Mom. Wow, are they ever expensive," he lied, looking out the window.

"Honey, then come home another time instead of paying top dollar for a last-minute flight. You'll save a lot of money."

"You know, Mom, I think you're right. Like always. I'll do that and let you know when I book some time off. Is Nana around so I can talk to her?"

"She's napping right now, dear."

"Then don't wake her, Mom. Just tell her that I called, and give her a hug from me. I'll send you my flight details when I book them."

His mother reassured him she would and the call ended.

Adrian opened his computer and went back to his project, but instead of feeling better after the call, he felt worse.

7:30 p.m.

Marcello hobbled over to his easy chair after returning home from Winnie's. He had just shared his first attempt at tiramisu with her, and she was in good spirits after a visit from Mason a few hours ago.

His back was particularly sore today from cleaning and cooking. His doctor told him to pace himself, but he liked to get his housekeeping done in one day. *Maybe I should listen to my doctor*, he thought as he leaned his head back and pulled the lever of his recliner to elevate his feet. He turned the TV on, and by the time the first commercial break of the game show aired, he was sound asleep. Michelangelo sat in the closed window well that opened to the fire exit watching Mona Lisa on the other side, her meows drowned out by the volume of the TV.

9:45 p.m.

Bryce returned from his evening shift at the call centre to a plateful of re-heated leftovers Talia had saved for him. Sometimes she shook the plate first so that the food portions overlapped each other. Elbows on the table and hands framing her face, Talia watched Bryce assess his plate, re-sort his food by colour and finish each mushy mound before progressing to the next. It frustrated both of them for different reasons.

"Why do you do that?" she asked.

Bryce knew exactly what she meant and offered the same response every time.

"Because it tastes better this way," he said with a smile. He moved a pea that had wandered over to his rice.

"Love you, Tal."

"Love you too," she sighed before they shared their day's events and gossiped about work.

Talia contemplated telling Bryce about Adrian inviting her out a few weeks ago, then decided against it. Bryce was a peaceful soul, and she didn't feel threatened or intimidated by either man. She would ignore Adrian and decline if he propositioned her again.

October 17th
Weather forecast: blowing winds and rain

9:10 a.m.

"Hell hath no fury like a woman scorned ..."

William Congreve

Gracie was offered and accepted the full-time position at the library. As happy as that made her, it also fuelled her frustration with Sonny, who continued to ignore her calls. Her last voicemail, left a few days ago, threatened him with legal action if he failed to meet her in the condo lobby today at 9:00 a.m. Gracie and Lily's mail was being delivered to their original units and both wanted this changed.

Gracie held Mason's card in her pocket for leverage. She retrieved it and looked at his impressive credentials again. He was just ten minutes away, not far from the fish and chips place, and Sonny was ten minutes late.

When Sonny finally made his appearance, it was not through the front door but from the first-floor hallway. He was dressed in paint-spattered jeans, a ragged sweatshirt and construction boots. His curly salt-and-pepper hair was crowned with the imprint of a hard hat. Throwing excuses and a weak apology her way, he said he assumed she had lost interest in the Loft, so he offered it to Lily. This contradicted Lily's explanation. When Gracie challenged Sonny, he immediately offered her Suite 1C at a discounted rate for a "luxurious two-bedroom unit," which was the identical cost of the one-bedroom Loft. He threw in one additional rent-free month. She balked at this, reminding him of her investment in rent and fees for the Loft. Feeling manipulated again, she demanded to see what condition Suite 1C was in. He declined, explaining it was still a construction site, but she nattered at him until he eventually conceded. She trailed Sonny down the hall, the scent of old sweat and garlic following him. As he unlocked the door and closed it swiftly behind them, Gracie pulled her sweater over her nose to filter out some of the charred stench and tried to focus beyond the damage. There was extensive restoration work in progress.

The pleasant surprise was that Gracie envisioned the condo, when finished, to be spectacular. It was spacious, with high crown-moulded ceilings and enormous windows. Her thoughts flashed back to the recent tragedy here, but in all honesty, Rosie was unknown to her. A month of free rent was enticing, and there were few other housing options in the neighbourhood. She walked quietly around, taking her time to avoid the construction supplies. Sonny, prematurely convinced she'd decline, enhanced his offer. He promised she could move in on November 1st, and if she committed to take it, he'd waive two more months, totalling three months of free rent. They both knew it would be difficult to lease locally, considering its well-published legacy. If this nagging woman accepted, he calculated, it would also save him the inconvenience and expense of listing it again.

Grace glared at him suspiciously as he worked hard to charm her into the deal. He followed her through the unit, pressing on. At one point they stood face to face and Sonny took one step closer to her, putting his hands on his hips. He raised his eyebrows and flashed a suggestive smile that repulsed her. She stepped back, and by the expression on her face, it was clear he had tried the wrong strategy. Even with what limited knowledge she had of construction, she knew it would be a miracle if the renovations were completed in thirteen days. A surge of adrenaline rushed through her. She took one more step away from him, then counter-offered.

"If this condo is not in move-in condition by November 1st, you must waive the rent for a total of six months," she said, producing Mason's card as a threat.

Another three-month extension was still cheaper than his own lawyer's quote to rectify the mess he created by ignoring her signed lease, refunding Gracie what he owed her and renting it out to someone else. Sonny ran his fingers through his unruly curls, examined his dusty work boots carefully and complained he was losing money. Gracie retaliated furiously. That was not her problem. He found his phone, pecked at his calculator and after his turn taking a slow walk around the condo, accepted Gracie's offer. He knew Gracie was right. She also demanded a new signed lease confirming what they just agreed to in her hand by day's end. If the unit was not ready by November 1st, she told him she was still moving in, rent-free, for a total of six months. He argued that this was still a construction site, and she reiterated her threat.

He promised Gracie the lease would be ready for her to sign by five o'clock the following day provided she kept their agreement confidential. She scoffed at him again and waved Mason's business card as ammunition. She took her phone out of her pocket, pointed out the window and warned Sonny that Mason was literally down the street waiting in his office for her call. Sonny knew the law firm but was unaware that Mason frequented this building. He finally conceded.

Grace took a final walk about the condo, again with Sonny following at a cautious distance. This time, feeling bold, she entered Lily's bathroom for the first time. She knew that Rosie died here. Impulsively, she picked up a hammer that was lying on the bathroom counter and pounded the porcelain ledge of the bathtub with blunt force, chipping out a large wedge that, ironically, resembled a heart. Sonny, defeated, made a mental note to add a new tub to his list.

Grace left Sonny in the condo, bewildered at what had just happened. Her confidence soared as did her level of anxiety. Gracie felt certain, based on her previous encounters with Sonny, that he would not return the contract the following day and that moving into the unit in thirteen days was a challenging, if not impossible, goal. But at least it was another hopeful start. *Thank you, Mason*, she whispered to herself as she left the building, leaving Sonny still fingering the bathtub chip.

9:30 a.m.

Sally lay silently in bed beside Mitch after they had made love. Even after some intimate weeks, he continued to remain distant. More distracted and less passionate. She wondered what she was doing wrong. She thought this marriage would work despite being forewarned that marrying a policeman was a complicated commitment. Mitch saved her from the mess her ex-boyfriend, Robin, put her in, and if it wasn't for Mitch, she'd be bankrupt, a potential accomplice to Robin's fraudulent activities and buried in legal bills.

Sally married Mitch because she fell in love with him and because she felt he protected her, which her father, brother and Robin hadn't. Yes, Mitch protected her, but she was unsure from what. Mitch never spoke about work or his ex-wife. He rarely mentioned his friends and had minimal contact with his sons other than obligatory gift-giving exchanges which excluded Sally.

Since their marriage, she also spent less time with her friends. Mitch didn't exactly discourage it, and although he was never condescending, she sensed he didn't approve of them. Or what she repeated that they said. These were long-standing friendships between women who had shared joy, hardship and dissolved marriages through death or infidelity. Friends who had coached each other through new beginnings. One friend gently asked if Sally was investing more effort in her marriage than he was. The comment stung but left her wondering.

Some evenings when Mitch worked late, she buried herself in a steamy romance to avoid feeling troubled, but she was unsure of what or why. On their rare outings, Mitch was more on edge, constantly looking around and impatient to leave. Not one to crave his attention, she longed to share an enjoyable evening out. Whatever defined a normal marriage, she was beginning to think it might not be reflective of theirs. Mitch rolled over and rubbed her back gently. He traced his finger up and down her spine, lightly across the top of her shoulders and then horizontally until he reached the small of her back.

"Are you okay?" Mitch asked as he kissed her shoulder blade.

"I'm good," she lied, choosing not to voice her worries and ruin the moment.

"Me too," he said as he squeezed her bottom and headed for the shower.

He sensed Sally was not herself, but why spoil a good start to his day.

10:00 a.m.

Mitch and Sally shared the morning paper over coffee and toast before he left for work. Sally was off today. She showered after Mitch left and put on her favourite jeans and a well-worn plaid shirt. She skipped the make-up, walked downstairs and out through the front doors. Shielded by the stone double arches of the front entrance, she breathed the wet air in deeply, looked down the street and saw a few feral cats. When the dampness chilled her, she returned inside and checked the mail. She heard footsteps clicking down the marble stairs behind her. She was surprised to see Lily unfolding her umbrella, dressed smartly in a long sweater and leggings.

"Good morning. Not so nice out there," Lily said.

"Not at all. I didn't think you'd moved back yet."

"I'm staying in the Loft for a while. At least until I decide if I'm okay staying there, I mean here, in this building."

"I understand. But I thought the Loft was rented."

"It was—or rather, is. Apparently, someone rented it, but there was a mix up because I moved in without her knowing. Anyhow, I'm not really sure how long I'm staying. I need some time to adjust, you know, after …" Lily didn't finish her sentence but, instead, walked over to the Suite 1C mailbox and checked it.

"It's nice to see you again. I'm sure these days are not easy for you."

"Thank you. Some are bad days and then there is a good one. There are still lots of loose ends to tie up."

"It must be overwhelming."

Lily said her goal today was to settle some of Rosie's bank accounts. She also mentioned Rosie hadn't changed her life insurance beneficiary. Sally said this was not uncommon at the bank where she worked.

They both agreed it would be nice to meet sometime again, and as Lily headed out the door, Sally thought about her own legal documents. Her aging but healthy mother was her beneficiary for everything. Mitch's life insurance was part of his work benefits. Sally suggested creating new wills, but Mitch laughed it off when he checked the underside of an old dresser drawer at their garage sale to ensure his old one wasn't taped to it.

Walking up the stairs, Sally wondered where Mitch's will was; maybe he really had taped it to a furniture drawer again rather placing it in the security of a safety deposit box. Sally had never searched through his personal effects because she had no reason to. She assumed she and his sons were included as beneficiaries. Curiosity tugged against her conscience as she entered her condo. She locked the deadbolt behind her, something she never did during the day.

Entering the spare room which doubled as Mitch's office, she opened the top drawer of his cherished oak desk, the same one his father used when the police station was still housed in this building. The top drawer was unlocked and it squeaked as it opened. His father's badge and an undated picture of Mitch and his father, both in uniform, laid side by side. Slips of paper, police logbooks and crumpled receipts were scattered randomly among office supplies. Sally slid the palm of her hand across the top under-surface of the drawer, feeling for anything that might be attached to it. There was nothing. Knowing Mitch, it wouldn't be that easy now. She opened the three drawers on the left. Nothing. Two deeper drawers on the right were stuffed with papers she felt uncomfortable rummaging through.

"Sally?" Mitch's loud yell pierced the stillness.

She tried to shove the desk drawers shut quietly, then she ran to open the front door. Mitch's expression was that of an officer on a stake-out, not a concerned husband.

"You scared me to death!" she exclaimed loudly.

"Why did you lock the deadbolt?" he questioned as she unlocked it.

"I don't know. Habit."

He knew she was lying. Mitch had reassured himself and Sally that the security system in this building was reliable.

"Why did you lock the door, Sally?"

It was Mitch the detective and not her husband asking. She wasn't going to lie again. She looked directly into his eyes but said nothing. It was easier than telling the truth. Mitch left his shoes on and walked to their bedroom. The bed was still unmade, and she watched him feel the temperature of sheets under the covers.

"Are you kidding me? You think I had company?" she asked weakly.

She felt his breath on her neck as he followed her to the living room. She curled up in a chair and fought tears as he checked the rest of the condo. She watched Mitch walk to his desk. The drawers were all shut, but his chair was not tucked into his desk. He turned around and glared at her as tears rolled down her cheeks.

"What are you crying about? Stop crying! You hear me? Stop it!" he growled.

She watched him open and shut each desk drawer, following the same sequence that Sally did as if he had somehow watched her. He slammed each drawer shut. Satisfied with his inspection, he shoved the desk chair hard against the desk and looked around the room. He slowly approached Sally, who was shaking. He firmly grasped her jaw with one extended hand. She had no choice but to face him. His other hand balled up into a fist so tight his knuckles turned white.

"Don't. Ever. Touch. My. Possessions. Again," he hissed.

Sally sank deeper into her chair, starkly aware that this version of Mitch was foreign to her. He held his grasp to emphasize his point, letting go only when a text ping distracted him.

Mitch left immediately and slammed the door behind him as Sally felt warm urine escape her. She had never wet herself before. She locked and deadbolted the door again and locked the bathroom door. She peeled her soiled clothes off and showered. She thought she heard the front door bang against the deadbolt chain again but purposely ignored it. She remained in the shower long after she was clean, and when she finally turned the tap off, she couldn't see beyond the steam. She stood, naked and shivering, and listened, not sure what she was expecting to hear. By the time she looked in the mirror, the residual finger indentations on her face had faded to a soft pink.

Sally dressed slowly in a baggy sweatshirt and jeans, dried her hair and, despite the tremors in her hand, attempted to apply a bit of make-up. She packed a gym bag with enough to clothe herself for a few days. To a casual observer, she was carrying what she needed for a workout. She noticed bigger chips out of the door paint from the deadbolt when Mitch had attempted to return. She walked over to the fire escape landing, briefly considering leaving via this exit, then changed her mind. She left via the door, locked it and walked cautiously to the front lobby. She researched the address for the women's shelter on her phone, then deleted her privatized history. She took a few deep breaths in the vestibule to reorganize the storm in her head. Taking one step outside, she spotted an unmarked cruiser parked discreetly behind a courier van. Backtracking, she leaned against the inside door, unable to formulate an alternative plan.

Sally walked back up the stairs and re-entered her condo, securing both door locks behind her. She walked over to the fire escape again and watched the unmarked car drive by slowly. She threw her gym bag back in its regular spot in the front hall closet. She cleaned the urine stain off of her chair, then slumped into another chair and remained there. She scrolled through her contact list in her phone, paused at a few of her close friends, then found her mother's number. She stared at it until the phone screen went black. She got up and walked back to the window that faced the front of the building and saw that the unmarked cruiser had parked there again.

She pulled her gym bag out again and returned her clothing and toiletries to where they belonged, taking care to replace her toothbrush to the same spot it was when Mitch returned. She put the kettle on and called her mother, who answered on the second ring.

"Hi, Mom," she said softly, putting a teabag into her favourite mug and fighting back fresh tears.

"It's Saturday morning, Dolly," her mother said. "You never call on Saturday morning. Are you okay?"

Her mother had called her Dolly since she was born.

"I'm fine, Mom. Never mind me. I just called to see how you were doing," Sally said, wiping tears and mascara away with one swipe.

She listened as her mother rambled about her new neighbours piling garbage up around their house, and that her housekeeper wasn't reliable. Sally stood up and walked slowly to the front hall closet door, resenting herself for not closing it completely when she took her gym bag out. She walked to her condo door to re-examine the missing paint from the deadbolt. She opened the door, wondering if other tenants would notice the marks. She gasped when she saw the arrangement of red roses standing in a vase on the floor beside the doorway.

"What's wrong? You're not listening to a thing I'm saying," her mother said.

"So sorry, Mom. I just opened the door. Someone delivered a bouquet of flowers."

"Flowers? What kind of flowers?"

"Ah, roses. Red ones."

Her mother was silent for a moment.

"Oh, my goodness. Now isn't that nice? Are they from Mitch?"

"They must be. Our building is quite secure."

"He's such a brave man to be in that line of work. And so handsome. I like him much better than that Robin character."

"Mom, I have to go and add water to these flowers," Sally lied as she struggled to lift the vase with one hand.

They exchanged hasty goodbyes, and Sally looked out both windows. The unmarked cruiser was gone.

11:45 a.m.

Talia woke up nauseated and achy all over but still went to work. She skipped breakfast and substituted weak tea for coffee, but didn't feel any better. Her supervisor, who was usually nasty and tended to hover over his sales team, noticed that she was not meeting her call targets. He observed Talia from a distance, then discreetly passed her workstation a few times, peaking over a modular wall. Unlike many others, she was not pre-occupied with her own phone, which laid untouched beside her tea.

He approached Talia, concerned she looked pale and encouraged her to go home, which was unusual for him. Talia rarely called in sick but acknowledged she was not herself. He escorted her to the elevator, also an unusual gesture. Even though sick time was unpaid, he told her that he would punch her timecard for the whole shift. She was an employee he did not want to lose.

Talia left work but couldn't text Bryce because she forgot her phone on her desk. Too sick to return to retrieve it, she walked home at a slow pace. She entered her building, dragged her wobbly legs up the stairs and just as she went to open the door to the second-floor hallway, Mitch forced it open quickly, narrowly avoiding slamming it against her. He apologized repeatedly, walked her to her door—more out of remorse than kindness—and apologized again before disappearing down the hall.

Talia unlocked the door and threw her bag on the floor. She expected to find Bryce stacking dirty laundry into little piles of matching colours because today was always laundry day. With the loud whirling of the machine's spin cycle, Bryce was oblivious to Talia's arrival.

Walking to the kitchen, she stopped abruptly in the doorway and stood there in silence. Bryce, his back to her, had removed everything from the pantry shelves and was sorting its contents. He had aligned all the cans, labels centred and facing forward on the top shelf by height. The tallest were on the ends and they sloped down to the shortest ones in the centre. He was doing the same with the boxes he was replacing on the second shelf and was counting aloud and repeating a sequence of numbers as he worked. He was totally immersed in his task. Talia waited for a few minutes until she lost her patience.

"Bryce, what are you doing?"

He recoiled and spun around.

"Tal, you just scared the shit out of me!"

He looked at the time on his watch.

"You're scaring me. Big time. What the fuck are you doing?"

"Just organizing the cupboards. You're always complaining you can't find anything," he said. "Why are you home?" he asked as he returned the remaining pantry contents haphazardly.

"I'm sick."

"Oh." He looked at her and frowned. "You look pale."

"Why are you doing that?" she asked more forcefully.

Bryce breathed deeply, trying to mask his frustration at being interrupted. He'd have to start again.

"So they're easy for us to find," he said.

With no energy to argue, Talia dropped her clothes all over the bedroom floor and buried herself under the blankets. Bryce followed her a minute later and, seeing the motionless top of her shiny hair, decided it was not a good time to defend himself. He looked at her piles of clothes, scooped them up and closed the door. He inhaled her scent from each article. Although they had been on her body only a few hours, he washed them anyway. He checked on Talia often, who was purring softly under the covers, while he finished his ritual of stacking the pantry contents in order. His order. He had to be careful. He couldn't bear to lose Talia.

OCTOBER 25TH
Weather forecast: partly cloudy

10:00 a.m.

"Most people choose which side they are on early in life."

Anonymous

Lily let Spencer into her Loft as pre-arranged. He was just checking in with her. He had nothing new to offer about Rosie's case and predicted there would be little to share in the future. It was unlikely, at this stage, that they could trace the supplier of the illegal substances Rosie had inhaled, and the cause of her death remained an accidental drowning. Feeling the heaviness in the Loft's air from his comments, she grabbed her wallet and escorted Spencer back to the main doors. He left, and she took in the crisp fall air, battling her craving for anything sweet from the bakery.

Lily checked her mismatched outfit, and instead of heading down the street, she returned to the Loft to process what the detective said. On her coffee table lay two condolence cards sent from Rosie's hotel corporate office. She insisted the officer take the rest. She didn't know the senders and had no desire to keep them. She had re-read each card an hour ago, baffled that her sister never mentioned these strangers.

1:00 p.m.

Marcello made some Italian wedding soup and delivered half to Winnie. Her compliments inspired him to share many of his dinner meals. She repaid him with heart-healthy, low-sodium commercially-prepared frozen meals that her children arranged to be delivered. They went to Marcello when her freezer section was jammed to capacity. She was a poor eater who hated cooking, nor was she skilled in the culinary arts. Marcello doctored these meals with herbs, salt and cream to make them palatable, and supplemented with wine, he enjoyed them with Winnie. Free was always affordable.

Winnie ate breakfast on her own time, which could be dinner leftovers consumed mid-morning, if and when she felt like eating. She would usually tell Marcello if she was going out by banging the same repeated pattern of loud knocks on his door each time she left and returned. This balanced out his increasing need of reassurance that she was fine.

Today Winnie told him she called the library and was going to there to pick up Italian cooking books that the new librarian found her. When she suggested she'd make dinner for Marcello from scratch, he wondered how and what someone with such a strong English ancestry might be capable of. Since moving, Winnie's literary interests had shifted from the monthly bestsellers her children sent her to church bulletins and junk mail. She passed the unread novels on to Marcello. He read and returned many of them, complete with a summary of the story and characters clipped to the book jacket. She was then duly prepared for when her children grilled her about them. Marcello also rated the books as excellent, okay, so-so or terrible. In turn, they kept sending the books and Marcello kept reading them, occasionally suggesting a new title or author of his own interest. It was a win-win arrangement. And as with the meals, free was affordable.

After consuming too much of a fresh baguette with his soup at lunch, Marcello cleaned up. The herb garden on the kitchen windowsill above the sink was dense and overgrown, obstructing his view of the street corner below. Had he looked carefully between the basil and parsley, he would have seen Mona Lisa on the sidewalk, positioned to cross the street between cars whizzing by. After a couple of false starts, she darted across the road in the direction of his building, narrowly missing the wheels of a tourist bus returning to its depot.

Marcello finished the dishes and turned his TV to *Rick Steves' Europe*. Ten minutes into his tour of the Vatican, Marcello was snoring and oblivious to Mona Lisa, who was sitting on the fire escape landing and meowing. Michelangelo listened for a while, then ignored her. He preferred to nap on Marcello instead.

Winnie decided to walk to the library; it was a colourful fall day, and she was dressed appropriately for the weather. As she exited the front door, a mangy looking tabby cat sprinted between her sturdy shoes, through the vestibule and into the front lobby. She returned to the lobby in an attempt to entice the cat back out the door, but it ran up the stairs. Knowing she couldn't outrun a cat, she abandoned Mona Lisa, leaving the task of evicting her to the next person entering the building.

Winnie stood on the street corner calculating her route to the library. She set off, passing Mason's office and reassuring herself she could stop by on her return if she wanted a rest or for Aida to make her some tea. Winnie soon realized that some of the offices and storefronts had changed since she last walked down this street. She passed a few more street crossings before she began to wonder if she should ask someone for directions. She walked into a pawn shop, which she remembered previously as a music store, and asked for directions to the library. A young woman with green hair, sleeve tattoos and an abundance of facial piercings checked her phone and pointed Winnie in the right direction. Two oversized bald men, dressed in ill-fitting jeans and motorcycle gang jackets, glanced at Winnie and decided she was oblivious to the shady business they were conducting at the back of the shop.

By the time Winnie arrived at the library a good hour later, it was near closing time. Gracie, stationed at the check-out desk, recognized Winnie's voice from her call and produced the heavy cookbooks she had asked about. Winnie presented an expired library card and then forgot her new address when Gracie attempted to update her membership. Grace recognized Winnie's last name from the Park Street resident list, and when Gracie described the building she was moving to soon, Winnie validated her address as the same.

Evaluating the heavy books against Winnie's stature, Gracie offered to carry them to Winnie's car. When Winnie said she walked over, Gracie worried whether she could find her way home safely and with such a heavy load; she offered Winnie a ride home when the library closed.

Winnie accepted the offer—and a glass of water—without hesitation. Winnie nestled herself between her books on a wooden bench near the front door and under the watchful eye of the library staff. The library always welcomed a varied mix of people, including the homeless, unwell and/or marginalized who used the facility as a quiet place to warm up or cool down, rest and feel safe. The staff were always cognizant of this, and on rare occasions they took action to protect vulnerable patrons who had become lost or were met by those who had less than good intentions.

By closing time, Winnie's head was propped awkwardly between her scarf and the wall behind the bench. Other library patrons ignored her gaping mouth and loud snores as they came and left. Gracie waited for the last employee to close up, then roused Winnie gently, taking note she was well-attired and cared for.

Gracie loaded Winnie and her burden into her front passenger seat. As they were approaching Park Street, Winnie told Gracie she needed to stop by her lawyer's office. Gracie had a long drive back to Tess's apartment, however, she agreed when Winnie pointed to the office with Mason's name etched in gold letters across the front window. She parked on the street and a refreshed Winnie sprang to life. She was out of the car and beyond the office front door before Gracie had fed the parking meter. Gracie opted to wait outside, regretting her choice of outfits and wishing she had washed her hair.

Standing in Mason's office waiting area, Winnie remembered her plan to stop by there, but forgot why. Aida was locking up her filing cabinets before setting the alarm on the front door. She messaged Mason that Winnie had surprised him with a visit. Aida guided Winnie to a seat opposite her, mostly for entertainment, but also to keep Winnie from distracting Mason while he was packing what timely documents he needed to bring home. Aida left when Mason appeared. He pecked Winnie lightly on the cheek and helped her stiff body to stand up.

"What brings you here today?"

"Well, I had some business to discuss, but it's slipped my mind."

"Why don't I give you a ride home and then maybe you can think about what it was," he offered, reaching for his trench coat.

"The librarian is driving me home. She got some Italian books for me, but they're too heavy, so she insisted she drive me."

"She did? You went to the library?"

"Why yes. Is there something wrong with that?"

"No. I'm actually glad you've got some books to read. Who took you to the library?"

"No one. I walked there."

"Winnie, you walked all the way to the library?"

"And I might add it was a very long walk."

"It is indeed, and I'm glad you got there safely."

Mason was not only concerned that she had walked this distance, but that she had managed to find her way there.

"Where's your driver?" he asked.

Mason picked up his briefcase, escorted Winnie out, set his security alarm and locked the door. As he turned to follow Winnie, he saw Gracie leaning against her car, blushing and flustered, working hard to straighten the creases out of her clothes. Her smile was as lovely as the first time they met.

"Mason, this is the new librarian."

They shook hands, their gentle hold generating the same warm feeling for both as before.

"Glad to meet you again," Mason smiled back.

Gracie opened the front passenger seat for Winnie, and Mason held her purse as Winnie sank heavily into the seat. Lifting her legs into the car one at a time, she gave a big sigh and exclaimed, "My goodness, it's been a long day."

"You've had a long walk, Winnie. Now rest up when you get home, and I'll call you in a few days."

He shut the door behind her and turned to face Gracie.

"Thanks very much for looking out for her. She should never have ventured out that far."

"With four cookbooks in hand."

"Cookbooks?"

"Yes. Italian ones."

Mason laughed heartily.

"Interesting. Because she hasn't cooked in years."

"So she's not making lasagna for you?"

Mason responded with a laugh.

"I doubt it." There was a long pause before Mason asked, "How's your dilemma with your landlord progressing?"

"He's got six days to have a unit move-in ready for me," Grace said, counting to six on her fingers, "otherwise he's supposed to let me live there, rent-free, for six months."

"That's impressive. If you negotiated that arrangement yourself, you certainly don't need my advice. Which suite is it?"

"1C."

"Is that where the fire was?"

Gracie nodded.

"Tragic story."

"Yes."

"Are you okay moving in there?"

"I feel terrible for what happened, but I'd never met the lady. And the property manager promised me the bathtub would be replaced."

"Then I hope things go as planned for you."

"It's still only a verbal agreement because I've not seen the new contract he promised."

"That's concerning."

"Well, I'm still banking on moving in early November, give or take a few days."

"I think it would be prudent to have a status update on the renovations. Can I make a phone call for you?"

Gracie's eyes grew wide with interest.

"Would you do that? I can still only pay you in fish and chips."

"Lawyers are pretty true to their words."

"Mr., ah," Gracie peeked behind Mason at his office window to call him correctly by his last name.

"It's Mason. Please call me Mason."

"Mason, I would appreciate that very much."

"Just so I've got this straight: You're moving in on November 1st or he's waiving the first six months of rent?"

"That's what Sonny promised."

"Okay, then. Let's see if I can make some progress with him."

"Much appreciated. And I'd gladly cover your lunch expenses."

Winnie impatiently opened her door and said, "I hope you're not talking about me. Let's wrap this up, Mason, because I need a bathroom."

"You're on your way, Winnie," Mason re-assured her, but she held the car door ajar with her foot. He turned again to face Gracie and said, "Give me a couple of days to make that call, and we'll arrange a meeting."

"Thank you. Again, I'm much obliged for your help."

Confident the conversation was ending, Winnie put her foot back in the car and Mason closed her door. He opened Grace's car door for her. Her scent today was representative of the library she'd spent her day in. She slid into her seat, started the car and rolled down the window.

"Enjoy your evening, ladies," Mason said.

Gracie drove off. Mason checked the office door lock again and walked to his car thinking he'd been on his own and in a comfortable routine for some time. Having lunch with a nice woman was something he'd done many times since his wife passed away five years ago, but, as usual, he was leery of any expectation beyond exchanging a meal for a bit of legal support.

Gracie parked her car in the vacant "Loft" parking spot. Winnie was in a real hurry to get to her bathroom, so she opened her own door and left Gracie struggling to keep pace with her. Gracie unlocked the front door for Winnie, who left Gracie in the lobby holding the cookbooks.

Gracie checked her mail and spotted an unkempt tabby cat sleeping in an armchair in the front lobby. With one crusty eye open, it watched Gracie as she approached her slowly. By the appearance of the feline's coat, she predicted it was a stray seeking shelter. Gracie's lunch reserve, part of a tuna wrap she saved for the drive back to Tess's apartment, was easy bait to lure the tabby back out onto the street. Gracie watched it devour the food as she clicked the front door lock. What she couldn't see when she returned to the lobby to pick up the cookbooks from the console table were the fleas that had made themselves at home in the lobby chair.

Gracie brought the cookbooks up to Winnie's condo and knocked on the door. She waited a moment, then anticipating Winnie may be like other hearing-impaired seniors at the library, she knocked on the door again. This time Winnie answered, her tunic top stuck partially in her pants.

"Oh, silly me. I was in such a hurry, I forgot about the books," she said, slightly out of breath.

"They are heavy. Where should I set them down?" Gracie asked.

"Of course they are. Come in."

Winnie opened the door, and Gracie walked into her beautifully appointed home. Although much of the furniture was old, it still commanded respect. She set the books down on the kitchen counter and paused by the grand piano positioned near the Palladian window.

"What a lovely home. And your piano against this window looks like a perfect setting for a portrait."

Winnie responded with a look of wonder, then motioned Gracie to follow her to a picture of her late husband hanging on the wall. The setting was different, but the piano was the same. Winnie adjusted the portrait's position even though it was hanging straight.

"My dear Alex bought this piano from our children's piano teacher once we could afford it. They lost interest in it, but he always played in the evening. When the windows were open in the summer, he had a neighbourhood audience of listeners. I didn't even know they existed or heard him until after he passed away."

"I'm sorry for your loss."

"When my Alex got sick, he put the piano top down to protect the insides until he felt well enough to resume playing, but that never happened. Do you play?"

"I did when I was young. I hated it, but now I love the sound of someone else playing. It makes me appreciate what a gift it is."

"I so miss him."

"I also lost my husband."

"You poor dear; you're such a young widow."

Gracie sympathized with Winnie, predicting the ages and circumstances of their deaths were as different as their grief, but this was not the time to fold that into their conversation.

"It was hard, but I have moved on."

"And I have not. He's near me every day, sitting at that piano."

"That's very touching, Mrs. Firestone."

"Please call me Winnie."

Gracie made her way back to the door.

"It was a pleasure to meet you, Winnie. And once I move back into the building, I hope to see you again."

The women shook hands, and Winnie, for lack of anything else to do, watched her leave.

6:30 p.m.

Mitch finished his fourth twelve-hour shift and headed to the liquor store. He was still on the rocky side of a bad week with Sally. After many roller coaster years of purging his bad habits and coming to his sober senses, he was sliding backwards again. It took years after leaving Georgia to return to the dry side of financial ruin instead of bathing in it. He had rebuilt some of his life but not the tarnished relationship with his sons. His oldest son "went bad" after Mitch bailed him out of one too many disasters. His younger son assumed Mitch would keeping fixing his mistakes, and the culminating argument was when Georgia refused to support Mitch's actions. After they separated and Georgia became their primary custodian, the boys cleaned up their acts. Mitch regretted keeping his sons out of the court system, which protected his family name from potential media exposure but didn't allow the justice system to do its job.

Mitch was desperate to restore whatever semblance of harmony he and Sally had left. He did not want to return to Georgia but, as before, knew she might help. And same as before, he had nothing, and everything to lose.

He parked his pickup truck a few doors down from her house and knocked on her front door. When there was no answer, he rang the doorbell, something unexpected solicitors used when he still lived there. Georgia, expecting to meet no one and surprised to find Mitch at the door, was wearing grey sweatpants and an old T-shirt. She recognized his solemn expression. It reflected one part vodka, two parts guilt and rarely, sadness. Mitch looked frumpy, wearing a suit she guessed he spent more than a few days in.

"Hmm. A front door visit. You look like shit."

Mitch hung his head and extended his hand above his shoulder to lean against the door frame.

"Can I come in?" he asked in a muffled tone.

Georgia looked beyond him and saw his pickup truck parked in full view on the street. This was definitely not a booty call.

"Trouble with the little missus?"

"Please don't."

Georgia unlocked the screen door and let him in. He looked around, not knowing where to sit, until Georgia motioned for him to follow her to the kitchen. A large casserole dish of something good was baking in the oven, and the ingredients for a Greek salad lay on the counter. He didn't know how hungry he was until now.

The kitchen chair Mitch previously occupied held a basket of dirty laundry. He picked another chair rather than moving it and sat down. Georgia leaned against the kitchen counter and faced him from an angle.

"Coffee or tea?"

"Coffee would be great. Please."

She filled their old coffee maker with water and measured dry coffee into the filter.

"You look like you could use a friend," she said as she pulled out the same worn mugs they had shared for years.

The kitchen smelled familiar, and he felt safe. He watched her fill the cups and pour the right amount of milk into his mug.

"I don't know why I came here," he said. Georgia remained silent. "I'm sorry to bother you."

"You're not bothering me yet."

"I'm fucked up," he said as he took the first sip.

"I'm guessing Sally found out."

He looked up at Georgia and shook his head slowly.

"No. No. She knows nothing about us."

He buried his head in his large, outstretched hands and rubbed his hair. He looked terrible. And older than his fifty-five years. Many of his seasoned colleagues that remained married to their first wives had retired. Those like Mitch needed to put in more years before they could afford to split a decent pension with their exes. Like Georgia, they were entitled to a substantial portion.

"Then what is it?"

"I don't even know how it got this bad. She was going through my stuff."

"What are you hiding?"

"Nothing. She wouldn't tell me what she was looking for."

"Did you ask her?"

"I did. But she wouldn't tell me. And I lost it."

"Did you lay a hand on her?"

His frown was defensive.

"I didn't hurt her."

"Did you threaten her?"

He remained still. He closed his eyes and slumped back in his chair.

"Not really."

"Not really? Or just sort of a little? Mitch," she said, crossing her arms over her chest and letting her question rest for a moment before re-phrasing it. "What did you do?"

"I turned the privacy function in her phone history off. She looked up the women's shelter."

"You did that? Through work?"

By not acknowledging it, Georgia knew the answer. He opened his mouth to start his list of excuses, and she put up both hands.

"Stop."

"Listen to me, Georgia."

"No Mitch. You stop. For a change, you listen to me. We've been through this movie too many times," she said, raising each finger in sequence to emphasize her point. "First of all, you smell like a distillery. To translate that into police code, you're driving under the influence. Second, emotional and physical and sexual abuse is abuse. One is no better or worse than the other. Period. Hear me? They are all bad. Third, a breach of trust ruins marriages. You already learned once the hard—and expensive—way."

Mitch stood up, interrupting her. Georgia knew enough to stop.

"Don't lecture me."

"I should know that. It never worked before."

Georgia pulled a business card for a counselling service out from under a magnet on the side wall of her refrigerator and placed it at the edge of the table.

"Look, you need help. You refused to get it before and it cost us both. No, that's wrong. It cost us all. You lost almost everything you had the first time. Don't do it again."

Mitch walked to the back door, pulling his keys out of his pocket.

"Where are you going?"

"Why do you care?"

"Because I love you, Mitch."

Georgia's words echoed against the walls of the kitchen and then against the walls in his head. He looked at her in disbelief. She walked over to him slowly and slid her arms around his shoulders. He did not resist.

"You're an ass, Mitch. But I love you. Your kids, in their own unspoken ways, still love you as well."

Georgia took the keys out of Mitch's hands and poured him another coffee.

"Go sit outside and make that call, Mitch," she said, pressing the business card into his hand.

Mitch went out the back door, and slouched into a worn lawn chair. He had not seen this yard in daylight for years. The trees needed trimming and the shrubs were overgrown, which, if anything, gave him some privacy from curious neighbours. He checked his phone for messages. There were no new ones. With the exception of a few curt texts, the last time he actually spoke to Sally was a week ago. Everything Georgia said was right, but he just didn't want to hear it. He scrolled through the messages he and Sally had exchanged.

"I'm sorry," Mitch texted Sally.

He saw that she read it and waited for her response. There was none. He leaned his head back and closed his eyes. The card Georgia gave him slipped from his hand and landed under his chair in the space between the patio stones as he tried to calm down.

Georgia opened the back door thirty minutes later and came out. She spotted the business card between the patio stones.

"Dinner's ready and you are welcome to stay," she said.

He looked up at her as she pointed to the card. He picked it up and put it in his wallet. Mitch got up slowly, realizing how stiff, cold and hungry he was. Georgia opened the door for him and as she followed him in said, "By the way, we've got company."

Mitch looked beyond the landing to see both of his sons already seated at the table. The basket of dirty laundry was off his chair, and his place at the table was set.

Georgia carried the conversation, and although the boys spoke occasionally, Mitch remained mostly silent. Georgia's chicken and rice casserole was delicious and brought back memories of this meal on Thursday nights before their boys played hockey. Mitch thanked her and the boys for allowing him to stay. With a full belly and a sobered mind, Georgia walked him to the front door and said quietly, "Mitch, if you really love her, you'll make that call."

She closed the door before he had a chance to respond.

I will, he said to himself.

He returned to his truck, and instead of calling the number on the card, he texted a retired detective who had used another counselling agency. His friend responded almost immediately with the number, a service with no affiliation with Mitch's workplace-funded program. As much as his association touted confidentiality and anonymity, Mitch needed to do it on his own terms and invest his own dollars. He decided to make the call on his day off, knowing Sally would be at work.

October 26th
Weather forecast: windy with partial cloud cover

8:30 a.m.

"All things are difficult before they are easy."

Thomas Fuller

Sally wasn't home when Mitch arrived the night before. There was no evidence of a recent meal, either prepared or eaten, so he assumed she'd gone out for dinner. Mitch showered when he returned, put his old sweats on and fell asleep on the couch, where he spent the night. When he woke up in the morning, the first of his rotation of days off, their bed had not been occupied.

Sally had gone to her friend's house the evening before and poured her troubles out over one too many glasses of wine. She read the text Mitch sent and chose not to respond, knowing it may not be the best option after drinking. She needed time to think with a clear mind to formulate a solid plan, and last night she had neither. Instead of risking being stopped for driving while under the influence and humiliating both herself and Mitch, she listened to her friend and spent the night. She borrowed some cozy flannel pajamas and fell into a deep sleep on her couch. When she woke up, she felt refreshed, having not slept that well for a week.

9:30 a.m.

Readying herself for her appointment at the bank, Lily dressed in the one pair of black slacks she owned and a grey sweater she had bought online. Both pieces of clothing were one size larger. She looked at her appearance, complete with her mother's pearls around her neck, in the full-length mirror. Matronly was an understatement. She looked just like her mother before she became ill. Her pants had a high-waisted, wide elastic band, a fake fly and no functioning pockets. She turned sideways hoping for a more flattering view only to find that her belly protruded farther than her breasts. She knew it was from what she'd been eating and everything that was eating away at her.

Out of guilt and gas in her car, Lily walked to the bank instead of driving. She arrived on time, perspiring from the activity and hair windswept in all directions. After re-assembling herself, she approached the courtesy desk. She was escorted to an office and introduced to Piper, a petite, well-dressed woman who was at least a decade younger. After ten minutes of small talk and one minute of business, the meeting ended. Despite what Lily produced, neither party could proceed without a will or consent.

Lily returned home dejected. She climbed the stairs slowly to the Loft and let herself in. She sat down in her new clothes and scanned the room, lost on how to proceed. She spotted the taped banker's box she had parked beside a shelving unit when she moved in. It held Rosie's possessions that were salvaged from the fire and wrapped in a clear bag to contain the smoky residue. Lily suspected it sat undisturbed long before the move from their childhood home.

Lily forced herself off of the couch. She heaved the heavy box across the floor to the glass door that opened to the tiny balcony that doubled as a fire escape. Balancing the box on the narrow door frame ledge, she slid it out of the garbage bag. Overpowered by the stench of smoke, she loosened her grip on the box and it tipped on its side. The tape on the lid disintegrated like her mattress cover and the lid fell off, spilling some of its contents out of the box. Yellowed papers and manila envelopes scattered across the small landing and others became airborne in the wind. Dropping to her knees on the grated steel, Lily scrambled to throw the papers and envelopes back in the box as others flew over the balcony, floating like leaves to the ground. Hoisting the box back inside, she slipped into her shoes and ran down the stairs as quickly and safely as she could, her breasts swinging in step with her movement.

Lily ran across the parking lot to the rear of the building and circled around the brush, landscaping debris and unkempt grass, scooping up the dozen or so papers as the wind competed to sweep them away. Satisfied she retrieved them all, she headed back to the Loft and soothed herself with a heaping spoon of peanut butter followed by a spoon of grape jelly. Returning to the balcony door to lock it, Lily spotted something shiny between the metal grates of the landing. She looked closer and saw a key ring, so she bent over and wiggled out the attached keys which had straddled the grate. *They must have fallen out of the box when it tipped over,* she thought. The first of five keys on the ring were for the side door at her family's home.

Two other keys were from her mother's old car, buried long ago in a scrapyard. The last two identical keys were attached to a separate ring with small metal tags looped to each key and imprinted with the same four numbers. Lily examined them curiously. Rosie's locker number at work had only three digits.

Unaware that Rosie had a safety deposit box, Lily dumped the box of papers on the kitchen table. Spreading them out, she threw Rosie's ancient tax returns back in the box. Other papers, such as employment contracts and performance reviews, copies of both deceased parents' wills and recent real estate transactions from the sale of their home were returned to the box. Rosie's contract to a safety deposit box was among the last of the documents she found.

Keys and newly-found evidence in hand, Lily returned to the bank two hours after she'd left it. A new attendant at the courtesy desk sighed loudly when Lily said she did not have an appointment. Piper was with a client, and Lily insisted she would wait for her. Parking herself in a chair within view of Piper's desk, Lily played with her phone and imagined what could be so valuable that Rosie would need a safety deposit box. Thirty minutes later, Lily helped herself to the free coffee and cookies at a table near the children's play area. As Lily finished her coffee and a second helping of cookies, Piper led her clients out and cleared her desk before allowing Lily in.

This time the meeting lasted a little longer. After a few rounds of negotiations and recital of bank rules, Lily followed Piper into a triple locked vault. Entering and matching the numbers to both, each inserted their key and Lily sighed loudly as the door opened and she slid the metal box out. Lily followed Piper back to her office, cancelled the safety deposit box contract and dropped the keys on her desk.

The contents of the box held three long, narrow, white, sealed envelopes which Lily was certain were wills. A few of her father's old coins and war medals were in a plastic sandwich bag, and a small black velvet pouch held her mother's inexpensive jewellery—all things Lily had forgotten about long ago. A smaller black sack held her parents' wedding rings. As they slid out of the sack, her mother's ring fell within her father's. Lily's eyes moistened unexpectedly.

Piper used the relationship the bank had with Rosie as collateral to open her will. Lily's mother was Rosie's executor, and because there were no other family members listed, Piper suggested the will be forwarded to the law firm on the envelope and, with Lily's permission, Lily's contact information.

A dozen worn bank account passbooks were the last items in the box. One bank account dated back to when the sisters were children. Monthly cheques were deposited into that account, which Piper said was a government child benefit. Only Rosie had this account, although this was also Lily's bank for years. In the event of her parents' and Rosie's passing, Lily was the beneficiary. Unsettled as to why only Rosie was listed under this account, it was balanced out by the few thousand dollars she could access quickly if she needed it.

Feeling slightly more hopeful than this morning, Lily followed Piper to the door, and Piper promptly locked the door behind her as the bank had closed fifteen minutes ago. An impatient bank manager lingered to comply with the "No Working Alone" policy, but was much more concerned about her children sitting on her front steps at home wondering where their mother was.

October 31st (Halloween)
Weather forecast: unseasonably warm

Noon

"The prime of your life does not come twice."

Japanese Proverb

Mason was not sophisticated at the dating game, but dining with female clients was routine. Lunches had a set agenda with no expectation to remain together beyond the diner door. Mason always returned to his office, and once his lunch guests were ushered out, they went on their merry way. He expected lunch with Gracie to be the same. She was early, and as usual, he was a few minutes late. Propped with an open novel in her hands at a corner table near the front window, their eyes met as he entered the diner. Dressed in a good suit on his tall frame, he approached her confidently and loosened his tie slightly as he sat down.

Gracie looked smart in a denim shirt dress paired with ballet flats. Her auburn hair, normally tied back in a ponytail, was styled into soft curls that framed her face. A bit of make-up and silver hoop earrings enhanced her features. Her genuine smile distracted him the first time he met her and did the same today. Judging by the soft lines around her eyes, he predicted she was half a decade younger than he was. When she closed her book, he recognized the well-known Swedish author.

"Coming from work?" Gracie asked nervously; it was a while since she had dined with a male other than in the library lunchroom.

"How did you know?"

"I watched you cross the street."

Mason nodded.

"I'm guessing you couldn't concentrate on your book?"

Gracie nodded and smoothed her hand across its protective cover.

"Even though he's such a good author."

"May I?" Mason asked, gesturing toward the book.

Gracie passed it across the table and Mason scanned the preview on the back cover.

"Is it as good as his others?" he asked.

Gracie's eyes lit up and she said, "It's his best one yet. You're familiar with his work?"

Mason greeted the waiter by name when he delivered water and menus.

"I am. My day ends best with a good book. And you must be able to critique all the new reads."

"I do have a slight advantage."

Lunch, followed by coffee, was delicious. Mason thanked Gracie again for taking Winnie home the week before, and their conversation drifted to Gracie's Park Street dilemma. Mason had to call three times before he received a response from Sonny, but he seemed to think that Gracie's condo would be ready for November 1st. Even though it wasn't.

She had met Sonny an hour earlier at Suite 1C, which had impressive upgrades, including the new tub. It was surprisingly close to being finished but wasn't yet. Sonny said he needed another week. After some colourful re-negotiations, they verbally agreed on three months free rent rather than his original promise of six months, which Gracie knew was fair.

Mason insisted he cover lunch because he scheduled this as a business meeting and Aida would be expecting the receipt. Their lunch ended with little excitement, and Gracie got the impression that it was just lunch—nothing more, nothing less. Gracie reassured Mason she would watch out for Winnie because, eight days from today, she would be living just down the hall from her.

7:00 p.m.

Both Talia and Bryce had a rare evening off together and were invited to a Halloween party. Talia found their costumes in a second-hand store. Bryce was dressed as a priest and Talia was a *Playboy* bunny complete with fishnet stockings and a bunny tail which took patience to attach. Not used to wearing stilettos, Talia walked gingerly down the stairs to the lobby, unaware that Adrian was watching her from the flea-infested chair that Mona Lisa occupied a week earlier. He remained still, hoping not to break her concentration and notice him staring at her. She carried a fake fur cape in one arm as the other rested on Bryce's arm for stability. Adrian was mesmerized by her iridescent skin, flawless under her revealing costume.

He discreetly held his phone and took a video of Talia. Exiting through the front door with Bryce following her, it wasn't until the last second that Bryce noticed Adrian. Bryce stopped short, watching Adrian's phone.

"Hey."

"Hey." Adrian froze in his chair but thought fast. "My ride just texted me. Is there a red car out there?"

Bryce looked out the door after Talia closed it.

"I don't see a car."

"Okay, thanks."

"Have a good night."

"Same to you."

Talia turned to Bryce as Adrian watched him shield what little flesh was visible of her fishnet-covered bottom.

"Did you just say something?" she asked.

"Nope, but I know I want to do something when we get home."

Adrian let out a loud sigh after the lobby doors closed and repeatedly watched the video clip of Talia until his ride picked him up for the night out.

Four hours, six bars and at least eight beers later, Adrian spent the night with "Darla," who bought his drinks at the last bar. She offered him a ride home, and he needed little persuasion when she invited him in to see her apartment. She became prettier after his last beer, but no match to Talia or any of the women he'd seen in his travels that night.

10:00 p.m.

Winnie put her cashmere sweater back on the hanger and into its plastic dry cleaning bag. She left it on the bed and put her nightgown on, not realizing she had it on backwards. She then conducted her night-time rituals with little thought. Her hair net always went on first. Occasionally she applied the expensive anti-aging products Annette bought her, but preferred her favourite night cream because Alex loved the scent of it when he snuggled up beside her. Tonight she missed him terribly. She remembered how they delighted in handing out candy to shy children at their door, then watched them run back to their parents with their loot.

Winnie lay down on the bed to complete her final beauty step. Years ago she learned that after she applied her night creams, she should hang her head over the edge of the bed to smooth out her wrinkles and let the beauty creams absorb into her skin. She positioned herself across the bed on her back and eased her head slowly into the "right" position, forgetting about the plastic bag holding her sweater. Digging her bare feet into the bedspread to give herself some traction, she pushed herself over too far, and with the aid of the slippery dry cleaning wrap, she slid right over the side of the bed. Her slippers and the carpet cushioned the blow to her head.

Winnie attempted to get up, but her head spun wildly. She managed to lift her head and shoulders up before becoming dizzy again and striking her forehead against her nightstand. She fell back down on the carpet, closed her eyes and waited, nauseated from the room moving in circles. She felt better if she kept her eyes open, so she lifted her head up, but put it down just as quickly. She waited a little longer, looking out her bedroom windows to see the sky and then a beautiful view of the moon. She remembered lying in an old boat with her Alex, who persuaded her to come out one summer night on the lake so he could fish and she could watch the stars. The moon tonight looked just the same. Winnie sensed that trying to move her head again would not be wise, so she just stayed there with her head cushioned by her slippers. She felt the tender spot where her forehead hit the night stand. It was sticky, and she tasted the metallic drop of blood she brushed away from her eyebrow. She looked around her, relieved she had already taken her last trip to the bathroom before bed, and fell asleep.

November 1st

8:30 a.m.

Darla woke first to the sound of Adrian's phone alarm and agreed to drive him back to his condo. He sent a text to Kelly at his office asking her to postpone his meeting for half an hour, which would buy him time to get home. He would dim the lights during this virtual meeting so no one would pay attention to his unkempt appearance.

As Darla drove him home in yesterday's dress and make-up, Adrian was cordial but repulsed that he had slept with her. He vowed to make better life choices. When she dropped him off two buildings away from his front entrance, he gave her an incorrect phone number and made her promise to call him in a few days. He waited until she turned the corner before he rushed home.

Adrian regretted not washing his new jeans before wearing them. Stripping naked, he miscalculated his aim for the laundry hamper, his clothes landing in a heap on the carpet instead. He blamed the clusters of itchy red dots forming on his lower extremities to the new denim fabric rather than the fleas that moved from the lobby chair onto him, his clothes and now his bedroom carpet.

3:00 p.m.

"If you rock the boat too much, you fall out."

Unknown

When Marcello delivered minestrone soup to Winnie for dinner, she told him through the door to leave the soup on the floor in the hallway. He refused, so she refused to open the door. They argued back and forth, neither of them hearing well enough to communicate effectively until Winnie finally relinquished and opened the door just a few inches. When Marcello saw her, he nearly fainted. She had a cut on her forehead, "raccoon eyes" and the imprint from the heal of her slipper clearly outlined on her cheek. She would have gotten away with telling others she was keeping her Halloween make-up on for another day, but Marcello knew better. She was also more unsteady on her feet.

Knowing she would fiercely refuse any medical assistance, he told her he would be right back with the baguette he was warming in the oven. After he told the ambulance dispatcher Winnie's address and what she wanted to know, he hung up and hustled back to Winnie, baguette in one hand and phone in the other.

He walked back through the door and pretended nothing had happened. And so did Winnie. It was a silent stand-off, each knowing better than to engage in any conversation about the elephant in the room. When Marcello heard the sirens, he excused himself and closed Winnie's door, expecting she would leave it unlocked.

He walked as quickly as his sore back would allow him down the hall and met the paramedics at the building's front door. They were weighed down with all manner of oversized bags, and he warned them that she would resist any care. They followed Marcello up the stairs, and after pointing to Winnie's door, the two burly men took over. They knocked gently but received no response. The second knock was also left unanswered. When Marcello divulged that Winnie may have a head injury, it was enough information to open her door and let them take control.

Winnie was sitting on her sofa when she saw the paramedics, and she immediately knew that Marcello had lied to her. As he leaned against the wall outside Winnie's door behind the commotion of the men setting up their equipment, she glared at him. There was fire in her eyes. Although he was certain he did the right thing, Marcello hung his head in despair because he had breached any trust he had earned from her.

Winnie refused to tell the paramedics what happened or where her medications were. When they turned to Marcello for answers, he quietly responded that he didn't live there. It was better than lying twice in one day; he would surely burn in hell if he betrayed Winnie again. Feeling helpless and hopelessly abandoned, Winnie did not resist the paramedics as they transferred her onto the stretcher like a fragile bird, tucking her in and accentuating her bruises with a bright orange blanket.

As they wheeled her out the door, Marcello's heart pounded. His friend shook her bruised and battered head, lifted an arthritic finger to point at him.

"You know this is the beginning of the end of me, and it's all your fault."

Marcello escorted the paramedics down the hallway and opened the door for them to pass. He turned back and walked back to his condo, closed the door and sank into his favourite chair. Head in his hands, he kept reassuring himself that he had Winnie's best interests at heart. What he failed to see if he would have opened the main entrance doors was one of the paramedics gently nudging Mona Lisa away from the lobby door to prevent her from getting in.

NOVEMBER 2ND
Weather forecast: cold, rainy, and miserable

8:30 a.m.

"Fear gives intelligence even to fools …"

Anonymous

Marcello woke up feeling worse than the previous day because Winnie had spent the night alone in the hospital. He showered and put on business clothes he would have typically worn if he was giving a tour. He drove to the hospital and found a parking spot on a quiet side street to avoid the fees that the hospital lot charged.

9:00 a.m.

Winnie was still in the emergency department when Marcello tracked her down. He paced in the waiting area until he was granted a short visit by a security guard who whispered Winnie's cubicle location and unlocked the door remotely. Marcello walked by a row of ailing patients, some with poor scores on the tooth to tattoo ratio, some vomiting and others feigning illness for the reward of a meal. Winnie's eyes were closed, and most of her exposed skin was a varied shade of purple. He stood quietly, knowing it was easier to leave than to stay. After a few moments, Marcello placed his hand gently over her blanket-covered toes.

Mason arrived just minutes after Marcello, visibly distraught by Winnie's appearance. As Marcello moved his hand onto the bed railing, he apologized to Mason for not getting his number previously. Mason quietly said that hospital had his information because he was listed as Winnie's power of attorney and point of contact. Hearing their voices, Winnie opened her eyes, which expressed nothing but hopeless defeat.

"Fancy meeting you here," Mason said softly.

Winnie alternated her gaze between her visitors and her hands; she traced the huge bruise on her forearm with her index finger. Her sight line followed the tubing from its insertion point in her wrist to the IV bag of fluid hanging on a pole above her head. She laid her matted head of hair back on her pillow and sighed quietly.

"What happened?" Mason asked softly. She mumbled something neither man could understand. Mason tried again. "Did you fall?"

"What does it look like?"

"It looks like you were beaten up. And then you fell," Mason said.

She nodded and both men raised their eyebrows.

"You were beaten up?" Mason asked, leaning in to listen more closely.

Winnie became impatient and turned away from them.

"No."

"Then you fell?"

"I want to go home," she said, looking directly at a guilt-stricken Marcello.

"The neurologist still has to read your MRI," Mason said.

"Who told you that?"

"The doctor. She said you were a little confused about what happened, so she needs to confirm what's injured so she can put a treatment plan together."

"I don't care. I just want to go home."

"We all want you home, but the experts must determine when you can go home safely."

Winnie crossed her arms defiantly then quickly uncrossed them because of the painful bruises.

"I'm going to die here."

"No, you're not," Mason replied.

"That's what they told my husband," Winnie mumbled, silencing them all.

Preferring to avoid their conversation, Marcello peeked out of the opening in the privacy curtain that separated Winnie from the other patient cubicles. Winnie's stretcher was located within sight of the nursing station, likely for good reason. His eye caught the fleeting glance of a middle-aged woman who was dressed in green scrubs. She looked vaguely familiar, and as she rose to leave the station, they exchanged cordial smiles. As Winnie was trying to convince Mason she would never leave the hospital if he didn't take her home now, Marcello searched his memory to identify the caregiver returning from a patient cubicle to her station.

Minutes later, the same woman returned, clipboard in hand, and told Winnie her blood work was fine, however, just as Mason had indicated, the neurologist still needed to review her MRI results. She smiled again at Marcello, who remembered her soft voice. The lanyard around her neck identified her as Raine.

"We've met, but I don't know where," he said, hoping she did.

"I'm not sure," she replied quietly, her eyes not leaving Winnie's chart.

"I know we've met," he repeated, hoping for a clue.

"We have."

"I'm trying to recall where. It's been years, but I can't place you."

He thought maybe it was at his bank or through his job.

"I worked somewhere else."

"Where?"

She looked back at him discreetly like she would prefer not to answer.

"Please tell me." He persisted. "I insist."

She glanced sideways in Mason's direction and then at Winnie. It was a non-verbal clue to Marcello that they would also hear her response.

She hesitated and whispered quietly, "Psychiatry."

Her answer hit Marcello like a rock. Mason's expression flattened, and Marcello was certain he'd heard the nurse's response correctly. Winnie, who was still complaining that she was dying, had not heard her. Nurse Raine smiled at Winnie and shut the privacy curtain behind her.

After an uncomfortable pause, Mason settled Winnie by promising to find her somewhere more private. Marcello told Winnie he looked forward to seeing her at home and asked Mason if there was something he could help with before he left. Mason shrugged his shoulders and appeared impartial. Marcello found one of two remaining business cards in his wallet, wrote his phone number on the back and exchanged it with Mason's business card. Marcello said goodbye to his neighbour and her lawyer. Neither responded, and Marcello left the hospital, wishing the morning had never happened.

Marcello parked his little green Fiat in his condo parking spot. His back paining him, he hobbled to the front of the building and unlocked the front door. Another surge of panic stopped him. He stood quietly, inhaling then exhaling deeply. A series of noises distracted him. A car drove by and he paused until other vehicles on the street had driven by and the day around him stood still. He heard one howl, or maybe a loud meow, and then another. Marcello turned his good ear towards the noises and listened. Once he established that they were coming from under the nearby railway overpass, he walked cautiously in that direction. The meows faded, but the stench of cat spray grew stronger as he approached the bridge. He looked up and saw the feline community tucked under the train bridge, complete with straw, boxes turned on their sides and the scent he recognized as dry cat kibble. Acclimatizing to the dark underpass, he counted at least a dozen cats staring at him, and a few more crouching deep into the crevice.

Marcello strained his aging eyes to search for Mona Lisa. He called out her pet names, and although a few curious cats inched closer, they were not his. If there was any comfort in his discovery, it was that someone cared enough to leave them food and water. He felt a soft brush of pressure against his lower legs and broke into tears when he saw Mona Lisa circling his feet and meowing hoarsely. He bent over and picked her up, nuzzling close to her before realizing how much her scraggly fur stank. Certain she had picked up more than one communicable problem, he took his coat off, securing her tightly in it to prevent a second escape and hustled her back to his condo. She had no intention of abandoning him, purring as he lovingly scolded her. Marcello isolated her safely in his guest bathroom to prevent contact with Michelangelo, who paced and meowed at full volume on the other side.

Following a call to his veterinarian, Marcello purchased whatever Mona Lisa needed to recover from her five-week escapade on the streets of Niagara Falls. Grateful for the unexpected reunion, it was an effective diversion for Marcello from his morning.

While Marcello consoled his reunited family, Mason spent another hour trying to appease Winnie, who eventually fell asleep. Before heading to work, he spoke with the emergency physician. In a crisp French accent, she described Winnie's many minor soft tissue injuries, bruising in the top of her head and a mild concussion. Because Winnie's medication included a blood thinner, her injuries appeared much worse than they were. Cautious about risk, she wanted to monitor Winnie's brain bump for another few days and ordered a neurological assessment. She placed both of her tiny, reassuring hands on Mason's and asked him if he could attend this assessment to provide corroborative details. Usually composed and well in control of his emotions, her kindness made him feel vulnerable. She looked up at Mason and spoke.

"I can see in your eyes that this little lady is special to you. I promise you we will do our very best to take good care of her."

Mason knew she was sincere and wondered why this young doctor had such an effect on him. They parted to continue with their days, Mason gently nudging Winnie to tell her that he was leaving. She opened her eyes, smiled at him and went right back to sleep.

Back at his office, Aida re-organized Mason's schedule so he could attend Winnie's assessment on November 4th. She also arranged a virtual meeting with both of Winnie's children. Annette was just getting up in San Francisco, and Allen was already in his office in Boston. Mason updated them on the events of the last thirty-plus hours, still confused as to how Winnie managed to fall off the bed and bruise the top of her head. Annette easily solved the mystery, outlining Winnie's ancient nightly beauty routine. Mason laughed loudly, now remembering his father mocking his mother for this identical beauty tip that both she and Winnie followed.

Allen and Annette asked Mason to check Winnie's apartment to see if she was taking her medication. Mason confidently repeated the emergency physician's comments that, based on her lab findings, blood pressure readings and her bruises, she was taking them. Annette asked him to check her freezer inventory to ensure she was eating her heart-healthy dinner packages. Annette and Allen wanted their assistants to send flowers, but Mason discouraged this until she was discharged. The florist Aida had already called to do the same informed her of the hospital's strictly enforced scent-free environment.

Allen resurrected the suggestion of a retirement home. Mason, very familiar with their previous arguments, redirected the idea until the hospital provided them with more feedback. Allen asked if her cleaning lady or others were concerned. Mason pulled out Marcello's business card and said Marcello was concerned enough to visit her this morning. They decided to send him a thank you card, and upon request, Mason spelled out Marcello's full name. Because the fire was in Unit 1C, where Gracie was moving in, and Winnie lived in Unit 1A, he knew Marcello lived in Unit 1B. He did not mention, nor was he concerned about Marcello's encounter with Raine, the nurse.

Satisfied with the questions answered, the children forwarded their well wishes via Mason and resumed their own lives. Mason endured both the pleasures and pains of caring for his parents, and he was grateful for the many positive memories he had of their aging years. He hoped Winnie's children wouldn't regret their physical and emotional distance from Winnie after she was gone.

6:45 p.m.

Winnie was more than cranky. She was still parked on her stretcher, rails up, across from the nursing station. She was dressed in a hospital gown and nothing else. Mason went to her condo after work and saw that the place was tidy and her freezer was almost full of meals.

In her bedroom beside her made bed, pillows lay on the carpet beside a sweater in a slippery plastic dry cleaning bag. What Annette assumed, and he saw, aligned with Winnie's injuries. Mason opened Winnie's bedroom closet and found a pretty pink housecoat and slippers. He refused to look through her dresser drawers for anything that resembled an undergarment.

He returned to the hospital and delivered her housecoat and slippers. Marcello had not returned, and other than being irritable, Mason was satisfied that Winnie was stable. Once she was assessed, a care plan would be determined. Mason listened patiently to her ranting until she ran out of things to say. He gave her a peck on her bruised forehead and headed home for the night.

11:55 p.m.

Winnie had had enough of everything and everyone. Because she had multiple naps, she was wide awake. She barked at the nurses to move her to a private room. She was angry when they couldn't turn the lights off. She questioned their competence. She complained about anything she could think of, whether it made sense or not. After a few concerning outbursts, the attending physician, two gruelling hours into his ten-hour shift, ordered a capacity assessment which would determine Winnie's mental ability to appreciate the consequences of her decisions and function on her own. He prescribed medication to settle her and help her sleep through her second night in the emergency department.

November 4th
Weather forecast: cold and dreary

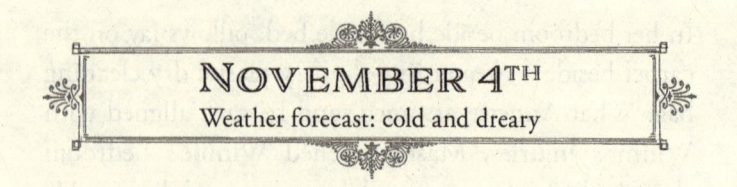

9:00 a.m.

"Nothing improves the memory more than trying to forget."

Anonymous

As requested, Mason was back at the hospital early to meet with a team that would complete the assessments on Winnie. As he knew her best, Mason's role was to provide details about Winnie. He had mixed emotions about attending and representing Winnie's children because they should have been present instead. Yet he was obligated to advocate for her rather than enforce the intentions and desires of her children.

Mason sensed that Winnie's foul mood was to mask her fear. A young nurse brought her via wheelchair, dressed in her pajamas and housecoat, into a small conference room. Mason asked if Winnie might struggle with her thought processes so soon after tumbling off her bed, however the neurologist felt that her injuries were not significant enough to skew the results. Winnie crossed her bruised arms over her sunken chest and interrupted the other three people in the room before they introduced themselves, including a seasoned clinician named Angela.

"Listen to me, people. I want you to know I'm refusing whatever this interrogation is."

"Mrs.—"

"Mason, take me home."

The neurologist glanced at Mason and then at Winnie.

"Mrs. Firestone, you and everyone else in this room want you to go home. We all have your best interests at heart."

"That's bullshit," Winnie mumbled under her breath, expecting no one to hear, then realizing everyone did.

Mason shifted uncomfortably in his seat. He had never heard Winnie swear. The others exchanged varied expressions of amusement across the table as the neurologist spoke again.

"Mrs. Firestone, if you decline, we may need to keep you in hospital longer to do some other evaluations. I'm really hoping that if you complete these activities today, we can discharge you sooner rather than later. What would you prefer?"

Winnie extended a trembling hand to Mason, the dread of failure clearly written on her face.

"I've known Mrs. Firestone for many years," he said, taking her hand, "and more recently, I became her legal representative. Our goal, whatever it takes, is to place Winnie safely back in her own home where she can continue to enjoy a quiet life."

"And that's exactly our hope too," the neurologist stated. After introductions, and a brief explanation of the process, he said, "Do you understand what we are offering you?"

Winnie looked at Mason and rolled her eyes as she nodded.

"Well then, you better get on with it," she said, glaring at the neurologist. Everyone left the room except Winnie and Angela.

Winnie sat through an hour's worth of tests and activities, led expertly by Angela. She drew a clock, a square shape like the one that had hung in her kitchen for thirty years. When Angela inquired about the clock she was drawing, Winnie told the assessor exactly that. She watched Angela replace an "X" on the form with a check mark. Winnie set the hands on the clock correctly.

"Please repeat the following five words," Angela said. "Face, velvet, church, daisy, red."

"Face, velvet, church, daisy, red," Winnie said.

When asked to repeat them again, she did so.

"Please remember these words, because I'll ask you about them later," Angela said. "Now, starting with 100, subtract by seven." Winnie hesitated, then responded, "100, 93, 86, 79, 72, 65, 61."

"You got most of them right. Good for you," she said.

How many does "most of them" mean? Winnie thought.

As the activities continued, Winnie's fatigue and frustration built. When Angela asked her to recall the five words she mentioned earlier, Winnie closed her eyes.

"Can you remember those words, Winnie?"

Winnie opened her eyes, looked directly at her and said, "Church … red … face … velvet …"

"One more."

Winnie worked hard to remain calm and searched her memory for the last word.

"Rose," she finally said.

"It was actually a daisy," Angela corrected.

"They're not in order," Winnie said, distraught.

"That's okay," reassured Angela.

"But it's not okay," whimpered Winnie.

As Winnie was being assessed, Mason sat in a separate meeting room and answered a barrage of questions from a social worker. How much of a burden was Winnie to her family? Did she drive? Did she get lost finding her way home? Mason pondered Winnie's recent walk to the library and chose his responses to weigh in Winnie's favour.

Winnie was flustered but no worse when she was reunited with Mason. The team interpreted the tests in another office. Mason kept picturing his own mother, frail and vulnerable, and he was grateful she did not have to endure this.

"I failed," Winnie said, slumped in her chair.

"I don't know if this is a pass or fail kind of test," Mason said, his mouth gradually turning into a smile. "Let's talk about something else."

"Like what? How many days before I get bed sores and die here?"

"Nope."

"How about funeral homes? Or naming famous people that kicked the bucket this year?"

"How about famous neighbours? If you could choose anyone to live beside you, who would you pick?"

Winnie rubbed her forehead with her fingers. Mason's distraction was working.

"I don't know. Who would you pick?"

"I've thought about it. Maybe a famous author."

"Hmmm. Why?"

"They hide in their house typing for weeks or travel to gather manuscript material."

"Okay, I'll pick Marcello."

"Your neighbour Marcello?"

"He's a good neighbour. Better who you know than who you don't."

"But that's boring to pick someone you know."

"That's my point. Besides, he's a great cook."

"How do you know?"

"He cooks for me."

"He does?"

"He sure does. A lot."

So Winnie's freezer was full for a reason, he thought.

"And how do you repay him?" Mason asked. He monitored her bank accounts and knew there were no suspicious withdrawals.

"Are you asking me if I have sex with him?"

Mason rolled his head back and burst into loud laughter.

"That's not what I meant," he said, his face flushed.

This amused Winnie.

"Well, if you're asking me if …"

"Stop. All I want to know is that he's not taking advantage of you."

"Here we go talking about romance again."

They both laughed.

"Why aren't you eating the frozen meals?" he asked.

"Why don't you come over and eat those crappy meals," she snapped.

"But Winnie, they're good for you. Your kids pay a lot of money to have them delivered."

"Mason, look at me. I'm eighty years old. I'm half-dead. Who cares what I eat? When you're eighty and want fish and chips every day, what difference will it make when you've got one foot in the grave already. And even deeper now that I'm here …"

The door opened and the team walked in, each with papers in hand. Winnie froze in terror, hanging her head and clasping her hands together to avoid them from shaking. Angela gently slid her hand over Winnie's, who pushed it away hard enough for everyone to notice. After a minute of calming talk, the neurologist started to describe the relevance of some of the testing.

"Just get on with it," Winnie burst in. "Did I pass or fail?"

Caught off guard, he spoke. "This is not about passing or failing, but if you want to put it into that simple context, you passed."

Winnie put her head back against her wheelchair and closed her eyes. A tear followed the wrinkles on her face, and the room fell quiet for what seemed like a long time. Winnie put her head back down, and as tears dripped on her housecoat, she whispered, "I just want to go home."

"And you will. I promise you," the doctor said.

"We need you to rest for another day or two, and then you can go home. Sometimes older people become anxious or depressed when they experience significant changes like losing a spouse or making a big move. Others around them mistake that for early signs of dementia, which we think has presented itself recently in your situation. So, to summarize your situation, Mrs. Firestone, we are not particularly concerned that your memory was affected either before or after you slipped and hit your head."

The meeting ended and the assessor returned Mason and Winnie to her little cubicle in the emergency department. Mason helped her step on a stool to crawl up onto her stretcher where she immediately fell asleep. He watched her sleep for at least thirty minutes before he left her. He gently brushed a stray strand of hair away from her face, still bruised but now serene. He didn't head to the office after he left, but rather returned to his house. He had breakfast and watched the bird feeder traffic through the glass doors in his kitchen until the clock on his fireplace mantle chimed twelve times. Like Winnie, he loved his own home, where he felt safe and was at peace.

November 5th
Weather forecast: sunny and mild

"When we take care of ourselves, we can take care of others better."

Unknown

Mason woke up feeling older than sixty. Between work, an upcoming trial, managing Winnie's needs and updating her children daily, he needed a break. In a rare moment, he strongly recommended Annette and/or Allen fly home and stay with Winnie to support her in her recovery after her discharge from the hospital. Although Winnie's test results were consistent with her eighty years, the doctor's interpretation of normal brain aging was different than her children's opinions.

Mason felt confident about his need to step away for a week to have Winnie's children see for themselves how desperately she wanted to remain independent. He emailed them copies of the doctor's discharge plan, which repeatedly recommended that the best place for Winnie was at home.

NOVEMBER 8TH
Weather forecast: sunny afternoon, overnight frost warning

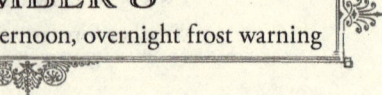

Noon

"You'll never find a rainbow if you're looking down."

Charlie Chaplin

As promised, Sonny handed Gracie the keys to 1C. Dressed in black yoga pants, a thigh-length grey tunic and sneakers, she toured the unit with Sonny, whom she silently praised for completing the renovations as promised. His effort to please her erased some of the negative thoughts she had formed of him. She signed two hard copies of the lease, kept one and allowed him to leave. As he opened the door, Gracie lifted a pink gift bag from the polished white granite kitchen island.

"Thank you for whatever this is," she said, skeptical again of his motive behind the gift.

Sonny looked at it, then shook his head.

"It's not from me."

"Then do you know who left it?"

"No idea. I figured it was safer inside than outside your front door."

"How do you know it's for me?"

"I don't."

Agreement in hand, Sonny closed the door behind him and disappeared.

The Park Street Secrets

Gracie inhaled the new smell of her condo with a deep breath. She felt happy—not quite skipping happy, but more content than yesterday. When she ended her relationship with Fred, both knew there was no resolution to the heavy strain their adult children placed on them. She had a job here she liked. She was in a new city she could finally explore instead of commuting to and from it. A clean start. Again, but with more security and no expectations.

Her not so new Volvo was packed full last night, and what little furniture she'd stored was scheduled to arrive later today.

It took five trips to unpack her vehicle, but it would have taken more if she hadn't met Lily in the parking lot, who offered her a wheeled moving cart, a kettle and a promise to meet soon. Gracie parked the last box, full of books, near the Palladian window, plugged in the kettle and peeked in the gift bag to find a hardcover book. She pulled it out, vaguely recognizing the local female author and her debut novel, which Gracie had not read. The dust jacket showed some signs of wear. Instinctively, she closed her eyes, opened the book and sniffed it. Yes, it had been read. Maybe several times. She chuckled to herself, knowing someone had actually created the term "bibliosmia" to describe the comforting smell of an old book. She saw a few yellow sticky notes marking some pages off.

Gracie steeped her tea in her travel mug, emptying the last teabag from the little metal container she kept in her purse for moments like this. She blew away the hot steam and took a small sip before placing the mug to cool on the windowsill. Already losing energy, she sat down on the box of books. She peaked out the window but was unable to see the street below.

Gracie looked at the book cover that showed a country road leading somewhere. Not a cover that would invite her pick to it up again or turn it over to see if the preview would entice her to choose it from the millions of books in existence. Gracie always volunteered to unpack new shipments of library books just to be the first to see newly published works, and she especially loved to feel her hand cross an unblemished book cover with a matte finish.

Gracie sipped her tea and opened the book in her lap. She unsealed a small envelope that was addressed to her and slid the card out. A watercolour of pale-yellow cabbage roses splashed across the white paper. The inside note was short and dated November 7.

> Happy Book Lover's Day,
> Here's a good read to end your day.
> Best regards,
> Mason

Gracie was touched by Mason's gesture. She opened the book to the first yellow sticky note. On the page, a few paragraphs had double lines pencilled vertically beside them. The sticky note said, "This part reminds me of you." It described a character that was vaguely similar to her who lacked self-esteem and was facing unexpected challenges. Mildly amused, she found the second note stuck to the beginning of a chapter, which Mason hinted might be helpful to her. In the first two paragraphs, Gracie read about the same character renting part of an old estate.

The movers interrupted her when they buzzed her condo from the street. Gracie flipped the open book over on the windowsill and approached the movers at the front door just as an elderly lady, her bruised face looking down and shielded by a stylish hat, navigated her walker through the lobby. She was accompanied by a well-attired but impatient woman with identical but younger facial features. She guessed that it was Winnie and her daughter, who held Winnie's upper arm as she conducted a business conversation on her phone. Sensing the daughter would not appreciate being interrupted, Gracie smiled at both, then opened the doors for the movers.

1:00 p.m.

Annette unlocked Winnie's condo door, entered and took a good whiff of the large room. It smelled clean and looked like the housekeepers were doing their job. She held the door open for Winnie, who parked her walker at the front door. Leaning against whatever was accessible, she inched her way to the sofa and sank into it heavily.

"You can take that back now," Winnie sighed, waving her hand in the direction of the walker.

"It's on loan from the hospital for a month, so there is no rush to return it yet," Annette replied.

Winnie leaned her head deep into the cushions and sighed softly.

"It so nice to be home."

"We'll see how you manage, Mom."

"I'm expecting I'll manage just fine. Can you put the kettle on, honey?"

Annette hung her and Winnie's coats in the closet and entered the kitchen while predicting the next four days would be long and arduous. She checked Winnie's fridge. The milk was sour, and the cold cuts in her meat keeper smelled rancid. She disposed of both of them as well as a sealed glass container holding some kind of Italian dish.

As their tea steeped, Annette contemplated ordering dinner in until she saw two chicken and pasta dinners in Winnie's freezer. She found a box of shortbread cookies, transferred some onto a plate and brought the offerings on a tray to the coffee table. She sat in the chair across from Winnie.

After an uncomfortable pause, the women's eyes met and both smiled, neither knowing where to start.

"Are you tired, Mom?"

"Not really. How's work?"

"Very busy."

"Well, I appreciate you coming even though I told Mason I don't need any help."

"We just want to make sure you're okay."

"We?"

"Allen and I."

"But he's not here."

"He had too much work to do, but he sends his love."

"Well, thank you."

"Mom, now sip your tea, and I'm going to catch up on a few messages."

"The phone's in the kitchen."

"No need. I'll use my own phone in the den, if you don't mind."

"Not at all. Make yourself comfortable."

As happy as Winnie was to see her daughter, she knew there was more than one purpose to her visit. Winnie was determined to stay put and prove to Annette she was doing just fine.

Annette left the den door open about a foot, and Winnie watched her, hand on one hip, talking loudly as her other arm flailed in the air to emphasize her point to whoever was on the phone and could not see her anyway. There was a soft knock on her front door.

"It's unlocked," Winnie said.

Marcello opened the door slowly, holding a clear package full of biscotti from the bakery down the street. By now, Winnie had softened her resentment of him for calling the paramedics when she fell, but Marcello was still a little wary. He approached her cautiously, expecting a less than pleasant conversation. He held the biscotti in both hands, extending them towards her. She took the package from him and set it on her lap.

"Is this a peace offering?" she said as she undid the gold ribbon holding the almond crusted confectionery.

"It is," Marcello said, standing a safe distance from her.

"Hmmm. You know these are my favourite."

"That's why it's important that the offering appeals to the victim in a comforting manner."

"You're lucky I'm forgiving you this time," she answered, patting the sofa for him to sit down.

Marcello noticed Winnie's visitor as his friend tore open the package of biscotti.

"She'll be on the phone in there forever. Just ignore her," said Winnie.

Marcello took Winnie's cue but sat at the end of the sofa, much farther away than he would normally sit when they played mah-jong or Scrabble. He looked at Winnie's fading bruises under her eyes.

"Thank you. I'm most pleased you have come home."

"Did you miss me?" she asked just as Annette ended her call and entered the room.

Marcello stood up, with some resistance from his back, as Winnie bit down hard on her indulgence.

"Annette, this is Marcello," she said, crunching loudly on her biscuit.

"He's one of the tenants in this building. Marcello, Annette has come all the way from Boston to babysit me for a few days."

Marcello knew all about Winnie's children and that she rarely spoke of them other than to acknowledge their successful careers. Marcello sensed their relationship was more functional than familial. He extended his hand to shake Annette's who, after a pause, reciprocated but retracted her limp hand as soon as it touched Marcello's. He waited for her to sit down before he did but got the distinct impression that she was less than pleased to see him. Winnie picked up on the tension between them.

"Marcello brought these from the Italian bakery," she said. "Remember the one around the corner from the hospital?"

"No, I don't," Annette said curtly.

Marcello took the cue from Annette that he was not welcome and stood up as cautiously as he could. He nodded at both ladies, excused himself and tried to walk without limping to the door. Annette looked directly at him, and in a tone of voice that meant business, she spoke.

"We're going to let Mother get lots of peaceful rest for the next week or two. She's been through a lot."

"Yes. She has."

Marcello looked at Winnie, who rolled her eyes as Annette spoke.

"I'll be good as new in no time at all," Winnie chirped, smiling like the old Winnie Marcello knew before her fall.

As Marcello was closing the door behind him, he overheard Annette say, "Mom, you don't let that man in your condo, do you?"

Marcello hesitated before closing the door completely.

"Don't get your knickers in a knot, child. He's harmless," Winnie said.

"He has a history, Mother," Annette said in a hushed tone.

Marcello caught Annette glancing his way, unsure whether her intention was for him to hear what she said. He closed the door, heard the lock click and waited, unable to hear what "history" Annette was about to share with Winnie. Winnie lifted her hand to stop Annette from speaking. Offended and not used to being shut down, Annette leaned forward and raised her eyebrows.

"Mother, I flew here to help you."

"And I appreciate that. I'm exhausted, and I'm going to have a nap."

"Don't you want to hear what I have to tell you?"

"Not particularly," Winnie responded, heaving herself off her sofa and towards her bedroom.

5:00 p.m.

Adrian sat in the office of the walk-in clinic, distancing himself from the other half dozen patients in various stages of discomfort. He hadn't worked for the last two days because the weeping, itchy welts on his skin were ruining his clothes. He was pre-occupied by his romp in Darla's bed, blaming her for gifting him with something terrible. When he asked Kelly at his office about seeing a doctor, she suggested the company physician. Leery of office leaks and gossip, he opted to attend a nearby clinic instead.

The clinic attendant, a middle-aged woman bursting out of her uniform, looked like she'd rather be anywhere else. When called, he followed her to a tiny room and sat on the paper-covered examination table for a long time with his shoes, socks and pants off as ordered by the attendant. He checked his messages and read all of the bulletin board posts, including where the sexual health clinic was, tacked under a bold sign that stated the clinic did not prescribe or keep narcotics on site.

The doctor who entered the room surprised Adrian. Expecting a crotchety old man in a tired lab coat, he instead saw an attractive young woman wearing scrubs that were covered by a disposable yellow isolation gown. Her lanyard confirmed her designation, and he suddenly felt embarrassed. She started the conversation immediately after donning purple examination gloves and zoning in on his legs.

"Wow. That looks uncomfortable," she said.

Instinctively, Adrian resisted the urge to scratch his backside.

"I can't stand it anymore."

"Do you know who the culprit is?"

"All I know is that her name was Darla."

"And does Darla bark or meow?"

Adrian caught a whiff of the doctor's shiny red hair as she bent down to examine his welts.

"What? I mean, pardon?"

"Were you around a dog or a cat? These are flea bites."

"They're flea bites? Way up here?" Adrian said, pointing to his inner thighs. He pulled away the back of his underwear to show her the biggest welts on his buttocks.

"Oh, those are nice ones. Yup, they're definitely flea bites."

She took a note pad from the desk and wrote the name of a few over-the-counter antihistamines and other remedies to soothe his bites.

"This should calm the itching, and if things don't settle down after a few more days, come back. But you must—and I emphasize the word *must*—get rid of the flea infestation in your house. Because they are on you, they're also in your house and will keep biting you. I'd call a pest control company if I were you."

Adrian had no idea where the fleas came from. He was thankful that Darla had no pets, so he wouldn't have to track her down.

The doctor flashed a mischievous smile, then asked, "Now, are you also worried about something Darla may have given you?"

Adrian knew he would feel better if the doctor also reassured him that he was okay. She carefully and thoroughly examined Adrian's private parts and told him she was unable to see any areas of concern. De-gloving, then scrubbing and drying her hands and arms thoroughly, she pointed to his crotch as she asked him, "Now, ah, Mr. Adrian Common, what's the moral of this story?"

Caught off guard, he shrugged him shoulders.

"The best gifts come wrapped. So next time, and every time it's sex time, wear a condom," she said, flashing a broad smile as she closed the door behind her, leaving Adrian to assemble himself and his ego.

6:30 p.m.

As frosty as it had been outside this morning, it was also the climate in Sally and Mitch's condo. Both had avoided the other, neither initiating the discussion that should have followed immediately after Sally searched Mitch's desk. The unchanged water had evaporated from the vase that still held the wilted roses Mitch left at their condo door three weeks ago. Mitch picked up extra shifts, mostly on the evenings and nights when Sally was home to avoid confronting their dilemma.

Sally had already changed from her work clothes into her pajamas and was settled on the sofa with a bowl of cereal for dinner when Mitch came home unexpectedly. Anxiety grabbed at her chest and tightened her throat as he locked the condo door after he walked in, including the deadbolt.

Mitch had a large pizza box in his hand. He kicked off his shoes, slid out of his coat while still holding the pizza and hung his coat on the front closet doorknob. He looked haggard, and like he'd been wearing the same clothes for longer than that day. He approached the common area where Sally sat in front of the TV and placed the pizza box on the coffee table. He loosened his tie as he went to the kitchen and brought back two plates. As he placed one on the table near her, Sally smelled the combined staleness of his sweat, socks and unwashed hair.

Both remained silent as Mitch opened the box and turned it so Sally saw that half of the pizza was vegetarian. She reviewed the conversation in her head that she had practised as Mitch placed a piece of pizza, laden with processed meats, on his plate. Sally put her half-finished cereal down. What little appetite she had was gone.

"I need to say a few things, and if you don't mind, I'd appreciate you hearing me out," Mitch said.

Sally's heart pounded furiously under her pajamas. She glanced at him and said nothing, but muted the TV. She ran her tongue across her teeth and swallowed the remnants of cereal lingering in her mouth.

"Look, I'm sorry. I am truly and deeply sorry," he said.

Sally absorbed his words, unsure if he was sincere or using a bargaining chip like the pizza in front of her. She stared blankly at him. Mitch watched her while he searched for the right words.

"I messed up. And I take full responsibility for it."

Sally didn't budge.

After a long pause, he continued. "None of this is your fault. I was on a tough case and running on empty. I was sleep-deprived and I ran out of patience. I should never have challenged you."

Sally became less afraid, but none of Mitch's words made her feel any better. The greasy shine from the pepperoni slices on Mitch's pizza disappeared as it cooled on his plate.

"Go on," she said quietly.

He stared at her, then hung his head. He was lost for words and the sequence of apologies he planned to recite.

"You said you had a few things to say."

"What do you want me to say?" he asked.

Sally saw that Mitch, who was always confident and self-assured, was losing his composure.

"I don't know what else to say," he said.

He watched for her usual clues of vulnerability but saw none.

"I know I screwed up, and I'm sorry, "he repeated.

"Is that it?"

Those didn't sound like Sally's own words. She was made of sweetness and light, and almost always found an excuse to explain an unhappy moment between them. Today there were no excuses. It was all about Mitch. He felt guilty for searching through Sally's phone history, which he had done many times for no good reason. He didn't divulge that so there was no need to apologize for it. There were no other red flags beyond her locating the shelter, and as many times as he had given the number to other women, he never saw Sally as a victim. But she was, and an innocent one.

Sally didn't know that Mitch had lied to her countless times and cheated on her. She didn't know he drank too much. She had no idea he was becoming more careless at work. He had made excuses for things he shouldn't have kept from her. He didn't want to go on vacation with her because, beyond sex, it would force him to spend uninterrupted time with her. Mitch had pursued Sally because she was like the Georgia he met decades ago. He could manipulate her like he did Georgia in their early years together. And knowing Sally now, he knew she would eventually become another Georgia because of his own mistakes. Her resilience and tolerance would be worn down eventually.

"I want you to leave," Sally said so quietly she barely heard herself.

"What did you just say?" Mitch asked. He was caught off-guard and was sure he hadn't heard her correctly.

"I want you to leave."

"Sally …"

"Please, don't. Just leave."

"Look, let's talk about this."

"I can't talk about this."

"We have to. I made a mistake."

"Mitch, I can't do this right now. Please leave."

"I don't have anywhere to go."

"I'm sure someone has a couch," she whispered as she turned up the TV volume.

Mitch slumped into his chair, blindsided. His elbows found his knees and he massaged his head with his hands, not bothering to smooth his hair back into place. Sally sat frozen, feet tucked under her, not daring to move or speak. Or cry. Mitch slid the cold piece of pizza back into the box and it landed on top of the vegetarian side. He walked to the kitchen and threw his plate into the sink. Sally jumped but remained where she sat, not daring to get up to see if the plate had broken.

Mitch walked to their bedroom, then to his office. He was out within minutes carrying a gym bag stuffed so full it wouldn't close and a plastic dry cleaning bag holding the suits and shirts she had picked up for him earlier in the day and purposely left on the bed. He came back into the living area and stood about ten feet from Sally. Despite changing into casual clothes, she could still smell the maleness of his sweat. It repulsed her. Cautiously watching him, she reached over to the pizza box, tucked the lid in and held it up for Mitch to take. He hesitated, then slinging his gym bag over his shoulder, took the box. Mitch closed the door and Sally listened, not sure for what other than the comfort of the normal sounds within and outside of her walls.

Mitch was stunned. In a state of disbelief. He had expected to make amends and carry on. He did not expect to be standing, unwelcome, outside the building his father so proudly had worked in. Beyond exhausted, Mitch left the building and sat in his pickup truck. The inside smelled of pizza. His windows fogged up and shrouded him from the rest of the world. He heard a car pull into the space beside him and waited quietly, for once sensing what it felt like to have someone watching him when he wanted to do nothing more than to hide.

Adrian locked his car and walked slowly by Mitch's truck, his own hot pizza box in hand. He noted a dark shadow in the driver's seat that was partially illuminated by the parking lot lights. He looked back, placing the vehicle in that spot before. It wasn't usually his practice to check on occupied vehicles, but he was in a helping mood after the walk-in clinic doctor helped him. Adrian cautiously approached Mitch's truck and tapped on the window. Mitch opened it an inch, recognized Adrian, and let the window down enough to see his face.

"You okay, man?" Adrian said.

"Everything's good."

"You sure?" Adrian asked, curious why this man, whose name he didn't recall, was sitting in his truck on a cold, dark night.

"I'm fine, thanks," Mitch said, starting the truck.

"Okay. Goodnight," Adrian said as Mitch rolled his window up.

He wasn't sure if Mitch heard him, but he walked with his pizza and anti-itch cream to his condo, convinced that the unkempt man in the truck was in worse shape than he was.

7:30 p.m.

Tonight was Talia's turn to choose which movie to watch. Bryce brought their regular Chinese food home and they ate quietly. Talia cracked open her fortune cookie and crunched on it while she read the inscription out loud.

"You are very persistent in pursuing your life goals," she read, smiling.

Bryce plucked his note from the sleeve of his cookie with tweezers, as he always did. He passed his uneaten treat to her, then read it while Talia ate.

"Very little is needed to make a life happy."

It was like the fortunes were written for each of them. Despite Bryce's peculiar habits, today Talia loved him. A lot. She rationalized that his odd behaviours really did not affect her other than her own occasional outbursts of frustration. She decided it wasn't helpful to worry about them because, as her fortune cookie told her, her career goals were moving in the right direction. She had attended an employee team meeting that day and learned that her company had re-configured her benefits into a flexible spending account that she could use for either health care or education. This was a gift—the gateway to pursue her master's degree. She shared this with Bryce, who was genuinely pleased for her. If Talia was happy, Bryce was happy. They cuddled under the blankets on the sofa until both found each other more stimulating than the movie, which they ignored as they made love. All twenty-four minutes of it.

8:30 p.m.

Gracie knocked on Lily's door. She had a bottle of wine tucked into the tissue and gift bag that had held the book Mason had given her earlier. She had successfully navigated up two flights of stairs with Lily's kettle, moving cart and the wine intact. Lily opened the door and greeted Gracie with a hesitant smile. She was unsure how Gracie would react to her still occupying the Loft, certain she had no intention of returning to the unit Gracie now occupied. Lily set the wine and kettle on her kitchen counter.

"Well? How is it?" Lily asked cautiously as she poured the Riesling into stemless wine glasses.

"It's beautiful. Sonny hustled hard to finish it and did a good job. In your own time, when and if you feel you're ready, you are very welcome to come and see it."

"Did he change the bathtub?" Lily asked anxiously.

"He changed everything. He replaced the, ah, old bathtub with a shower, then installed a new tub in the bathroom that used to have a shower. It's like two new bathrooms."

Lily pictured the changes with mild curiosity, then changed the subject.

"Maybe I will visit, but not just yet. Did you meet little old Winnie yet?"

"I did, initially when she walked all the way to the library I work at and I drove her home. I saw her briefly in the hallway today as well. I wonder if she had an accident because she has a bunch of bruises on her face. I think her daughter was with her."

"Hmm. I didn't know she had family. I've only seen a man that occasionally visits."

"Tall, with grey hair and glasses? And well-dressed?"

"Sounds like the same guy. All business and stingy with his smiles," Lily said.

Gracie hid her smile, thinking of his sticky notes in the book.

"He's her guardian."

"I'd like a guardian like that."

Each woman found a comfortable chair, toasted new beginnings and started to unravel their lives to each other, ending their evening when the wine bottle was empty.

9:00 p.m.

Mitch literally had nowhere to go. He drove slowly through deserted streets as the tourist attractions closed for the evening, the box of uneaten pizza sliding across the passenger side floor warning him when he rounded a corner too fast. Two hours later, he sat slouched in his parked truck in front of Georgia's house, weighing two dismal options. He could check into a two-star hotel for the night, hopefully without being recognized, or approach Georgia and hope Sally wouldn't find out. He left his belongings and the pizza in his truck, and walked to the front door. Through the sheer living room curtains, he recognized Georgia getting up off the sofa. She must have heard something or seen his vehicle because she walked to the front door and opened it before Mitch had a chance to knock.

"Oh boy."

"Georgia ..."

"The second front door visit in less than ten days, and you still look like shit."

"Don't."

"Let me guess. She kicked you out."

Mitch turned his back to Georgia and stood facing his truck. More than anything, he wanted to head for the nearest bar, but the light taps of Georgia's hand on his shoulder stopped him.

"Get in here."

Mitch kicked off his shoes in the front hallway and dropped his jacket on the floor on top of them. He eased himself into the chair nearest the door while Georgia picked his coat up and hung it in the entrance closet. She put the kettle on and brought Mitch coffee in an old mug his sons gave him for an occasion he wasn't around to enjoy with them.

"There's leftover meatloaf from dinner. I can put it on toast."

"That would be nice."

Mitch sat in silence as Georgia busied herself in the kitchen. Minutes later she passed him the mustard-dressed sandwich. Neither spoke while he ate. When he could finally breathe calmly, he put the empty plate gently in the kitchen sink.

"Now go have a shower. You stink."

Mitch was at her mercy, with no energy to object.

"I have clothes in the truck."

"I figured that."

Mitch retrieved his gym bag and locked his truck; he was beyond caring if anyone saw him. Georgia sipped her tea, watching him purge his bag for what toiletries he needed and head down the hall to the bathroom. He found a clean towel in the bathroom cupboard and stripped off his clothes. The hot shower beating full force on his body soothed him. Clean and smelling of Georgia's shower gel, he rubbed himself dry and donned clean sweats from the final load of laundry that Sally had washed for him.

"Ah, you're human again," Georgia chirped, pointing to the opposite side of the same sofa she sat on.

Mitch closed the living room curtains, locked the front door and sat down, feeling somewhat more like he could participate in the conversation Georgia initiated. She started with a safe topic.

"Are you on a day off?"

"Yup. Finished my last shift of four today. I've got four days off."

"You look like you need the break. How's work?"

"Same messes. Different players."

"Did you have a chance to call the number I gave you?"

"No, because I don't believe it's confidential. A guy I work with suggested another counsellor."

"And?"

"And nothing."

Georgia watched Mitch as he stared blankly at the closed curtains. She contemplated her words carefully.

"Look, I'll make you a deal. You make that call, whether it's the number I gave you or your buddy's contact, and you can stay here tonight. Simple as that. No more questions asked, and no expectations from me. The number I gave you is still on the fridge."

"What good will it do me?"

"Mitch, I'm not the person to answer that question. But I can tell you that it took me months of talking to someone with no emotional ties to you or me, friends or otherwise, to put my life back in order after you left."

Mitch wasn't aware of that. Georgia breathed deeply.

"Neither of us are perfect," she said, "and now is not the time for either of us to re-hash the mistakes we made. But if you love Sally, you at least owe it to her to make the effort."

"Their office is closed," Mitch said, checking his watch.

"I'm sure they have voicemail."

Mitch went to the closet and found his phone in his coat pocket. No attempt from Sally to reach him. There was one text from his supervisor offering him an extra shift tonight. Working would be easier than making that call, but tomorrow would bring a repeat of today. As would the next day after that. He walked down the hallway to the bathroom and sat on the ledge of the bathtub. He scrolled through his pictures for the screenshot of the card his buddy sent him. He stared at the number. The area code was a local one. He could lie to Georgia that he made the call, but he would be no further ahead. And she would eventually find out.

It was almost 9:30 p.m. when he dialled the number. To his surprise, a female answered the phone.

"Carrie speaking."

He almost hung up.

"Hello?" she said again, her voice sounded kind, yet businesslike.

"Yes, hello. I understand you do some counselling."

"Yes, that's correct."

The conversation flowed through a series of intake questions, including his agreement to pay her rate. It was more than he expected, but he did not want to use the police program. She gave him a choice of a cancelled appointment the following day or a regular appointment in ten days. He accepted the first choice, certain he would change his mind if he waited longer.

Georgia was washing the few dishes they used when he came into the kitchen.

"How did you make out?'

"I have an appointment tomorrow."

"Perfect. Now take the garbage out."

"What?"

"You think you're staying here for free?" she said without turning around.

Without speaking, Mitch obeyed. When he came in, Georgia handed him two new light bulbs with instructions to replace the ones in the basement guest room ceiling. When he completed that task, she invited him to watch the evening news with her in the downstairs family room adjacent to that bedroom. After the news, she announced she was going to bed and he was welcome to sleep in the guest bedroom. She was all business, and for the first time in a long, long time he appreciated her for that.

NOVEMBER 10TH
Weather forecast: light dusting of snow

9:00 a.m.

"No matter how bad the weather is, the sky always makes room for it."

Anonymous

Mason buzzed the doorbell to Winnie's building, and Annette let him in. She had invited Mason and Allen to meet with Winnie and herself. Allen linked in virtually and was chatting with Winnie when Mason entered the living room. Niceties were exchanged as Allen and Annette took turns bragging about their children's accomplishments. Mason's briefcase was organized with many documents, including Winnie's current will, as he knew little more than his presence was requested. As his eyes met Winnie's, he sensed she had no idea what Annette's agenda was either.

Annette called the small gathering to her attention and started by saying how pleased she was that, with the exception of one fading raccoon eye, Winnie had recovered from her fall. She felt it was inevitable she would fall again, and the alert button on the lanyard Winnie refused to wear around her neck was not an effective safety measure. Winnie rolled her eyes in Mason's direction but said nothing. Annette's concerns about Winnie's well-being overshadowed Allen's, and the siblings engaged in an exchange of polite words that became more accusatory until Winnie lost her patience.

"Stop it!" she shouted. "Stop this! Right now!"

"But Mother!"

"Stop mothering me. I'm the mother here, and I can hear everything you say!" Winnie yelled louder than she had in years.

Mason smiled proudly at Winnie for standing up for herself, which Annette misinterpreted as him being amused by her mother's outburst.

"Mother, we want what's best for you," Allen offered.

"No, you don't! You want what's best for the both of you. And if you don't think I don't know what's going on here, you've got—"

"What exactly do you mean by that?" Annette interrupted.

Winnie looked at Annette, then at Allen.

"You're trying to lock me away!"

"We are not. Mother, we just want—"

"I said, do not "Mother" me! Mason, what was all that nonsense I did at the hospital? What was that called?"

On cue, Mason produced the document he was certain would come up today.

"It was a capacity assessment," he said.

"And other than asking me questions that a second grader would know, were we not told I could come back and live at home?"

"Yes, we were."

Winnie glared at Annette, then faced Allen, inches away from Annette's laptop screen.

"Did you hear that, son?"

Allen nodded, retreating in the background.

"Then what do you think you're both doing?"

Allen remained quiet, silently blaming Annette for roping him into this meeting. Winnie took the papers from Mason's hand and shook them in the air.

"This says I'm not demented and that I can take care of myself. It also says I can do whatever I want. If I want to eat cookies for breakfast and drink brandy for lunch, then I sure as hell don't need you to tell me otherwise!"

Internally, Mason beamed with pride. Winnie had command of her own court, and in his eyes, was winning her case.

No one heard the soft knock on the door above Winnie's voice. Marcello knocked louder a second time, mostly concerned but also a little bit curious. When Mason answered the door, the room fell silent. Winnie got out of her chair, bracing her hand on her thigh as she straightened up. She approached Marcello.

"Come in," she said.

Marcello searched Winnie's face for clues but did not move.

"I see you have guests," he said.

"I do, from near and far, and even in the clouds," she said, pointing to Allen's face on the screen.

"Mother, perhaps your visitor—"

"Marcello, these are my children. And, of course, you know Mason."

Marcello nodded sheepishly. Annette glared at him, then made faces at Allen, readjusting her laptop so he could see Marcello in the doorway. Annette took to her phone, texting furiously. Almost instantly, the ping of a text was heard on Allen's screen. The siblings bobbed their heads between screens and phones, nodded to each other and, as if on cue, both asked Marcello to come in. Sensing danger, he didn't move.

"No thank you. I'll let you get back to your visit."

"I insist you come in," Annette said firmly.

Winnie and Mason looked puzzled. Marcello stepped into the room but left the door open.

"It's Mr. Portobello, correct?" Annette asked, using her business meeting voice.

"Yes, but please call me Marcello."

"Marcello, how did you come to meet my—ah, our—mother?"

Mason, Winnie and Marcello's faces tightened. Marcello faced Winnie as he answered.

"When I moved here in September, as her neighbour."

"And my friend," said Winnie.

"Mr. Portobello, I understand that there was a time when you were not well."

"Yes, Winnie knows that my back is fragile," he replied, moving his hand to his hip.

"And your mind, is that still fragile too?" Annette snapped.

Mason searched the other faces for clues, settling on Marcello.

"What are you talking about?" Winnie asked Annette loudly.

"Mother, did your friend tell you that he spent a few months on the psych ward?"

Winnie rolled her eyes again but turned to see the colour drain from Marcello's face.

"And, Mother, did this man tell you he stood on a railing, ready to jump over Niagara Falls before the police rescued him, drunk and despondent?"

A text pinged on Annette's phone in that frozen moment. She ignored it. As an attorney, Mason, equally cognizant of the law and his need to protect Winnie, did not interrupt Annette's interrogation.

Seeing only heartache in Marcello's eyes, Winnie faced her daughter.

"What are you trying to do here, Annette?"

"I'm trying to make you aware that this man is unstable."

"This 'unstable man,' as you call him, looks after me," Winnie said, looking to Mason. "As does this man. They both look after me. You," she pointed to Annette and then Allen, "you look at me, not after me. At least one of these two men see me daily, and you, and that goes for both of you, you don't. You don't make me soup. You don't share what I need to know, only what you think I should know."

Winnie stood between the men and took one of their hands in each of her fragile ones.

"Unlike you, these men really have my best interests at heart."

Mason squeezed Winnie's hand, then gently released it to slide the document Winnie handed him into his briefcase. If her children had any question about Winnie's ability to speak for herself, she had just proven them wrong.

Marcello felt no need to defend himself or explain his tortured years after Valentina abandoned him. He had planted healthy roots in Canadian soil with the intention of beginning their newlywed lives here. When she ended that dream, he became stricken with a depression so severe he was bedridden for weeks. His life was not worth living, and he envisioned jumping over the falls as the only way to escape his grief. This unknown woman would not force him to relive the years it took him to bury his grief in his own private place. How she found out was beyond him, but it was not a topic he was willing to explore.

Head hung low in humiliation, Marcello backtracked three steps and left the group. Winnie, as angry as she had been with him for calling the paramedics, knew that he, like Mason, was not the enemy in the room. Marcello regretted knocking on Winnie's door as much as Mason regretted asking Winnie's children to become more involved. Marcello closed the door behind him and went home to his cats, his heart as heavy as his mood.

Winnie sat down, her lips pursed so tightly they disappeared. Livid, she turned to Annette.

"Why on earth would you invade this man's private life?" she asked.

Annette turned her phone over and quickly scrolled to something she saved for this conversation.

"It's right here, Mom," she said smugly. "When I did a search on him, an old news article came up about him trying to jump over the falls. And do you remember my friend Terry from high school? She's a nurse on the psychiatry unit, and she confirmed the story."

"Whether that's accurate or not, your friend Terry breached Marcello's privacy, and if he decides to pursue legal action, it could result in her losing her job and her license to practice," said Mason carefully.

He was well-versed in people bringing up lurid details and was cautious about what he said.

"If Mr. Portobello acts on this complaint, she better hope she has substantial liability insurance."

Annette put her phone down; she didn't expect to hear that. Allen interrupted, stated he was being called to another meeting, whether imaginary or real, and quickly said goodbye.

Not wanting to be party to any more of the dialogue between Annette and Winnie, Mason found his own excuse to head to his office. Both women thanked him for coming, and Mason said he would check in with both of them soon. He let himself out, closed the door and exhaled deeply.

9:45 a.m.

Mason hesitated for a moment in the hallway, wagering if having a private word with Marcello would help him gauge if, or how, to address Annette's concern about him. Opting to let things settle first, he started down the hall. As he opened the door to the stairwell, he heard a female voice say "Good morning" behind him. He turned to see Gracie closing her condo door. She was dressed in black slacks, warm outerwear and sneakers. He held the door open for her.

"Good morning. It's a good thing you're dressed warmly; we're expecting our first dusting of snow today," he said, looking curiously at Gracie's shoes.

"Walking to work wakes me up. And reading your book before bed helps me sleep," she chirped.

"Would you like a ride?" Mason offered.

"Why, thank you. That would be much appreciated," Gracie replied, wishing she'd spent more time on her hair, which was tied in a loose knot.

She followed Mason to his black Cadillac, where he opened the door for her, as he had done for Winnie.

"That's very chivalrous of you, thank you."

"My mother always told me to treat a woman with the respect she deserves."

"You had a good mother."

"She was a wonderful woman. Full of wit and wisdom."

Mason navigated his big car out of the parking slot assigned to Winnie and took the side streets to the library, which was a short drive and provided little opportunity for more than small talk. After exchanging opinions about the novel he lent her, Mason asked if she was settled in her new condo.

"It's beautiful. I felt a little uneasy for the first couple of days, but the bathtub where—ah—the lady—ah—drowned was removed, and both bathrooms were reconfigured. It's all new. I convinced myself that another life's tragedy was not mine to own, so I'm making my own memories here."

"That's very insightful."

"It's what all those self-help books I've read told me to do."

Mason didn't ask why she needed to read them. He didn't want to know, especially after his morning at Winnie's.

Mason pulled into the parking lot, and after a few pensive moments, Gracie thanked him for the ride.

"If you're visiting Winnie, you are welcome to see the renovations," she said.

Mason's shoulders tensed slightly, and he paused before saying, "Thank you."

The conversation ended there. Gracie let herself out of the car, and Mason watched her until she entered the library safely. She waved back, curious why he lingered. Driving to his office, Mason thought about his deceased wife, this morning's meeting and how he and Marcello shared the trauma of a lost love and the pain of recounting it. His wife filled his lived history, in good times and in bad. Letting those memories fade to make new ones made him uneasy. He was also uncomfortable thinking about physical intimacy despite having only pleasant thoughts of Gracie. He imagined what she might share about her own history and about losing her husband. Perhaps inviting her for a hike on a nearby trail would be a safe way to learn more.

Gracie had a few extra minutes before her assignment to the front desk began. Instead of joining the others in the lunchroom, she walked among the aisles of books, not looking for anything more than some quiet time to think about Mason. Was it nothing more than a willingness to share their love of reading? He was deeply connected to his beloved wife, unlike how she felt about Blair. And leaving Fred was a significant but different loss. A loss she chose; an exit she planned. And as painful as it was, it solidified her goal to move on. She wondered if Mason might join her for a walk one day as a tourist to see the falls. It was safe, healthy and an opportunity to critique other novels. Or the beginning of writing their own? Hearing the sound of the library doors unlock brought Gracie back to the day ahead of her.

10:00 a.m.

Lily sat on her living room sofa in her bathrobe, flipping mindlessly through another rotation of TV stations. There was nothing she wanted to do today. Two coffees in, her mind was shifting from 'Park' to 'Go' with nowhere to be and nothing to spend money on. Her bank balance was small but better managed. She muted the TV and scrolled through the social media posts on her phone. Other people were getting on with life, but hers was standing still.

The things she took for granted when she and Rosie lived together were gone. Familiar routines like her shopping list on the fridge, her travel mug on the counter or her bras drying on the cupboard knobs in the laundry room were now a memory. Lily missed the harmless Rosie today, or maybe what was harmless between them. But none of that would change now. It was Lily who needed to change. She needed to find a job. She needed to fit back into her clothes to wear to a job. She needed to find someone to ask her how her day was after she came home from her job. Lily needed a plan. So that was what she decided she would do today. She would make herself a plan.

Lily got up off the sofa and looked out the window to the parking lot where Gracie's car sat. She texted Gracie, inviting her to come up for coffee. She saw Gracie as kind, patient and organized, personality traits that Lily needed help with. Maybe Gracie would help her with her plan.

Gracie texted back that she could meet her after work. The burst of caffeine prompted Lily to start with another plan—finding a boyfriend. She sat back down on the sofa and started her search by typing "How to find a good dating website" into her tablet. A barrage of ads for dating websites distracted her from her original inquiry. Common themes flowed through many of them. They could all find her a perfect match. They would find her quick hook-ups or true lasting love, sometimes for free. They could even find a meaningful relationship, no strings attached, with a wealthy, seasoned professional. A whole buffet of options to suit her every desire.

It all sounded very exciting, and all Lily needed to do today was build and submit her dating profile. And she could use the same one for multiple sites. She didn't have a current picture, so she went through her skin cleansing routine, applying lotions and potions, then a face full of make-up. She snapped a few selfies but despised them all. She found an old picture in her phone that was five years and twenty-five pounds ago; much different than this morning's selfies. She rationalized that once a guy tagged her, he would look beyond the pretty face she was posting and magically find her the fascinating, fun-loving person that she wrote she was.

Lily typed in more generic information about herself. She paused at the question asking her about what her most important and positive character trait was. She wrote that she was creative and outgoing, especially when shopping was involved. She would add more later and maybe embellish a little. She couldn't describe her career because living off her ex-husband's alimony would not be a character trait intriguing to other men. She skipped to the next question about what she was passionate about. She didn't like animals, and when she thought about it, she didn't like many people either. She liked to travel, but the means to do so evaporated after the divorce. She enjoyed music. Ah ha! She filled that line in quickly.

The section about the type of man she wanted to meet was also tricky. Her nails clicked on the tablet that she typed in her desire to meet a handsome man with a good physique, hair and a solid income, but what she really wanted was someone who would not intimidate her with his education and experience. A red flag popped up on the screen, suggesting she was listing characteristics rather than the type of character she wanted. Lily ignored the prompt. Once the Mr. Wonderfuls saw her picture and her notes, they would be lining up to date her. Under her own character trait, she typed "loyalty." She was loyal—unlike Elliott, who wasn't. When another yellow flag flashed across her screen and suggested she eliminate anything that was negative, she deleted the part that said Elliot wasn't.

The next question asked her to indicate ways she had fun and lived her life. Lily couldn't remember that last time she had fun, so she skipped this question as well, because answering honestly would result in a another flag popping back to tell her that was negative and wouldn't land her the guy she wanted to meet.

Setting up her profile was much harder than she expected. She moved on to the next question, which asked her who she cared about. Lily put the screen down. She had no one, two or four-legged, to fill in that space. She cared about Gracie, who she'd known for only eight weeks. She wrote that she liked helping others even though she hadn't really helped anyone, including herself.

The next tip encouraged her to be honest about who and what she was looking for. She reviewed what she had written, and it struck her that her profile reflected the very person she didn't want to meet. Would the right guys find a match in her? Would any guys be matched with her? She saved what she wrote and would ask Gracie to review it when they met that evening. Lily popped a bagel in the toaster, unmuted her TV and flipped through another rotation of channels to see if anything would hold her interest her this time.

11:30 a.m.

Adrian was out of bed at 8:55 a.m. and working from his home office within five minutes. He let his phone go to voicemail once he checked the number. It was his mother calling. He finished the project he was working on just about the same time his stomach started growling. He dressed and left his building but stopped to check his mailbox. As usual, it was empty. He still hoped one day to find a message from Talia. He did notice someone had removed the chairs from the front lobby and replaced them with plastic lawn chairs. Because he never opened the occasional tenant email communications, he didn't know the chairs were being cleaned to rid them of fleas.

He walked to a high-priced café for breakfast, then to his office to meet green-eyed Scarlett, the new associate who had recently transferred from Texas. She wore a checkered shirt dress and cowboy boots. Her waves of ginger hair were woven into a thick, loose braid that ended at her waist. Adrian introduced himself, noticing the sprinkle of freckles across her cheeks. She was an anomaly who did not meet his typical dating criteria, but she might be interesting enough to share a meal with. Kelly called her away to finalize some personnel details, and their interaction ended.

Walking home, he regretted wearing his best shoes because the salt and melting snow were staining them. Adrian walked into his condo just as his mother was calling him again.

"Hey Mom, sorry I missed your first call."

"Oh, Adrian," her voice wavered.

"What's wrong, Mom?"

"Did you get my message?"

He felt a small pang of guilt for ignoring it.

"Sorry, I was tied up at work. What did it say?"

"It's your father."

"Dad? What happened?"

"He's had an accident. And he's in the hospital … and I think you should come home."

"Oh no. That's too bad. What kind of an accident? How much time do I have?" Adrian asked, thinking more of his own agenda.

"He fell off a stepladder while hanging Christmas lights on the eaves-troughs. We're waiting for the doctor to tell us what's broken and what all the test results show, so we'll know more then."

Adrian did some quick calculations. He had planned to meet friends over the next two nights and had just signed up with the local basketball league, but he could skip the first game.

"Hope he's okay. I'll take some personal time off and give you a call when my flights are booked."

"That would be very much appreciated."

Adrian and his father, a very hard-working man who, unlike Adrian, was loyal to the same company for decades, did not have a close bond. Describing them as opposites was an understatement. His mother, whose main domain was the kitchen, had always been the mediator and the peacekeeper between them. As he hung up, he decided that a trip home would be a good idea not only to see his family, but to meet an old girlfriend who always hooked up with him for old times' sake.

Adrian went for drinks with his friends and postponed booking his flights until the next day.

Noon

After Mason left, Annette sequestered herself in Winnie's study, barely exchanging a word with her until lunch. Annette and Winnie competed in the kitchen over who was making lunch, until Winnie succumbed, retreating to a living room chair where she watched Annette muddle through a kitchen she had never been in before. Annette had already moved her flight up by four days to this evening, feigning an emergency work meeting the next morning. This also gave her the opportunity to remain in the study to pack her clothes. Both mother and daughter knew neither was fooling the other, and the atmosphere in the condo would lighten when only one person remained.

Annette brought Winnie's canned tomato soup and sandwich to her on a cookie sheet lined with a place mat. It was easier than asking Winnie if she had a tray, or worse yet, eating together at the tiny table in the kitchen. Annette poured the remaining soup into a mug and sat across from Winnie on the sofa in the same seats they occupied this morning. Both were armed and ready to continue their battle, but didn't. Winnie finished her meal completely even though she wasn't hungry, because if she was eating, she didn't need to speak. She didn't want to hear that she had lost or gained weight, resurrect the debate about meal delivery costs or, heaven forbid, Marcello cooking for her. Annette sipped her soup and supervised Winnie, satisfied that at least her mother had consumed some semblance of a meal, albeit processed food, before she left her.

The pair sat in silence for another few minutes before Annette spoke.

"Look, Mom, this isn't easy for either of us."

Winnie, lips pursed into a thin line, said nothing.

"If Allen or I lived closer, we wouldn't be as concerned. I know I said it earlier, but we really do worry about you living here by yourself."

"I didn't pick this. You did. And now you're worried about a place you insisted I move into? I would have been much happier not living here either. But I am not moving again unless I leave feet first. And hopefully they'll both be stone cold, like Mason's parents."

"Mother, don't say that. You have years ahead of you."

"Precisely why I didn't want to leave the home where your father and I raised you and your brother in the first place. You've moved more times than I have room for in my address book. You say each house is bigger and better, but let me tell you, fancy houses don't buy happiness. Have you ever asked your kids if they're happy? How many bedrooms have Dallas and Savannah had? And how many times have they switched schools? I've lost count."

Annette recoiled. She and Richard, both her real estate and live-in partner after her divorce, traded up their Boston addresses regularly to boost their net worth. Annette's kids never complained to her and always seemed happy to come home after weekends with their father. Annette did not have the time or energy to defend herself or tell her mother any more than she felt she needed to know. Which is exactly what Winnie had said this morning.

"I'm sorry. That was uncalled for," Winnie said, further surprising her daughter. "But the point here, Annette, is that I don't interfere in your life, and I'd appreciate it if you don't interfere in mine. My health matches my age, as does my judgement. The doctors proved that. As long as I can walk and talk, I will be your parent, and you and Allen will be my children. So, let's be civil and carry on remembering we're what's left of this family."

Winnie, triumphant at putting her daughter back in her place, sat back in her chair and reset it to the reclining position.

"Now if you don't mind, I'm going to have a nap."

If Winnie was going to nap their last hours away, then Annette felt no need to stay. Even if her flight was not leaving for six hours, she did not want to waste her time here. She moved her suitcase to the front door and lied that her ride was coming shortly. She kissed her mother goodbye and tucked her in with the blanket she had shrouded herself in as her mother lectured her. It was not yet cool, and both Winnie and Annette knew that was the only warmth they would share before she left. Annette put her designer coat on, hoisted her oversized laptop bag over her shoulder and wheeled her matching luggage into the hallway.

"I love you, Mom."

"Love you too, honey. Safe trip," Winnie said, only her head peeking out from the blanket, the last of the bruising under one eye all but gone.

Their eyes met, and Annette blew her a kiss across the room before she shut the door behind her.

By the time Annette was booking a taxi from the lobby of Winnie's building, both she and Winnie were sobbing. They were just a hundred steps from each other but miles apart emotionally.

Marcello left his condo unlocked and sauntered into the lobby to pick up his mail in his slippers and favourite over-stretched sweater, which was covered in cat hair. He did not anticipate seeing anyone, and certainly not Winnie's daughter. One encounter was sufficient enough for his lifetime. Annette quickly turned to face the front door when she became aware of someone entering the lobby. Concentrating on her task, she wiped her eyes and nose with a used tissue. If it wasn't so cold, she would have waited outside to avoid the person. Marcello, thinking it might be better if he returned later, changed his mind when he was certain Annette had heard the hallway door click. Ignoring her, he first checked his empty mailbox, then opened the hallway door. He was a man with manners, so he faced Annette and offered a confident nod to make it clear he did not fear her. Glaring at him, red-faced and tear-stained, she threw her last words across the lobby at him like a weapon.

"Stay away from my mother," she hissed as he closed the hallway door and shuffled back to the security of his home.

Winnie was exhausted both physically and emotionally, and sleep wouldn't settle her. Her world had been turned upside down since her fall on Hallowe'en night. More than anything, she missed Alex. And then Marcello. While Mason replaced Alex as her model for logic, Marcello was her voice of reason. He validated her thoughts. He guided her, especially when she questioned her judgement. She wrapped her blanket around her shoulders, flipped off the new slippers Annette had brought her and slid into her old ones. She opened her door and was startled to see Marcello in his own favourite sweater and slippers as she stepped into the hallway. As grateful as she was to see him, Marcello's stance became guarded. As if she was the one to be feared. He bowed his head and opened his condo door.

"Stop!" she called to him. "What's this about? No 'Hello, how are you?'"

Marcello remained still, both in movement and with his words. He saw her familiar, exasperated expression. The blanket around her shoulders was not a familiar sight.

"Can I come in?" she asked.

He hesitated, Annette's order still resonating in his head. Yet, he rationalized, it was Winnie inviting herself to meet with him, not the reverse when he would check on her.

"Very well. But the cats are restless."

"I don't care if they're restless. I'm restless too."

Marcello opened the door slowly to keep Mona Lisa from escaping down the hall. Since her taste of freedom, although unpleasant, Marcello was cautious that she might escape again. Still in recovery from her assortment of street-acquired afflictions, she was as skittish as Marcello was right now. He scooped her up in one arm and held the door open for Winnie. His condo was clean and messy. Newspapers lay scattered on the floor where Marcello had just inventoried the obituaries for familiar names. Mona Lisa rejoined Michelangelo in pouncing on and shredding the papers. Marcello removed an upside down metal colander from the one antique chair cushion not covered in yellowed plastic wrap. He gestured for Winnie to take that seat as he pointed to the colander.

"If it sits here, the cats don't."

One of the reasons Winnie admired him was how he managed his small world so efficiently. Winnie sat down and scanned the room. She had often knocked on his door to tell him she was going out but had only been inside a few times. Today something was amiss. Nothing was simmering on the stove, and the only scent in the air was suspicion.

"Are you going out?" she asked, her elbows on the chair arms and palms facing the ceiling.

"Not today."

"You're usually whipping up something divine in there," she said, pointing towards the kitchen.

She saw an open decanter of red wine and a half full glass on the counter.

"I know it's five o'clock somewhere but not usually this early in here. That's not like you."

Marcello rubbed his eyes and forehead with one hand. He looked at Winnie, then down at his hands, which were now resting on his lap.

"Would you care for a glass of wine?"

"By the look on your face, I think that might help both of us. What's wrong, my friend?"

Calling Marcello her friend settled the anxious tremor of his hands. He poured the elixir into a second glass and set both on the table between them.

"Your daughter warned me to stay away from you," he said quietly, his chin sagging into his chest.

Winnie's mouth dropped open as she shook her head.

"I don't remember hearing that."

"She was calling a taxi."

"Where?"

"In the lobby when I went to get my mail."

"When?"

"Five minutes ago."

"She told me it was already booked."

Marcello was frank with Winnie. He would never lie again to her.

"She was upset. She was crying," he said.

Winnie's eyes saddened. They both took a long pull of their wine and set their glasses down simultaneously.

"Well, I'll be damned. She still has a heart."

Marcello didn't ask, and Winnie saw no reason to explain. She took another big gulp of her wine and immediately changed the subject.

"Now, I don't need to know any more about your hospital stay after Valentina dumped you, do I?"

Marcello breathed a loud sigh of relief and shook his head.

"When you lose your one true love, you want your world to end with them."

Winnie had felt that way many times after Alex passed away. For months she would have been happier not waking up to face another lonely day. Like Marcello, she understood that grief was the price they paid for true love. Marcello raised his glass, and as they clinked, they toasted the things they were grateful for, including each other.

What neither heard was Annette knocking on Winnie's door. She was remorseful and wanted to apologize to her mother for interfering. She did not want to leave without making amends. When Winnie didn't answer, Annette assumed she had fallen asleep. She whispered an apology softly as she left, knowing only she would hear it. She did not realize that Winnie had cast aside her new slippers and was drinking with her neighbour, thus ignoring the alcohol warning Annette had highlighted in yellow on Winnie's prescription bottles.

6:30 p.m.

After splitting the grilled chicken wraps and salad Gracie picked up on her walk home from work, Lily and Gracie settled across from each other at the kitchen island in the Loft to do their homework. Lily passed her one of two copies of the dating profile draft she had put together earlier that day. The first odd thing Gracie noticed was that Lily's photo did not resemble the woman sitting across from her.

"I know what you're thinking," Lily said, looking at her copy. "It doesn't look like me now."

Gracie wasn't familiar with online dating, so she was not qualified to be a critic.

"You do look a little, ah, different," she said.

The word "different" was kinder than "younger" or "thinner," and the purpose of their meeting was not to undermine Lily but to offer her guidance.

"Honesty is the best policy," Gracie suggested.

As Gracie perused Lily's answers, she flashed back to her very brief but steamy romance with her deceased husband's friend Simon, who had met her at her worst. Forever stamped in Gracie's mind, Simon's intentions did not align with hers, and she made wiser decisions after that. Gracie imagined what Simon's profile would look like. Had both played the dating game, they would never have matched. Skipping the intimate details, Gracie briefly told Lily about Simon, her long marriage to Blair and moving in with Fred. It was not the twenty-six years with Blair but the two with Fred that were the most complicated. Although she and Blair grew into and out of their marriage, she knew exactly what she was facing when Fred proposed.

"I'd take any of them right now," Lily laughed haughtily.

She instantly apologized for her inappropriate comment. Lily and Gracie revised her profile answers, and by evening's end, most of it was accurate. When she pressed the Send button, she squealed. They toasted their efforts with more wine, and by bedtime, Lily was so excited she couldn't sleep.

Gracie took her time walking the two flights down to her own unit. She didn't see the package tucked into her door frame until it fell on the floor when she let herself in. On a sealed yellow envelope bearing the name of Mason's law firm, she saw "GRACE." It made her smile. Only after she prepared for bed and slid under her covers, did she open the envelope. Inside was a guidebook about The Bruce Trail, a popular hiking trail. She flipped through the guide to find one yellow sticker attached to a page that gave novice hikers advice. A pencilled circle marked the start of the trail, which was just a few kilometres away near the Niagara River. On the sticker, she recognized Mason's writing, which said,

> *As novices, we could start here ... and sunny skies are forecasted for the weekend.*
> *M.*

Gracie browsed through the paperback then read a bit of the history of this 880-kilometre trail, which ended in Tobermory, Ontario. The thought of spending a few hours with Mason excited her so much that she, like her neighbour two floors above her, had trouble settling herself to sleep.

November 15th
Weather forecast: warm and sunny

10:00 a.m.

"What seems to us as bitter trials are often blessings in disguise."

Oscar Wilde

Adrian sat restlessly in the passenger seat of his mother's car as she drove him from the airport to the hospital where his father had spent three nights following surgery to repair a fractured leg. Adrian felt most comfortable being the driver in any vehicle, and on the list of worst drivers he knew, his mother ranked second only to her own mother. As she weaved in and out of traffic, her lack of skill was compounded by her anxiety and unfamiliarity with her surroundings. Adrian opted to keep the conversation light, hoping they and those in proximity to his mother's vehicle would all arrive safely.

The hospital was an hour's commute from the airport in the opposite direction from the home that Adrian had grown up in, so by the time they arrived at the hospital, both Adrian and his mother were frazzled. He wondered how he would survive the three days he had booked off. After finding the orthopedic floor, his mother calmed down, cautioned Adrian to be prepared and entered the hospital room first as if to protect him.

Adrian's vision of his father, who was normally dressed in a department store suit with all hairs in place, lay asleep in a hospital gown, dishevelled and unshaven. One leg was in a cast to his hip and elevated on pillows. Both men were used to being in control, but neither was today. Adrian wasn't expecting to be as affected by his father's vulnerable appearance as he was. He stood quietly and absorbed what he saw. Both parents had aged considerably in the six months since Adrian was home. The silence was interrupted only by the beeps of medical equipment in the room. His mother slumped into the chair between the bed and the wall and wept quietly.

"What's wrong, Mom?"

"How am I going to look after him?" she asked through her tears.

Adrian had no idea how to respond.

"It's only temporary. He'll get better."

Adrian's father stirred, a painful expression breaking his sleep, and he opened his eyes. He looked first in the direction of the chair that his wife had occupied since his admission, and then to his son.

"Well, look who's here." His father's weak voice was forced from his throat.

Adrian moved closer to the bed and awkwardly shook his father's extended hand. He couldn't remember what their last conversation was about, only that it was unpleasant. His father attempted to shift his position and his gown without exposing himself, and his mother jumped out of her chair to help him. It appeared that they had gone through this routine a few times; Adrian's mother putting her own worries aside to help him. His father ignored her teary eyes and turned back to his son.

"Good flight?"

"Yup."

"Did you use your flight miles?"

"I did."

"That's good."

Their conversation continued about nothing meaningful for another twenty minutes until his father received another dose of pain medication. As his mother predicted, he fell asleep shortly after that. Adrian walked beside his mother as they left the floor, then he sat in a waiting area while his mother worked herself into a frenzy looking for her parking slip. Finding it in her pants pocket, she then tried to recall which floor in the parking garage she had parked on. Adrian reminded her it was the yellow floor, and she followed him until he showed her where she had parked. He suggested he drive her home.

"Your father won't like that," she said nervously.

"Why not?"

"He thinks you drive too fast."

"When's the last time he saw me drive?"

"I don't know, but he said I should drive."

"Well, what he won't know won't hurt him, right, Mom?"

Reluctantly, Adrian's mother surrendered her keys and her parking slip, and gave Adrian the exact amount to cover the parking cost. Adrian edged her domestic car out of the parking garage much slower than he would have driven his own import and was unimpressed by the effort the engine required to achieve the legal speed limit. Adrian's mother sat beside him, white knuckles clinging to her purse. He turned into the subdivision he knew well. Nothing had changed other than a new stop sign on a street he didn't expect. He slammed on the brakes, his expensive suitcase sliding off the back seat and hitting the back of his mother's seat before landing with a thump on the floor. His mother jumped, and Adrian resisted the urge to yell at her, like his father often did, to calm down. Both remained silent until he drove into their garage beside his father's newer, more expensive car. A little, well-worn car was parked on the street in front of their house.

As Adrian's mother composed herself, she misunderstood his intentions when he came around to her side of the vehicle. He retrieved his suitcase and checked it for damage before he realized his mother was still in the car. He opened the door for her.

"Thank you," she said, deciding to lie when her husband asked her who drove home.

Entering the house from the garage, Adrian was surprised again to see a middle-aged female dressed in a uniform in the kitchen of his parent's two-storey house.

"Hi Ida," his mother said. "How did it go?"

"Good. It's all good, Mrs. Common."

"That's reassuring. Ida, this is our son, Adrian. He lives in Canada, but he came home to see his father."

Adrian waved with his free hand after replacing his mother's keys on the hook where his parents had kept them forever. He placed his coat and shoes in the closet on the far right, where he had also parked them for years.

"Why, you are the spitting image of your father, Adrian."

"Thanks," he said, walking past her to the fridge.

There was no beer on the shelf where his father usually kept a few cans in the event that company came over. His mother, knowing what Adrian was looking for, looked at the clock, which was a half hour short of noon, and didn't re-direct him to the bar fridge in the garage.

"Ida, I think we can manage from here, but why don't you brew something hot for your drive?" his mother offered, seeing the unfamiliar travel mug on her counter.

"I'll do just that, thanks," she said.

She was familiar with where the tea and coffee was stored. While Adrian's mother stayed in the kitchen to send Ida off, Adrian walked to the living room, smelling the unfamiliar combination of powder and antiseptic. The chair where his father usually sat had been moved away from the window, and in its place was a powered lift chair. Dwarfed in the chair's seat was his maternal grandmother, who was staring blankly into the room. He approached her, stripped of whatever compliments he had intended to give her.

"Hi, Grammy," he said softly, leaning over closer to her face.

She looked at him, unblinking. Her expression didn't change. Adrian thought about the last time he saw her, which was at least six months ago. His mother paused at the kitchen doorway to watch Adrian watch her mother.

"It's me, Grammy, it's Adrian."

There was no response beyond the weariness in her eyes. Adrian's mother came over and took her hand, rubbing it gently until his grandmother looked at her. Her lips turned from a thin horizontal line to a tiny smile. When his mother kissed her on her forehead, the smile broadened.

"There we go," his mother cooed softly.

She transferred her mother's cold and gnarly hand into Adrian's firm, warm one. He didn't know what to do with it and felt strangely uncomfortable holding his own grandmother's hand—the same hand that had changed his diapers, and baked his favourite cookies.

"Why is she staring at me like that?"

"Because her brain can't process information like it used to."

As Adrian looked around the living room, the walls still resounded from lectures his father gave him, mostly deserved. His mother's voice was the same now as it was then. Alternating between anxiety and reassurance, but always kind. Patching up his mistakes to make them right, even when he was the one that was wrong.

"Then who's sending me the money?"

"I didn't want you to know how bad she was," his mother said, shrugging her shoulders. "You have such an important job. I thought it best not to distract you."

Adrian gently replaced his grandmother's hand in her lap and covered it with her blanket. He sat down on the sofa and absorbed what his mother just said. His mother had been caring for his Grammy for many months, and in a few days, her burden would be doubled when his father came home.

"How often does the helper come in? What was her name?"

"Ida. Usually once a week so I can run out and get groceries. Sometimes if I hurry, I can do a little shopping too. The kettle's hot. I'm making tea. Do you want some lunch? There's a pork chop and some potatoes left over from dinner."

"Sure. But I'll have coffee."

Adrian watched his mother return to the kitchen, put her hand on her back and lean heavily on the kitchen counter. Adrian got up and followed her.

"What's wrong with your back?"

"Oh, it's nothing. What do you want in your coffee?"

He was about to tell his mother he drank it black, when he hesitated. She had doted on him since his birth, much more than his sister. He was the only son, and if he bore the grandchildren his parents hoped for, he would carry on the family name. Today it was very obvious she was looking after everyone but herself. He leaned on the counter and watched her as she tried to straighten up without wincing.

"Mom, sit down. I'll make lunch."

"You can't do that. You were up so early."

Adrian clicked his tongue against his teeth and ignored his mother. She gave up, then sat at the small kitchen table and observed him muddle through the preparation of hot leftovers. As he placed two full plates in front of them, he remembered his grandmother.

"What about Grammy? What will she eat?"

"Ida fed her before we got home."

Adrian checked on his grandmother, who was sound asleep in her chair, legs elevated and mouth sagging open.

He sat down across from his mother, picked up his fork and saw that his mother remained still.

"What's wrong?" he asked.

"I think we should pray," she said softly.

Adrian hadn't prayed since his last meal with his family. He put his fork down, bowed his head and waited for his mother to start.

"Bless us, O Lord, and these, thy gifts which we are about to receive from Thy bounty through Christ our Lord, Amen. And God bless our dear Adrian, who is home with us. And, Amen again."

His mother struggled through her tears to finish the prayer. Adrian, who usually felt entitled and in control, kept his hands close to his face so his mother wouldn't notice that his lower lip was quivering.

12:30 p.m.

Gracie was up early and couldn't decide what to wear, what to do with her hair, how much make-up was appropriate to wear on a hike in November, and whether a hike fit the definition of a date.

Mason slept in and read the morning paper with his breakfast before picking Gracie up. He also wondered if a hike fit the definition of a date.

Gracie dabbed a bit of cologne on from a new sample she had no special reason to try before. She rarely wore cologne anymore. The scent was lovely but strong, so she washed some of it off. She used her bathroom one last time, hoping her bladder would co-operate with the availability of outhouses—or whatever a public trail would offer—before switching her phone to the silent mode and heading to the lobby to meet Mason.

She had packed energy bars, nuts, cheese and fruit in a weathered knapsack discarded by Tess. Mason, assigned to keep them hydrated, brought a thermos of coffee, some water and two cans of beer. Mason planned for a three-hour hike each way, which would give both parties ample time to gauge if this would be a pleasant or painful adventure. Or a date.

Early into their hike, Mason learned he was seven years older than Gracie. They spoke enough of their past marriages for Gracie to know how deeply committed he was to his wife. In between negotiating the trails and catching glimpses of curious wildlife, both shared the opinion that everlasting happiness was an elusive goal. They had accumulated enough life experience to be realistic, tread carefully and trust their own judgement. Mason's comfort level improved when Gracie said she was not chasing rainbows or an easy ride into her sunset years.

Celebrating their halfway point with food and drink, each silently but cautiously felt connected by a common sense of optimism. The hike back to Mason's car was enjoyable because the pressure of spending a day with someone new was gone. Mason delivered Gracie back to Park Street. Surprising himself, and after asking permission, he kissed Gracie lightly on her cheek, and after a tentative pause, very lightly on her lips. It was the first time he had wanted to kiss a woman since his wife passed away.

6:30 p.m.

Lily texted Gracie a few times, with no response, to tell her how elated she was that so many men tagged her profile. She owed many thanks to her. When she knocked on Gracie's door later in the day, she found she was still queasy from being so near to where Rosie passed away. When there was no answer, she returned to her Loft, made eggs and toast for dinner and began scrolling through her responses.

7:00 p.m.

Georgia handed Mitch the plate of homemade burgers to barbecue for dinner. It had been a week since he'd parked his truck in her driveway and his clothes in her basement. He calmed down, caught up on sleep and worked through a growing list of neglected chores. Sally did not respond to his texts, and until he saw his counsellor again, he was hesitant to do more than cover his portion of the condo expenses. His first counselling session involved unpacking his history, and as uneasy as he was answering the questions—because he was usually the one asking them, he felt some relief when it ended.

Today was the first day both Mitch and Georgia were off. They avoided any opportunity for physical contact. Georgia attended her book club and pottery classes, while Mitch stayed home, which for years had been their home.

Georgia had the table set and salad ready when Mitch brought the burgers in. They sat as far apart as the table allowed, exchanging small talk about what he repaired in the house.

"Good burgers. Thank you," Mitch said.

"They were good. Any word from Sally?"

"No."

"How's it going with Carrie?"

"My second session is tonight."

"Good. How's work?"

"Calm for a change."

"Do your buddies know you're here?"

"Only Stewy."

"You two have worked together for a while."

"He's a smart guy. He'll make a good sergeant one day."

Mitch helped Georgia clean up after dinner, and after their shoulders brushed against each other, he knew he was too close to her, so he left the room. He showered and left early for his appointment, opting to stop at the hardware store instead of driving by Park Street. He arrived early for his appointment, against the advice of the counsellor, and recognized another police officer leaving her office as he was parking his car. He regretted compromising a co-worker's privacy. A minute before his session, he called Carrie, who let him in.

The counsellor and client got right down to business. He shared that he was staying with Georgia, hadn't heard from Sally and whether she knew where he was staying.

"This is like trying to preserve fire in a bottle," she said. "Either it will shatter in your face, or if left long enough, it will melt. Neither outcome is good."

She commended him for his sobriety, continuing to work and meeting his financial obligations to both women.

She asked what he would say to Sally. He thought about their first months together, their insatiable sex and the silent cheers from his friends and co-workers when they met "such a pretty girl." He'd already told her countless times he was sorry. He'd asked for forgiveness and got none. His worst nightmare would be if she reported his hard grip on her jaw to the police, as there would be nothing more humiliating than his co-workers knowing about it. He felt that what women reported and what actually transpired were often interpreted differently.

Right now he knew he was safer at Georgia's, except for their lingering flame, which was as inviting as a warm bed on a cold November night.

9:00 p.m.

It had been a rough week since Sally had asked Mitch to leave. She hadn't done laundry, gone to work or eaten anything that required more than five minutes to prepare. Mitch left in a hurry, and in that haste, neglected to lock his office desk. Walking into Mitch's office brought flashbacks of her old boyfriend Robin hiding illegal files, which eventually led to Mitch entering her life. Contrary to what Mitch told her, his desk contents contained no case files or anything linked to his job other than his pension statements, insurance forms and expense claim records. What Sally did discover was that Georgia was still his beneficiary on his life insurance and his pension. And, as Sally predicted, he had never changed his will after they had married. The most influential men in her life—her father, Robin and Mitch—had all deceived her.

What Sally also accomplished this week was calling a new lawyer. And then she curled up in a blanket on her sofa where she had slept all week, wondering if Mitch had left the desk unlocked on purpose.

November 18th
Weather forecast: sunny and humid (in the southwest US)

11:45 a.m.

"Wisdom is easy to carry but difficult to gather."

Anonymous

Adrian offered to pick up his father from the hospital when he was cleared for discharge, so his mother could remain at home with his grandmother. A hospital bed and other medical equipment were set up in the family room, ready and waiting for him. A commode was placed discreetly behind the door, which his mother expected his father would need until he could safely navigate his walker to the powder room at the opposite end of the house.

Adrian parked his mother's car in the patient pick up zone and entered via the main entrance. In his pocket were explicit directions he didn't need that his mother had written on how to get to the orthopedic floor. His father had already been released and sat restlessly waiting for him in a wheelchair, with his left leg elevated. It took some effort for father and son to express their opinions about the best way to get in the car, and both men were exasperated by the time they were seated and on their way home. Their moods were subdued, and beyond Adrian's father telling him how to drive, there was no interaction.

Adrian backed his mother's car into the driveway to allow his father closer access to the front door. His mother literally circled around her husband until he was safely in the house, then exploded into tears after closing the front door. His parents embraced like re-united lovers, and Adrian was humbled by the bond they still shared. Adrian's sister Chrissy had arrived home, and the house had the same festive atmosphere he remembered in childhood. Something delicious was roasting in the oven, and all gathered around his father, who sat on display like a Christmas tree in his borrowed bed. For a change, Adrian was not the focus of his mother's attention. Chrissy shooed his mother out of the kitchen and Adrian, not quite sure where he belonged, escaped to the kitchen and hovered around Chrissy when his father needed the commode. Adrian dutifully set the table for a late lunch, followed his sister's orders to slice the bread thinly and found serving dishes in the china cabinet. His jaw dropped when Chrissy passed him the bowl of puree to feed his grandmother and told him to be sure she finished it without choking.

Adrian held the mush and bib in his hand, wanting to delegate this to his mother until he saw her sitting beside his father in bed, hand in hand and facing the window. He pulled the ottoman close to his Grammy, set her meal down and put her bib on. The expression on her face was unchanged until he touched her lips with the warm food as his sister had instructed him. Unaware his mother was watching, his grandmother slowly opened her mouth and he slid the first plastic spoonful in. She rolled the food around in her toothless mouth, swallowed it and opened her mouth for more. A tingle of accomplishment warmed him, like completing a difficult work project, until the bowl was empty. When she opened her mouth again and again, he returned to his sister for more food, who explained that it was a repetitive activity, and her declining brain function stopped sending the message that she had eaten enough.

The family said their prayers before their own meal, gave thanks for their day and ate as Adrian's grandmother slept in her chair, oblivious to the commotion around her. His father remained reserved but content, and for a change, Adrian did not feel the need to boast or say anything except that he was truly grateful for the family he had.

Adrian's flight itinerary meant he had to leave in about an hour, and he regretted leaving home for the first time in years. His mother didn't load him up with treats, and even his father wished him well instead of finding reasons to fault him. Adrian gently asked his mother not to send him his grandmother's money anymore. His sister offered to drive him to the airport, but Adrian knew her time would be better appreciated at home. When the cab pulled out of his parents' home, Adrian felt despondent but loved.

4:00 p.m.

Marcello brought the chicken cacciatore through Winnie's front door, which she had left open for him. The penne came second just as Winnie set her best wine glasses and china on the table. He poured the chardonnay and then grated parmesan cheese over their food. Winnie inhaled the steam from her feast, then raised her glass.

"With the exception of dinners at *The Capri*, I have never been so well-fed in my life. Here is to the chef and the weeds in his window," she said.

"And of course, don't forget the garlic!" he said with a graceful smile.

"To the garlic!" Winnie smiled, content with what she had accomplished that day.

Winnie had been unsettled since Annette's visit and had done some serious soul-searching. Earlier that day, she had walked over to Mason's office, unannounced, and ambushed him about her will. She was secure financially, even when factoring in a full-time caregiver in the event she needed one. Long before Alex passed away, he and Winnie appointed Mason as their executor and power of attorney to relieve their younger children of this burden. Her recent assessment at the hospital boosted her confidence that she wasn't losing her mind. She was determined to live independently until her doctors and Mason, but not her children, decided she needed a different level of care. Her trust in Mason had never wavered.

Her will currently divided her assets equally between Annette and Allen. Winnie already had names written on snippets of masking tape stuck under furniture and figurines with whom she bequeathed it to, which was not necessarily the person who wanted it. She also warned them to bicker about it after rather than before her death. She inventoried the contents of her jewellery box and taped that list of intended recipients to its bottom as well.

Before Annette left Winnie, she had shown her dozens of pictures of her and Allen's home renovations. Her children didn't need what she and Alex had worked hard for, but Winnie hoped her four intelligent grandchildren would have bright futures and be well-educated. So today she directed Mason to amend her will and establish a generous trust fund for each grandchild. Mason asked Winnie to take extra time to decide where the remainder of her estate would go.

Winnie shared her decision about leaving money for her grandchildren as opposed to her children with Marcello, who was very reluctant to offer any comments.

"But I want your opinion," Winnie responded.

"Regardless of your plan, my opinion is irrelevant because your children will continue to be part of your life and I won't," he said.

"And why not?"

"Ah, my friend, even though you have ten years on me, there are days where you are the younger one. My health does not allow me to do the things I used to do."

Winnie swept her hand across the meal they had just consumed.

"And who does this at your age?"

Marcello grinned, the wine mellowing his Italian dialect.

"My medication allows me to do this."

"What, a few pain pills here and there?"

Marcello's grin widened. He hid nothing from her.

"I take more than a few pain pills," he said.

Winnie walked over to her kitchen counter and returned with a blister pack of her medication. Annette had arranged the switch from pill bottles and ordered Mason to check her compliance.

"Don't tell me you take more than these."

"If we're competing, it's a tie. But after dinner, shall I beat you at Scrabble or mah-jong?"

Dinner progressed through easy debates, second helpings and loading the dishwasher together. They moved to more comfortable chairs by Alex's piano, which had been silent for years, where Winnie easily walloped Marcello in Scrabble. Winnie walked Marcello to the door and locked it behind him. Today was a very good day. She felt like she was back in control of her life again, and she was happy to have such a fine neighbour.

9:30 p.m.

Talia met a girlfriend for a run before working the afternoon shift, which allowed Bryce to successfully implement each of his cleaning rituals. Somewhat envious of her for running regularly, he was devoting more time to cleaning and less to his own fitness and leisure activities with friends.

Bryce also checked the huge withdrawal from their bank account for the sixth time today. Talia's tuition was the largest withdrawal that had been made since they moved in together. He had always been a bit of a miser, hoarding his money for some unknown future catastrophe. He was happy for Talia yet fearful that something could happen and they wouldn't be able to finance their way out of it. He had lost control of that.

Of Talia and Bryce's two bedrooms, Bryce claimed one as his, filling shelving units with broken appliances, old school books and assorted collections he refused to part with. Before Talia left today, she asked him to unclutter this room to allow her a corner to study, but he couldn't bring himself to part with anything more than duplicates of textbooks his college roommates left behind. Even though it compromised his own space, he appreciated that Talia needed some too. When she came home, brain drained of the capacity to do more than feed herself, she was disappointed. She didn't argue but went to bed. He returned to his room, and after an hour, managed to transfer a dead toaster and a laptop to their basement storage unit, which was already overstuffed with Bryce's other stashes. As he climbed into bed after Talia had fallen asleep, he promised himself to try harder to make her happier tomorrow.

11:00 p.m.

Lily was spinning with excitement in her Loft. She had posted enough good things on her profile to match her up with ten men. Ten! She sent them all identical messages about common interests and welcomed their response. Over three days, five ignored her message and five answered back. Five men! She paid her fee and baited them all with identical emails to gauge their response and avoid confusing herself. She reminded herself that she was new to this game and to tread carefully. She logged out of her email, turned on a yoga video and concentrated on calming herself down. She decided to give her five potential dates a few days to respond while she worked on herself. A face-to-face date might be just around the corner.

November 23rd
Weather forecast: partly sunny with mild winds

9:30 a.m.

As scheduled, Mason rang the lobby doorbell to Winnie's condo, and she let him in. Revised draft of her will in hand, he planned to review it with her before returning to the lobby to meet Gracie to hike another leg of the Bruce trail. Winnie, used to seeing him in a smart business suit, commented on his casual attire.

"It's Saturday, Winnie."

"Yes, it is. Why are you working on a Saturday?"

"I was in the neighbourhood and decided to drop by."

"It's a good thing because I'm not getting any younger. Did you bring the will?"

"I did."

"Did you tell my kids?"

"I didn't."

Winnie directed him to the sofa, and he unpacked the coffee and raisin scones from the same bakery where she and his mother would meet to gossip on Saturday mornings.

"Well, Mason, can I afford to educate all of my grandkids?"

"Every one of them."

"And will there be anything left over after someone helps me with my bath when I get old and decrepit?"

"There will be."

"Then that's good enough for me."

The lawyer and his client reviewed the draft. Her judgement was sound and her intentions sincere, but he was concerned when Winnie leaned back in the sofa and asked his advice about leaving a small amount for Marcello.

"I can advise you, not only as your advocate but as someone who cares about you," he said, letting the statement marinate for a moment.

"Go on," prodded Winnie.

"He seems like a nice person, but you've known him for less than three months."

"He's more than nice. He's kind and honest, and he watches over me more than my children do."

"Well, in fairness to them, they live far away."

"That's not my fault. Did you know their secretaries send my birthday cards? And the flowers?"

Mason knew she was correct. She told him her cards arrived buried in bigger envelopes from her children's office addresses.

"I'm not making excuses for them, but some people do that because it's a business expense."

"Hah, so I'm also their tax deduction?"

Winnie also told him that when she interrogated the local florist, she said that Annette and Allen's receptionists ordered them. Mason felt a stab of guilt when his own mother refused to accept flowers from him after finding out that Aida sent them. It was also the last time he did that.

"Sometimes they're busy, Winnie."

"Mason, I'm their mother, not their customer."

"Is that why you're excluding them from your will?"

"That's part of it."

"Are you comfortable sharing any other reasons?"

"Because they forced me to leave my home," she snipped, folding her arms across her chest defiantly. "They told me the market was hot and I had no choice but to act on it. They made me move here against my wishes."

"I can appreciate your frustration," he replied, recalling the scenario well.

"But the good news is that I found Marcello—or rather, he found me. A new friend who is just steps away. He keeps me safe, feeds me and asks for nothing in return. Not even an onion. So, he deserves at least something."

"Does he visit often?"

"Almost daily."

This was news to Mason.

"And does he ever make you feel uncomfortable?"

She cocked her head and frowned.

"Uncomfortable? In what way? You're not going to ask me again if he wants to have sex with me?"

Mason struggled to keep a straight face.

"That's not what I mean. Does he ever ask you things that you feel he's not entitled to know?"

"Never. Never. Never."

"You seem pretty clear about that."

"I am. The best thing this man did was to disobey me and call 911 when I fell."

"As you said, he was worried. I would have done the same thing."

Winnie raised her eyebrows.

"That's beside the point. If I hadn't slid off the bed and landed on my noggin, I wouldn't have had all those stupid tests in that hospital meeting room. But Mason, those tests were the best thing that could have happened. When you brought me here on moving day, I cried myself to sleep. I missed Alex so much, and I was convinced my body and my brain would rot here. I wasn't eating, I wasn't sleeping, I didn't know what time it was. And I lost hope."

"I'm sorry to hear that."

"I thought I was losing my mind. And then I met Marcello. He was just as miserable and lonely as I was. And you know what he told me?"

"I'm curious," Mason replied, although he wasn't.

"He said I was depressed. When he told me that, I wanted to smack him right upside his head."

Mason laughed in spite of himself, then quickly regained his composure. Winnie forged on.

"Then he told me about Valentina."

"And who's Valentina?"

"His fiancée in Italy."

"His fiancée?"

"Yes sirree. She strung him along forever then dumped him. She decided to stay in Venice with her mama," said Winnie, full of fire. "He became depressed and wanted to die. Just like I did. I always thought about my future, until there wasn't one." Mason's eyes softened because he also remembered that painful feeling. "When I was down, he made me the best soup. And do you remember the day when I lost my dinner all over the kitchen floor? He cleaned up after me. And one night when I was convinced I was going to die, he stayed with me all night."

"All night?" Mason said, raising his eyebrows.

"All night long," Winnie said, arching her own eyebrows in response.

"I'm afraid to ask where he slept."

"Then don't," she said with a wink.

"Oh God, Winnie, not in your bed ..."

Winnie didn't respond and Mason didn't want to know.

Mason gathered his documents and left a little more rattled than when he'd walked through her door. They agreed Winnie needed to do a little more thinking about how to disperse the rest of her assets, but she was adamant about including a little something for Marcello.

10:30 a.m.

Mason met Gracie in the building foyer, a more neutral setting than the dozen or so steps between Winnie's and Gracie's front doors. He also wanted to leave Winnie's documents and his briefcase at his office rather than in his car at a public trail. Gracie packed their lunch and came down to the lobby after Mason texted her that he was there. As previously, Mason was in charge of refreshments.

Mason parked on the street in front of his office. He gave Gracie the option of coming in with him, and, after disarming the security system, he held the door for her. His office decor represented the era when he and his two associates first established their practice. Judging by their portraits on the wall, they were called to the bar at about the same age. Behind his desk on a credenza sat five pictures, three of a formally-dressed Mason holding different awards. The fourth picture looked like a standard cruise photograph of a smiling, youthful Mason with a woman of similar age. The last picture was a formal portrait of the same couple.

"She was a beautiful woman," Gracie said, smiling.

"She was. We had everything, except children," he responded, thinking this would be an opportune time to disclose more about his wife.

"I'm sure it was a devastating loss."

"It was. One evening she fell off a step-stool while she was reaching for something in an upper kitchen cupboard. She got up, put the stool away, took a headache pill and went upstairs to sleep. I heard her get up during the night, assuming she was going down to the kitchen for another pill. But then she fell down the whole damn flight of stairs and lost consciousness."

"Oh no!"

Gracie watched the pained expression on Mason's face as he repeated the story.

"What made it worse was that the MRI showed that a leaking brain aneurysm had affected her balance and may have caused her to fall. That was compounded by the brain injury from falling off the step-stool and then down the stairs."

Mason sat down behind his desk, and Gracie took the chair facing him. She noticed the small tremor in his hands as he spoke.

"That's terrible."

"She survived only twenty more hours," he said, breathing heavily, looking at the ceiling and working hard to maintain his composure.

"I'm so very sorry," she whispered.

Mason closed his eyes and bridged his thumb and forefinger across the top of his nose. Gracie sat quietly, giving him some space to recover.

"We don't need to go hiking today," she suggested.

"That's very kind of you to say that."

"I can walk home and let you rest."

"I think it would do us both good to carry on as planned."

"I actually agree with you."

"Then shall we?"

Mason locked up, and the pair drove quietly to their destination. Because they arrived an hour later, they shortened their hike and returned before sunset. Their conversations were more subdued, ending with Mason declining Gracie's offer to make an easy dinner. Dropping her off at her front door, he thanked her for tolerating his quiet mood. She let herself out, and the closest thing to any exchange of intimacy was a cordial wave goodbye.

6:30 p.m.

Gracie walked into the lobby to find Lily, smartly dressed in a new, simple black dress, high heels and her mother's pearls, pacing the floor.

"Wow. Look at you! I barely recognized you," Gracie remarked as she held her muddy hiking boots in one hand and her knapsack in the other.

"I've got a date!" Lily squealed. "How do I look?"

"Amazing," Gracie said, surveying her own soiled clothes.

"Where have you been? Digging in the dirt?"

"You're sort of right. I went hiking with a friend."

"Did she get as dirty as you did?"

"Yup," Gracie said, purposely keeping her companion's identity to herself.

"You probably deserve dinner more than I do."

"Don't be so hard on yourself. You also deserve a nice night out. Where's dinner?"

"His place. He's barbecuing."

Gracie flinched, thinking of her own safety protocols.

"Have you met him before?"

"Nope. First date."

"Aren't you breaking the dating site's safety rules about always meeting somewhere in public?"

"Grace. Look at me. I'm forty-five years old and forty pounds overweight. I can't be too choosy."

"Not being choosy and not being safe are two different things. When is he picking you up?"

"In fifteen minutes," Lily said, checking her phone.

"Do you know where he lives?"

"Somewhere near the falls."

"Why don't you call him and tell him you'll drive yourself there? Then at least if you arrive and get the feeling that all is not as it seems, you can just keep driving."

"We've only emailed each other."

"So, am I understanding that you don't know where he's coming from, where you're going and you have no phone number?"

Lily unlocked her phone and turned a picture of a presentable looking male towards Gracie.

"Does this face look dangerous?"

"Lily, just because he looks good doesn't mean he won't hurt you."

"You're making me nervous."

"I'd rather scare you than bury you," Gracie said, instantly regretting how she phrased her statement.

Lily re-considered her plan.

"What if I email him and he doesn't respond?"

"Then he might be driving. Still, I would think very carefully about getting in that vehicle."

"Now you're really scaring me."

"Good. Mission accomplished." Gracie pointed to Lily's phone. "Go ahead. Email him, and I'll wait until he shows up."

"What for? What are you going to do?"

"What do you think I should do?"

Lily stared blankly at Gracie.

"Maybe take a picture of his car?" Lily asked.

"That's a start," Gracie said, nodding in an exaggerated motion. "And then take a picture of his license plate and of him. Hopefully he's enough of a gentleman to come in and get you—or at least open your door for you."

Lily typed furiously, pressed the send key and looked anxiously at Gracie for more direction.

"Okay. So you're staying with me until he gets here?"

"I'm not moving," Gracie said.

She dropped her boots and knapsack on the floor, then checked the backside of her pants before sitting down. Lily resumed pacing.

7:05 p.m.

Both Lily and Gracie heard the big pickup truck before they saw it stop at the curb, and both approached the entrance like window shoppers at a jewellery sale. They stared at a mid-sized man, dressed in jeans and a navy sweater covering a protruding belly get out; Lily grabbed her coat and purse.

"Not so fast," Gracie cautioned. "Why don't you ask him to come in?"

"Why?"

"So we can compare him to his picture."

"What difference does that make?" Lily asked, then gasped. "Oh, shit!"

"What?"

"He doesn't look like his picture. Look. Here he comes."

"Give me your purse."

"Why?"

"Just give it to me."

Lily relented, handing her purse to Gracie. Holding it as collateral, Gracie shoved her chair deep into the lobby corner and crouched into it, wishing the man would come in so she could quickly evaluate him before he spotted her. Lily opened the outer and vestibule doors. Gracie heard Lily's voice but was unable to see the pair or hear their conversation until the inside lobby door opened.

"Just let me get my purse," Lily said, then waved her hand impatiently as Gracie reluctantly handed over her purse. Lily disappeared through the door as Gracie snapped a few blurry pictures of Lily awkwardly climbing into the black truck, stressing the slit in the back of her dress. Gracie couldn't see the vehicle make or the license plate as it sped off. Like an overprotective mother, Gracie texted Lily to send her at least the address when she arrived so Gracie could rescue her or call police if she felt unsafe.

Gracie gathered her belongings, unlocked her front door and set her soiled boots on a newspaper outside it. She stripped down to her underwear and ran a hot bath, hoping to soothe her muscles and her mind. She kept her phone close and tried to relax.

Feeling slightly better after bathing, she donned her bathrobe but set out fresh clothes on her bedroom chair in case she needed to rescue Lily. She ate some toast with peanut butter, then crawled into bed with a steaming mug of herbal tea; it was much earlier than her usual bedtime. She opened the new book she had brought home yesterday, but she couldn't concentrate. Her phone pinged, and she sat up. The text from Mason said, "My apologies for doing little to cultivate our friendship. I wasn't the best company." Gracie thought for a minute before tapping her reply.

"I was glad you shared your day with me. Looking forward to the next one."

"Have a peaceful evening."

"Goodnight."

She put the book down and watched an old *Seinfeld* episode and the evening news with her lights off. Still wide awake at midnight, Gracie blamed Lily for how she would feel in the morning.

November 24th
Weather forecast: high winds and snow squalls

8:30 a.m.

"Get back on the horse and ride again."

Old Adage

Gracie readied herself for work. Her tired muscles and a look outside at the blowing snow persuaded her to drive instead of walk. She left her hiking boots from the night before in the hallway, opting to clean them and put them away after work. Lily had not responded, and Gracie weighed her options as she scraped enough crusty snow off her car windows to get herself safely to work. Because Rose perished from a foolish trust in someone, Gracie expected Lily to be more cautious around others. She decided to wait until her lunch-break before texting her. She may well have had an exciting evening with her new date and even spent the night. Gracie thought about her own naïvety when she accepted Simon's offer to stay at his house until her place became available. It was a lesson in how a one-night stand could last for ten days.

10:00 a.m.

Lily rolled over, relieved to be in her own bed rather than with the dude from last night. Gracie instilled enough fear in her to be cautious, yet when her date picked her up, she remained excited about her evening. Even though he was not the man in the dating profile, she gave him the benefit of the doubt because, after all, her own picture did not accurately represent her. It wasn't until he began having difficulty finding his way around the kitchen that she sensed the house they were in was not his. A trip to the bathroom led to a peek in the medicine cabinet which held pill bottles prescribed to someone with a different name. By then, two glasses of wine were seeping into her bloodstream. Dinner was commercially-made burgers and hot dogs served with a boxed salad, which she gladly ate to help dilute the buzz in her head. Her date kept his distance until after dinner, when he sat down and patted the spot on the sofa beside him. By then, he was much less handsome. She chose a nearby chair where he couldn't reach her. She declined a third glass of wine but watched him finish his and switch to beer as she planned her exit.

Lily complimented her date's barbecuing, and for lack of a better idea, went to the bathroom again. Her stomach was upset. She waited a full two minutes and returned to her chair in the living room.

"I was hoping you would sit beside me," he said.

"I think I should sit here for a bit," Lily said, splaying her hands over her stomach.

"There's more room here," he said, winking at her.

"I know you would prefer me to sit here for a while."

"Why?"

Lily's thoughts flashed quickly to a recent TV advertisement.

"Gas. I'm feeling a bit gassy," she said.

"What?" he asked and took a big swig of his beer.

"Your hot dogs were delicious, but I have sensitive bowels."

"What does that mean?" he asked, unimpressed.

"I forgot how bloated hot dogs make me," Lily said, treading carefully.

"Are you kidding me?"

"I wish I was. And I can see you worked so hard to make such a nice meal," she gushed. "Excuse me, but I have to use the bathroom again."

She got up as he guzzled his beer.

"You've been there twice already," he muttered as she closed the bathroom and locked it.

After silently counting to thirty, she put both hands across her inflated cheeks and stood close to the door. Slowly, she pushed against her cheeks to make a sound that she felt very effectively mimicked a prolonged fart. She waited a bit longer, washed her hands, took her time drying them and left the bathroom.

Her date was back in the kitchen with a new can of beer, far away from the bathroom.

"I apologize, but I need to go home and take my medication," she lied.

By then, he had written off the evening. Lily pretended to call a cab and not aggravate him further by asking the address. With two beers and a lot of wine lubricating him, she knew she was safer finding her own way home.

Lily apologized again and escaped, not realizing he had locked the door until she left. Her date kept his distance, never leaving the kitchen. Waddling in high heels and wearing a coat that was too small and inappropriate for the weather, she planted each step carefully on the slippery sidewalk until she reached a convenience store almost a block down the street. Shivering but intact, she called a taxi and gave the dispatcher the address the clerk gave her. She stamped the snow off her shoes as she arrived home, then figured it was better to take them off to climb the two flights of stairs to her Loft.

Lily assumed Gracie went to bed early after her hike, so she delayed texting her until the morning. She put a movie on, warmed up with hot chocolate and thanked her lucky stars for arriving home unscathed. Her face illuminated from the bright images on the television screen, she promised herself to ask Gracie's advice before planning her date with Match #2.

5:15 p.m.

Mitch arrived at the condo as pre-arranged with Sally. On the advice of her lawyer, Sally texted him the day before to pick up his clothes and personal effects while she was at work. She asked Sonny, the building manager, to change her locks, let Mitch in and remain with him until he left. As a courtesy, Sally left empty banker's boxes for him to use. When he walked in, Mitch was immediately offended by the new deadbolt and a second security lock on the fire escape door.

Sonny sat at the kitchen island and watched Mitch, who packed up his office first. Sally had left his will and other documents appointing Georgia as his beneficiary on top of his desk. After years in policing, he was certain Sally's lawyer had instructed her to make copies of everything she felt was important as well as a list of what was not so important. Mitch's desk contents filled one box, and arrangements were made with Sonny to pick up his father's desk and a few other heavy items. Packing took less than an hour, and while Sonny helped him carry the boxes to his truck, he asked again about Rosie's death. Mitch repeated the same concern about the transient drug underworld. Because of the fire, there was little evidence to work with. Sonny lingered, worrying aloud about his four teenagers.

"Are they home most nights?" Mitch asked him, recalling his own sons' misadventures.

"They've got a curfew. They hate it, but they stick to it."

"Good. Do you see them most nights?"

There were countless nights his boys were asleep before he got home.

"Dinner is at six, and nobody breaks that rule unless they're working or playing hockey."

"Sounds like you're doing a great job, Sonny."

Mitch pulled a fifty-dollar bill from his wallet, which he would normally have spent on beer. He offered it to Sonny who kept his hands in his pockets.

"No strings attached. Just take this, and buy your kids a pizza," Mitch said. "And tell them that you love them, no matter what."

Sonny looked around, then took the money discreetly just before both men saw Sally drive into the building's parking lot. Because she and Mitch shared adjacent spots, her options were to choose someone else's spot or park in hers. Always one to follow rules, she backed into her designated spot so her door opened away from Mitch's truck. Sonny stayed put, eager to support or defend either party. Sally exited her car, purse and lunch tote in hand. She stood at her door, remembering her lawyer's advice to avoid any confrontation. Sonny spoke up as Sally worked to avoid eye contact with her husband.

"I just helped your, ah, Mitch with the boxes."

"I can see that," Sally said softly.

After sixteen days apart, Sally looked haggard. Instead of her fluffy blonde hair framing her face, it was tied back, which made her greying roots more visible. She wore little make-up, and no rings. Her clothes hung loosely under her open coat.

"I've got to check the furnace room. Anything I can carry in for you?" Sonny asked, offering her protection without being direct.

Sally looked at Mitch and sensing no danger, she thanked Sonny and dismissed him. He sauntered to the building's side maintenance door, glancing back to capture Sally's nod that she felt safe. Mitch, aware and humiliated by that interaction, leaned against the cargo bed of his truck and shuffled a few boxes around. He chose his words wisely, expecting Sally would have also been educated to report any litigious comments. The longer and more awkward the minutes, the colder and darker it felt. Mitch, having done this before, finally spoke, starting with a safe topic.

"How was work?"

"Same as usual."

"Anything you need?"

"No."

"Do you want to talk?"

"No."

"For what it's worth, I'm seeing someone," Mitch said.

She glared at him, confused and hurt, until he quickly clarified his statement.

"A therapist."

Her expression went flat again.

"Good."

"Look, I'm sorry."

"For what?"

"For everything."

"You're a little late for that."

Their conversation ended there, and Sally wondered how she had become so mesmerized by this man who she now despised. She locked her car and walked briskly to her front door, still monitored by Sonny from his tiny, barred window in the furnace room.

With both parties dispersed, Sonny went back outside and cleaned up garbage. He collected discarded drug paraphernalia in the shrubs around the building's perimeter, then walked half a block and tossed it into a large dumpster behind the nearby bus stop. He carried on his routine, feeding the cats living under the railway bridge. Someone else was still replenishing the straw and water supply. The meagre profits he made from selling his mother's fentanyl patches to buy cat food was much easier than listening to his wife chastise him for wasting good money. But since Rosie's death, he was becoming more concerned about selling the patches, even though his "regular" buyer swore he only used it for himself.

5:45 p.m.

Gracie came home from work; her dirty hiking boots were still on the mat outside her door. Lily had finally texted her that she was fine, and needed more advice before going out on another date. Gracie put her things down on the counter, changed into comfy clothes and retrieved her boots from the hallway. She walked to the balcony and slapped one hiking boot against the other. A bit of the dry mud fell away and dropped onto the bushes below. Reaching deeper into her boots to grab them more firmly and avoid dropping them, her fingers touched something. A pale yellow envelope was tucked into one boot. As she pulled it out, she recognized Mason's handwriting. She opened the envelope, a variation of the floral card he'd previously given her. His note read:

Still feeling badly about yesterday.
We'll chat soon.
M.

Not sure how to interpret the note, she kept whacking her hiking boots against each other until the rest of caked mud came off.

6:00 p.m.

Mitch pulled into Georgia's driveway and opened the garage door with the remote she had issued him earlier, his reward for getting rid of the junk in his old bay. He stacked boxes along the back, save for the important files from his desk. By now, the neighbours recognized Mitch's truck, but neither he nor Georgia were offering explanations.

Georgia arrived home from work and parked in her own garage bay. She walked by the boxes and into her house just as Mitch was kicking off his shoes, still holding the remaining box. She kept her thoughts to herself, knowing his emotions were raw before he retrieved his things. Mitch placed the box on a bookshelf in the basement and returned upstairs. Tempted to open a beer, he made coffee instead as Georgia went to change from her work clothes. He sat on the sofa, spent, and looked down the hall to see his first wife, in her worn housecoat, cross the hall from her bedroom to the bathroom. Restless, he stood up and looked outside across the street at his old neighbourhood. Not much had changed since he left, except now his salary was paying for two residences and he was borrowing a small corner of one.

He returned to the sofa and sat down again. Glancing down the hall, he heard the shower and saw that the bathroom door was slightly ajar. An unexpected rush stirred his loins. He sat for a few more minutes trying to reason why she'd left the door open. Arguing with himself, he stood up, went to the front window again, then padded silently down the carpeted hallway, stopping just before the door. He heard the sound variations of the water as it splashed against Georgia's skin. Edging closer, he saw the round curves of her silhouette in the steam; he fought the desire to undress and join her. Instead, he returned to his side of the sofa, sitting down just as he heard the water shut off.

Georgia emerged from the bathroom soon after, hair in a towel and bathrobe wrapped tightly around her waist, the heady scent of body wash and shampoo stoking his fire. Georgia returned to the bathroom and dressed in yoga pants and one of their son's old school T-shirts. He heard the hair dryer, and some cupboards were opened and closed a few times before she came into the living room and sat opposite him on the sofa. Her face was still flushed from the shower. He could easily reach over and touch her.

"I haven't planned anything for dinner yet. Any suggestions?" Georgia asked.

"I'm good with whatever. We can order out," he responded hoarsely, fighting his urge to say something more.

Georgia picked her phone up and scrolled through some local eatery menus.

"Are you okay with Japanese?"

She looked at him for approval and then stared at her phone without moving the screen. Then she looked back at him and studied his face. He watched her breathe deeply, part her lips as if to speak, then say nothing. He waited, knowing that once they crossed that fragile line, things would change. She switched her phone to the silent mode, turned it over and put it down. She slowly placed her arm along the top of the sofa so that her hand was easily touchable if he did the same. And he did. He reached over and kissed her palm, inhaling her clean skin. He moved closer to her, kissing the inside of her forearm where it still felt like velvet. She moaned softly and leaned into him, feeling his fingers gently touch her hair. He pulled her closer and she responded. He kissed her on her lips, which he hadn't done in years. He remembered their early years together when just a brush against her skin would make him want her.

Georgia moved her lips across the grey stubble on his lower cheek. There was more definition in the lines on his face, but in his eyes she saw a different need, more than passion. Perhaps companionship, and maybe some of the good in him that he lost somewhere along the way. She kissed him back, deep with desire and the longing that was lost when their marriage did not survive the changes that came with time.

"I'm not sure this is a smart thing to do," she whispered.

He responded by kissing her lips again. Then he moved to her forehead and put his hands on her face before moving on to kiss her neck and her ears.

"Look at me, Mitch," she said quietly, her own need increasing.

Mitch drew back and looked at her chin.

"Look here, in my eyes."

He glanced directly at her, then away.

"I know that's hard for you to do."

Mitch looked at her slowly.

"There we go. We can do this, but it can't be just about sex anymore. It's the canary in the coal mine, and it's dangerous for both of us."

Mitch pulled away and sat up straight.

"Come back here," she said, watching his shoulders sag. She took his hand and felt the tension in it. "You're not listening."

Mitch moved closer because it was easier to avoid confrontation than face it. His physical desire was waning.

"You left the door open when you showered," he said.

"I've left the door open since the boys moved out."

"Oh."

"Did you think I left it open for more than to let the air circulate?"

"I didn't know what to think."

There was a long pause, and, feeling the hand she was still holding relax, Georgia moved closer to Mitch.

"Look, if you're willing to give this another go, then I'm willing to do my part. But this time, we're not hiding behind the boys or our jobs, anyone or anything else. If we're on the same page, maybe we can grow this relationship again from our mistakes."

After three sessions with the counsellor, who mirrored what Georgia just said in more technical terms, Mitch knew he had some serious decisions to make. Sally had already made the first one for him, and Georgia offered him the second. Georgia leaned back on the sofa and opened her arms to him. Hesitantly at first, he leaned into her. They shifted positions a few times until he eventually laid down on the sofa on his back with his head on her lap. He looked up at her, and she outlined the features on his face with her finger, slowly calming him. She felt the tension ease out of his shoulders and his weight grow heavy against her.

"I did some homework," she said.

"Oh no. What kind of homework?"

"Statistics. Research."

"Oh?"

"Do you want to hear about it?"

"Sounds complicated. Do I have to think?"

"Nope."

"Do I have to listen?" he asked, eyes closed.

"Nope," she smiled as she ran her fingers through his fine hair. "You've just had some caffeine, so you should be wide awake."

"Okay. I'll listen."

"Did you know that most couples who divorce each other and then reunite stay together?"

"No."

"The key word is 'most.'"

"What made you look that up?"

"Because in my heart, I think you're here for a reason, and it's not just for a place to park your butt until you find someone new."

"Are you telling me you're not just my port in the middle of this storm?" he asked, almost comically.

Georgia thought about his statement and decided it wasn't said to offend her. She circled his lips with her index finger.

"What I meant was that you're the lighthouse. And I'm the lighthouse keeper."

"Ah."

She paused, then became serious.

"Neither of us want a future to re-create our past. We've grown far beyond that."

"I agree," Mitch said.

"If you take me as I am, not as you think you want me to be, there's hope for us. I am now my own person, not your person."

"I'm sorry."

"We're both sorry."

"I failed you. I failed the boys."

"We both failed, especially the 'until death do us part' clause."

"You've got this all figured out."

"I wouldn't have opened the door two weeks ago if I hadn't."

December 1st
Weather forecast: snow flurries

Unit 2A
10:00 a.m.

"We have one life to live, and it goes by rather quickly."

Anonymous

Talia was still fuming from earlier that morning. She and Bryce had re-negotiated his deadline twice to clean up the second bedroom so she could study undisturbed. He did nothing but shuffle things around. When he suggested she use the library—or worse, the conference room at work—she blew up. So far what she had learned in her leadership courses was ineffective on Bryce. He called her out for trying to manage him, and she was losing patience. She was starting to wonder what he did at home on the days she worked other than cleaning. He never went anywhere and had distanced himself from his friends. He stopped running, and when she asked about his day, he always said it was fine. Some days when she got home, he was still wearing the pajamas he'd slept in. He looked distressed if she arrived home early. One of her friends suggested she leave her laptop camera on at home when she went out, which Talia knew would break their trust. Her parents divorced over trust, and she wasn't going down that road. At least he always went to work.

Despite this morning's war, he went through his usual routines, then headed off to work.

Talia loved Christmas, and to offset her misery, she decided to start decorating today. Full of adrenaline, she ran down the two flights of stairs from their condo to the basement storage lockers, which were converted from jail cells when the building was a police station. The lockers still had the original barred metal doors. Another surge of frustration fueled her when she began to rummage through more of Bryce's stuff in their locker to get to her decorations. They would be impossible to access unless she moved some of Bryce's boxes into the hall. Determined to get this done, she tried to lift the first two boxes together and couldn't. One at a time, she moved a dozen weighty boxes into the hall, having no idea what they contained. A half hour later, still with no pathway to her decorations, she kicked a box in frustration. Met with solid resistance, she yelled out in pain, followed by a long string of profanity.

Adrian didn't hear Talia until he opened the basement fire door and wheeled his bicycle down the hall to store it in his own unit. He was surprised to find anyone there, and then hear the barrage of words more suited to rival fans at a hockey game. Unable to wheel his bike beyond the blocked hallway, he would normally spit words back, but hearing a female yelling like that humoured him. He propped his bike against the wall and made enough noise to let the culprit know she had company. When Talia popped her head up over the boxes, Adrian was the last person she expected or wanted to see. Adrian still had her video on his phone.

"I'm surprised you know all those words," he said, grinning.

"I didn't expect anyone to hear me," she scoffed.

"You look like you could use some help."

He could only see her head behind stacked boxes, hair clipped up and bobbing when she moved. He hoped for a better view.

"I'll be fine," she said, wincing as she took a step.

"Are you okay?"

"I will be. I just stubbed my toe."

Talia didn't like Adrian standing in the doorway and blocking her exit.

"I want to store my bike, but my unit is on the other side of your boxes."

"Sorry. I'm trying to get some decorations out. When I find them, I'll put everything back. Can you come back in an hour?"

Adrian saw her pain when she tried to walk.

"With that foot, it'll take more you than an hour."

"I'll manage," she said defensively.

"Your man should be helping you," he said, not letting up.

"If I need help, I'll call him," she lied, not wanting Adrian to know Bryce was working.

After this morning, she didn't want either to help. Accepting Adrian's help might mean more than a thank you. Re-positioning her foot caused another stab of pain, which Adrian couldn't ignore. She felt her foot tightening in her sneakers.

"Last call," he offered, and she ignored him.

It was like a stand-off with no winners.

He spoke again, putting his hands on his hips.

"I don't really want to carry this bike back up two flights of stairs, and you don't think you need any help. So, maybe I'll leave it here, and when I come back in about a half an hour, if you're still here, you can put your foot up and tell me what to move, and where. Is that fair? No strings attached. I promise."

Talia shrugged her shoulders, which he took as a concession.

Adrian left a defiant Talia stranded where she was, confident she wouldn't resolve her dilemma in thirty minutes. He climbed the stairs two at a time, brushed his teeth and checked his messages. He walked to the specialty coffee shop around the corner and picked up one black coffee and a caffè latte. Exactly thirty minutes later he returned, whistling loudly, to find his bike moved beyond a narrow passage of boxes littering the hall.

He found her there perched on a box with her right shoe off, assessing her bruised and swollen great toe. Her red running shorts ended where her well-toned legs met her hips. A snug white T-shirt from a charity run outlined her perfect shape. Beads of sweat glistened on her forehead, and she looked defeated. He extended both hands to offer her a choice.

"Black or latte?"

She sighed, exhaled through pursed lips and accepted the latte. He sat down on the concrete floor about six feet across from her.

"Thank you," she said.

"I'm impressed with what you accomplished."

"Obviously not enough."

"Did you find your decorations?"

"One box. There's two more on the bottom right against the back wall."

"Would you have any objections if I got them out for you?" he asked politely.

He seemed less arrogant than at their last encounter, but she remained guarded.

"I guess not. They're labelled."

Adrian put his coffee down and weaved cautiously through the boxes until he pointed to the ones she needed. He began lifting Bryce's heavy boxes.

"What the ... ? What's in these? Bricks?" he asked, amazed that she had moved what she did.

"Old books, I think," she sighed.

"That's quite the collection."

"He refuses to part with them. Or anything."

"I'm sensing some frustration."

"I'd rather not discuss it."

"I apologize. It's none of my business."

Adrian navigated the cramped path to lift and carry Talia's two boxes out of the cell and park them beside the other one in the hall. They were the lightest ones he had lifted. He then moved another heavy and unlabelled box and set it down on the floor apart from all the others.

"If you sit here, I'll move the rest of these that you don't need back in your storage cell," he offered.

Talia looked at him, trying to judge his real intentions. He looked back, bearing an apprehensive smile. She stood up, and with one bare foot, limped to the spot Adrian set up for her. He passed her cup back to her, her cold fingers briefly touching his.

"I know I'm not in a pleasant mood, but I do appreciate this."

"My pleasure," he said, gulping his coffee, then tackling his next assignment.

As Adrian started putting the boxes back, he noticed each box had a tiny, pencilled number in one corner.

"Am I supposed to be replacing these in a specific order?"

"No. Why?"

"Because they're numbered."

"What?"

"They have numbers in the corner," he said, picking up the Christmas box closest to her and examining it. "Except there are no numbers on this one, nor on your second or third box."

"Fuck."

"There's that word again."

"These are mine," she said, pointing to the three beside her.

"And those?"

"They're his."

"He's ordering."

"Pardon?"

"He's ordering, which is an OCD trait. Same as hoarding. And cleaning," he said matter-of-factly.

Talia stared at him blankly.

"One of my university roommates had it. Really bad."

She leaned back heavily against the concrete wall. She looked less angry but more morose. Adrian decided not to elaborate more on his friend's rituals. He waited to see if she would.

"So, am I putting these back in numerical order?" he asked innocently, bringing Talia back to the present.

"No. Please no. Just put them back."

Talia sat quietly and processed how she managed to adapt to Bryce's behaviours as Adrian obediently restacked his boxes. He locked her cell for her, feeling a rush when his hand crossed over hers to return her key. Talia watched Adrian's well-defined muscles move under his sweat-drenched T-shirt as he wheeled his bike into his storage cell. He then stacked her boxes of decorations on top of each other and picked them up. Together they weighed less than one of Bryce's.

"You lead the way," he said, carrying the boxes awkwardly to avoid hitting Talia as he watched her navigate the stairs.

Her movements looked painful, and despite wanting to walk near her, he worried about her stumbling. Both were winded when they reached the second floor. Talia unlocked her condo, and Adrian lowered his load onto her front lobby floor. A quick glance around gave him the layout of her unit; the sparse hodgepodge of furniture took Adrian back to his university days.

"Thank you, really. And I'm sorry for being such a bitch," Talia said.

"Glad I could help," Adrian said, looking at the beautiful woman across from him, face flushed.

Instead of taking the liberty of kissing her without permission, he pictured his mother scolding him if he did.

"Ah, what do I owe you?" she asked.

"Just a smile," he responded.

He received what he asked for, and with a gentlemanly nod, started down the hall.

"Talia?" he said as he walked away.

She popped her head out the door, expecting that he wanted something more. A pang of guilt stabbed her.

"Are you going to get that foot looked at?"

"I'm hoping it settles with ice."

"Me too. But if you need help, you have my number."

"Actually, I threw it out," she confessed.

"I don't blame you. That was bold of me to ask when you're with someone."

There was a silent gap. She didn't request another business card, and he didn't have one to give her.

"If you need me, you know where I live," he said, laughing.

Talia watched him saunter down the hall to his condo. He turned and saw her in her doorway balancing on one shoed foot with her other lovely bare foot resting on it. She waved and he reciprocated.

Talia found an ice pack and applied it to her elevated foot while Adrian floated through her head. As she read websites on obsessive-compulsive disorder, Adrian slid his card under her door, unnoticed, until Talia moved the boxes. She looked at the card, imagining having her own card with similar credentials. Unlike the first one, there was no message. She tucked it in her textbook in the chapter titled "Cultivating Harmonious Business Relationships."

Adrian's goodwill gesture saved him a trip to the gym. He wondered how his parents, who were polar opposites, maintained such a solid bond while Adrian's long string of girlfriends attached, then quickly detached themselves from him. He never felt connected enough to anyone to be more than entertained. Something was changing in him and he was curious why.

5:03 p.m.

Winnie ignored her doorbell ringing the first time because she was more interested in finding out who won on *Jeopardy*. When it rang again, she checked the calendar, and as sure as December follows November, one of her children had sent a Christmas arrangement. By the magnitude of it, Annette and Allen were competing again. It was too large for her coffee and dining room tables that she and Marcello were making daily use of, so she directed the delivery man to set it on the grand piano. She reached for her change purse as he mentioned the second one. Marcello was bringing veal parmigiana down the hall, and he kept watch at the door until the young man, laden with a second and even bigger weight, set it on another corner of the piano lid. Winnie doubled the amount of change and handed it to the unimpressed courier. Because the flower shop was closed, she would threaten the florist again tomorrow into confessing who actually ordered them.

"How morbid. I feel like we're dining in a funeral parlour," she quipped, joining Marcello at the table and ignoring the little envelopes tucked into the flowers.

After dinner, they studied the arrangements. Some water from one of the containers had spilled onto the grand piano and trickled into its interior. Alex had last played it more than five years ago. It was difficult for both Winnie and Marcello to move the heavy arrangements, and Winnie silently cursed her children—then herself—for not being more attentive when the courier set them down. Marcello figured out how to lift the lid and keep it open while Winnie dried the spill.

Inside the piano, Marcello spotted a faded purple tin, embossed with a familiar label displaying chocolates. Cautiously plucking it out, Winnie remarked that she and Alex met when both lived in England. Alex worked at a famous chocolate factory before his immigration to Canada post-war. On their dates, he brought Winnie chocolates. Soon after meeting, he proposed to her on her seventeenth birthday with a gold band of five diamonds he paid for with his meagre earnings. Her parents declined for her. When she turned eighteen, he proposed again with a bigger box of chocolates, his grandmother's heirloom ring and her father's permission.

"That was sixty-three years ago," she sighed aloud as Marcello handed her the dented tin.

She had no idea when Alex had stashed the box in the piano. Winnie carried it to the coffee table and they sat on the sofa as, fighting tears, she attempted to pry the box open. Rust corroded the lid and sealed it to the container. Gingerly, Marcello loosened it with his pen knife and passed it over to her. Her hands were shaking. Inside were old English coins, Alex's lost war medals, love letters and the tiny ring of five stones which she thought was returned to wherever it came from. It no longer fit on her gnarly ring finger but did on her baby finger. Marcello passed a small, yellowed envelope addressed to Winnie that had been tucked into the bottom of the box. Sensing her hesitancy, Marcello thought it best that he leave. She insisted he stay, unsealed the envelope with a brass letter opener and removed the card. The words were scribed with Alex's hand.

My dearest Winnie,
No matter in which order I lose myself,
Be it my mind first, or my life,
Remember I will always love you.
Alex
xoxox

Winnie held the card to her lips and closed her eyes as tears followed the creases around her eyes. She inhaled Alex's faint Old Spice cologne blended with the mustiness of the other treasures. Marcello was moved by the moment, and he marvelled at how such simple words could still stir a heart's song. It made him think of his own loss. He watched Winnie sift through the other remnants, of little value, that would give her more joy and outlast the expensive arrangements.

"He was such a kind man," Winnie whispered.

"You were lucky to have him for so long," Marcello replied.

She saw the emptiness in Marcello's eyes.

"You deserve someone special, too, my friend," she said, nodding her head slowly.

"Ah, that time has come and gone. Now they have four legs—and even then, one escaped me!"

Winnie filled her best tulip glasses with cognac.

"Are we grieving or celebrating?" Marcello asked as they toasted.

"Both, with a splash of melancholy," she chirped, plucking the envelopes from the flower arrangements.

Both typed cards had identical inscriptions from her children and their families:

We will always love you, Mom.

"They won't be saying that after I croak," she groaned while looking at the same decorative theme of the arrangements. "What am I going to do with these?"

"Admire them," Marcello suggested humbly.

He'd never received such a gift in his life.

"You'd be sadder without them."

"Hmm, now there's that splash of melancholy," she said, sipping her drink.

"I have no family to argue with. My cousins in Italy might send me a nice pair of socks, and I visit them once a year. But that's it. Some days I'm lonely, but many days, when I fill it with music, a good book or some decadent pastry from the market, my day has been made complete with things that people who don't know me have given me of themselves. Those are my gifts, Winnie, which I have learned to cherish. And you? What do you cherish?"

Winnie sighed.

"This," she said pointing to Alex's card.

"And what else?"

"Are we getting philosophical?" she asked, peering at him over her glasses.

"Just because someone is delegated to send you flowers, doesn't mean the person they represent doesn't care for you."

"I suppose."

"The florist took great pride in putting these together. I doubt they make these every day—and they probably took the whole day to create."

"I'm still going to call them and see who ordered them."

"And what difference would it make?"

Winnie didn't answer, so he continued.

"If I made these beautiful pieces and someone badgered me the next day about something I had no influence over, it would make me unhappy. Then, if you complained to the receptionists who ordered them because they did the job they were assigned, on time and within their given budget, they would also be unhappy and tell your children. You would also scold them and add another layer of unhappiness. So, instead of just you being unhappy, you add one florist, two receptionists, two children and, of course, that young man who wasn't happy with his tip because you weren't happy with the arrangements." Marcello raised each finger as he counted them. "You have made seven unhappy people from a gesture initiated to give one person—you—some generous Christmas cheer."

"I think we should watch some TV," Winnie responded, finishing her cognac and handing Marcello the remote.

"Something light-hearted."

Marcello scrolled through the menu, and after some negotiation, they agreed upon a remake of the Dr. Seuss book *How the Grinch Stole Christmas*. Winnie remembered reading the bedtime Christmas story to her children. Marcello had never seen the movie or read the book.

"What's it about?" he asked.

"It's a comedy."

"I thought it was a cartoon."

"It was, and then it became a movie about a Grinch who hates people and despises Christmas and plans to ruin it for everyone. A little person persuades him to stop destroying the holiday and become a happier person."

"Hmmm, that sounds very familiar," Marcello mumbled, as Winnie replenished their glasses, returned to the sofa and threw the other half of her blanket over him.

December 3ʳᴅ
Weather forecast: partly cloudy and miserable

11:50 a.m.

"Courage is always greatest when blended with meekness."

Anonymous

Mason's complicated meeting with a demanding client ended earlier than planned, and his afternoon was reserved to prepare for a court hearing. On a whim, he gave Aida the afternoon off and then drove to the library. Entering through the glass doors, he didn't need to ask if Gracie was working. She was perched on a stepladder, thumb-tacking banners of Santa Clauses riding sleighs under the clock behind the front desk. As if on cue, she turned to ask her co-worker if the Santas were evenly spaced. Mason gave her a thumbs up, his broad smile causing her to float down the ladder.

"Excuse me, could you show me where the Bruce Trail guidebooks are?" he asked, for lack of something better to say.

Gracie's co-worker stood to escort him to the self-help desk, so he politely said, "This kind lady has helped me before."

Mason followed Gracie to the secluded geography section, far from other employees.

"What a nice surprise," Gracie said, propping her elbow on a shelf with a gap between books.

"I hope you don't mind."

"Not at all. There's lots of Bruce Trail books here."

"Have you got a lunch-break?" he asked.

"Today's a short day," she said, shaking her head.

"I've had my lunch already, but I'm off at three."

"Hmm …" Mason said, propping a book open, and taking one step back to allow a librarian to pass between them.

"I'm making chicken pot pie and salad for dinner," she said. "If you'd like to join me, I won't have to eat leftovers all week." She then realized her suggestion would be more intimate than dining in a public place. "It's dinner, Mason. Two chairs divided by a table. No expectations other than for you to enjoy your meal."

"Gee … homemade chicken pot pie?"

"My mother's recipe."

He was wavering.

"Full disclosure: I buy the crust," she said.

He rolled his eyes in an exaggerated manner.

"But the salad dressing is from scratch. And the dress code is comfy casual, so you'll have to change."

She saw acceptance in his nervous smile.

"And I can bring refreshments in their original bottles?"

"Of course."

"And what time?"

"Six-ish?"

"Six it is."

"And Mason?"

"Yes."

"We don't need to call this a date. We can just have a nice dinner. Like book club people do."

"I'd like that."

Gracie finished hanging the Santas while Mason lingered around the new book section before leaving empty-handed. He gave a coffee shop gift card he had in his wallet to the pregnant teen that was sitting on the sidewalk outside the front doors asking him for change.

Mason bought wine on the way home and surprised himself by focusing enough to finish his work. With little time to spare, he showered and changed into jeans and a pastel plaid shirt.

When her shift ended, Gracie stopped at the market to upgrade her dinner menu with more colourful salad ingredients and fresh rolls. She bought white wine to add to the red she had at home. She prepared dinner, showered and dressed in her favourite jeans and a white shirt, sparing ten minutes to put her feet up before the doorbell rang.

6:00 p.m.

A flutter of pleasure warmed her as she opened her door to see Mason looking so handsome. Both were initially skittish without the distractions of other diners or a hiking trail. Their conversation hovered around the commonalities they previously shared until the wine started to melt them down.

Gracie's great room included a sofa and two armchairs that captured spectacular views of the river and the falls tourist area, all framed by tall Palladian windows. Her dining alcove extended from this room, and an island divided it from her kitchen. Mason sat at the island opposite Gracie as she tossed the salad, their awkwardness fading with more wine at dinner.

Mason returned to the island with his assignment to dish out lemon squares while Gracie packaged leftovers into containers and made tea. Mason balanced his dessert and tea as he sank carefully into his chair, pre-warned that it swivelled, while Gracie took the other chair. Both faced the colourful hotel-lit silhouettes against the night sky. They talked about the diverse culture of the city, generations of residents mixed with transients that shifted between bordering countries depending on when and where they had worn out their welcome. Mason's tree of life was full and honourable with a solid but childless marriage and firm roots in a house filled with joy, then grief. Gracie's baggage was messier. Her mundane life was turned upside down after Blair's death, the denial of his life insurance payout and her job loss. She told him about Fred's choice to remain involved in his ex-wife's matters.

"That's not your fault," Mason said quietly, finishing his dessert.

This caught Gracie by surprise.

"What isn't?"

"About marrying young, about your job or about your husband's error in judgement."

"Whew. There's my life summed up in one sentence."

Mason smiled.

"It's what I've learned litigating divorces. Infidelity, addiction, violence are someone's choices. Cancer, messing up your—not his—insurance benefit and that consequence was not your fault."

"What about incompatibility?"

"Now that's a little more complicated. Each case is different, and in divorce wars, even those who declare victory are not always winners."

"Interesting. Do you still like what you do?"

"Most days. And you?"

"Yes. But dealing with noisy people, thefts and those who can't pay their fines is less stressful than your job."

"Being compassionate to those who are marginalized can be heartbreaking."

"Giving them a smile and a safe place to warm up is the easiest part of my job."

"And most admirable."

"They all have a story. As you said, it often unfolds through no fault of theirs and sometimes for the same reasons that lead to divorce."

"You're very insightful."

Their conversation cycled through safe topics—mostly books—until they eventually ran out of things to talk about. Knowing they both were working the following day, Mason thanked her for the evening and rose to leave.

"I think we did well, considering this was not a date," Gracie said, taking Mason's coat out of her closet.

"Do you think it was more like a dinner meeting?"

"We could call it that."

"I'm sure you know by now that I rarely share my private life," Mason replied apologetically.

The Park Street Secrets

"And like the library, mine's an open book," Gracie quipped.

She grabbed a container of leftovers from the kitchen and handed them to Mason.

"Why, thank you. Good thing the housekeeper is off tomorrow. I'd have trouble explaining myself."

Their eyes met for longer than the few times it had happened that evening.

"With your permission, may I kiss you?" Gracie asked.

Mason responded by moving closer. She could feel the warmth of his breath against her cheek. He kissed her cheek first, inhaling her scent that was mixed with the aroma of dinner. He then kissed her on her lips, softly at first, feeling her respond. She took the leftovers out of his hand and kissed him again as his arms moved around her. Tightening his embrace, Mason held the next kiss, feeling more emotion than he had in years. Gracie leaned against the wall as he held her silently in his arms.

"I'm a little rusty at this," he whispered in her ear.

"And I was afraid you'd drop your leftovers," Gracie said, setting the container on a nearby table.

"That would be such a waste," he replied, kissing her again and again.

Gracie slid her arms under Mason's coat and around his back. They embraced, remaining where they were.

"This is lovely," she said softly.

"Most certainly."

"Worthy of another dinner?"

"Absolutely."

"Then we can make that happen."

"I'd like that."

8:45 p.m.

Once they separated, Gracie tucked the leftovers back in Mason's hand. After another series of kisses and a warm embrace, he opened the door and they agreed to make plans on the weekend. Mason kissed her a last time, and passionately, before she closed the door.

Yearning for more, Mason headed down the hall. As he arrived at the fire door, he looked back, hoping that Gracie would open her door and invite him to return. Instead, he saw Marcello leave Winnie's condo holding an empty cooking pot in one hand and his keys in the other. Marcello and Mason both heard Winnie's door close. Marcello scratched his forehead, gave Mason a polite nod and hobbled down the hall to his own door, whistling loud enough for Mason to hear him. Neither man was interested in sharing the details of their evening.

Sally acknowledged the man dressed in jeans and a muted plaid shirt leaving her building as she was entering it. He was either Winnie's guardian or he worked in the same office as the lawyer she had retained to arrange her separation from Mitch. Or maybe both. Mitch had signed the legal agreement without dispute, and other than dissolving their marriage and meeting his financial obligations, there was nothing else to ask for.

Sally wasn't sure she wanted to stay in the condo, but she could only manage one major decision at a time. She walked up the stairs and unlocked her door. Fear stiffened her as she walked in, and it wasn't until after she replaced the bed linen and towels that she and Mitch both shared

The Park Street Secrets

that she felt less afraid. His heavy items, including father's desk had been removed under Sonny's watchful eye. She kept his office door closed despite the view. Once she could afford to pay Sonny to paint it a pastel pink, she would feel more comfortable leaving it open.

Lily had texted Gracie a few times that day, disappointed that she had not responded. She had arranged a date with Match #2 but needed some advice about avoiding the pitfalls of her date with Match #1. Texting her again, she was thrilled when Gracie asked her to pop by in ten minutes.

Gracie would have preferred to savour her evening alone than meet Lily but ultimately negotiated thirty minutes to sort through her questions. As Gracie hurried to erase any evidence of having company, she was puzzled how Lily, in her mid-forties and divorced for years, could be so naïve.

Gracie opened the door to a very excited Lily, who was dressed in leggings and a sweat shirt, clutching her tablet. Lily took in her surroundings. Sonny's renovations, Gracie's decorating and Match #2's profile in front of her made it easier to return to Unit 1C. They sat down at the kitchen island, Gracie choosing the stool where Mason sat an hour earlier. Gracie slid the remaining lemon squares in her direction.

"Oh no," Lily said, hiding them behind the computer screen she was scrolling through.

"I gotta get another five pounds off before Friday."

"What's on Friday?"

"I'm meeting Mr. Match #2. He looks like a good catch, and he's a local boy," she squealed, turning the screen for Gracie to see a more impressive photo than Lily's first choice.

"Very nice. And where are you going to meet?"

"At a bar for cocktails near the falls. Safe and public, just like you suggested."

"Great," she said as her phone pinged with a text from Mason. She switched it to the silent mode and turned it over.

"And dinner?"

Gracie was more concerned about the dater's character and intent.

"We'll decide that later. If I don't like him, it gives me an early exit."

"Smart thinking. I hope he's nice."

"Me too. What do you think of him?" Lily asked, showing Gracie his details.

"Everything seems to line up," she replied, still wondering why Lily would be asking for her approval. "Have fun. Be smart, and if things work out, hopefully a second date will follow," Gracie responded, hoping the same of Mason.

"Okay. I bought another new outfit, so he better be worth it."

"If I'm home, pop by and show me before you leave."

Within twenty minutes Lily was back home, loaded with confidence.

Gracie flipped her phone over and read Mason's text:

"If I eat your chicken pot pie for lunch, can I take you out for dinner tomorrow?"

Gracie smiled as she texted back, "Wow. So soon?"
"Too soon?"
"Not for me."
"Whew."
"Is this dinner? Or a dinner date?"
"I think we could call it a dinner date after those tender moments."
"They were lovely. And I accept."
"A date it is. Can I pick you up around six-ish?"
"Six-ish it is."
"Sleep well, Gracie."
"I know for sure I will. And you too."
"Goodnight."

December 8th
Weather forecast: snow (and lots of it)

6:15 a.m.

"Life's tragedy is that we get old too soon and wise too late."

Anonymous

Bryce wrapped his coat and scarf tighter around him as he attempted to follow the same footprints in the deep sidewalk snow that someone before him had made. He was walking to the station to take the train because he hated driving. On those rare occasions where he had to drive, every imperfection on the road gave him the overwhelming fear that he had struck something living, like a dog or a person. He would always circle back to where he felt the bump hit his wheel—or park if he could—to check around and under his car. He always imagined the worst, and hearing a siren shortly after terrified him. So, despite his heavy backpack and the snow, it was easier to walk than to drive.

Bryce was taking the 7:00 a.m. train to Toronto for a two-day project his employer, who had acknowledged his perfectionism, sent him on. He was never happy being away from the security and routines of his own home. And Talia, although their last few weeks had been tough. She was becoming less tolerant of his need to get things done, and although their co-workers were curious about a wedding date, Bryce needed to be sure he was marrying the right person.

Trudging through the snow, he saw that today was also garbage day. Although he usually ignored it, he was drawn to a red plastic bin a woman was pushing toward the curb. She then re-entered the law office she was cleaning. Bryce paused until he heard the door lock click, and then he approached the bin, which was full of outdated books and journals. He sorted through the box and chose a couple of thick journals on matrimonial law. Only one fit in his overstuffed back pack, so he carried the other, thrilled with his find. His sidetrack delayed him enough to arrive just in time to catch his train.

9:35 a.m.

Winnie walked from window to window, content to watch the snow as it swirled through the air. She was happy she had no plans other than to watch the day pass by. She walked down the first-floor hallway, through the fire door and to the lobby to get her mail. Marcello had been a big help in discontinuing the junk mail and flyers she was getting after she realized she wasn't reading them anymore. She also took Mason's suggestion and donated to the local groups Alex supported. Opening her mail, she was touched by a card from the food bank, which included fond memories of Alex. Winnie also peeked through the little window of Marcello's mailbox. Since he rarely got mail, she would remind him at dinner to check.

Gracie zipped up her practical boots and bundled up for the walk to work. She passed under the train bridge and the cat colony. A dozen of them watched her pass, the smell of hay and cat food reassuring her that someone continued to nurture and nourish them.

Gracie had spent four of the last five evenings with Mason. They were drawn to each other like old souls. Quiet evenings apart became quiet evenings together, with each meeting peeling away another layer of discomfort that came with acclimatizing to someone new. Mason was a realist, and his calmness blended nicely with Gracie's appreciation of all things quiet. They preferred documentaries over action thrillers and the popular paranormal films. Although they were still far from bringing their intimacy to the bedroom, Gracie awakened a desire in Mason. She knew he loved his wife very much and remained loyal to their circle of friends.

Gracie stopped by an office window on her walk to peek at some coloured paper stuck to the glass front door. A new thought-provoking line was posted each week, and today it said:

GRATITUDE TURNS WHAT WE HAVE INTO ENOUGH

Today she was full of gratitude. She enjoyed her job, had settled into a new home she could afford and was loved by a daughter who was building her own life. But today, she was most grateful that Mason had come into her life.

Meanwhile, Talia was feeling more and more helpless. She had altered her expectations of Bryce after what Adrian told her. But being empathetic and compassionate wasn't working anymore, and more often than not, her emotions were compromising her ability to reason with him. Bryce was putting up more barriers, and they agreed that his two days away would give them a much-needed break. Instead of risking an injury by going for a run, she went for a brisk walk, and by the time she got home, she was drenched in sweat and snow. She kicked off her boots and put them outside her condo door on a mat to dry. She was off today, and her only plan was to shower and read trashy tabloids. Clothes soaked from sweat and hair wet from the snow, she debated whether to shower first or eat. She decided when she turned the music on and a good song started to play, pouring herself a generous helping of sugary cereal she reserved for days like this. Just before she poured the milk in, she thought she heard a faint knock on the door.

Talia squinted into the peep hole to see Adrian standing on the other side, then opened the door. He was unshaven, hair uncombed and white as a ghost. Her feet, bare like his, were dwarfed next to Adrian's.

"Are you okay?" she asked, looking directly into his eyes.

"I'm sorry. I just …" he stuttered, on the verge of tears.

"What's wrong?" she asked opening the door and allowing him into her front entrance. A month ago, she would not have done this.

"It's my dad."

"What happened?"

"He's in hospital with some blood clots."

"Oh no. That sounds serious."

"I can't believe it. My poor mom."

Talia gestured for him to join her at the kitchen stools after she quickly spaced them farther apart. Adrian hadn't showered, and she desperately needed one. She set another cereal bowl and spoon beside him. She partially faced him, picking at the sugar-covered letters in her bowl as she listened to his story.

Adrian spoke of his rare visit home three weeks ago, not being close to his father, and how his mother worked overtime to keep them connected. Returning from seeing his father after he broke his leg, Adrian saw himself as an outlier. Normally unfazed by things that didn't affect him directly, this did. He told Talia that his grandmother's dementia forced her to move into his parents' home, and with his father's re-admission to hospital, his mother's caregiver roles depleted her ability to care about herself. Usually silent as stone about her own well-being, it was the desperation in her voice that crushed Adrian.

"I'd be going home," Talia said, pouring milk over what remained of her cereal and passing the carton to Adrian.

"I don't know what I'd do if I went, or if I can even get the time off."

"If my boss wouldn't give me time off to see my ill father, I'd be looking for a new job."

"They need me."

"And your mother doesn't? I don't think it's about you right now, Adrian."

Her comment hit Adrian hard. She pushed the cereal towards him again, then watched him check flights between mouthfuls.

"Eight o'clock," Adrian said.

"That's when your flight leaves?"

"Yup."

"Good boy. And your flight back?"

"I didn't book it."

"Good. Because I'd be spending Christmas there if I were you."

As soon as his bowl was empty, Talia headed for her door and Adrian followed, fuelled with food and advice.

"I'm sorry for interrupting your day."

"No worries. It's payback for helping me with that mess in the storage room."

"Hey, how's your foot?"

"One hundred percent," she said.

Adrian stood quietly by the door, knowing it was inappropriate to touch her.

"I'll probably see you after Christmas. And I hope you have a good one."

"Me too," she said, thinking briefly about her own holiday plans.

She watched Adrian pad barefoot down the hall, waving back to him when he entered his condo. Lifting her arm high and frowning at her stench, she hung her damp clothes over the bathtub to dry and hopped into the shower.

3:00 p.m.

Marcello looked outside and decided the ingredients for his main meal would have to come from within the walls of his kitchen. He had enough cat food for three days, so there was no urgency to leave until then. He poked his head in the fridge, both cats responding to the sound of the door opening.

"No, no, it's not time yet," he scolded them quietly.

He decided to make gnocchi and pan fry the defrosted chicken breasts with the red and yellow peppers that hadn't yet been used in any other meal.

Dressed in old clothes that he would not normally leave his unit in, he decided to check his mail. Opting to remain in his slippers, he put his favourite sweater on and buttoned it, ignoring that the buttons did not line up with their holes. He unlocked the little door and pulled out a thick letter from his cousin in Italy, which was postmarked in his hometown twelve days earlier. For a change of scenery, he settled into a wing-back chair in the lobby. Guessing it was a Christmas card, he was correct when he opened the envelope. The card was ornate, made by a local artist in the market he visited every time he returned. Nostalgia washed over him as he glanced outside at the heavy snowflakes, which were almost non-existent in his part of Italy. If he was there right now, he'd be savouring a pastry at an outdoor café with friends against the backdrop of noisy multi-generational families in a nearby courtyard. He missed that, and he ruminated again about his decision to remain in Canada.

Marcello's cousin included updated school pictures of his great nieces and nephews. He also opened a newspaper clipping from the sports section of the weekly paper. The article took up more than half the page and included three colour photos. The first was a team of boys holding a trophy. He scanned the players and located his nephews beaming at the camera. The second featured an older woman surrounded by a bevy of boys dressed in various soccer uniforms.

Marcello was instantly drawn to the woman. Yes, it was indeed Valentina. The headline showcased her and thirteen grandchildren, mostly boys, who played on regional teams. Aging well, her plump arms enveloped two identical pre-schoolers who occupied her generous lap. After he took the time to absorb her features, he read the story. Valentina had four sons: Rocco, Antonio, Severio and—Marcello caught his breath when he read the last one's name—Marcello. The boys shared Valentina's surname, which was stamped on the back of their uniforms, and they were assembled from tallest to shortest in various stages of development. The man identified as Marcello stood behind the boys, resting his hands on the middle boys' shoulders.

Marcello stared blankly out the window to the snow-covered street while trying to piece together what little he knew. The man whom Valentina first married was not the name in the article. She must have become single through divorce or death and re-married soon enough after to have at least four children by the same man. And all those grandchildren!

Shuffling in his slippers back to his condo, he laid the greeting card and photos on his table, tucked the newspaper article back in its envelope and placed it in a drawer. He argued with himself that it didn't matter what Valentina had, but it only emphasized what he didn't have.

Later that evening, Marcello's dinner was better than his company. He usually bathed and dressed before coming to Winnie's, but today he smelled like stale clothes and garlic. It took some effort to pry out the cause of his sadness.

"So that was your mail?"

"It was."

"Thirteen grandchildren—and so many boys. I wouldn't remember who belonged to which father, let alone their names."

"And they all looked alike."

"Sooo, now the big question. What did she look like?"

"Older and fat, like me," he mumbled.

"I thought most older women in Italy stayed voluptuous and alluring," she said, looking for the humour in his misery.

"And that's what she was."

"That's what she was fifty years ago. When's the last time you saw her?"

"Forty-five years ago."

"Look on the bright side: Maybe she's become a wretched old woman with all those grandkids."

That didn't make Marcello feel better.

"One of her sons has my name."

"You're joking."

"I'm not."

"Now I'm really curious. May I see the article?"

Marcello returned shortly with the envelope and passed it to Winnie. She unfolded the article, put her reading glasses on and took her time scrutinizing the paper in front of her.

"Marcello, she's still beautiful," she said as she passed the paper back to him. "I think you have some homework to do."

"And what's that?"

"Don't you have your cousin's phone number? Can't you call him and ask him—he must know something to have sent you this."

"His nephews are in the picture because they won the trophy."

"I'll bet my cognac that his nephews have won more than one trophy. I think he sent this to you for a reason. Did he mention anything in his Christmas card?" she asked, looking over her glasses.

"Nothing. Not even one thing."

"And this other Marcello? Are you sure he's not yours?"

"Winnie, listen to me," Marcello said with his arms spread apart and pleading for reason. "If I was caught kissing a girl fifty years ago, I would have been thrown out of the house. Sleeping with her was sacrilegious. I'd be tossed right out of my village!"

"But that doesn't mean people didn't sleep together. How do you think Mary had Jesus? Let's face it, Marcello, it wasn't divine intervention."

Marcello rolled his eyes and head in an exaggerated manner.

"How did religion become a part of this? Are you going to mock the Pope next?"

"Pope schmope. Now let's get back to business here."

Both well-saturated with cognac, by the end of the evening Winnie had convinced Marcello he needed to know more, so he promised to call his cousin to fish for explanations. Marcello opened Winnie's door and was startled by Mona Lisa laying sprawled on the hallway carpet across from him. Because she easily outran him, there was no use in trying to catch her. He hobbled home and left his door open until she sauntered back in, ignoring him and heading right for her food dish. Marcello took one long look at the picture of Valentina before leaving it on the table. She was a stranger to him now, but a beautiful one at that. Winnie was right. He needed to find out more.

5:15 p.m.

Lily stood on the scale wearing nothing but her curiosity and was pleased with the number flashing back at her—the same number as this morning and the day before. She starved herself most of the week, and her reward was the new outfit for her date tonight. She showered and prettied herself up with a generous application of perfume and make-up, taking a final check of approval in the hallway mirror before heading out the door. The snow had stopped and city crews were busy clearing the streets. Thinking back to her first date, Lily chose more practical shoes and a warmer coat this time. She cleared the snow from her car and drove carefully to the bar where she and Match #2 had agreed to meet.

Lily sat down on the bar stool and ordered a martini, her feet nervously treading empty air. It wasn't long before a tall, slightly overweight man dressed in a casual manner that Lily found appealing arrived. Best of all, he looked like his profile photograph, although with just a little less hair.

Unlike Match #1, Match #2 was really named Rob. He was smooth with his words, and the first hour passed quickly. He invited her to dinner at the café next door. It was usually packed with diners during the warmer tourist season, but only a handful of tables were occupied. They were fortunate to get a table overlooking the falls, and the combination of Christmas lights and the heavy snowfall made their view magical.

Rob attended a different local high school than Lily and was also a few years older. Over appetizers, when Lily mentioned her maiden name, he tilted his head and paused.

"Miles, you know, that sounds familiar," he said as he explored her facial features more carefully. "Are you—I mean, were you—any relation to Rose Miles?"

"She was my sister," Lily responded, swallowing her food carefully to avoid choking.

"Sorry for your loss," Rob said.

"Thank you. Did you know her?"

"We dated for a little while."

Lily's heart sank.

"Oh? How did you meet?"

"I had business meetings in the conference rooms in the hotel she worked at."

"I see."

"She was a really nice person," Rob said as Lily tried to remain positive.

"I lived in the States for a long time, so we didn't see much of each other until the last few years."

Lily was pleased with how she worded her response. The conversation drifted to Rob's job, a divorce and his adult children. Through dinner, Lily kept hoping he would share more about Rose, and she occasionally slipped in a question about her. Taking her cue, he said he dated her for a few months.

"How did she die?"

"She drowned," was all Lily said.

"That's a shame. The details in the news were kind of sketchy."

Lily was unwilling to share any more details. They finished dinner, and Lily resisted the urge to have dessert. She watched him eat cheesecake—the kind the bakery around the corner sold. The rest of the dinner was little more than small talk. Lily's thoughts were getting soggy after Rob said he dated Rosie. Rob paid for the bill and appreciated Lily leaving the tip. The evening was pleasant enough, and at the end, he asked her if she would be interested in meeting again. She looked at her feet, then at him.

"It depends."

He looked surprised. "On what?"

"How honest you are with me."

He looked puzzled. "I don't understand. I have been honest with you."

"And I appreciate that."

"So, what's your concern?"

"Did you sleep with her?"

"Ah, that's what's bothering you."

Rob thought for a moment, then gave her more than she needed to hear.

"Yes, I slept with her. She lived with your mom, so we met when she could book a free room at the hotel."

"You're disgusting."

"Heh, when booze oozes in, common sense oozes out."

Lily was halfway to her car before Rob finished his sentence. Ignoring the thin layer of frost on her windows, she turned her car on, repeatedly pressed her windshield washers until she could see enough to drive and headed home, her eyes glazed with tears. On her way, she stopped at the grocery store and bought enough sugary snacks to overdose her hungry heart. It would be some time before she would think about connecting with Match #3.

7:00 p.m.

Adrian arrived at the airport with time to spare before his flight home. He checked his suitcase at the baggage counter, then headed to the nearest bar for a beer and some pub food. He was unable to concentrate on anything important, so he glanced through the newsfeeds, none of which interested him. Moving on to his photos, he looked at past family get-togethers and anything his mother felt worthy to send him. He zoomed in on his parents instead of selfies. Adrian stopped at the video of Talia he had taken in the lobby and played it again. He felt as if his mother, coincidentally pictured in the screens before and after the video of Talia, was sending him messages of shame and guilt. And it worked. He deleted it, instantly feeling relief.

December 10th
Weather forecast: cold (actually, bitterly cold)

7:30 a.m.

Mitch drove to Georgia's house from his overtime night shift. His plan was to pay down his credit card bill, and with six more shifts, he could breathe easier about his debt and continue counselling. He was starting to atone for his mistakes. He had dinner with Georgia and his sons the night before but needed to feel more grounded before meeting their partners. He apologized to them privately and together for being absent when they needed him and for not supporting Georgia when the family needed to make tough decisions. *Things were improving for a change*, he thought as he stripped off his clothes, showered and crawled into bed next to Georgia. Yes, things were looking up.

1:45 p.m.

Bryce got off the train from Toronto and headed home. He knew that when Talia returned from work, they would have to have the overdue conversation about the fragile state of their union. He didn't know how he would effectively explain what started deep in his brain, one soft whisper at a time, and progressed to an unstoppable storm. Since the condo move, he had succumbed to the repetitive sequence of behaviours that now dominated his life. As much as he tried to find his old self, he couldn't bring himself to stop.

Bryce buried the two books he had pilfered from the recycling bin two days ago behind other books in the spare room. The closer to the time of Talia's arrival home, the more agitated he became. When she opened the door and met his sleepless eyes, it felt like both sides had abandoned the battle before the guns were even drawn.

Talia poured two glasses of water and handed Bryce one. They exchanged bits of their days apart to delay the inevitable. Talia made the first move by saying she would be honest with him and appreciated him doing the same. She said that she found the quirks about his cleanliness secretly endearing in the beginning, but she gradually grew intolerant of his obsessions and compulsions. And finally, because his hoarding was interfering with the progression of her own life, her happiness was unsustainable. Talia would stay but only if he got help. She sobbed, saying she'd hoped things would improve after they moved in together, but instead they got worse.

Bryce was speechless. His head hung low, immobilized by Talia's ultimatum. He was oblivious that it had come to this. His knees started bouncing and his breaths came faster and deeper. His heart pounded like a drum. He tucked his trembling hands under his thighs in an effort to control the only part of him he felt able to. In the background, a city bus drove by full of people carrying on with their daily lives while he tried to make sense of his. Talia finished her water, put her glass in the sink and faced Bryce.

"If there's anything you'd like to say, I'm willing to listen."

"I just want to be normal," was all he could manage.

"I just want you to be normal too."

Talia changed from her work clothes to her running gear in the bathroom because she didn't want Bryce to see anything more than her sadness. She walked into the spare room, her guts churning from the sight and mustiness of Bryce's books. She picked up her textbook from her tiny pile of possessions that sat on the unopened boxes of Christmas decorations.

Adrian's business card marked the chapter where she had left it. She tucked it into the tiny back pocket of her leggings. She zipped her phone into the front pocket of her running shell and left Bryce on the sofa with his knees still pumping up and down. She walked quietly down to the lobby and stretched out her taut muscles there. She sat down in an armchair and pulled Adrian's card and her phone out. She keyed in his mobile number and a message.

"Hi. It's Talia from across the hall. Arrived safely? Is your dad stable?"

She re-read her words, then pressed the Send button.

He replied instantly.

"Nice surprise. My dad's in ICU. Will know more soon."

"Planning to stay?"

"At least 1 wk. Waiting for an OK re: Xmas."

"Good. I might need a favour."

"Anything."

"Will text if I do."

"Glad to help."

"Good luck with your dad."

"Thanks. Will keep you posted."

Talia pulled her hair into a ponytail and covered her head with a hat. She took a deep breath and started to run, pacing her steps slowly at first. Three blocks in, she was running harder and faster than she had in months. It was an exhilarating sensation, and by the time she returned to the lobby, she was spent. She pulled out her phone, privatized her conversation with Adrian and changed her password.

She walked back upstairs, her lungs burning and her legs like rubber. Leaving her runners outside the door, she walked in, not knowing what to expect. All was quiet, and Bryce had left the couch. She looked around and found him standing in the spare room, hands on his hips. Their eyes met but no words were exchanged. Talia had rehearsed what she had said to Bryce earlier, but she had no idea how to proceed after that. She waited a minute, returned to the kitchen and gulped a tall glass of water down before heading to their bedroom. She chose a change of clothes and took them to the bathroom with her, locking the door behind her.

3:00 p.m.

It was 8:00 p.m. in Venice when Marcello got off the phone with his cousin. After catching up on the few relatives he remained connected to, it was his cousin that brought up the newspaper article. Winnie was right. He had sent it for a reason, and his nephews in the photo were the segue to the rest of the story. His cousin started by bragging about his grandsons and the other boys they played with. He then asked Marcello if he recognized the woman in the picture. Because his cousin served as his best man at his wedding, Marcello wavered between feeling insulted and injured. He acknowledged he knew it was Valentina and despite his own bitterness, many others involved in their nuptials were also affected by Valentina's scandalous escape. There was so much chatter in the town for months after that Marcello, bearing his own sorrows an ocean away, managed to avoid much of it.

It took some time for his cousin to relay what he gathered about Valentina by being a spectator in the bleachers and speaking with her assorted family members at the soccer matches. He said Valentina's first marriage ended shortly after it began for reasons unknown. She remarried and became pregnant with her first son, Rocco. Her husband, who Marcello and his cousin both knew from school, perished in an industrial fire and left Valentina a young, impoverished widow with an unborn child. She wasted no time in meeting her third husband, who adopted Rocco and, according to Marcello's cousin, was not a pillar of the community. She bore three more sons: Antonio, Severio and, lastly, Marcello. Her husband was in and out of jobs as often as he was in and out of bars and brothels, so Valentina was forced to take on odd jobs to support the family. It was a marriage of convenience, according to the village gossip, because Valentina's chances of finding happiness and a fourth husband were slim. So, she remained married and miserable until, much to her relief, he died of liver disease a few years ago. By that time, her only interest was her grandchildren.

It was Marcello's cousin who told Valentina's son, the one also named Marcello, that he was related to a cousin with the same name. One discussion led to another, and eventually Valentina approached Marcello's cousin to learn more when they were far away from the inquisitive ears of others. When Marcello's cousin linked himself to Marcello, Valentina became curious. At the end of that conversation, she confessed that she named her last son Marcello because of the fond memories of her fiancé Marcello, who moved to Canada. She still had regrets, hoped he was well and felt certain he would never forgive an old woman who had little more to offer him than a picture of his namesake.

When Marcello hung up the phone, he wasn't certain how much of what he had learned was helpful, but he knew two things that made him feel somewhat better: that Valentina never forgot him, and that she had enough positive thoughts about him to name a child after him. Marcello stood up, stiff from sitting for the last hour, and walked to his table where the article sat. He picked it up and substituted his bifocals for a magnifying glass, which didn't make the photos clearer. He sat back down, having lost interest in making or eating dinner. He called Winnie, lied that he had a queasy stomach and was staying home. She balked at microwaving a freezer-burned meal and offered him her stash of remedies if he needed them. Just before she hung up, she asked Marcello if he had called his cousin. Hoping to delay that conversation, he only acknowledged that he did. When she asked if they'd had a long talk, he also confirmed that they did. He heard Winnie sigh loudly and then forgive him for taking the night off from cooking. Just before she hung up, she said she thought it was his heart that was queasy, not his stomach.

7:00 p.m.

Today was a first for Mason. He was making dinner for Gracie, with the discreet but encouraging support of his housekeeper. Other than preparing soup and sandwich meals, he was not a connoisseur of the kitchen. He came home early and stood at the counter reading the warning not to burn the chicken casserole that was prepped for him to bake. As curious as she was about his dinner guest, out of respect, his housekeeper would never ask. She had worked for Mason and his late wife for many years and had rarely seen him so fidgety. She brought a potted orange kalanchoe to serve as a table centrepiece, set out extra bath towels, and washed and air-dried his sheets outside in the event he and his guest found their way to his bedroom. Based on his predictable routines since his wife's passing, there had been no overnight guests, and she secretly hoped he'd find someone nice. Her last instructions before she left—and she looked directly at him when she said it—were to relax and enjoy the evening. Mason wondered if she actually winked at him before she left him to his own devices.

Gracie set her vehicle's navigation system to guide her to the prestigious neighbourhood where Mason lived.

Admiring the architecture and the sprawling umbrellas of oak trees lining it, she pulled into the driveway behind his black Cadillac. She slung her purse over her shoulder, gathered up a new bestseller and the white wine. She skipped up the front steps and clacked the antique door knocker.

Mason answered the door wearing a pale pink shirt tucked into khakis that were protected with a clean white apron that was so small he couldn't tie the strings.

"My oh my, look at you," Gracie exclaimed, delighted at the sight of him outside of his element.

Mason held the door open for her at a distance. He waited until they were hidden from the attentive eyes of the elderly widow across the street—the self-appointed neighbourhood watcher—before greeting her with a generous kiss. He hung up her parka as she handed him the wine before removing her shoes. He kissed her again on her lips, and then on her neck. She placed her arms around his neck and returned the kiss, filled with an overwhelming desire to feel his body against hers. Pulling away first, Mason invited her to follow him to the kitchen, where a timer was going off. Mason stood in front of the stove, unsure how to cancel it until Gracie gently suggested which button to press.

The pair exchanged highlights of their days as he poured the wine. Mason periodically opened an upper cupboard door to peek at handwritten instructions taped inside at his eye-level. Gracie found this amusing, as she watched him broil the grated cheese bread, toss the salad and transfer the casserole and roasted vegetables to the table. He suggested she wander around and give him a few minutes to focus on his tasks. If she hadn't known otherwise, Mason's home gave the distinct impression that there were still two occupants. There were dozens of photographs of Mason and his wife, solo and together, in various life stages, impeccably coiffed and dressed in casual or formal attire. Some included dogs, vacation destinations and events with dignitaries. Such an admirable couple. Two well-worn leather recliners were positioned beside each other in the den, and there was a half-full basket of knitting between them.

Mason cleared his throat behind Gracie.

"I've had a hard time changing things," he said.

"I don't blame you. This is your, and ah, was her home."

"I don't have kids to give them to, and I feel guilty about putting them away."

"Then don't."

"I appreciate you saying that. I felt nervous inviting you over."

"I think I hear another timer going off," Gracie said as Mason retrieved his phone and shut the alarm off.

He pulled out the pre-sliced cheese bread from the oven, the final menu item to go on the table.

Dinner was perfect, and ice cream waited in the freezer. Mason relaxed considerably after they cleared the table and loaded the dishwasher. As he spoke about the neighbourhood, he encouraged her to peek out the front window to check if Mrs. Gray, his neighbour across the street, was spying on them. Gracie pulled the living room curtain back to see a lamp-lit face looking out her front window. She waved at the woman who, after a moment, returned the gesture before Gracie shut the curtains again.

"Did you see her?"

"Sure did. I gave her a big wave."

"You didn't."

"I did."

"That will keep her going for a week."

"What time does she go to bed?"

"That'll depend."

"On what?"

"On how long your car is in the driveway."

"Oh, mercy." Gracie said, smiling.

She set her glass down and embraced Mason from behind as he folded a dish towel and left it on the counter.

"What's that song about giving them something to talk about?"

"She's eighty-eight. We'd give her a heart attack," Mason said, chuckling.

He turned around, cupped her face in his hands and kissed her gently. She enveloped her arms around his back and leaned into him, the scent of his skin taking her to a place she longed to be. His arms circled her waist, and she felt his hardness swelling against her. They held each other until Mason became overwhelmed with emotion. She hugged him tightly, then looked into his watery eyes.

"Are you okay?" Gracie whispered.

"I'm not sure."

"I know I am."

"It's been a while," Mason groaned softly, his breath moist against her ear.

"I'm no spring chicken either."

"You still feel like one."

"I'm assuming that's a compliment."

They both giggled softly as he took her hand and walked towards the living room, but did not sit down. He embraced her again against the living room doorway. They kissed deeply and passionately. He lowered his arms down along her back and hesitated before moving his hands down to the small of her back.

"This is even better than dinner," she said with a smile.

He slowly moved his hands to her bottom, his breathing deepening. He then pressed her up towards him. She moaned softly.

He pulled back slightly, and whispered, "I can offer you Plan A or Plan B."

"I'll take Plan B."

"You don't know what Plan A is."

"It doesn't matter," she whispered back.

Mason held her hand, led her quietly to his bedroom and sat down on the bed beside her. The room was dark, save for the reflection of the night sky illuminating their soft shadows. He asked permission to unbutton her shirt, and Gracie smiled.

"You have my permission. Full consent or disclosure or whatever the right legal words are."

Mason unbuttoned Gracie's shirt with trembling fingers and slipped it off, kissing one shoulder and then the other. He inhaled her scent as he kissed her neck and then her cleavage. She unbuttoned his shirt and helped him out of it. He chuckled quietly that bras were never his area of expertise as he fumbled to unfasten hers. Both were acutely conscious of the assorted ways their bodies had aged as they awkwardly, then passionately, explored each other. They broke their moments of progressive silence with whispered sprinkles of humour about hoping nothing would fail them, apart or together. Protecting their nakedness under the covers, Mason took comfort in holding Gracie in tender embraces as their passion intensified. The scent of clean laundry and Mason's faint cologne deepened Gracie's senses. When their bodies united, he performed cautiously, increasing his thrusts until eventually she felt him shudder and then grow calm. She held him in her arms for a long time, the moonlight outlining their silhouette across the wall.

"I can only tell you now how afraid I was of this," Mason said quietly in her ear.

"Why? What were you afraid of?" Gracie whispered, stroking his fine grey hair.

She buried her head in his neck, listening to his pounding heart grow calmer.

"Oh, of everything. And nothing."

"And now?"

"Only one thing."

"And do I need to worry about that one thing?"

"You most certainly do," he replied, breathing heavily in her ear.

Gracie pulled her head up and asked, "What is it?"

"You'll know soon enough."

"Mason, tell me what it is," she asked again, pressing the palm of his hand firmly against her chest so he could feel her accelerating heart rate.

"The wandering eyes—and wagging tongue—of our chatty Mrs. Gray," he whispered in a spooky voice in her ear.

"Hmmm, I wonder if she has a library card I can, um …"

"Compromise? Oh, she's still an avid reader," he replied, nuzzling his face in her hair and inhaling its heady scent. "And she loves steamy historical romances," he growled, moving his mouth to her breast.

Gracie mumbled as she stretched out on her back, Mason next to her, and savoured the moment.

It was late at night when they left Mason's bed, blaming each other for ignoring the clock. Gracie convinced Mason that showering together was a time-saving measure to allow them to sleep in longer before work the following day. He jokingly asked her not to call 911 if he had a heart attack in the shower. While Gracie massaged his back with soap, Mason was reminded of a tender moment he shared with his wife many years ago. A wave of guilt enveloped him. After they left the shower and began drying each other off, Gracie noticed that Mason was more reserved.

"Are you okay?" she asked quietly. Mason smiled silently. "Did I say something wrong?"

"You did nothing wrong," he whispered, "until I have to confess to Mrs. Gray that I slept with a librarian."

Gracie rubbed Mason's back with her towel, then pressed herself against him. He turned around and embraced her lovingly, covering her back with his towel. She followed him back to the bedroom where he slipped into his bathrobe as she dressed, leaving her bra off and tucking it in her purse. He smiled broadly as he watched her preparing to leave.

"Is there something funny, Mason? What is it? You're grinning like a Cheshire cat," she said, eyebrows raised as he helped her into her parka.

"I hope you don't get stopped on the way home and have to explain yourself," he said, chuckling and pointing to her lacy pink bra.

"I'll drive carefully," she said with a grinned. "Oh! I forgot something!"

"What's wrong?" he asked.

Gracie picked up the library book she had propped against the front door and forgotten. She passed it to Mason, who immediately recognized the author as among his recent favourites.

"Ah, thank you."

"I put your name on the list as soon as I knew we ordered it. You're the first of twenty on the wait-list to read it. You have two weeks to return it or I'll slap you with a hefty fine."

"If I have trouble getting it back on time, I'll just ask Mrs. Gray to return it for me," he teased, flashing her a mischievous smile.

"You wouldn't dare."

"Just watch me."

"Then I'll have to tell her how you seduced me …"

Mason kissed her passionately before opening the door. He left the outdoor light off, hoping to avoid any attention of his dinner guest leaving so late. Gracie's vision acclimatized quickly to the night as she walked to her car. She caught a glimpse of Mrs. Gray peeking through the window, so she waved goodbye to her and watched her quickly disappear behind her drapes. Gracie waved at Mason as she left, relishing the wonderful evening she had shared with this very handsome and charismatic man.

December 12th
Weather forecast: high winds with lake effects and winter squalls

6:45 a.m.

"Giving up doesn't always mean you are weak ... sometimes it means you are strong enough to let go."

Anonymous

Talia spent a second consecutive night on her couch, and between its lumps, the city's lights and her sharp stabs of doubt, she barely slept. She showered and dressed quickly for work, hoping to be gone before Bryce woke up. She grabbed leftovers from the fridge for lunch and found her phone, which was buried between the sofa cushions while it charged. She bundled up for the walk to work and waited until she was in the lobby to unmute her phone and check it.

Adrian's message was short and to the point: "Heh, hope you're okay. Staying here for Xmas. Still need that favour?"

Talia's heart skipped a beat. Or maybe a few.

"Hi. Glad you'll be spending the holidays with your family."

He answered immediately. "My dad is still in ICU, sedated and full of blood thinners. You OK?"

The Park Street Secrets

Talia didn't know how best to respond. As she considered how and what to write, her phone rang, piercing the lobby silence. She answered Adrian's call in a whispered hello, moving from the cold stone steps to the vestibule where her words were protected between two sets of doors.

"Heh, how come you're up so early?" he asked in a gravelly voice.

"I'm heading to work."

"Where are you now?"

"In our building vestibule."

"Alone?"

"I am."

"I sense that something's wrong."

"I don't even know where to start."

"You didn't answer when I asked if you were okay."

"I think I am. Sort of," she said, checking the time. "Look, without getting into details, Bryce and I are going through a rough patch, and I need to give him time to sort through some stuff."

"Like literally?"

Adrian's comment was not what Talia expected to hear.

"Yes and no. But I have a huge favour to ask you."

"Yes, you can stay at my place."

"What? How did you know I was going to ask you that?"

"It doesn't really matter. The place is yours."

"Really?"

"Really."

"Is there a spare key somewhere or should I ask Sonny?"

"Go up there right now. I don't often lock it."

"Really?"

"Really. Go now. I'll stay on the phone until I hear from you."

Talia ran up the stairs and walked quietly down the second-floor hallway she and Bryce shared with Adrian and Sally. His door was, in fact, unlocked. She opened the door gently, walked in and closed it behind her.

"I'm standing in your front entrance."

"Open the closet door and you'll recognize the extra key hanging on the hook. Take it and lock the door behind you."

"Adrian, I'm not sure this is the right—"

"I don't want to know. Just take it. If you need it, great. If you don't, no harm done."

"Thank you."

"For you, anything."

Talia locked Adrian's door, wrapped the key in a serviette and placed it at the bottom of her lunch tote. She ran silently down the hall, the stairs and most of the way to work. She was grateful her injured toe had heeled quickly and allowed her to keep running. And that Adrian, despite her initial impression of him, was there when she needed him. More than once.

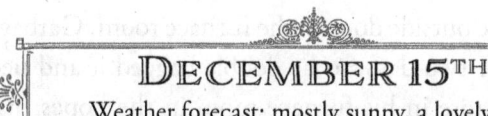

December 15th
Weather forecast: mostly sunny, a lovely day

8:30 a.m.

*"A blind person who sees is better than
a seeing person who is blind."*

Anonymous

Sonny had breakfast with his wife and sons, just like he did every morning. He had a long to-do list, including picking up cheese for his mother at her favourite Italian deli. It was also a less obvious way of her knowing that he was checking up on her, even though she knew he was. He worried about her declining health and increasing reliance on her pain patches, which decreased what she gave him. This, in turn, lowered his income from his fentanyl buyer and barely covered the cost of food for the cats under the bridge. The buyer also started threatening him, which made Sonny think that he would have to make some changes sooner or later. But he didn't expect that to happen today.

After his deli trip and visit with his mother, Sonny drove to Park Street. He emptied the trash in the public garbage bin on the street near the front of the building. It was installed as an incentive for people passing by to use it rather than throwing trash on the street, but he felt it also detracted from the building's prestige. He set the bag beside the outside door to the furnace room. Garbage day wasn't for two days, so he double bagged it and tied it tightly to store in his furnace room in the hopes that rodents wouldn't rummage through it.

Sonny walked around the perimeter of the building cleaning up debris. A young unkempt woman, who was leaning against the building, was as frightened to see him as he was to find her. He was ready to order her to move on until he saw the fresh bruises around her eyes, which were streaked and crusted with old mascara. *She might look like a sex worker*, he thought, but *she is still some mother's child*. He coaxed her out from between the bushes and asked her if she had somewhere to go. She was leery of his motives, so she said nothing.

"Look, I have four kids about your age. And a wife."

That got him nowhere.

"Are you from around town?" he asked.

That prompted a slight shake of her matted dreadlocks.

"Then let's get you somewhere safe."

She looked up at him long enough for him to notice her bottom lip was quivering. He took her arm gently and asked her to come inside until he could find her somewhere warm to go. He didn't want to bring her into the lobby and disturb the occupants, so he offered her the furnace room to warm up. She hesitated. He asked her if she had a phone. She produced one and said the battery needed charging. It was the same brand he had, and she agreed to follow him to use his phone charger.

The slight, shivering woman limped as she followed him around to the side of the building. He unlocked the door, picked up the garbage bag and held the door open for her. She followed him past a few storage cells and waited while he unlocked an unpainted steel door that had a hand-written 'Property Manager' sign taped to it. He left the garbage bag outside the door and rolled out the old oak office chair towards her; it was a relic from the warden's office when the cells housed overnight prisoners.

Sonny pointed to the shelf where the charger sat. She plugged her phone in and whispered a thank you. He hoped she would stay long enough for him to figure out how to help her. She scanned the large room and saw that part of it opened to one of the furnace areas. The other side served as his combined office and tool room. He watched her as closely as she watched him. He passed her his half-finished coffee and the muffin his wife packed for him two days ago. She gulped the tepid coffee down, and within a minute, she stared up at the ceiling and began to have a seizure. He tried to brace her fall, but she still landed heavily on the concrete floor. He called 911, then began to panic. He placed a grimy seat cushion under her head, and within minutes, he heard the welcome sounds of a siren. He propped the side exterior door open for the paramedics, then prayed as he paced frantically between the young woman and the outside door. A police cruiser arrived first. Instantly relieved to pass her care on to someone more qualified than him, he hurried the female officer to the motionless woman. When he heard more sirens, he ran outside to flag down the paramedics.

By the time the paramedics saw the young woman, she was regaining consciousness and resisting their involvement. Sonny blurted out what happened to whoever would listen, unplugged her phone as evidence and passed it to a paramedic. As the woman was transferred onto a stretcher and out of the building, an unmarked car pulled up. Mitch got out and scanned the parking lot for Sally's car as he talked on his phone. Sonny left him and returned to the female officer, who was also on the phone speaking police language. Her eyes met his and she ended her call. Sonny turned around and was startled to see Mitch standing in the doorway.

"Quite a set-up you got here," Mitch said.

"Yup. Lots of things still to be done," Sonny said, pointing to the tools hanging on hooks or on shelves.

The female officer walked around the room with her hands on her hips while Mitch asked Sonny casually what was new in the building.

"Not much, same old stuff," he answered.

Mitch's phone rang and he walked out of the room, leaving Sonny and the female officer facing each other.

"So, tell me a little more about what happened," she asked, leaning against his work bench but still keeping her hands on her hips.

Sonny started from the beginning but was interrupted by a dog barking, which became progressively louder and harsher until an enormous black King Shepherd named Knox barrelled into the room. He was leashed to his uniformed handler and barking furiously at the black garbage bag as well as other parts of the room.

"Hey, that's not fair!" Sonny protested, pointing at the bag. "This is from the street! I swear it is. I just brought it in!"

"I believe you, Sonny," Mitch said. "But Knox is telling us there's more of it in here."

"What do you mean?" Sonny asked, feigning innocence.

"What are those sharp needles and things in the jar over there?" Mitch asked.

"That's what I pick up off the street and behind the building. They're all over the place. I'm trying to keep things clean over here!"

"And what about those?" Mitch asked, pointing to another clear package holding fentanyl patches.

"Those are my mother's. She gives me a few to use when my back gets really sore."

"I also believe you. But there's also another small problem here," Mitch said.

"What's that?" Sonny's eyes were on fire.

"The guy you're also supplying just got picked up for trafficking. Apparently, he had a bone to pick with you and confessed that you're selling him fentanyl."

Sonny slumped down hard into his chair, forgetting the grimy cushion was still on the floor. Of all the things he regretted doing in his life, this topped the list. He pointed to the large bags of cat food on the floor that Knox was hanging around, and tried to explain himself. Mitch bought none of it.

"Selling opioids to feed street cats so your wife won't yell at you doesn't cut it. People are dying from overdoses at record numbers around here."

"But those are street drugs!"

"Sonny, I thought you were smarter than that. Especially with four teenagers. And if you're not listening to everything they're saying, then you're an even bigger fool. Where do you think that woman Rosie who died in this very building got it from?"

That struck a raw nerve.

"My kids? You leave my kids out of of this!" Sonny screamed, rubbing his hand over his face repeatedly in hot surges of anger.

"Your kids are in the middle of this because they now have a father who's a criminal! How are you going to explain that to them?"

Mitch nodded to the female officer who responded with a grip on Sonny that was firm but quick. She handcuffed him and read him his rights as he followed Knox and his handler out of his work room.

Mitch growled loudly after Sonny, "I thought better of you, but now you're nothing but scum."

He felt no satisfaction from having the last word.

Two cruisers left, one with Sonny in the back and the other with Knox and his handler. Mitch and his partner returned to the furnace room, secured the scene and gathered evidence. He returned to his office and wrote up his report, silently grateful for re-establishing ties with his sons. He texted Georgia that, barring a crisis, he would be home for dinner. His phone pinged with a response from Georgia.

"Great. We're having leftovers. I've also made my list, and I've checked it twice."

She listed five gift items, including a book, small spatulas, a metal strainer, wool socks and a new fleece housecoat. She attached pictures. The wish list totalled just over $100, the limit they agreed upon for Christmas.

He texted back: "Are you going to wear the housecoat and those socks at the same time? That is not sexy."

"Of course I will. No one likes cold feet."

She added a heart emoji and Mitch estimated he could tackle her shopping list in a couple of hours. He had booked Christmas off, for the first time in forever, and was looking forward to it.

1:00 p.m.

Bryce had an unexpected meeting with his new boss and Human Resources. He could barely breathe as he left his tiny call centre cubicle and headed to the HR administrative offices, tapping every wall outlet and light switch on his way. He checked in with the receptionist, who led him into the office where his old and new supervisor sat along with his HR representative. In a short meeting, the three women took turns complimenting his work performance and his attention to ensuring every quality measure of his job was met. This was not what Bryce was expecting, so he calmed down. They offered him a new position related to his recent training, and a pay raise. He accepted it without hesitation or consideration that he should ask Talia. He needed good news to offset the misery he was experiencing at home. Then, as if the HR representative read his mind, she asked him a very open-ended question about how things were going outside his job.

"Fine," he lied.

His new boss, prefacing her statement by acknowledging she had no right to ask about his personal life, stated she wanted to share something personal with him. She said that her father had some health problems, and she noticed some similar behaviours in Bryce. She reiterated that she had no right to interfere unless it affected his job performance and offered him confidential support if he needed it. They thanked him for coming in on short notice, and Bryce escaped as quickly as he could.

Even though Talia said he needed help and his employer offered him help, Bryce did not feel he needed fixing. *I'll just have to try a little harder to keep things under control*, he thought as he repeated the sequence of touching the wall sockets and outlets on his way back to his workstation.

4:45 p.m.

Gracie's days at the library were happy ones. The excitement of Christmas just around the corner lightened everyone's spirits. Mason was meeting old friends later that day, at Gracie's insistence. Both kept their relationship private, and Marcello had remained silent about seeing Mason a few weeks ago.

Gracie hurried home and met Lily at her Loft with a hot box of pizza, mostly to lift Lily's mood after her second disaster of a date. She knew that Lily's desperation was partly about companionship but mostly about her alimony arrangement ending soon. She was looking for someone new to support her. Gracie was just about to suggest Lily consider other options when there was a soft knock on the door. It was Sally, and she was holding a letter from Lily's bank that she found in her own mailbox. Lily invited her in, and the three women who had not been together since the reunion dinner in the lobby after the fire, didn't take long to catch up.

Gently, Gracie and Sally convinced Lily that working gave them financial independence, self-worth and a broader social circle. Lily hadn't worked since her teen years, and she last volunteered when she was still married. She also had no resume, so, instead of scrutinizing Match #3's profile, who sounded as exciting as a stack of cardboard, the three women created one. The evening ended on a positive note.

December 18th
Weather forecast: freezing rain

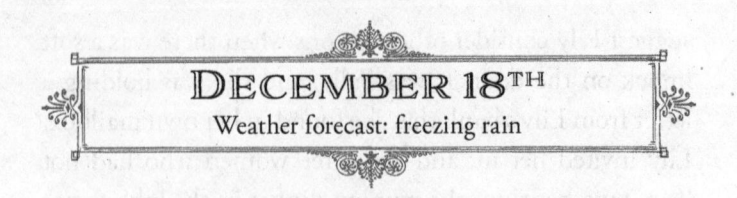

4:00 p.m.

*"May you never be too grown up to search
the skies on Christmas Eve."*

Unknown

Winnie decided she was staying home for Christmas, and despite her children's invitations to fly her to Boston, she preferred the calm of her own little world. At dinner, Marcello said he wasn't going anywhere, and Winnie wondered how many others at Park Street were spending Christmas alone. She suggested that if the others wanted to share a meal on Christmas Eve, perhaps Marcello could cook the turkey. He balked at her because eel was served at Christmas in Italy. Winnie quickly reminded him that him he didn't live in Italy anymore. With cognac saturating the roasted walnut gnocchi in their bellies, Winnie pulled out her best Christmas stationary and wrote out one invitation as pretty as her arthritic fingers could manage. Marcello watched her pen move across the paper as he rambled off excuses. Others would have somewhere else to go, and why would Winnie want to host guests she barely knew? What if none—or worse, too many—responded? Winnie called Marcello a Grinch, pulled out a second sheet of festive paper and created a chart of rows and columns.

She numbered the first column from one to ten. The middle column asked for the attendee's name, with the last column for their pot luck contribution. In bold letters, she wrote "RSVP by December 21st."

Winnie was quite proud of herself; she hurried down to the lobby with a pencil and a roll of tape to post her invite while Marcello was still wondering how he got coerced into cooking a whole turkey, something he had done only once in his life.

5:30 p.m.

When Talia saw Winnie's handwritten invitation in the lobby, she was charmed. She planned to meet her family only for Christmas Day dinner because she didn't want them to know about her war with Bryce. Despite them discouraging Bryce and Talia from moving in together, she didn't want to prove them right—especially now. Bryce decided to go home, hoping it would buy him more time. The longer Talia slept on the couch, the more possessive he was about keeping his prized book collection intact, which Talia called hoarding. A better job with higher pay boosted Bryce's confidence that he was normal.

Bryce was working tonight. He and Talia worked opposite shifts and all but stopped communicating. Talia made it clear that if Bryce had not cleaned up his messes, which at this stage was almost impossible, she was leaving him after Christmas. Bryce didn't know, nor asked where Talia would go. Talia and Adrian had progressed to texting daily, keeping it cordial rather than intimate.

They firmed up Adrian's offer to allow Talia to stay at his condo if needed.

6:00 p.m.

Talia inhaled her veggie sub, chased it with liberal gulps of wine from the bottle, then hauled her boxes of Christmas decorations down to the lobby. She erected the artificial Christmas tree, which popped open in ascending layers like an upside-down umbrella. Cast-offs from her mother, the lights and decorations brought back mixed memories of her childhood. She assembled the tree as well as a matching Santa and Mrs. Claus that was as tall as she was and set them beside the mailboxes. She fussed over a wilted table arrangement until it looked almost new again. She was surprised to find a switch under it, and she giggled when the tiny white bulbs lit up. She set it on the table in the window between the lobby chairs. She also plugged the Christmas tree lights on and sighed as the lights sparkled intermittently.

Talia then took the pencil Winnie had attached to a string beside her dinner invitation. She put her name on the list and added cookies under Winnie's veggies and Marcello's turkey. She would bake her favourite shortbread, and if she changed her mind, the bakery was always well-stocked.

Talia propped the outside door open and stepped onto the sidewalk to see her efforts from the street. As a calm washed over her, a tiny bit of hope touched her heart, and Christmas became a little less sad.

Mason arrived just as Talia was heading back inside. She recognized him and held the door for him, catching his smile as he scanned the decorated lobby and empty boxes.

"Is this your hard work?" he asked.

"Yup. I'm pretty surprised myself," she quipped.

"This street corner has never looked so festive," he said as his curiosity drew him to the dinner list.

His finger followed Winnie's entry to make vegetables. He shook his head.

"Good for Winnie. The last time she cooked at Christmas was before her husband passed."

"She's changed a lot since she first moved in," Talia said.

"Oh? In what way?"

"No disrespect intended, but I thought she was more scattered—kind of forgetful—and maybe a little unstable to be living here alone. But she's really perked up. She's less confused, and she's much happier."

"That's good to know."

"For all it's worth."

"Actually, it's worth a lot. I know we've met, but I've forgotten your name."

"It's Talia. I live in Unit—ah—on the second floor."

Mason glanced at the mailboxes and said, "Yes, of course. Unit 2A."

Talia smiled at him and nodded. *Not for long in 2A*, she thought.

She cleaned her boxes up as Mason walked down the hall and knocked on Winnie's door. Marcello had left by then, and her table was set for tea. Inhaling the lingering aroma, Mason was glad she had eaten a tasty dinner. He observed her with interest as she reheated the kettle. She was nicely dressed and had regained the weight she shouldn't have lost when Alex died. Where they had both spent the last five Decembers running away from anything remotely related to Christmas, things were looking more hopeful for both of them.

Winnie and Mason sat down to tea and digestive biscuits. He commented on how well she looked and then for planning a Christmas Eve dinner. She grinned like an elf when she told him about conning Marcello into cooking the turkey.

"I even told him to buy a big one," she said.

"How many guests are you expecting?" he asked.

"Hopefully six or seven, which is better than one," she said. "Mason, you should join our lonely hearts club band."

"I'll have to check my calendar," he replied as Winnie eyed him over her glasses.

"It's Christmas. Your calendar will be empty," she said with a wink.

6:30 p.m.

Mason finished his paperwork with Winnie and sent a clandestine text to Gracie to let her know. With Talia corroborating his own observations, he was worrying less instead of more about Winnie's well-being. They exchanged goodbyes and he closed her door behind him. Hesitating for a moment on whether to return to the lobby first or go directly to Gracie's, he opted to tiptoe down the hall to Gracie's. Her door was partially ajar, and just as he turned to walk inside, he caught Marcello popping out of his own door. He nodded to Mason and closed it again. Mason was greeted with a heartwarming embrace as he closed Gracie's door.

"I think our secret is over," he whispered in her ear.

"I've said nothing."

"But Marcello's seen something."

"What?"

"Me. Here. Twice."

"Hmmm, twice. That might be problematic."

"And Winnie's invited me to a pot luck Christmas Eve dinner in the lobby."

"That's nice. Can you bring a guest?" Gracie asked, leaning into Mason's well-dressed frame.

"Ah, I'm thinking I would be the guest."

"And whose guest would you be?"

"Well, if you don't invite me, then I'll have to be Winnie's," Mason murmured, inhaling Gracie's fragrant, slightly damp hair.

"And then I'd take Marcello?" she asked, her arms enveloping his neck.

"Well, he's a much better chef. And he knows how to cook a turkey."

"Hmm. If he's roasting the turkey, am I making the stuffing?"

"Would that be from scratch or out of the box?"

"If you come to dinner, you'll find out for yourself," Gracie said, taking Mason's hand and leading him to the kitchen where her pot roast was resting and waiting for him to slice it.

By the time Mason and Gracie sat down to dinner, Marcello was back at Winnie's debating how big the turkey should be.

10:30 p.m.

Marcello was already home and asleep in his own bed by the time Mason left Gracie's bed, his tie and socks tucked in his coat pockets. He walked quietly down the hall and into the lobby. He was mesmerized by the snow falling outside the lobby windows, so he sat down in the lobby chair and gazed at the tree lights while he put his socks back on. He walked over to the Christmas dinner list and added Gracie's name and "Gracie's amazing homemade stuffing" beside it. Underneath it he wrote his own name and added red and white wine. Shutting off the lights on the little table arrangement and the Christmas tree before leaving the building, Mason left Park Street with a full belly and a happy heart.

December 21st
Weather forecast: sunny skies

8:45 a.m.

"The future belongs to those who believe in the beauty of their dreams."

Eleanor Roosevelt

Sally got up early, downed a banana and a glass of milk for breakfast and packed her lunch before heading out the door to work. She was distracted by the notice near the lobby mailbox, fearing an increase in the building maintenance fees. She was pleasantly surprised to see Winnie's invite instead. She reviewed the list, added her name and wrote "Surprise" in the menu column, which gave her time to figure out what was needed to round out the meal. The invite was a welcome diversion; she recently became aware that Mitch was back with his ex-wife. *So much for changing his beneficiary on his legal documents,* she thought as she walked to work.

9:45 a.m.

Lily skipped her way down the stairs from the Loft to her second ever job interview at a bank down the street. She was feeling a little more optimistic because things weren't eating away at her as much. A few of her old clothes fit, and she managed to put together a conservative ensemble from her closet rather than buying something new. She saw Winnie's invite posted in the lobby, added her name and a tossed salad to the menu without hesitation before leaving the building. She wasn't the best of cooks, but it was pretty hard to mess up a salad.

10:30 a.m.

Winnie went to the lobby to get her mail and was thrilled to see the growing list. It was the happiest she'd been in a long, long time. She looked closer, impressed that Mason not only was coming, but he was bringing wine. Gracie, the librarian who drove her home one day, was also coming, and she noticed Gracie's handwriting looked like Mason's. *Mason needs to meet someone nice, maybe even the librarian*, she thought. She unlocked her mailbox and pulled out some Christmas cards from old neighbours. Returning to her condo, she wrote a note to herself to remind Marcello that he definitely needed to buy a bigger turkey.

Noon

Through a slot in his cell door, Sonny was served baked beans, rice and drowned vegetables on a melamine tray, the same thing he ate on his first day there. He was allowed two phone calls to his wife—who cried through both conversations—and three calls from his lawyer—who was still trying to negotiate bail and could not guarantee Sonny would be home for Christmas. Sonny didn't know that his buyer was well-established in the underground drug culture, which created even more obstacles to Sonny's release.

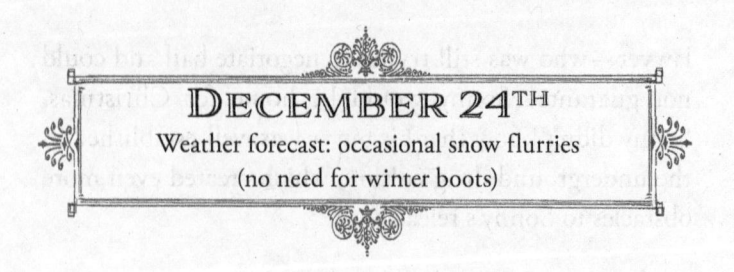

December 24th
Weather forecast: occasional snow flurries
(no need for winter boots)

3:00 p.m.

"It's not what's under the Christmas tree that matters, it's who's around it."

Anonymous

Marcello seasoned his twelve-pound turkey, blessed it as well as himself, and put it in the oven. He eased into his recliner and put his feet up. Mona Lisa was quick to find his lap, and as both were nodding off, the phone rang. Marcello moved the cat, heaved himself up and answered his cousin's call on the fourth ring. After a medley of Italian salutations from his noisy family, Marcello's cousin found a quiet room and quickly progressed to tell Marcello that he had met Valentina at the Christmas market. After their polite exchanges about nothing, Valentina asked Marcello's cousin about him. She narrowed in on her life's regrets, and towards the end of their conversation, she asked Marcello's cousin to ask Marcello if he could find it in his heart to forgive her. He promised the message would get to Marcello, but she also understood that Marcello may want nothing to do with her. Marcello quickly found his glasses and wrote her phone number down on his newspaper; he said he would think about calling her.

When he hung up, he picked up the newspaper clipping of her and stared at it. Any hope of a nap had vanished.

The bank closed early for Christmas, which gave Sally time to set up the folding table and chairs in the lobby, just as she did when the residents moved back after the fire. Winnie's list totalled seven guests for Christmas dinner, but she set an extra plate just in case. Just in case of what, or who, she didn't know. She found festive table accessories at the dollar store, and when the table was set, her meagre investment made the table look elegant. She then headed upstairs to make the garlic mashed potatoes she had added to the list.

Because Bryce was out of town, Talia switched shifts to work the early one at the call centre. She purchased cookie cutters, gingerbread and shortbread ingredients and took the liberty of doing her baking at Adrian's. The end result yielded dozens of cookies, and she put the extras into Adrian's empty freezer.

Lily was moping because she hadn't heard anything from the bank. She took her frustration out on the salad ingredients, chopping furiously. She reasoned that getting a job was more involved than applying for one. Today she also missed her sister very, very much. And her parents. And even her dog that had died before everyone else did. She would spend tomorrow eating and watching movies, but at least she wouldn't be alone today.

Mason closed the office at noon and bought five bottles of good Niagara wine, including a late harvest ice wine which he last purchased to share with his wife. He found boxes of glasses stashed in his kitchen pantry, washed enough for everyone and repacked them to bring for dinner. He felt a mix of nostalgia thinking about past Christmases with his wife and tonight's dinner with Gracie, and others, in a building lobby.

4:30 p.m.

Winnie took a leisurely bath, bubbles and all, and consciously anchored each foot safely on the bath mat to avoid falling as she got out. She put curlers in her hair, ironed a white blouse and set her coral pink suit on the bed because her red one didn't fit. She blamed Marcello for that. With a little guidance from him, she prepared Brussels sprouts for roasting. She despised cooking, but today was an exception. Feeding six other people who she knew would appreciate her effort was worth it. Because Mason was coming, she wouldn't have to worry about him being alone, and he could brag about her cooking when her children called him to check up on her.

Winnie put her feet up and the TV watched her have a little snooze until Marcello knocked on her door to remind her to preheat the oven before putting the vegetables in. She set the temperature and admired the falling snow outside until the oven was ready. She wondered if Mason would take her to Christmas mass tomorrow.

Because Gracie was always the designated stuffing maker in her family, her recipe was locked in her head. The library closed early, and any lingering street people were escorted out with a Christmas card and a goody bag of holiday treats. She enjoyed her peaceful walk home through the sparkling snow. She prepared the stuffing and put it in to bake, then headed for the shower. She and Mason arranged to meet in the lobby at dinner and to avoid any displays of affection while they were with the other people in the building.

6:00 p.m.

"Dinner is served ..."

Unknown

Marcello took great pride in how his turkey turned out. He carved and arranged the bird on an ornate serving plate he had borrowed from Winnie and kept it warm under foil. Cautiously and proudly, he carried it to the table Sally had set up and then brought gravy and serving utensils for tonight's meal.

Winnie drizzled her Brussels sprouts with maple syrup, tossed in the crispy bacon Marcello had prepared for her and loaded it into her best covered serving dish. Wedging herself into her outfit, she paraded down the hall with her offering and placed it on the table like a newborn baby.

Lily decided not to dress her salad, but instead brought bottles of dressing and spaced them apart on the table. She wore the same black suit as she did for her job interview.

Sally, still sweaty from draining and mashing the potatoes, put them on the table and wiped the perspiration from her brow. She didn't have time to shower and hoped no one would notice that she smelled like garlic.

Talia beamed as she brought her offering down to the lobby. She set her cookies on the table between the armchairs that were next to the window. She was pleased with how they turned out and had already decided that her New Year's resolution was to do things she enjoyed more often.

Gracie's stuffing smelled like Christmas at home. She made a batch for tonight and a second for Christmas dinner with her daughter, sister and niece the following day.

Mason put a fresh shirt on and reasoned with himself that he would rather be overdressed than too casual. He saw Gracie looking out the lobby window pretending she wasn't waiting for him when he parked his car. She opened the door for him, feigning surprise to see him and offloading the wine glasses as he returned to his car to carry the wine in.

6:30 p.m.

Sally lit the candles, and Talia plugged in the lights on the Christmas tree and the arrangement in the window. The guests assembled around the table, each noticing the extra setting and wondering who the mystery person would be. Winnie invited whoever felt comfortable to join her in prayer. All bowed their heads and prayed in their own way, including Marcello in his native tongue. As Mason poured the wine, Winnie toasted everyone for their contribution and for making her Christmas dream come true.

When the question of the extra setting came up, Sally explained that it was her family's custom to leave a place for those who were missed. Mason rolled Sally's story into the second toast for those who had passed or who were unable to join them. All became still, and eyes became misty with memories of other lives that would have made this evening very different.

After the calm, the tinkling of glasses resumed, as did the passing of plates and serving dishes. The conversation shifted back to Christmas traditions.

8:00 p.m.

With worries set aside, even if for a few hours, the party was so focused on each other that no one noticed the group of eight peering from the outside window in.

Winnie's family had flown in from Boston and San Francisco to surprise her for Christmas. They left multiple messages on her phone, which was in her purse in her closet. Mason deliberately set his phone on silent at noon when the office closed, and because Gracie agreed to meet him at the door, he consciously decided to leave it that way for the evening.

Annette wanted to make things right after their last visit, so it was her suggestion that everyone surprise Winnie. As Annette grew increasingly more impatient, Allen stopped her from rapping her knuckles against the window to catch Winnie's attention.

"Look at her, Sis," Allen said. "I haven't seen her this happy in years. Watch the way she's laughing. That's real."

"We should have called her to tell her we were coming," Annette snipped, standing so close to the window her breath was fogging it up.

"And get her in a frenzy?" Allen's wife Kim asked.

"I agree. And remember, you said you wanted to surprise her," Allen said.

"I've all but lost my parents," Kim said. "They don't know who I am anymore, and that vacant stare they give me every time I go home crushes me. I think we should just let her enjoy her friends and come back tomorrow morning. Twelve hours won't make any real difference, will it?"

"But we flew all this way," Annette fussed while texting her receptionist about a business deal.

Annette's partner, Richard, gently put his hand on her arm to remind her that she promised to leave her work in Boston. Annette's daughter, Savannah, shivering in the cold said, "Mom, it's not Nana's problem that you decided to surprise her. I agree with Uncle Allen. We should leave her alone and come back Christmas morning. She obviously doesn't have her phone with her, so why ruin her party."

"Is that the guy you said was in the psych ward that's sitting beside Mom?" Allen asked.

"Why yes, it is," Annette said, stewing.

"And isn't that Mason sitting across from Mom?" Allen asked, his nose as close to the window as Annette's.

"You're right. It is. And they're toasting something. And oh—oh look! Mom just put her arm around that guy and—oh! Look—she just pecked him on the cheek," Annette snorted, grasping her brother's arm.

"That's gross," Savannah said. "I can't believe Nana would kiss anyone after Grandpa died. And someone that's an old fart like that."

"Annette, it's cold out here, and I agree that we shouldn't interfere with Mom's plans," Allen said.

"I'll leave Mason another message and we'll proceed as planned tomorrow. We've got reservations for brunch and dinner at the hotel, and we'll just stick with our original plans. I'll come back and get Mom in the morning."

Savannah took a number of pictures of Winnie through the window, and in the last photo, she realized that the man Winnie had kissed on the cheek was looking in the direction of the window. Annette and the rest of the entourage had already headed back to the shuttle bus. Savannah was the last to board the shuttle, and she sat in front of her mother. She scrolled through the photos she had just taken and zoomed in on the last one. Sure enough, that man was staring straight out the window as if he had seen the Grinch steal Christmas.

Marcello glanced discreetly out the window twice before he recognized who he saw a few minutes ago. He thought about nudging Winnie to look, confident she would have mentioned if she knew her family was coming. He listened to Winnie's happy rambling and decided not to spoil her rare moment in the spotlight. When he looked toward the window again, the entourage had left.

Near dinner's end, Talia's cookies were half-gone and everyone's mood was mellow and kind. Lily overheard

Winnie ask Mason if he planned on attending the early Christmas mass. Before Mason could answer, Lily offered to take her. Winnie looked to Mason, who looked to Lily and then back to Winnie. He said he planned to go later. Winnie accepted Lily's offer, which gave Mason the opportunity of sleeping in with Gracie.

8:15 p.m.

Talia, Sally and Lily remained after dinner ended to clean up and finish a bottle of wine Mason had left for them. Mason brought Marcello and Winnie's contributions back to Winnie's condo, overhearing Winnie asking Marcello to help her clean up. Marcello asked Winnie if her family called. She said they would call tomorrow as she poured their rum and eggnog. She desperately wanted to send Marcello home to get out of his stuffy clothes because she could barely breathe in hers.

"Do you know what the rule was in my old neighbourhood?" Winnie asked.

"I'm curious," Marcello responded.

"It was called the 6:30 Rule. After 6:30 p.m., if it was raining, it was socially acceptable to put your pajamas on. I think the snow would qualify as rain tonight."

"I couldn't agree with you more," Marcello responded, his belt cinched much too tightly around the waist of his good pants.

"Then you have fifteen minutes to change and get back here or I'll finish your eggnog."

"I'll be back in ten," Marcello said, leaving the door ajar as he walked out.

Winnie was most relieved to take her fancy bra off. She cursed herself for putting it on and tossed it in the wastebasket so she'd never have to put it back on again. She put a matching nightgown and housecoat on, and, as promised, Marcello was back soon in flannel pajamas, bottoms creased from the new package he just removed them from. He covered them with a shiny navy and burgundy paisley smoking jacket, rounded off with his favourite floppy slippers. She patted the sofa beside her for him to sit down, and he did.

"You know what I like best about you, my friend?" Winnie said, their glasses clinking.

"I'm afraid to know."

"As those young people say, there's no drama."

"I don't understand."

Winnie kicked her slippers off and placed her varicose-veined feet on a pillow on the coffee table, toes pointing sideways in opposite directions.

"I never worry about you."

"Is that good or bad?"

"Good. It's very good, and I thank you."

"My pleasure, I think."

"Now, what did you watch on TV way over there in Venice on Christmas Eve?"

"We didn't. We strolled as a family through the Christmas market and bought lots of fish. Then we ate and drank all night, just like you do here."

"Well, in Canada we eat and then watch *It's a Wonderful Life*, so I think we should do that."

"Very well."

Winnie replenished their glasses, sat down close enough to Marcello that their shoulders and hips eased into each other and turned the TV on.

"Did you call her?" she asked.

"Who?"

"You know who. Your Valentine."

"Not yet."

"What are you waiting for?"

"Christmas."

Winnie almost spit out her eggnog.

"That's tomorrow."

"It is?" he looked at her with eyebrows raised.

"Promise me you'll call her?"

"Very well. I will call her."

"All right then. Now turn the volume up."

Fifteen minutes into the movie, both Winnie's and Marcello's heads were leaning into each other and against the back of the sofa, the food and drinks effectively putting them both to sleep.

9:00 p.m.

Mason was hoping to walk unnoticed by Winnie's door to get his overnight bag from his car, but he saw that her door was not shut completely. He peeked in and saw the sleeping pair propped up against each other in their pajamas. He was quite touched by the scene. He quietly turned the door lever so it would lock behind him and made his way down the hall. Standing at the door which opened to the lobby, he heard nothing. The lobby was cleaned and empty. He retrieved his bag from his car and turned the Christmas lights off in the lobby for safety's sake. He again hesitated at the door between the lobby and the hall, listening for any movement. There was nothing. He hurried quietly down the hall like a teenager and breathed a sigh of relief when he was safely behind Gracie's door, deadbolt locked. She had already changed into something comfortable, poured more wine and programmed *It's a Wonderful Life* into her TV.

Talia, Sally and Lily, cozy in their Christmas flannels, relocated to Lily's Loft to admire the falls view and the holiday lights. None of them wanted to be alone, so they exchanged life stories, which prompted Talia to realize that, apart from texting and a few short and not always positive encounters, she really didn't know Adrian. She needed to consider alternative arrangements if she left Bryce unless she felt very confident and safe around Adrian. When he called, Talia was cautious with her words. His flight home wasn't scheduled until New Year's Eve, which gave her some more breathing room.

CHRISTMAS DAY
Weather forecast: sunny (good weather for driving)

8:40 a.m.

"It's not how much we give but how much love we put into giving."

Mother Theresa

Lily was up and ready for church. When Winnie wasn't waiting in the lobby as planned, she knocked on her door. Winnie opened it immediately, apologizing as she fumbled with her boots and coat. Her phone spent the night in her purse and had no battery life. Lily hurried Winnie along, and by the time she brushed the snow off her car and pulled it in front of the building, Winnie was waiting for her outside the front door.

As Lily escorted Winnie up the stairs and into the church, they were greeted by the same priest who led the funeral services for Winnie's Alex and Lily's sister Rose. His words of support, comfort and joy were good to hear.

Mason was up by 8:00 a.m. and made coffee for two. When he switched his phone from the silent mode, he saw Allen's messages. He called Allen back at 8:30 a.m. apologized for not picking up his message sooner, and advised him of Winnie's plan to attend church at 9:00 a.m. with another condo resident. Winnie's family decided to join her, which bought Mason and Gracie time to share breakfast and exchange new novels before she headed to Toronto to see her family.

9:02 a.m.

Annette and Allen arrived at the church just as Christmas mass began. They sauntered up the aisle expecting to see Marcello sitting beside their mother, who they expected to see wearing her red coat and matching pillbox hat. It wasn't until they took aisle seats that they recognized her sitting one row up and ten feet over, with a female.

Mass began and ended without Winnie noticing them, and it wasn't until the aisles were clearing that Allen gently touched her shoulder. Overjoyed to see them, Winnie burst into tears. Lily began crying as well; she missed her own family. She chauffeured Winnie, Annette and Allen back to the hotel and then graciously declined their invitation to brunch. She couldn't bring her own family back but felt blessed to have witnessed the happiness of others.

10:30 a.m.

Marcello woke up on Christmas morning in his own bed. He remembered leaving Winnie's sofa after one woke the other one up for snoring. He then tossed and turned in his own bed until his cats woke him up for breakfast.

He anguished for about thirty minutes before making the call, rehearsing what he thought he might and might not say. He tapped the number in carefully on his new mobile phone, a gift to himself. He touched the Call symbol and almost dropped the phone when a young male appeared live on the screen and greeted him in Italian. As Marcello tried to process what he was seeing, he saw his own image in a tiny square. Marcello identified himself and where he was calling from. The young man said he was Valentina's grandson, and asked if Marcello would like to speak with her. Marcello quickly combed through his thin hair with his fingers, relieved he was at least dressed, and said yes.

The image of the woman that appeared startled Marcello, and she instantly read his discomfort. She looked so much older than the smiling woman in the newspaper photo. She was wearing a black sweater buttoned to her neck and a simple gold cross. Her hair was almost white and was pulled away from her face. And the voluptuous Marilyn Monroe lips he pined for had withered into crevassed lines. For a moment, Marcello regretted making the call.

"Ciao, Marcello."

"Buon Natale," he responded, holding his breath as he absorbed every inch of what he was able to see.

Valentina shooed whoever was in the room away, and in the background, he heard a door close. Conversing in Italian, Valentina's raspy greeting gave Marcello pause and made him wonder how much his own voice had changed. Her head moved slowly from side to side as she spoke.

"I'm looking at you looking at me and I sense you don't like what you see," she chirped.

"Many years have passed since we were young. You are looking at an old man," he said.

"But you are still a handsome man. Time has favoured you …"

"I didn't believe your flattery then, nor do I now, Valentina," he replied, her name rolling off his tongue like velvet.

"Those Canadian winters have preserved you."

Their expressions softened, and then their words flowed more freely. Valentina carefully unfolded her history. She had indeed endured decades of conflict, abuse and poverty. She moved often, sometimes living in shelters or any place safe and warm for her family to sleep. She was readily accountable for her choices, confessing that leaving her homeland for Marcello proved to be a far greater hardship than she imagined. In the end, the dissuasion of her family and the uncertainty of an unknown country was why she remained. The other men, she bargained with Marcello, were a means to survival. She fingered the cross Marcello realized was one he gave her for Christmas decades ago. She said it had never left her neck and often gave her strength to keep living. The more she spoke, the more he understood the cause of each fine line that was etched into her face. His solitude paled in comparison to hers, despite being abandoned.

"Marcello, I am deeply sorry. I've made many mistakes in my life," she said for the first time. "And most I regret. But here we are, and we speak again."

Almost an hour passed before the lapses between sentences became longer. Valentina was called to dinner by her family, and a moment passed before Valentina spoke again.

"So," she asked quietly as he watched her cautiously.

"Will you come?"

Marcello paused, unsure of her intent.

"To visit?" he asked.

"To visit. Maybe, at first."

"And then?"

"And then, maybe to live?" she asked.

"That is a question I cannot answer. Canada is where I have made my home. But perhaps I will visit one day," he said, aware of the despair in her eyes.

"I want to see you, Marcello. Maybe sooner than later?"

"I will need to give that some thought."

A second call to dinner from Valentina's family brought their conversation to its end.

"Thank you for the call. You have given me hope," Valentina said with glassy eyes.

She blew him a kiss, her once slender knuckles now thick and aged from hard work and time.

"I hope that you will come."

Before he said, "Then I will come," she hung up.

Marcello made his breakfast and knew his day's thoughts would continue to migrate to Valentina. He was most puzzled about why she asked about him after so many years, and why he needed to come home soon. Had her life's burdens shortened her final years? Was she indirectly professing her renewed love or running out of male companions? He sat in his chair and clicked his TV remote until he found the Pope celebrating Christmas mass. Perhaps a little help from God might help him make a good decision. When the choir started singing, a tiny tear trickled between the creases in his cheeks; he lost patience with his own thoughts. It would have been easier if he had not made the call, especially today.

11:00 a.m.

Adrian was up to help his father dress while his mother tended to his grandmother. Three months ago, he would have rather paid others to care for family members. Three months ago, he was only focused on what was best for Adrian.

He knelt down and carefully pulled the white compression socks over his father's swollen ankles while trying to keep him steady on his bed. Adrian then watched his father try to brush his teeth. He caught glimpses of his mother coax the last spoonful of oatmeal into his grandmother. Chrissy was in the kitchen pre-occupied with arranging brunch onto serving dishes. Adrian wondered how they would manage when he left. And the shorter the hours came to him leaving, the heavier his heart felt for doing so.

Adrian helped his father stand up and lean heavily against his walker, which accompanied him when he was discharged home on Christmas Eve. With trembling hands, he shuffled to the dining room with Adrian hovering behind him, just as his father did when Adrian took his first steps. How their roles had reversed. Six months ago, his father hinted he needed a grandson to carry on the family name. Adrian had dodged the roulette wheel of unprotected encounters with his various and transient bed mates. His thoughts shifted to Talia, who he envisioned sleeping in his bed, showering in his bathroom and watching the sun rise and fall from his window.

His mother raised her glass of orange juice, as his father gripped his plastic cup. Adrian then joined the toasting, silently wondering who would occupy these chairs next Christmas.

11:30 a.m.

Winnie was famished by the time they sat down to brunch at the hotel. Because she had experienced indigestion from the night before, she had skipped breakfast. Allen helped her out of her good coat and hat; she was oblivious to the veiled scrutiny of her family when they inspected her elastic-waisted, mis-matched pant suit underneath.

With grace said, they charged to the buffet. Winnie politely declined Annette's offer to bring her meal to her, neither mentioning the crusty thoughts from their last visit. Winnie was relieved that she mailed her generous Christmas cheques early; they were acknowledged with sincerity. Winnie opened presents of framed family portraits. No one mentioned the night before or Marcello. Winnie's families brought her back to their large hotel suites where she settled in for a post-brunch nap.

12:50 p.m.

Lily had changed twice before she left for her first volunteer shift at the food bank. Uncertain what to expect, she opened the front door to a flurry of happy activity. Red-shirted people in all shapes and sizes were bustling around. A volunteer approached Lily, and once she established Lily was a volunteer and not a patron, she was immediately escorted to a large kitchen and assigned to dish out salad and packets of dressing onto disposable plates. The meal assembly rolled on as quickly as the noisy banter over it. By 4:00 p.m. when her shift ended, a new team of happy people arrived to carve the turkey and scoop hot veggies onto the Christmas dinner plates. When Lily left, people were lined up as far as she could see. Her heart was full from feeding the hungry, something she'd only done for philanthropic photo opportunities to promote her ex-husband's family.

5:00 p.m.

Sally enjoyed a peaceful day with her mother. Dinner for two, with enough to feed four, was delivered hot and delicious from their favourite restaurant. Later, they took a sunset stroll through Sally's old neighbourhood. Christmas lights illuminated the street and fond memories. While Sally appreciated her mother's physical health, her mother appreciated the improvement in Sally's mood after she found out more about that hellish detective and sent him packing.

Talia's mother and sister spent Christmas in the tropics with her step-father, which left only her father to visit. She rang the doorbell, fingering the silver heart floating around her neck that he gifted her last Christmas. She stood alone on the porch, her weary eyes telling him and his girlfriend that all was not well. He led Talia to the sofa in his office, closed the French doors and sat quietly beside her until her breathing became normal. Without criticism, he asked enough open questions for her to spill her troubles out. Much to Talia's surprise, he praised her for not compromising her own happiness.

A gentle knock on the office door welcomed them to a peaceful dinner prepared earlier by her father and his girlfriend, who she watched with equal parts of envy and curiosity. After more heart-warming words of encouragement and good advice, Talia was offered refuge at their home, once she had the difficult conversation with Bryce.

Unlike the exchange of holiday wishes between Adrian and Talia, Bryce had been silent. Adrian had even sent a picture of himself with his wounded family, something he had never shared with a woman before.

6:00 p.m.

Mason accepted the invite to dinner with Winnie and her family at the hotel, which offered all the pleasantries of dinners together in years past. It was his escape from being alone and a chance for Winnie's children to corner him for a status update. Mason was honest and frank, but said nothing about Winnie revising her will. Winnie was not depressed but, in fact, had flourished since her move. Mason also praised Marcello's consistent, unbiased and unselfish support, which he divulged made him worry less about her.

9:30 p.m.

Bryce left his father's house early and was home when Talia returned. He was dressed in a new shirt and sweater from his family. Talia retrieved his gift from the closet after she saw a wrapped package sitting on the coffee table. He moved the present towards her and said it was something from his family. She had nothing to give him from hers and asked him if she should open it. He said he didn't care. Leaving the gift where it sat, she asked about his visit. He said it was tense and he was happy to be home. When she asked what made him happy, he became still, scratched his head and returned his hand to his lap.

"You. You make me happy," he answered, looking away.

"And what about *us* being happy?"

"I want that too."

"So do I. But the only way we can survive, Bryce, is if we resolve to work at what's making us fall apart."

"But I can't do what you're asking me to do," Bryce said. "I need my space. I need structure. And I need my routines."

"So, are you telling me that those are things that you need most?"

"Yes."

"And where do I fit in this picture?"

"Here, with me."

"Within your space, and your structure and your routines?"

"Yes. No, no ... I mean our space."

"Bryce, I'm willing to work with you if you are willing to get some help."

"I don't need help."

Talia glared at Bryce and took a few deep breaths. She had cried enough today. She stood up and pointed to the room that she had removed her school things from a week earlier. She also noticed Bryce had since moved more boxes of books in and eliminated any room to walk beyond a few steps.

"You don't need help for this?"

"Talia, that is my life," Bryce said defensively.

"Well, maybe you can clarify what is more important: that part of your life or me?"

"I am not getting rid of my books."

"Bryce, this is a fire hazard."

"I'm not getting rid of them. That's 10,024 books."

Talia shuddered at Bryce's obsession with numbers.

"Then move them somewhere else. Anywhere. Your dad's house."

Bryce shook his head and said, "We just packed up all of my books from there and I brought them home."

"On the bus?"

"My sister drove me."

"She drove you three hours here and then three hours back?"

"She didn't mind. My dad paid me to take my books and for her to drive me home."

"He paid you?"

"A thousand dollars."

Talia put her head in her hands and rubbed what little make-up was left away.

"He actually paid you? I don't believe it."

Bryce took the small wad of money out of his pants pocket to show her, which further frustrated her.

"Bryce, I can't do this anymore." The outer corners of his eyes sagged. He was losing the battle. "I can't stand the smell of those mouldy books. I can't stand paying what we can barely afford for space that I can't even use, and I can't stand the look you give me when you think there is nothing wrong. I'm sorry it's gotten to this, but it's over, Bryce. We are done."

Talia picked up her phone and tapped at the screen for a minute before putting her phone down.

"Look at me, Bryce." He looked at her, quickly looked away again before his eyes focused back on her. "I just transferred all the money I saved that was in my education account into your account to cover two months rent. The cash your dad just gave you will cover the third month. I'm breaking my portion of our lease and will pay whatever it takes to get me out of it. I just can't live like this anymore."

Bryce's jaw dropped.

"But where will you go?"

She hesitated, then said, "My father's house."

"Oh. I thought you didn't get along."

"We didn't, but things are better now."

"Oh."

"Are you still working the day shift tomorrow?" she asked Bryce.

"Yes."

"Then I'll have my stuff out by the time you come home. Whatever I don't take is yours."

Bryce's shoulders slumped as he sank deep into his chair.

"How are you going to get all of your stuff moved in nine hours?"

"I'm not you, Bryce," she said, as she gathered a few things out of the bathroom, a change of clothes and her purse.

Talia closed the door quietly behind her, leaving Bryce still sitting on the pull-out sofa they had made love on many times before.

Talia dialled her father's number, checked the time and then instantly cancelled the call. Her father had probably turned in for the night. She walked quickly to Adrian's apartment, let herself in and locked the door behind her, feeling the weight of a room full of books off her shoulders. Meanwhile, Bryce felt the added weight of them on his.

Talia walked over to the huge window in Adrian's living area and gazed at the calming flakes of snow that were putting the city to sleep. She pressed her forehead against the coolness of the glass, wondering how many people had asked someone they loved to share the rest of their lives together and then changed their mind. She texted Adrian that she was moving out the following day and thanked him for being there when she needed him. She would leave his key on his kitchen counter.

Adrian texted her back immediately to say he wished he could be there to help her. He also encouraged her to store anything she couldn't move on her own at his place. They exchanged words of sorrow, encouragement and a commitment to continue to support each other. She made herself some hot chocolate and hoped her own thoughts would rest enough to let her sleep.

March 2nd (Three Months Later)
Weather forecast: mostly cloudy

6:30 a.m.

"Here's to the future because I'm done with the past."

Anonymous

Talia rolled over and turned her alarm off. She sat up in bed, reorienting herself to the beautiful guest room in her father's home. Her homework covered the antique desk that faced a backyard filled with busy bird feeders. She headed to the ensuite to shower before work, still awestruck by her father's offer to fund her tuition. She also planned to find a job away from Bryce. He kept persisting that they continue to share Chinese food on Fridays, which she consistently ignored once she realized it was another ritual. She and Adrian were communicating, mostly about their changing lives and their visions for finding happiness in the future. Neither mentioned that they hoped it would include the other, however, they committed to a celebratory dinner when she was finished her first semester. Adrian was certain she was worth the wait.

8:45 a.m.

Sonny put his foot on the imaginary brake in the back of the police car as it rolled to a stop in the underground parking lot of the courthouse. His handcuffed wrists fidgeted in his lap. With no indication of what the outcome of today's hearing would be, he tried to be optimistic; he had no other choice. He was escorted into a courtroom as his distraught family, all dressed in black, watched from the back row. His sons squirmed in their seats while their mother's face remained frozen in disgust.

He sat in a chair beside his lawyer as the judge called both attorneys to the bench. Hushed words were exchanged before the lawyers returned to their seats. The judge's furrowed brow focused on Sonny as he announced that due to the convoluted mix of players involved in this case, more time was needed to prepare for trial. Sonny's lawyer reassured him that this was not a bad thing, even though he had no idea why. As he was unable, and his wife unwilling to raise enough funds for the outrageous bail payment, Sonny was returned to jail, and his family to their routine of carrying on their lives without him.

9:00 a.m.

Winnie removed her cholesterol and blood pressure medications from the white paper bag the pharmacy had just delivered them in, then set the bag down on her kitchen counter. In it she placed one unopened sleeve of digestive cookies and a dozen pills in a tiny envelope.

She sealed it and wrote "Pills for nausea and pretty good for sleep too." She then gathered the spare euro bills and coins she would never use and sealed them in a sandwich bag. She found a pretty card, wrote a note in the blank space inside and signed her name. She sealed the envelope, then wrote Valentina's name on the front in her shaky calligraphy. She walked down the hall to Marcello's condo door, which was propped open with his suitcase. She tested the heavy weight of the luggage by attempting to lift the handle, then pummelled him with unsolicited advice about ruining his back. She babbled on about his suitcase contents, ordered him to check his passport expiry date, then fretted over him like a mother sending her first child off to school. Marcello took it all in stride, secretly relishing the rarity of someone worrying about him. His doorbell rang on time, and Marcello buzzed his driver in.

Mason arrived at Marcello's door as planned. Coincidentally, Mason had a meeting in Toronto the same afternoon as Marcello's flight left for Venice. Winnie procured Mason's services as soon as Marcello booked his flight and before Mason could object. Winnie shifted her orders from Marcello to Mason, wagging a crooked finger at him to drive safely because two of the most important men in her life would occupy the same vehicle. She then handed Marcello the little white paper bag. As he peeked into it, she warned him about constipated travellers, advised him to ration the digestive cookies into daily portions and to eat vegetables every day. When he held up the clear bag of currency, she said it should cover his airport shuttle. Marcello protested and attempted to return the euros because his cousin was picking him up, she pushed his hand away and said she'd like a nice red silk scarf.

Mason was entertained by the two friends' antics, knowing their month-long separation would weigh heavily on them. Marcello didn't examine the rest of the bag contents but rather tucked it in his carry-on luggage. Winnie smothered both men with affection and sent them on their way. She walked back to her condo, mopping up tears with one of Alex's old cotton handkerchiefs she had specifically hidden inside her sleeve for this moment.

Mason took Marcello's large suitcase as Marcello wheeled his carry-on into the front lobby. Gracie, bundled up and heading to work, bounded into the lobby, greeted the men and feigned innocence when Mason politely shared their plans. It wasn't until Mason dusted the snow off his car that Marcello realized that Mason and his vehicle spent the night at Park Street. Gracie declined Mason's offer of a ride to work, and when she wished them a safe journey, she caught Marcello winking at her.

12:50 p.m.

Lily had already completed her first task of the morning. She met a stonemason at the cemetery who added Rosie's name and dates to her parents' and infant brother's gravestones. She watched from a distance as the tradesman etched the phrase "Beloved Parents and Sister of Lily," then carved a rose and a lily into the top corners of the granite. She changed her mind about adding her own name and birthdate under her sister's. Her future was ahead of her. When the stonemason left, she used the snow and her gloves to rub the residue off the black stone until it glistened. She touched her hands to her lips and then to the names on the stone before dusting off her own clothes and heading to the food bank.

Lily arrived early at her third shift since Christmas. Among the regulars was a man close to her in age. Lily observed his kind demeanour as he floated throughout the patrons, some of them strangers and others he greeted by name. He was not particularly attractive, nor was his appearance offensive. He blended into his tired surroundings, wearing worn jeans and a navy flannel shirt that was just a little snug around his middle. He introduced himself as an outreach worker and sparked her curiosity when he asked her to stay for coffee after his shift ended. He was recruiting volunteers for a new program which he hoped would evolve into paid work, if and when some funding for it was approved. Lily felt a surge of confidence when she agreed to stay. She had nothing to lose.

12:56 p.m.

Sally sat in her bank manager's office after formalizing all her legal papers. She was officially single again, and determined to stay that way. With Mitch off the lease, she could plan her next move and the rest of her life without him. She had learned many lessons from her mistakes, most she hoped to never repeat.

2:05 p.m.

Bryce scanned his badge under the time monitor outside his locker room at work. He was late again and hoped his new boss would overlook it. He had been so preoccupied re-arranging his books in alphabetical order that he lost track of time. He loved his new job, which required a great deal of organization, something he prided himself in. But he loved Talia more. The thought of losing her was devastating, and it distracted him during his routines. He would just have to try harder to persuade her to come back because he was unsure that he could make room to accommodate someone new.

6:05 p.m.

Mason promised Winnie they would share dinner when he arrived home from his meeting in Toronto, even though she had a hefty stash of frozen leftovers that Marcello made for her. Her family finally abandoned the meal delivery service when they discovered there was no room in the freezer for any more of them. Winnie also told her children she was staying in her Niagara Falls condo rather than moving into either of their big homes. It was either home or heaven for her, and nothing in between.

When Mason rang Winnie's doorbell and let himself in, she had yet to set the table. She noticed the abundance of food he brought, frowning when he asked her if there was enough room at her table for three. She chirped that whoever number three was, they had better get there in a minute or less. As she busied herself setting out the plates and cutlery, Mason sent a quick text, then sauntered over to Winnie's front door and opened it.

Gracie, still wearing her name tag from the library, walked in holding a wine bottle in one hand and a cookbook in the other. While choosing wine glasses from her china cabinet, Winnie spotted Gracie, then glanced wide-eyed at Mason, her mind processing what was happening. Mason took the wine and pecked Gracie lightly on her cheek.

"Is there something I don't know?" Winnie asked both of them, glasses still in her hands.

"Not anymore," they replied simultaneously.

Mason held the chair out for Winnie to sit down before he did the same for Gracie.

6:30 p.m.

It was a dark, starless sky on the evening Mitch was called to follow up on another money laundering lead at an exclusive mansion that was shielded from the street by mature evergreens. He had been following this case for most of the last two months. He was on his last of four shifts before four days off and was met at the door again by the same beautiful woman he'd seen there before. In broken English, she said the boyfriend she lived with was still out of the country. Mitch was certain that she understood her circumstances, and if the opportunity presented itself, he could easily take advantage of her invitation. He thought of Sally first, then Georgia, and the risks he'd taken with those relationships. The woman asked him in, and Mitch removed his shoes out of respect for the opulence that enveloped him.

He followed the petite woman through a large foyer with a grand central staircase to the huge kitchen. Dressed in black leggings and a cropped top, Mitch doubted she was wearing underwear. Her blonde hair was piled into a knot high on her head, and when she stopped, he almost bumped into her. She pointed towards two stacks of papers that were neatly arranged on the granite kitchen island. She then stood opposite him and slid both piles toward him. She said her signature was forged on the left stack and asked him whether he thought they were different than the documents on the right. This was not the reason Mitch came to investigate, but gave him cause to be there longer and use the excuse that it could potentially provide him with new clues. She leaned over, her round, unfettered breasts touching the counter as she pointed to the signatures on each pile with her long, red fingernails.

Mitch, distracted by the view, met her inviting eyes. She batted her eyelash extensions, and asked him to look carefully at the documents, as she appreciated him giving her his expert opinion. Mitch bent over and tried to focus his aging eyesight on the documents without spoiling the moment and pulling out his reading glasses. He was oblivious to the gun she aimed at the top of his skull. She repeatedly discharged the bullets through the silencer.

Mitch felt nothing as his torso slid off the granite and onto the floor, aided by the pooling of his own blood. She quickly disappeared through to the garage and into a waiting car that took her to the airport. She would arrive on another continent before anyone realized Mitch was missing.

7:30 p.m.

The feral cats under the abandoned railway bridge not far from Park Street went back to their old way of life. Instead of being served cat food regularly, they were re-adjusting to fending for themselves, if the waiter at the local diner didn't deliver fish and chips or other food scraps on his way home.

Sonny rotted in his jail cell and would never find out that the waiter at the diner traded meals for fentanyl; the fentanyl that Sonny used to sell to the waiter's dealer who lived in the exclusive mansion where Mitch's body was growing cold.

Something to Consider

In Ontario, Canada:

- 91% percent of seniors are determined to remain in their own home (Home Care Ontario, July 2020).
- There has been a substantial increase in opioid-related harms and death since the beginning of the COVID-19 pandemic due to changes in the illegal drug supply, less access to supports and services for users, and more use as a way to cope with stress (Government of Canada, June 23, 2022).
- Although there is an overwhelming number of people that struggle with food addiction, as of this writing, it has not been recognized as a diagnosis in the *Diagnostic and Statistical Manual of Psychiatric Disorders* (DSM-V).
- Numerous scholarly articles report that older adults are often mistaken to have memory impairment when they actually develop or increase pre-existing anxiety and/or depression after a significant adverse event.
- It is also well-documented that many people who have a mental illness do not seek help because they are not in a stage of change that allows them to do so.

Acknowledgements

This novel was completed near the end of my long nursing career. For years, I witnessed people face and overcome incredible adversity. Their stories are forever etched in my memory.

We are all human. We have feelings. Some of us are more resilient than others. Everyone deserves respect and understanding regardless of how, why and when they reach the point of needing help. Studies suggest that hearing the stories of others overcoming challenges can save a life, and engaging in that conversation can motivate change.

There are many people to thank, and I do so in no particular order, as they are all important. Stanislaw Fiedorek, who at the time of this writing was the owner of the old Dominion Public Building, known in this novel as Park Street. He shared many interesting tales, which included buried treasure and stolen money. Unfortunately, I was unable to find any factual data to substantiate these claims. Thank you, Mr. Fiedorek, for your permission to use the building as the setting for this book (Dec. 21, 2019). The building was also used for a number of movies, including *Niagara*, featuring Marilyn Monroe.

Many thanks also to Mr. Sherman Zavitz, retired historian for the City of Niagara Falls, and Cathy Roy from the Niagara Falls Library for their knowledge and the articles they forwarded to me about 4177 Park Street.

I had the pleasure of meeting Mr. Jim Healey (now deceased) on a number of occasions when I worked in Niagara Falls. Jim was a police officer with the City of Niagara Falls, and he spent many working years in the Dominion Public Building. His stories inspired me to plant my characters within the walls of 4177 Park Street.

I became aware of the cat colony and made a point of walking by it often on my lunch hours. As mentioned in the beginning of this novel, it still exists at the time of this writing.

Thank you, Kristen, for teaching me about safety deposit boxes.

Thank you, Ursula Kehoe, for your edits before I finally hit the "send" button and let the Tellwell experts make this novel a reality. And last, but most important, I thank my precious family.

You allow me to live well, love me unconditionally and inspire me to keep writing. Thanks to Lee and Melanie for being such wonderful people and parents. Thanks to my munchkins, Alexa and Max, for giving me never-ending moments of joy. Thank you, Craig, for eating your vegetables so I don't have to worry about you being so far away. Finally, to John: thank you for not vacuuming when I was writing, and for giving me really good advice. All the time.